Resounding Praise for Schutt and Finch and Their Thrillers

"Schutt and Finch are filling the void left by Michael Crichton."

—James Cameron

THE DARWIN STRAIN

"For those of us with a taste for fantastical adventure grounded in real history and authentic science (think Jules Verne and Arthur Conan Doyle). . . . I can't help feeling that Charles Darwin . . . would delight in this . . . page-turner."

—James Morrow, author of *Galápagos Regained*

"*The Darwin Strain* makes readers rethink history and the world they know and imagine the possibilities of what can be unlocked through evolution. At the very least, it's hard to look at an octopus—whether on the other side of the glass or on a dinner plate—the same again."

—Criminal Element

HIMALAYAN CODEX

"Schutt and Finch provide a textbook example of how to make the fantastic easy to buy into with their superior second Crichton-esque thriller featuring field zoologist R. J. MacCready."

—*Publishers Weekly* (starred review)

"I reviewed [*Hell's Gate*] and compared it favorably to Michael Crichton's science-infused thrillers. This great sequel is more like Jules Verne's *Journey to the Center of the Earth* . . . There is a fantastic line in the book—'the strangest band of travelers since *The Wizard of Oz*.' Readers will find to their fascination that the description is completely accurate. Highly readable and great fun!"

—*Historical Novels Review*

"While *Hell's Gate* was a brilliant start to this terrific new series, Schutt and Finch top themselves with this nerve-wracking, heart-thumping thriller that is perfect for fans of Michael Crichton and James Rollins."

—The Real Book Spy

"James Rollins and Steve Berry fans who relish a heaping dose of scientific and historical intrigue in their thrillers will find plenty of both here."

—*Library Journal*

"It's unavoidable to call on Michael Crichton as a comparison for this smashing semi–science fiction adventure series—but add in some Indiana Jones to get nearer to the full flavor. (It's just after World War II, for one thing.) The first novel, called *Hell's Gate*, felt like the discovery of a short tunnel into an enormous new world—one couldn't wait to charge through their next tunnel. And this is that, and it's even better."

—*Sullivan County Democrat*

HELL'S GATE

"Scientifically accurate, and chillingly real; Schutt and Finch amplify the many perils that come with any expedition into the unknown. I dashed through *Hell's Gate*—cover to cover—with white-knuckle fear of what might be lurking on the next page. I'd be surprised if this thing weren't made into the scariest movie anyone ever saw. It's written cinematically, and it's full of surprises, and with a story depth that makes it relatable on so many levels. Brace yourself, this is no ordinary thriller."

—Darrin Lunde, author of *The Naturalist*

"A World War II thriller with plenty of action and suspense in a most unusual setting. Just think Indiana Jones. For that matter, this yarn evokes more than a few reminders of Stephen King, Joseph Conrad, and Bram Stoker's *Dracula*. If this book is ever made into a movie, and it should be, it will have plenty of spectacular visuals and gross-out scenes. Fast-moving fun for thriller readers who enjoy a bit of horror and seeing bad guys get what's coming to them."

—*Kirkus Reviews* (starred review)

"Saying this book is hard to put down just doesn't do it justice. That'd be like saying Oreos are hard to stop eating after just one cookie. In reality, both are nearly impossible! *Hell's Gate* has a little bit of something for everyone and should appeal to a wide and diverse audience. Thrilling and suspenseful, with a touch of creepy and a dash of terrifying, *Hell's Gate* is a fun read with an original plot and a unique cast of characters."

—The Real Book Spy

"The authors adeptly balance science and suspense, and a detailed afterword lays out how much of the story line is based in history. Michael Crichton fans will be pleased that the ending leaves room for a sequel."

—*Publishers Weekly* (starred review)

"Coauthors Schutt and Finch are experts in the sciences, and the scenes involving the biology behind what's really going on in the jungle—there's a touch of horror in the mix—are fascinating."

—*Booklist*

THE
DARWIN
STRAIN

By Bill Schutt & J. R. Finch

The Darwin Strain
The Himalayan Codex
Hell's Gate

By Bill Schutt

Dark Banquet: Blood and the Curious
Lives of Blood-Feeding Creatures
Cannibalism: A Perfectly Natural History

The
Darwin
Strain

An R. J. MacCready Novel

BILL SCHUTT &
J. R. FINCH

𝒲𝓂

WILLIAM MORROW
An Imprint of HarperCollins*Publishers*

This is a work of fiction. Names, characters, places, and incidents are products of the author's imagination or are used fictitiously and are not to be construed as real. Any resemblance to actual events, locales, organizations, or persons, living or dead, is entirely coincidental.

First William Morrow premium printing: August 2020
First William Morrow hardcover printing: August 2019

Print Edition ISBN: 978-0-06-283548-2
Digital Edition ISBN: 978-0-06-283549-9

Cover design by Richard L. Aquan
Cover photographs © Rich Carey/Shutterstock (ocean); © ArtColibris /Shutterstock (squid); © wawritto/Shutterstock (hammer and sickle)
Chapter illustrations by Patricia J. Wynne

For Donald Peterson—

whose principles of kindness

are the hope of our species.

Socially inept, I was—like most of my friends, driven mostly by a child-like sense of wonder about the world. We were beat over the head for our strange ideas—told that the answers we sought from nature were impossibilities . . . that we must put away childish thoughts, and curiosity, and "grow up." Some of us resisted. We never did finish growing up. But we never stopped growing.

—SIR ARTHUR C. CLARKE

It's kind of fun to do the impossible.

—WALT DISNEY

1N73LL1G3NC3 15 7H3 4B1L17Y 70 4D4P7 70 CH4NG3.

—573PH3N H4WK1NG

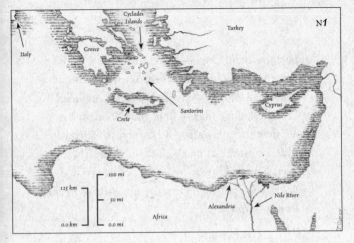

The East Mediterranean, 1948 A.D.

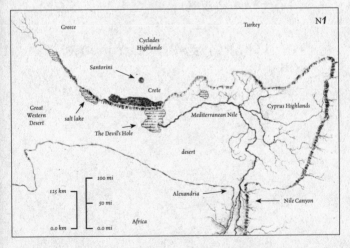

The Great Mediterranean Canyon and Nile River, 5.3 million B.C.

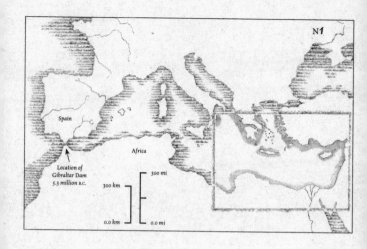

Spain

Africa

Location of
Gibraltar Dam
5.3 million B.C.

300 mi

300 km

0.0 km

0.0 mi

Santorini Island
1948 A.D.

Therasia

Nea Kameni

Town
of Fira

Fira
Quarry
(5.3 million
B.C.)

Aspronisi

Mesa
Vouno

Lost City
1630 B.C.

Village of
Akrotiri

THE
DARWIN
STRAIN

PROLOGUE

June 23, 1948
U.S. Surveillance Ship Argo, Eastern Mediterranean
120 miles south of Santorini, Greece

The Devil's Hole was a gash so deeply cut into the seafloor that generations of Greek fishermen simply considered it to be bottomless. The young technology officer at the controls of his ship's experimental sonar array knew otherwise. With the highest resolution of its kind, his equipment revealed a rim of ledges and hills nearly eleven thousand feet beneath the surface, with the hole itself descending some four thousand feet below that. These findings were fascinating, but he knew they were utterly classified. Only a select few were permitted to know that such an instrument even existed.

As with most great discoveries, those who first glimpsed the lost world had started out looking for something else. During an earlier practice run for a planned deployment in the Atlantic, the new sonar system had easily revealed the locations and dimensions of Allied submarines, ordered to run silent at various depths as part of the test. An unexpected benefit was that the device also peered *beyond* its targets and into the seabed itself, revealing details that had, until then, been completely hidden from human eyes.

The sonar technicians aboard the *Argo* had already named the largest of the riverine features east of the Devil's Hole, Lethe and Styx. But beyond their references to the ancient Greek underworld, no one really believed rivers had ever flowed along the seabed. "Not really," they all agreed. Until they didn't—until it became difficult to agree on the meaning of anything they were observing.

Near the western foothills of a seamount overlooking Styx, a series of perfectly circular shapes in the seafloor should have been easy to dismiss as natural formations that by sheer coincidence merely resembled unnatural figures. But unlike Germany's Ries Basin and the Great Hudson Bay, these circles seemed too perfect. And then there were the straight lines crossing tangentially and radiating away from the circles, like ancient canals or roads, created on a cyclopean scale and with mathematical precision. The sonar men knew from experience that nature seemed to abhor perfectly straight lines scratched into the earth, perhaps even more than it abhorred perfect *circles*. Yet there they were, *both* shapes together.

Ultimately, the engineers agreed that until someone built a submarine capable of descending two miles and with the ability to collect samples, nothing more could be said beyond the fact that the peculiar geometry appeared to resemble an unnatural phenomenon.

Nonetheless, in private thoughts and hushed conversations, no one aboard the *Argo* could make even a reasonable guess at who could have built such a thing at that depth.

CHAPTER 1

Hephaestus Awakes

The first thing that must be asked about future man is whether he will be alive, and will know how to keep alive, and not whether it is a good thing that he should be alive.
—CHARLES DARWIN

We tend to think of ourselves as the only wholly unique creations in nature, but this is not so. Uniqueness is so commonplace a property of living things that there is really nothing at all unique about it.
—LEWIS THOMAS

June 23, 1948
The Greek Isle of Santorini, Eastern Mediterranean

Jacques Yves Cousteau had never been seasick in his life but something told him that this was probably what it felt like.

"Merde alors," he muttered, walking unsteadily away from the twin-engine light transport.

The French Air Force was grooming the ten-passenger Dassault "Flamingo," including its newly modified glazed nose, for use as a trainer and light bomber. Cousteau, a thirty-eight-year-old former naval officer, had called in a favor to be flown from Tunisia to an airstrip on the Greek island of Santorini, as quickly as possible.

He turned back to see two of the ground crew hauling his baggage out of the cargo hold. One tall Greek was lugging an oversize canvas bag that contained his clothes and wet suit, while the other struggled with a pair of steel air tanks.

Cousteau called a warning to the one wrestling with the cylinders. *"Monsieur, soyez prudent avec ceux."*

The man gave him a quick disinterested wave, before muttering something to his coworker. Cousteau ignored him, turning his attention instead to the pilot, who had already climbed outside to inspect one of the plane's duel six-cylinder engines.

A bit underpowered, isn't she? Cousteau thought.

Lieutenant Cousteau knew that if not for a horrific accident a decade earlier, *he* should have been the one piloting the plane, perhaps even flight-testing one of the newer models. His dreams of becoming a naval aviator had been derailed in a single moment of random chance—a car crash that broke both of his arms. Even now, Cousteau cringed at the memory, cognizant that few people knew how very close he had come to dying. The young gunnery officer had nonetheless adapted quickly, steering a new path during the remainder of the war, toward his lifelong fascination with the sea and diving. Working with the French Resistance, he had also found time to codevelop the regulator apparatus that made Jules Verne's Aqua-Lung a reality.

On land, "Gravity is my enemy," he sometimes told friends. The damage to Cousteau's bones made him feel like a man at least thirty years older—*yet beneath the water, I am free, like a child.*

These days, in an alliance with the American navy, his government was assigning him to form what someone had already christened the Underwater Studies and Research Group. Cousteau and his small team were field-testing improvements on their equipment while simultaneously exploring and mapping the remains of a Roman shipwreck—the first such scuba expedition in history. The project was not yet complete when two members of his team were called away from the Tunisia wreck site and flown to Santorini with instructions to investigate the aftermath of seismic shifts offshore. Reportedly the quakes were associated with "some interesting biological phenomena." Cousteau, still recovering from a serious infection he'd contracted in Tunisia, had planned to sit this one out. Now, though, a message from his called-away friend Vincent had changed the plan.

From the air, it had been easy to see that Santorini was the outer rim of a caldera nearly eight miles wide, the remains of an ancient cataclysm that had literally blown a hole in the earth. Long before the first words were written or even spoken in Greek, the northern Mediterranean filled in the wound, creating one of the planet's most picturesque lagoons. But beauty could not hide the violence or the potential for it to awaken again. Near the center of the lagoon, the isle of Nea Kameni ("the new burnt land") had risen in smoke and flames during the time of Napoleon. More recently there had occurred a series of small but progressively stronger quakes, and although geologists debated whether these might be ushering in a new period of island building, they all agreed on one thing—Santorini was not dead.

But volcanic islands awakening do not normally attract the attention of both the French Navy and the Greek Orthodox Church, Cousteau told himself, shaking his head at the incongruity.

Twenty minutes after landing, he checked into what his driver described as "the only hotel in town." The clerk—his eyes conveying the expression of a man who had perhaps seen too much during the war—passed Cousteau a sealed envelope. The Frenchman shot him a questioning look but the man simply shrugged.

The message inside was in neat, handwritten English.

"Heard you were dropping by. Have made remarkable discovery in local quarry. Your old friend MacCready should be here soon. Hope we can compare notes (and share Mac stories) tonight over a bottle of grappa. —Cordially, Wang Tse-lin"

Cousteau smiled. At the bottom of the sheet,

the Chinese scientist had written a phone number and the local address for a restaurant, in what was apparently another "only hotel in town."

Tse-lin was a paleo-anthropologist with a brontosaurian appetite for all of the sciences—including zoology and gemology. During the war, he had lived through the darkest, most tenuous days of the resistance against the occupation of northern China by the late empire of Japan. Recently he had also survived some undisclosed adventure with R. J. MacCready, apparently settling now into what the Frenchman considered to be a rather tame existence collecting fossils and gems. Evidently the only mission Tse-lin cared about these days involved the peace and quiet of fossil-studded cliffs offering skyscraper-high views of the Aegean Sea.

A good plan, Cousteau told himself. *Until it wasn't.*

The Frenchman was looking forward to a meeting with the newest member of the MacCready gang—but that would have to wait. As if to drive home this particular point, he turned toward a commotion at the front door. It was Vincent, trailed by Laurent. Their excitement was unmistakable, and urgent.

"Jacques, *finally*!" Vincent exclaimed, rushing in to hug him.

"Are you ready to dive?" Laurent chimed in.

Cousteau gestured to his bags and equipment, which had been deposited beside the hotel's front desk. "Yes, I am ready this very minute," Cousteau responded. "No food. No rest. Still sick. A dive sounds like great fun."

"Great!" they exclaimed in unison. Cousteau nodded, reminded that sarcasm had never been one of his strong skills.

The clerk had apparently moved past any concerns about the odd luggage and was now looking quite amused at what was unfolding. Shooting the man a suspicious look, Vincent gestured for Cousteau to come nearer, then began whispering something in his ear. During the next minute, the newly arrived Frenchman became even more animated than his two friends. Five minutes after that, the hotel worker was staring at Cousteau's open canvas bag—which looked as if it had just ejected a small assortment of clothing onto the floor. The strange guest and half of the even stranger tanks that had arrived with him were gone.

C*ela semble microbien*," one of the Frenchmen called out, over the protests of an aging inboard engine. His two compatriots nodded in response.

As the little fishing boat motored away from the waterfront village of Fira, its owner, Antoninus Stavracos, thought it odd that the newest member of the trio was ignoring the spectacular multicolored cliffs bordering a crater lagoon nearly three times wider than New York City.

"*Une espèce de Rhodophyte, peut-être?*" a second Frenchman called out. He and his friend had hired Stavracos to take them on an identical dive trip several days earlier.

"*Je ne pense pas*," the new man responded, with a head shake. Though the Greek boatman could barely track more than a few phrases of French at a time, it was clear that this one was the leader.

They're talking about the arrival of the red waters, Stavracos thought. *His Holy Blood.* The Greek found it impossible not to fixate on the amazing events that had occurred during the two months since "the Reddening": *The fish in the markets are larger and healthier, and those who eat them have been cured from all manner of ailments.* "A miracle," Stavracos said, beneath the sound of the motor. Then, shooting a quick glance skyward, he crossed himself.

He knew that, unlike these Frenchmen, most of his recent clientele had been locals—parents mostly, accompanied by their sick or crippled children. He'd taken them to the exact spot where his Holy Blood poured from wounds on the seafloor. Stigmata, some were calling the red plumes, though no one, save for these Frenchmen, had dared to investigate any deeper.

Nearly all of the pilgrims who hired out his boat were poor, like he was, and although he felt bad about taking advantage of their misfortune, he sometimes took a few coins or an item that had been bartered. Often, though, and this was something Stavracos kept from his wife, he charged them nothing at all—the sight of mothers and fathers gently lowering their loved ones into the red water was incompatible with the collection of a fee. He shook his head, remembering how some poor souls, too weak for even a brief immersion, had been splashed with the red-tinted water.

Using the relative positions of the three islands that surrounded them, Therasia looming ahead, Nea Kameni port side, and the cliffs of Santorini far to the rear, Stavracos throttled back briefly before turning off the engine. Satisfied that he'd pinpointed the desired location, he gestured toward the anchor, but none of the men took notice. They were either struggling into black rubber dive suits or adjusting the equipment and bulky air tanks that would allow them to remain submerged for nearly half an hour.

Shaking his head, Antoninus Stavracos moved forward and lowered the anchor himself, feeling for and finding the bottom. He allowed himself a smile, pleased that he could now pinpoint the initial section of shallows, bordering a drop-off estimated to reach at least a third of a mile.

Several minutes later, the boat owner's concerns about the divers and their questionable motives were interrupted by a rapid series of splashes as one by one the men tumbled backward over the gunwale and disappeared.

He watched three sets of bubbles rise through the dark water. *God prevent these strangers from desecrating this site*, he thought. Then Antoninus Stavracos crossed himself yet again.

As Cousteau followed Vincent and Laurent toward a gentle slope strewn with rocks, he managed a quick review of all that he had recently learned. Two months earlier, there had occurred a small earthquake. There were no fatalities and little damage beyond some cracked masonry and smashed glassware. In the aftermath, though, the waters near the lagoon's central cluster of islands gradually began to change color, and within a day or two a sharp-eyed fisherman had determined the source—a shallow spot near the shore of Nea Kameni. Here the stained waters were indeed flowing toward the surface, warm and red—like blood. Soon after came the first claims of rejuvenation and healing, with local doctors perplexed at their apparent validity. About a week after that, the Greek Orthodox Church got into the act and several elder representatives arrived from Crete to begin an investigation.

"They're calling it a Greek version of Lourdes and Fatima," Vincent had explained with a shrug.

"At first we thought it was just superstitious nonsense," Laurent had added.

But the mystery only deepened after one of the town physicians discovered that the so-called miracle fish all contained a strange red material in their guts, at which point Cousteau was alerted. By the time he arrived, his men discovered the source of the material—a series of vents on the seafloor, sixty feet below the surface.

As Cousteau equalized the pressure in his ears and descended toward a rocky incline, he could see it for himself—strange, cauliflowerlike billows of red smoke escaping fissures no wider than his fist. Heard above the distant propeller whine of a fishing boat were the sounds emanating from the vents themselves—a steady rumble of water, accented by the occasional clicking and snapping of rocks trapped within.

Pulling up beside Cousteau as they reached the bottom, Vincent pointed to a boulder several yards from the nearest vent. Like much of the surrounding hillside, it had the appearance of being covered in lush scarlet-hued velvet, and as they moved nearer, Cousteau could feel a significant rise in water temperature. Knowing that his men had taken only a tiny sample of the material on their first dive, he could also see that someone—in all likelihood a free diver—had been there as well, apparently using a blade to scrape away sections of the red mat. Whoever did this had exposed a series of organic strata, the outermost of which were clearly alive. The curious formation reminded Cousteau of the fossilized algal mats called stromatolites, whose modern descendants thrived in the most saline water on the planet.

He peeled off a small piece and brought it close to his face mask. *Perhaps this is an even more extreme life form than the stromatolites*, he thought, before turning his attention toward the near-boiling-point water pouring from the vents. *Microbes from deep in the earth, flourishing in the most difficult of environments.*

His thoughts were interrupted by Laurent, who swept one arm in a wide arc. Cousteau allowed his gaze to follow it. The same material covered the rocks downhill and in every other direction for as far as the eye could see.

He nodded, the message quite clear. *This has been*

escaping into the sea far longer than a few short weeks—
probably at a much-reduced rate—until the earthquake.

Cousteau gave the thumbs-up sign, gestured for his two friends to collect samples of the material, and then swam off a short distance to examine another formation. The Frenchman noticed more scratches on the rock surfaces, where the velvetlike material had been torn away in long strips.

Locals, searching for their miracles, he concluded.

Glancing back, Cousteau could see Vincent and Laurent turning over red-tinted rocks, their wet-suit-clad bodies set against an even darker backdrop as the shallows dropped off into deep black water.

As spectacular as all of this might have been to his friends, Laurent was quickly growing bored.

Bringing ancient Roman artifacts into the light for the first time in two thousand years—now that *was interesting,* he thought. *But a smoke-spewing exhaust pipe—not so much. And collecting more samples of algae?* Merde alors.

He checked his dive watch and air supply. *Great, we'll be heading up soon.*

As his hyperactive colleague Vincent continued to examine the scarlet-stained surroundings, Laurent drifted toward a relatively flattened section that fell off into a far steeper incline. He steadied himself against the current and stared down into the abyss.

There is no red tint there, he thought, noting this with an involuntary shiver. Instead, the water was Bible black and noticeably colder.

How deep is it really? Laurent wondered. *They say four hundred meters but I'm betting more.*

In response to his own question, Laurent pulled loose a bowling-ball-shaped stone, briefly struggled to maneuver the microbe-sheathed boulder into position, then gave a final push. Kicking gently back, he watched as it rolled down the precipitous slope, trailed by an avalanche of dust and red gravel. He followed the path of the rock until it disappeared and until the avalanche he'd created had subsided, leaving only the impenetrable darkness.

Turning, he could see that Vincent was working his way slowly uphill toward another smoke-spewing vent. The man stopped and gestured for him to follow.

Excellent suggestion, Laurent thought, before turning to take a final glance over the cliff edge.

What he saw held him spellbound. A section of the darkness below appeared to be shimmering—a black sheet fluttering in the breeze. *No, not black. More like a violet so deep as to only* seem *black. And so beautiful that no camera I know will ever capture the hue.*

Laurent spun around and began waving his arms wildly, and Vincent, seeing immediately that his friend was either excited or alarmed, swam toward him at full speed. Laurent turned back to face the disturbance from below, barely noticing Vincent's arrival. Both men stared into the shim-

mering transparency, unable to shake the feeling
that it stared also into them, while one thought
from their dive training came immediately to the
forefront: *La panique et vous êtes mort!*

The shimmer ascended the slope and now
seemed to hover, suspended before them like a
great dark curtain.

Jacques Yves Cousteau perceived no indication
of violence. It was as if his two friends were
simply standing beside the drop-off, in front of a
gently shifting and transparent curtain. He would
have described the movements as graceful—right
up to the moment in which Vincent and Laurent
were snatched off the rim. They were not dragged
downward, or dragged anywhere for that matter,
as they would have been if seized by a shark or
another known predator. Instead they seemed
to come apart—to peel open before Cousteau's
eyes—leaving behind ribbons of curled flesh and
a new hue of red clouding the water.

Without turning his back on the shimmering
transparency—there was no one to be saved—he
began backing away from the vent, moving cautiously uphill. He resisted the urge to rise too fast,
a move his experience had taught him would cause
a crippling or even lethal case of "the bends."

Under the direction of his sympathetic nervous system, Cousteau's body had already initiated a fight-or-flight response—the former action
neurochemically circumvented by the latter. He'd

decided to escape the immediate area before surfacing, but the shimmering whatever-it-was appeared to have another idea—gliding closer to Cousteau's position.

An incredibly cryptic predator, he thought, *or predators*—since he had no idea if there were more than one of them.

As if to answer this particular question, the curtain seemed to split in two, each section more or less rectangular. Now they were drifting apart.

Having paused between two boulders, Cousteau was painfully aware that the breath-generated bubble trail he was producing served to advertise his position as effectively as a neon sign.

They're flanking me, he thought. *Like lions stalking their prey.*

A disturbance from above froze the shapes in place.

The boatman's seen something. And as if to affirm this realization, streaks that Cousteau recognized as bullet trails knifed downward through the water in quick succession.

The diver's subconscious steadied him, during that critical moment, by focusing on an irrelevant oddity: *Where did the gun come from?*

The response to the gunshots was instantaneous—the sheets of distorted water changed direction and charged up toward the boat.

To his simultaneous relief and alarm, Cousteau realized that he had just been provided with a distraction. Deciding not to give away his location any more than he'd already done, he took two last deep breaths, shed his scuba tank, then his weight belt, and resumed his swim up the incline, exhaling as he advanced toward shallower water. His subconscious had already performed the vital calculations: *You can stay underwater three minutes on one lungful of air—four at the outside, if you remain calm.*

The commotion on the surface had evolved into a confusion of inexplicable movement. After initially shaking itself from side to side, the boat was snatched downward. Through a semitranslucent blur, Cousteau could see the hull disassemble into a chaotic mélange of smashed timber, boat gear, and motor parts. There was also a human figure, its effort to reach the surface overwhelmed by something (or several somethings) that held it in place, as if caught in a bear trap.

The boatman.

The Greek was flailing and struggling some twenty feet under the lagoon, and in that moment Cousteau decided to swim toward him. Then, as Antoninus Stavracos reached down toward Cousteau pleadingly, his entire body was engulfed in semitransparent sheets, now taking on the reddish-blue hues of the water's surface.

Though his lungs were beginning to ache, Cousteau had a single thought: *They camouflage themselves.* Continuing to back away from the hellscape, and uphill, he saw the roiling shapes glow blindingly bright for an instant, then wink out.

Inexplicably, the man had simply disappeared—as had the sheets of distorted water.

Now the only movement came from the slip-stream of the descending boat parts as they rained around the sole human survivor.

Unable to sustain a calm sufficient to provide the hoped-for maximum of four minutes, Cousteau surfaced far too quickly, barely noting the painful tingling in his fingers.

He gave a loud, involuntary cough, his imagination anticipating the sudden tug that would come just before his body was snatched down and dissected. *Like Vincent. Like Laurent. Like—*

There was a loud squawking sound to his right, but a moment later he realized that it was only seagulls. *Fighting over*—Cousteau turned away.

Now, as the Frenchman wondered what had just taken place, while simultaneously preparing himself for an array of rapid ascent symptoms that would never come, he scissor-kicked smoothly, propelling his body toward the rocky shore of Nea Kameni.

I might just survive the bends, he thought, *if I don't get eaten first.*

Jacques Yves Cousteau had already choked down several mouthfuls of water stained with the red microbes. He would swear until his dying day that it tasted like human blood.

CHAPTER 2

From the Graves of Eden

Looking back across time, through all those fossils . . . I can equate natural selection with just two members of the Hindu Triad—with Siva the destroyer and Vishnu the preserver, but not with Brahma the creator.
—Charles Lyell

Past, present, and future are only an illusion, albeit a stubborn one.
—Albert Einstein

Two Days Later
June 25, 1948
Metropolitan Museum of Natural History, NYC

The fifth-floor office door was open, so Major Patrick Hendry decided that clearing his throat would be an effective way to announce his arrival. R. J. MacCready and two familiar "museum types" had their backs turned to him and were examining what appeared to be a pair of football-sized skulls.

As Hendry's pharyngeal house cleaning abruptly turned into a prolonged, phlegmy cough, the trio turned toward him, wearing an assortment of disgusted looks.

"I'll have some of that on a cracker," Mac said, eliciting additional groans from the pixyish woman in black sitting to his right.

"Go ahead, Mac, make fun," Hendry said, after finally catching his breath. He was carrying a shoe-box-sized package and made an exaggerated showing of gently placing it down on MacCready's desk.

"Well, Major, that *was* a rather unique entrance," said Patricia Wynters. She had flipped up a pair of jeweler's loupe-equipped eyeglasses and was now wearing a genuinely concerned expression. "Are you ill?"

"Sounds like he needs an oil change," grumbled a white-haired man, who quickly turned his attention back to the skulls.

"Nice to see you too, Knight," Major Hendry grumbled back.

Seventy-three-year-old Charles R. Knight was the world's foremost artist of prehistoric life. Without turning around, he granted Hendry a wave with his cigarette.

"Personally, I think *both* of you should quit smoking," Patricia said quietly.

"Second that," Mac added, now waving his arms

in a vain attempt to break up the smoke screen that Hendry and Knight were laying down.

Ignoring Patricia's and Mac's comments, Hendry moved in closer to an enamel tray holding the skulls. "Prehistoric horses again, huh?"

"Yeah, and no touching," Mac added. Though the major had certainly improved over the years, Mac remained mindful of past trespasses that included the conversion of a triceratops into a *bi*ceratops, and most infamously, tripping over and fracturing three of T. rex's toes. Some of Knight's colleagues believed a convergence of disease and an upheaval of the world's oceans had killed the dinosaurs. "If so," Knight had assured one of them, "it took Hendry to finish the job."

Putting down his cigar and leaning in toward the specimens, the major placed both hands behind his back—assuming the "museum looking" position Mac had demonstrated for him on too many occasions for Hendry's liking.

"*Mesohippus* and *Parahippus*, huh?" he asked.

"You got it," Mac said, with an appreciative nod.

"Show-off," Knight muttered under his breath. "Ask him what species they are."

Patricia ignored her grumpy friend. "We're off to central Brazil next month, Major," she announced, excitedly. "Yanni too."

Instead of responding, Hendry flashed her a tight-lipped smile and nodded slightly.

"What?" Mac asked quickly, his voice carrying a hint of alarm.

The major gestured toward the specimens. "Those formerly extinct horses you're looking to study have been around a long time—right, Mac?"

"About fifteen million years," MacCready replied. "And yeah, that's a lot longer than anyone believed possible."

Hendry took a deep breath, then let it out slowly. "Well, then—"

"You *can't* be serious?" Mac said, interrupting what he knew was bound to be bad news.

Major Hendry said nothing.

"Come on, Pat. I mean . . . I'm on quasi-semi-active duty."

Hendry cupped a hand behind one ear. "What was that last thing?" The major turned to Knight and Wynters. "He *did* say 'active duty.' Am I right?"

The researchers stared back at him, blankly, so the major continued. "I'm *sure* there was an 'active' in there somewhere."

"But the permits, the equipment, the . . . the—"

Hendry shook his head, still silent but wearing an expression that said, *Save it, Mac.* He turned back to the package he'd brought and opened it. "This came for you in the mail today," he said, gently removing some packing material before spreading out several items on an empty tray. "They're from Greece. Your pal Tse-lin dug 'em up."

"Wang Tse-lin? And what are *you* doing with it?"

"Let's just say, someone in your mailroom gave me a call when it came in. I did them a little favor by making the delivery myself."

The three scientists moved in for a closer look. Hendry had laid out a pair of strange-looking hand tools—obviously ancient. "They're made of volcanic glass," he said, watching as the trio reacted with something several notches below astonishment.

Knight was the first to turn away, adjusting the easel that held his latest reconstruction on canvas—a prehistoric horse species with beautiful golden eyes.

Mac picked up an obsidian blade. "Umm . . . these are nice, Pat. But you can find stone tools all around the Mediterranean."

Instead of responding, Major Hendry broke into a smile that Mac had seen only rarely—and he hated it. It said, *Gotcha!*

"What?" Mac said.

Hendry replied by lifting away another layer of cardboard and cotton packing material. Then he carefully withdrew an object and held it out to MacCready and Patricia.

"Well, here's your tool maker, smart guy."

Reacting to the odd silence that followed, Charles R. Knight turned around, adjusted his glasses, and stood so quickly that he knocked his easel and brushes to the floor.

"Holy shit!" he cried. "You have *got* to be kidding me."

"No kidding, Chuck," Hendry replied. Then, turning to Mac, he handed him an envelope with two folded pages sticking out and jerked a thumb toward Knight. "Now, before *you* get excited and start knocking stuff over, I need you to read this."

Mac read it quickly and handed the telegram back.

"What is it?" Patricia asked, concerned.

R. J. MacCready remained as silent as the Sphinx—his face giving away nothing. *Well, Pat,* he thought. *I wonder what new level of hell you're dropping me into this time.*

M ac decided even before he repacked the stone tools into Hendry's box and tucked it under an arm that there was no choice but to cancel his expedition to Brazil. The telegram Hendry had received from Cousteau in the eastern Mediterranean did not leave much time to tear up the equipment checklist for a South American expedition and reprovision for the new island destination. Stepping out onto Eighty-First Street and glancing toward a subway entrance, he found it difficult to plan a way through the train delays that had been plaguing the system lately. Reaching for his wallet, he voted for speed over an inexpensive subway token and hailed a cab heading downtown on Central Park West.

"Castle Garden, Battery Park," he told the driver, then sat back and closed his eyes. Mac knew that Yanni had been looking forward to the Brazil expedition. He also knew that she preferred to receive bad news promptly.

All things considered, she took it better than he anticipated.

"And no helicopters, right?"

Mac grimaced. "Yeah, well, Hendry didn't exactly mention helicopters."

As she spoke, Yanni Thorne was simultaneously treading water and adjusting a hydrophone array at one end of a large saltwater pool. Several months after the death of the Central Park Menagerie's last elephant, Yanni had applied for and been transferred to a Navy-affiliated project at what used to be the New York Aquarium.

"So where to?" she asked, switching off the underwater microphones. At the deep end of the pool, an enormous shape responded by making a sharp turn. A five-foot-long, gleaming white hump broke the surface and began steaming toward her at high speed.

Mac took a protectively reflexive step forward, watching as the beluga whale he'd nicknamed "Moby-Dick Jr." generated a large V-shaped wake. It had taken Mac several visits to get used to the immensity of the creature—which Yanni's late husband might have referred to as "a Buick with fins." In truth, Mac knew there was no real cause for concern. The animal's trainer was, after all, Yanni.

"An island off the coast of Greece," Mac responded, as the whale pulled up and raised its domed head out of the water. The humans were suddenly facing a mouthful of peglike teeth.

"Which island?" she asked, before turning to address the cetacean. "Hold on a minute there, big guy."

Yanni swam to the side of the pool and after

gracefully hauling herself out, Mac handed her a towel.

"Santorini," he said, before gesturing to a poolside bucket. "So what's Junior havin' for treats today?"

"Coupla bluefish and some mackerel," she said, reaching into a mélange of sea life, fresh from the Fulton Fish Market. "There's an active volcano there, right?"

"Yeah, semiactive I'd call it. Not like—"

"And a civil war going on too?"

"Yeah, it's a weird one."

"Well then gimme the thirty-second version."

"Let's see. On the right we've got the Greek government army. Their leaders were exiled during the war, and while they were gone things went to shit. Of course, that's who we're backing. And on the left, there are the communist partisans."

"Who weaseled their way into the vacuum left by the Nazis."

"You got it," Mac said.

"Lemme guess. Backed by Stalin and his mob."

"You'd think so, right?" Mac said, flashing the smile he reserved for the rare occasions when Yanni got something wrong. "But actually, no— it's been mostly Yugoslavia and their own commie heartthrob, Tito. Stalin actually opposes the fight."

"Why's that?"

"Hates Tito, plus Stalin's picking his fights carefully. And Greece ain't it."

"Got it," Yanni said.

Mac watched as Yanni flipped the tail half of a

"cocktail blue" into Junior's waiting maw, which chomped closed with a crunch. "We should be okay, though. Most of that political shit's taking place on the Greek mainland and north of Athens."

"Oh yeah, sounds completely safe," Yanni said, sounding somewhat less than convinced. "So why Santorini then?"

"Well, you remember the white stuff and the red stuff in Tibet?"

"You're such a zoologist," she replied. "You mean the fungus that could speed up evolution?"

"Yeah, among other things."

"So?"

"So, a coupla weeks ago Hendry gets a message from Tse-lin, of all people."

"At Santorini? Wasn't he tracking down fossils in Africa?"

"He was. Until he gets sent to Greece."

"Wouldn't a thunk there'd be much paleoanthropology to be done near a volcano."

"No, you wouldn't think so. But there he was—following a lead about weird fossils—digging away nice and peaceful like."

"And then?"

"And then he learns about some big ruckus that's got everyone worked up. Long story short, sounds to him like the red stuff."

Yanni shot him an incredulous look. "Coming out of the volcano?"

"Sort of," Mac replied. "In the water—spewing out of a thermal vent on the lagoon floor."

"This is the *same* microbe we found in Tibet?"

"Something similar but I can't imagine a fungus from Tibet blowing out of a thermal vent all the way in the Mediterranean. Tse-lin says it acts the same—cures, healing, the whole shebang."

"As in 'The world's greatest cure or its deadliest weapon.'"

"Yeah, that shebang," Mac replied with a nod. "Darwin amok."

Yanni let out a deep breath and glanced back at Junior, who was clearly anticipating his next course. In response, she tossed a baseball-bat-length eel toward the middle of the pool. Then she crossed her arms above her head, signaling that snack time was over.

"Look," Mac continued, "we knew we couldn't keep a lid on this forever—that we'd be drawn back in somehow. I guess we just convinced ourselves we had more time, stopped believing it could be so soon."

"Great," Yanni said, staring across the pool. "What else?"

Mac gave a funeral laugh. "Well, this is the part where things go to hell. Seems three French divers head down to investigate the discovery . . ."

"Yeah, and?"

"And two of 'em got torn apart."

"What, sharks?" Yanni replied. "I *hate* sharks."

"No. Not sharks. Apparently something a bit more—well, more exotic. I happen to know the guy who survived—solid credentials. And he says this is something *none* of us have seen before."

"Wonderful."

"Knew you'd think so."

"So is Tse-lin still there?"

Mac nodded. "Barely. Until Hendry doubly re-assured him we were going in, he was lookin' to get out of Dodge."

Yanni shot him a quizzical look.

"Santorini," Mac corrected himself.

"You blame him?" Yanni said. "The return of our 'red stuff,' something tearing divers apart." She shook her head. "Sounds like the perfect vacation spot."

"And don't forget the civil war," Mac added cheerily.

"Sure," Yanni said. "We can't have the locals gettin' along."

"Nah, that would set an uncomfortable prece-dent," Mac said. "Hey, look on the bright side: at least we won't be freezing our butts off this time, right?"

"I suppose," Yanni said, watching skeptically as Mac unfolded the top of a cardboard box he'd brought.

"But there *is* one more thing."

"How'd I guess?"

"No, this one's okay. In fact it'll give us an in-teresting cover story."

Mac gently removed a small, beautifully pre-served fossil skull from the box.

"That looks familiar."

"It is. It's a chimp, or something close to it. Tse-lin thinks it's some lost branch of the bonobos. Knight agrees with him."

"That's nice—those little pygmy guys, right?"

She lifted the skull and gently turned it over. "But why's that so important?"

"The kicker's what our Chinese pal found *alongside* the bones."

"Go on," Yanni said, allowing impatience to creep into her voice.

Mac reached into the box again, withdrew a small object, and held it out to her. Then he gestured toward the skull. "Seems like Cheeta made this."

"Ancient chimps crafting stone tools. Get the hell out of here!"

Mac replied with a wry smile.

"How long ago?"

"Oh, we're thinking something like five million years—give or take a million."

"Holy shit," Yanni said. "You *are* kiddin' me, right?"

Mac stifled a laugh.

5 MILLION YEARS TO SANTORINI

When the great sea was already ancient, of an age most people scarcely dream, continents were being reshaped and the stage was being set for a focus of human forces. Two million years before the arrival of Santorini's tool makers, Africa had been a raft of land, adrift on a collision course with southern Spain. At the point of impact between Morocco and Gibraltar, the seabed crumpled and a new mountain range bulged four thousand feet into the clouds, forming a natural dam that completely sealed off the Atlantic from the Mediterranean.

As rocks and continents measured time, the Gibraltar Dam formed and the entire Mediterranean Sea began to dry out in a geologic heartbeat; yet, from Mac's and Yanni's perspective on time, that single heartbeat would have lasted twenty thousand generations. Aside from the occasional earthquake, no ancestral humans could have noticed the change—given even a whole lifetime of watching, even as it happened before their eyes.

The universe was filled with such contrasts, and in Mac's generation, Harold "Doc" Edgerton reveled in them. Having invented a method for filming the first split second of an atomic bomb test in ultra-slow motion, he next time-lapsed entire years into seconds. Thus did he reveal the previously unobserved wonder of autumn reds and yellows alternating with flashes of snow and bursts of green while his cameras slowly panned across Massachusetts landscapes. By the time Mac and Yanni departed a Grumman airfield on Long Island for the isle of Santorini, Edgerton had already begun advising stop-motion film animator George Pal, who would soon transform H. G. Wells's novel about a time traveler into a feature-length film depicting a journey across 802,701 years.

To Edgerton and Pal, even the slow and stately transitions of ancient Gibraltar could be perceived as a symphony of motion. To them,

the centuries required for the entire Mediterranean to evaporate behind the dam and form
a canyon deeper and wider than any the planet
had known in more than a hundred million years
could be viewed across the span of a minute.
Below Santorini and Crete, and as far south as
Egypt, deep blue waters flashed to desert. Forests flowed in, spreading across the land like
puffs of green vapor. And then, blue floodwaters.
And desert again. Forests.

By 5.4 million years B.C., a chancy sort of balance had been achieved in the uneasy marriage
between two continental plates. For more than
600,000 years, now, the Gibraltar Dam stood
strong. Two miles beneath the limestone plain
on which the pyramids would make their stand
against time, the Nile flowed north along the
Mediterranean floor. It fed scores of lakes and
oases, before being stopped near Crete and the
deep waters of the Devil's Hole. At the hole's
edge, great fissures yawned open. Volcanic fountains sent forth streams of water laced so thickly
with red microbes that they grew like wool on the
rocks.

In the incomparably dense, humid, and richly
oxygenated air, relatives of clams, snails, and
squids evolved to fill niches never occupied by
their kind before. Insects and spiders failed to
thrive in the great Mediterranean canyon. There
were no ants, no termites, and no mosquitoes.
The mollusks had seen to that.

Sea butterflies transitioned from graceful
swimmers into the air—first as gliders, then

exhibiting powered flight. With no aerial competitors, they diversified into myriad shapes and sizes—convergence imparting them with color patterns that would have seemed familiar to any twentieth-century birdwatcher.

But the land two miles below Spain, Greece, and Africa remained inhospitable to outsiders and so the ancestral elephants that occasionally migrated down from the green Sahara highlands did not stay for very long. They were smart enough to know better.

CHAPTER 3

Adaptation

I was very careful in the selection of my ancestors.
—ERNST MAYR

*A hen is only an egg's way of making
another egg.*
—SAMUEL BUTLER

But only God can hatch a dragon.
—FROM A GREEK ORTHODOX TRADITION
REGARDING THE APOSTLE PHILIP'S TRAVELS

June 28, 1948
The Airstrip at Santorini, Greece

R. J. MacCready and Yanni Thorne exited the dual-engine Cessna Bobcat and stood on a pebble- and shell-strewn tarmac. Dubbed the

Bamboo Bomber by airmen, the light transport had pounded down hard onto a short, war-time airstrip. Although most visitors still arrived by boat, the flight from Athens had saved them at least two full days. While Mac and the pilot hauled supplies out of the plane, Yanni could see two men exiting a nearby truck. Mac paused in his hauling and gave one of them, their friend Wang Tse-lin, a handshake that turned into a bear hug. Tse-lin broke from the hug and waved excitedly toward Yanni.

Yanni returned the wave but after shooting the Chinese scientist a warm smile looked away from the second man—whom she'd never seen before—with the awkwardness she usually felt upon meeting new people.

"We will see you later at the hotel," Tse-lin said to his companion, who seemed to sense Yanni's unease and headed promptly for the stack of de-planed supplies. Without a word of greeting, the stranger began carrying their gear toward the truck, whistling a distinctly creepy rendition of "The Colonel Bogey March" as he went.

Yanni watched as the balding whistler loaded a canvas bag packed with a rather unique assortment of field gear and automatic weapons. "So, Wang, who's your pal?"

"That is Pierre."

"Okay," she said, "*another* French guy but not *the* French guy?"

"Right. This one is my colleague. Plants rubber trees. Blows things up. Now he digs fossils."

"Interesting resume," Mac added, with a touch of genuine admiration. "Pierre who?"

"Boulle," Tse-lin replied, then turned to Yanni. "Other *real* French guy is Jacques."

Yanni nodded. "And he's still being held by the authorities?"

"Yes," Tse-lin said, somberly. "They have many questions for him."

Their friend ushered Mac and Yanni to a car he had rented, and held the door as they climbed in. The car was prewar, well maintained, comfortable. "You go to the hotel, get an hour's rest? A meal?"

Mac shook his head. "Where's Cousteau being held?"

"Police station."

"Then we're going to the police station."

"This ought to be fun," Yanni said, staring out the window at the lagoon.

"Could be big trouble," Tse-lin said. Yanni could not see his face, but she had no doubt that he was trying to size up Mac's mood through the rearview mirror, as a compass setting for what was to come.

Like every other building on the island, the Santorini police station was a low, white, and boxy affair. Like most of his countrymen, Jacques Cousteau understood at least a grade schooler's level of Greek but, in keeping with French tradition, pretended not to. He simply listened, and assessed.

Cousteau had been inside for more than six hours, much of that time spent sitting on an uncomfortable wooden chair while the head gendarme looked for someone who could more fluently speak and translate French. Once this was accomplished, Cousteau had been grilled unceasingly about the incident in the lagoon—reported as a strange accident that claimed three lives, one of them a well-known local. The real problem arose after he explained that several large sharks, in some sort of feeding frenzy, had destroyed the boat.

"I do not believe you are telling me everything, monsieur." This became the most oft-repeated phrase in what had rapidly degenerated from a polite conversation into *un interrogatoire*.

"*Il ne reste plus rien à dire*," Cousteau insisted. There was nothing left to tell. *Nous avons été attaqués par plusieurs requins*. He turned from the translator to the policeman. "Καρχαρίες! Sharks!"

The policeman crossed his arms. *No translation required*, Cousteau thought.

The problem was, that after a tearful meeting with the boatman's wife, the Greek officer was now intent on sending his own divers down to recover whatever remains the widow might be able to properly bury.

But also, Cousteau reasoned, *to see if perhaps I murdered my own friends and someone's beloved husband*.

With their safety in mind, Cousteau had been adamant that they must not send divers. However, in retrospect, he now believed he had probably been a bit *too* adamant in that regard.

Sometimes saying the right thing doesn't change anything, Cousteau thought. *Except to make everything worse.*

Okay, who's running the show around here?" Mac said, barging into the sleepy-looking police station and waking the man behind a clutter-strewn desk from his midday reading.

The man shouted something in Greek. Tse-lin, who had entered with Yanni, scrambled forward to translate. "He wants to know who the—who you are?"

MacCready produced a handful of official-looking paperwork and waved it at the man. "Captain R. J. MacCready, U.S. Army. Does anyone speak English around here? We haven't got all day."

Tse-lin relayed the message and the man quickly ducked into a back room. A fireplug-shaped bruiser emerged, his face well tanned and unsmiling. "What this is about, Mr.—?"

"*Captain* MacCready. And what is your name, sir?"

"Sergeant Demetrius Papandreas," the man announced, in clear but heavily accented English.

Yanni started writing in a small notebook. "Is that two *p*'s or one, Sergeant?"

The officer shot her a suspicious look. "One *p*," he said. "And who are *you*?"

Mac jumped back in. "This is Special Agent Thorne. Sergeant, are you aware that the man you're currently holding prisoner is working on a joint mission of international importance—a collaboration between the French and American governments and one that has the full cooperation of your own government?"

"I . . . I . . . he is not a prisoner," the cop shot back, defensively.

Yanni, who continued to write, looked up and shot the man a mirthless smile. "Then please bring Lieutenant Cousteau out here immediately so we can verify that he has not been harmed."

"Harmed? Nobody touched him," the officer replied.

Mac stepped in. "Sergeant Papandreas, I'm sure you know that Lieutenant Cousteau has recently gone through a horribly traumatic experience in which two of his close friends were violently killed in a shark attack."

"Yes, but—"

"Excuse me," Mac said, shuffling through the papers he was holding before stopping to read one. "We know that a local man was killed as well, a husband and father of three children."

Yanni addressed the man solemnly, their bluster momentarily set aside. "Our commanders noted that this heroic individual did not flee when the trouble began, and died trying to save our people."

Mac continued: "Somehow the word 'condolences' is not big enough."

The policeman nodded in appreciation.

Cousteau appeared in the doorway.

"Lieutenant Cousteau." Mac came to attention and saluted.

"Ma—Captain, MacCready," Cousteau responded, returning the salute and a rather confused expression.

Mac turned to his two friends. "Of course you know Dr. Wang Tse-lin. And this is Special Agent Thorne."

Yanni snapped off her own salute, which Cousteau returned.

Mac handed the policeman a slip of paper. "Sergeant Papandreas, if you have any further questions, you should call this number. If not, on behalf of the U.S. Army and President Truman, your cooperation is greatly appreciated."

He gestured to Yanni, who held up her notebook and tapped it with a pen.

Within a minute, and with no further fuss at all, the quartet was headed toward the waiting car. "Special Agent Thorne?" Yanni said, under her breath.

Mac allowed himself a wry smile but remained silent.

"Whose phone number did you give that sergeant guy anyway? Not Hendry's?"

"Nah," Mac said, finally. "It was something I saw on a poster in the Athens airport. I think it's a cab company."

Once they pulled away from the police station, Mac turned to Cousteau, who was looking morose. "Jacques, long time no see. Too long."

The Frenchman shook off his sorrowful expression for a moment. "Mac, I want to thank you. Thank you all for—"

Mac held out a hand that said, *No need*. "I'm

sorry to hear about your friends," he added. "And we can talk about that later, if you like."

"*Merci*," Cousteau said, with a nod.

"Jacques, this is my friend Yanni Thorne."

Cousteau, ever the gentleman, reached across his friend to shake her hand. "Special Agent?"

"Yeah," Yanni replied, looking past him in the direction of the lagoon. "Just got promoted about ten minutes ago."

P*hysiquement*, I think I am feeling better than I should," Cousteau said, once they'd arrived at the hotel, and after Mac and Yanni had checked in to their rooms.

"How's that?" Mac asked.

"After all of that happened . . . down there. After all I saw, I came to the surface *trop vite*." He turned to Yanni. "Too fast."

She nodded.

Cousteau continued. "And yet I feel perfectly fine—I have no, and this absolutely should *not* be, *no* aftereffects? And the strangest thing—though there is plenty of strange about this—is how my arms feel better also."

"Jacques was in a car accident sometime back," Mac explained, heading off Yanni's question.

Wearing an expression of disbelief, the Frenchman shook his arms, then reached upward and wiggled his fingers. "But now there is no pain."

Mac and Yanni exchanged looks and shared the same thought. *The red stuff.*

Cousteau did not seem to notice.

Mac could see easily that his friend appeared to be drifting off into a nightmare. *"Mentalement, c'est une autre histoire,"* Cousteau muttered.

Mac nodded sympathetically. *"Another story"* indeed.

JUNE 29, 1948

_____

Not very long after sunrise, while Cousteau lay low at the hotel, Mac and Yanni accompanied Tse-lin to the excavation site where he had been at work, above the western shores of Santorini.

They made their way down the steep, rocky trail until Tse-lin came to a halt at around the midway point. From here the feeling that they were standing on the rim of an enormous caldera was all too clear. Mac thought it was a perfect spot to take in a spectacular view of the lagoon and the smaller islands. But it was also clear to him that Tse-lin had not stopped to admire the view.

"I have something important to tell you both," he said.

Given recent events, Mac and Yanni expected the worst: the full spectrum from *being black-mailed into service by Mao's communists* to *joining a cargo cult* came to mind.

"What is it, Tse-lin?" Mac asked.

"I . . . I am so uncertain," he said.

"We're your friends," Yanni said. "Tell us what's eatin' you."

Tse-lin paused a moment, seemingly to summon

his courage. "I am now American," he said proudly, before pausing. "And now . . . I need an American name."

Mac and Yanni released the collective breaths they had been holding but managed to maintain their solemn expressions.

"That *is* serious," Mac said.

"Very serious," Tse-lin said, with a nod.

"You got any ideas yet?" Yanni asked.

"I was thinking . . . maybe Seymour."

Mac, who'd been prepared to offer whatever support he could, started to bite on his lower lip. "Um, anything else make the short list?"

"Maybe Poindexter too."

Now Mac turned away, feigning a coughing fit, and Yanni threw him a dirty look.

"Those are . . . swell names, Tse-lin," she said. "But what about Alan?"

"Ah-lan?" Tse-lin repeated.

"It was my husband Bob's middle name. And I've always loved it."

Mac, who had gone pensive at the mention of his late best friend, managed a smile. "I think it's a lulu," he said at last.

Now Tse-lin smiled too. "Alan. From now on I would like to be called Alan."

"It'll be my pleasure," Yanni responded, trying unsuccessfully *not* to tear up.

"Me too . . . Alan," Mac said.

They found Pierre Boulle working in the shade of a blanket-sized canopy that had been rigged to allow the fossil diggers to remain out of the direct sunlight. The men who quarried volcanic ash for the Suez Canal's concrete had taken a giant chunk out of the island, like a slice out of a layer cake. From the bottom of the quarry, one could either look out across the lagoon or straight up into the layers of alternating volcanic and sedimentary deposits. The youngest layers, near the top, enclosed part of a Crusades-era church. Twenty feet below the church floor lay graves of the first humans to reach Santorini. The farther down one walked toward the bottom of the mine's geologic layer cake, the deeper one descended into time.

Pierre Boulle and Alan Tse-lin had set up camp at the very bottom.

"So this is where that chimp skull came from?" Mac asked.

"The skull, the spear points, the hand axes," Pierre replied, not bothering to look up.

"Couldn't they have been made by early humans and then gotten mixed up with your primate bones? Maybe by a stream eroding through and washing them down to this level?"

Now Pierre turned, appearing to size up the American zoologist. "That idea is *merde*. Do you know what is *merde*?"

"I'm familiar with it."

"Then you know there were no tool-making humans here five million years ago, or any humans. But these tools *were* here."

"Can you tell us what else was here five million years ago?" Yanni asked.

"A very different world," the newly minted Alan replied. "These fossils, these artifacts, and even the rock that surrounds them, they are beginning to tell us a story—of our past and perhaps of our future. It is our job to decipher that story."

With that, Alan Tse-lin picked up a stainless steel dental pick and knelt beside his colleague, who was scraping and brushing earth away from a newly exposed skull.

"She is a beautiful lady, no?" said Pierre.

"It's a beautiful *specimen*," Yanni replied, "but how do you know it's a female?"

In response, Boulle drew an index finger along a ridge that ran along the top of the cranium. "This we call a sagittal crest," he said.

"In this species, females were larger," Alan chimed in. "Bigger crest. Bigger jaw muscles."

Boulle turned to Mac. "And *monsieur*, these tools we collected are related to funerary rites. *Je suis absolument certain!*"

Mac nodded. "Whose funerals?"

"Well, the tools are not from people across the water. And they were *not* mixed in with stone artifacts from humans who lived here in more recent time."

"So who—"

"As I say, they were *buried* here, *monsieur*. *Délibérément!*"

Yanni moved in for a closer look. "Meaning these creatures had some belief that tools might be needed after death?"

"Who knows? Perhaps they are just for decorative purposes," said Alan. "But what a possibility to raise!"

"And I have not seen such quality stonework since the American Clovis points they recovered in '29," Boulle said, then pointed toward higher strata. "The first humans are way up there—one hundred, maybe two hundred thousand years before today."

"And crude, crude tools are what you find there," Alan Tse-lin added. "But here is a most amazing thing—"

"The more *ancient* culture is the more *advanced* culture," Boulle interjected, stealing his colleague's punch line.

Alan nodded in affirmation, before continuing, very gingerly, to expose the bones of a hand, placed evidently with loving care, over the "beautiful lady's" chest.

Boulle turned back to the skull, brushing soil away from a blackened layer beneath it. "This dark here is plant material," he said, reverently. "Someone made a soft bed of olive leaves before laying her body to rest."

Mac and Yanni watched them for a few moments more before turning their attention to the red stains in the lagoon, the phenomenon plainly visible even at this distance.

Yanni took a step toward MacCready. "So you think there's a connection, going all the way back, between these fossils and the red stuff?"

Before Mac could answer, there was a rumble in the sky and four heads turned to the north.

Flying in tandem, two silver jet fighters streaked

across the lagoon. As if intentionally overflying the excavation, they dropped altitude and let out a unified roar. The drawn-out, artificial thunder rattled the eyeless sockets of a skull that had never lived to see (or even to imagine) a plane. Before the jets circled back over the island fragment called Therasia and disappeared again into the north, Mac identified their origin by the large red star adorning a vertical stabilizer. *Russians.*

"I don't know, Yanni," Mac said, answering her question, "but we need to get to work—and fast."

CHAPTER 4

Dead of Night

*Call it mother, if you will—but Earth is
not a doting parent.*
    —ISAAC ASIMOV

5.33 Million B.C.
On the Bed of the Eastern Mediterranean

The dust came down like
snow—came down with twi-
light, as gentle and fine as
mist. It tasted faintly of salt, and it rode in each
afternoon on a wind from the western desert.
Proud One had seen the desert once, after the
Stone-throwers chased her clan down from the
highland savanna and watering holes. The desert
was endless. When the sunlight struck it in the
morning, it shimmered like a wonderful horizon-
spanning lake, but to enter the lake and travel
west was slow death.

Proud One, her surviving child, Seed, and her

entire clan were in retreat. The lands above the canyon floor—two miles above—belonged to the Stone-throwers now, belonged to a stockier and much stronger clan that was spreading like a conquering horde from the distant plain of black rock.

"Stone-throwers," Seed signed with her fingers, expressing recollection of past horrors, and fear.

"They will not follow us here," the mother signed back. She raised two calloused, hair-covered hands above her head, so all could see her assuring reply. They had paused on an outcrop of siltstone, overlooking a vast river. Proud One, the clan of forty's leading matriarch, flared her huge nostrils wide, breathing deeply of the strange new scents of the forest, of ripening fruits near and far, and of nectars she had not smelled in such abundance since before she was Seed's age.

For just a little while, Proud One felt like a child again, at the beginning of a fantastic adventure.

For only a little while, she felt so.

Her kind had long ago reached a stage in brain development by which past experiences could be compared, one to another, to anticipate the future in reasonable detail. She also knew that the clan's retreat into new lands had produced more bad memories than good and so her moment of excitement was all too brief. Proud One looked at her daughter and then to the unknown world ahead with a renewed sense of loss and fear that was the ancestor of worry. And with that emotion the first lies entered the world.

"We will be safe," Proud One signed to Seed, and to the rest of the clan.

She repeated the sign and gestured toward the river's edge and the northern route that lay beyond.

Now Proud One's greatest concern was putting distance between her group and the Stone-throwers. Urgency drove her forward, but an inner, almost equally urgent instinct seemed to be crying out that this new world was far from safe.

Each day, in this canyon refuge miles below sea level, the planet's warmest and most complex air currents drew up mountains of moisture from the west, piling trillions of water droplets together above the eastern oases, forming towering anvil clouds. At night the clouds collapsed into torrents. In air two times thicker than on the continents above, raindrops fell with curiously lazy speed, barely faster than leaves falling from trees.

This particular night, predators arrived with the rain. They came down from the trees, black as the clouds above, revealed against deep shadows only by the suddenly intensifying flicker of lightning. There were only three of them, but they were enough—each so much at the peak of its species's pack-hunting skills that had Seed not been wide awake and looking in precisely the right direction, the creatures would have fallen upon the encampment without even the faintest scuttle against a tree trunk for warning.

Proud One was also awake, but her attention had been directed elsewhere. Hearing Seed's whimper, her head snapped toward the child and followed her gaze upward. She could sense that the rest of her clan was also awake and scanning for movement.

Proud One expected to see a large, arboreal cat, though there had been no sounds or smells anywhere along the oasis of anything even vaguely reminiscent of a panther. Instead, a particularly long series of lightning flickers seemed to reveal nests of snakes descending from the canopy. Each nest possessed a head, not much larger than her own, and roughly the same shape. But these "heads" were surrounded by groping, wiggling black tendrils—which projected toward her from the shadows.

One night visitor's eyes—like none Proud One had ever seen—reflected the shimmering sky fire and held her momentarily transfixed. The child clutched her mother's waist, while she and the rest of the clan bared their canines, preparing for a fight. Reacting to the threat display, the three intruders froze in place—demonstrating an uncanny ability to blend in with the forest's dark nooks and crannies.

But for a shimmer of lightning, Proud One would have seen little or nothing of the actual attack, which began when one of the night stalkers uncoiled two snakelike limbs—and sprang toward her and Seed.

Against this, the matriarch's keen hearing and sense of touch guided her more deftly than sight. In an instant she had sidestepped the strike and bitten a soft strip of flesh from the very beast that had dropped from the trees in a failed attempt to prey upon her child. The wad of tissue writhed in Proud One's mouth, tasting simultaneously salty and sweet.

It seemed impossible that the monster could have survived such a wound—yet, as the mother stood in the rain and blackness, there came to her a slow recognition that the creatures had not failed in their hunt. Through the intermittent lightning Proud One could see that while she momentarily engaged one of the creatures, other predators used the distraction to their benefit. Two clan members, who had been standing nearby, simply vanished—they and their attackers disappearing into the night as if swallowed by it.

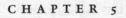

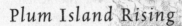

CHAPTER 5

Plum Island Rising

We all agree that your theory is mad.
The problem which divides us is this: is it
sufficiently crazy to be right?
—NIELS BOHR

June 30, 1948
Metropolitan Museum of Natural History, NYC

For Dr. Nora Nesbitt it had been a tremendously busy few days. The lack of sleep was difficult enough, but her training had helped her to adapt. The hardest part of all was the knowledge that she was now a traitor to people she had thought of as friends. Tired and burdened with what she called "a bit of that bad dog feeling," she bumped into the corner of an awkwardly placed table while retrieving a stack of MacCready's field notebooks. A framed picture almost fell onto the floor, an amiable-looking guy with a ponytail, but she caught it and repositioned it on the tabletop—or, rather, what had looked like the top of a table.

Theremin, she thought, with a grimace. That *ugly thing, again.*

Fortunately, although Nesbitt had made plenty of noise, no one along the museum's fifth-floor corridors seemed to have heard anything. In the absolute wakefulness that often crept in behind periods of extended fatigue, she scanned speedily through the first notebook, then a second and a third. It was clear to her by the time she rifled through another desk drawer full of loose notes and correspondence that during all of two years, Mac had written down nothing about the last expedition—nothing about a Himalayan grotto or what he'd referred to as the red stuff—nothing except the most obscure, self-coded references.

Has he hidden those records? she wondered. *Or is he now able to keep it all in his head?*

For her own part, Nesbitt reveled in the knowledge that her previous exposure to the red stuff had the side effect of giving her a photographic memory. She could recall and cross-reference hundreds of pages from Mac's notes in search of anything relevant.

Does he realize, yet, that he came out of there with something more than a cure for the common cold in his veins?

Mac and Yanni had suddenly abandoned expedition plans that appeared to be more than two years in the making. And from the moment her colleagues at the (officially nonexistent) Plum

Island lab learned this, it was clear their own research was at risk. Nesbitt had assigned code words of her own to the enigmatic red microbe: the Darwin Strain. And to her, those two words spelled *Oh, mother.* The lock that Nesbitt's team thought they held over the world's supply of the substance had seemed absolute. Now that Mac had flown off to the Mediterranean with no warning at all, she was not so sure.

Nesbitt was scanning through another volume of "notes about irrelevant oddities" when the door to R. J. MacCready's office opened. She looked up from the papers and screwed on her best *I'm-sure-Mac-would-be-delighted-to-see-me-rifling-through-his-notes* smile.

Two familiar figures stepped inside.

Neither of them was smiling.

"Patricia. Charles," Nesbitt said, cheerily.

"Find everything you need?" Patricia asked.

"The gold jewelry from Troy is in the east wing and you'll find the Star of Ceylon in the southeast turret," Charles Knight said, loudly.

"We keep the silverware on the ground floor," Patricia added.

"You don't understand," Nesbitt protested.

"I'm afraid we do," Knight said.

"How long has it been, Nora?" Patricia asked. "Two years?"

"Yes, well—"

"Now here you are, back again," Patricia said, "coming in here really sneaky-like, and going through Mac's expedition notes." She gestured toward a stack of suddenly well-organized papers.

"And *so* nice to see both of you, as well," Nesbitt said.

"Save it, Nora," Knight said. "Why don't you just tell us why you're here?"

"The truth is, I'm doing a follow-up to the Himalayan expedition and I needed to check a few things."

"Follow-up for whom?" the elderly artist shot back.

Their former museum colleague ignored the question. Instead she took a quick glance around the room, which was in an even greater state of disarray than usual. "Looks like Mac left in a hurry. He must be in the field, huh?"

"Back to central Brazil," Knight replied, a bit too quickly. "Looking for prehistoric horses."

"Bit of a homecoming too," Patricia chimed in, attempting to salvage the story. "For Yanni, that is."

Nesbitt responded with a wry grin. "Personally, I think you're going to need a better cover story."

"Well, then I guess you got some bad information," Knight said, once again trying to sound convincing, but failing miserably.

Instead of attempting a further rebuttal, Nesbitt produced a color photograph from her bag and passed it to the artist. It showed a single elongated digit—a finger, though far too long to be human. Seemingly tanned like leather, the flesh was covered in what appeared to be red velvet. The two researchers examined the photo silently for several seconds before Nesbitt cleared her throat. "Look familiar?"

Patricia shook her head. "Not in the least."

Charles Knight gave a slight shoulder shrug. "Haven't got a clue."

"Look," Nesbitt said, making no attempt to hide her disappointment. "I'm trying to have a serious conversation here."

"Please hurry, dear," Patricia said. "We've *really* got a ton of work to do."

"Okay, then let's get right down to it," Nesbitt said. "You *do* remember that red microbe I discovered in Tibet? The one that can speed up the process of evolution, maybe extend life, cure the sick?"

Patricia Wynters clenched her teeth, as if trying to keep her jaw from dropping open.

"*You* discovered?" Knight said, with a derisive laugh, his response eliciting a near-instantaneous wince from Patricia.

Dr. Nora Nesbitt smiled her unpleasant smile again. "You two would make terrible spies," she said, shaking her head.

"Maybe it's because we deal in facts," Patricia followed. "In our world, deception is a bit harder to see—kind of gets lost in the peripheral vision. Can you say the same?"

"All right, so let's kill the BS," said Knight. "Get to the point or get out!"

The biologist remained calm. "You both know as well as I do that we have to keep a lid on something."

"That's an interesting concept," Patricia said, gesturing toward Mac's notebooks.

Nesbitt ignored the comment. "On Plum Island,

my coworkers and I have been running tests on a small sample of the red microbe that came into my possession. You can see it in that photo."

"You mean the photo of the sample you *stole*?" Knight interjected. "And then smuggled out of Tibet?"

Nesbitt shrugged. "Collected/stole, exported/smuggled. It's all semantics."

"As I understand it," Knight said, "one mission requirement was *not* to bring anything alive out of those valleys."

"And how do you know *what* my mission was? Have you been given clearance, up to that level?"

Silence.

"Well, let me fill you in," Nesbitt said. "You *have*."

"Clearance by whom?" Patricia asked. "And why?"

"Not that we give two . . . licks," Knight said, angrily.

"The first part of that question isn't important right now. As for why: For one, you already know most of the story. Plus you've all developed a little more expertise on the biology and history of to-day's lost worlds than I'd been led to believe."

"*You'd* been led to believe?" Knight said, growing even more annoyed.

"Yes," Nesbitt continued, "just like I believe—*know*—that Mac's nowhere near Brazil, and that Yanni's involved in this little excursion as well."

"And what if she is?" Patricia asked.

"Such an interesting woman. You know, I've heard from one of our contacts in Brazil that she was a *very* strange child. That would be consistent with her incomparable, empathic connections with whales and elephants—and who knows what else in the pantheon of animals."

"So what?" Knight said.

"So," Nesbitt replied, "a little birdie tells me Mac's meeting up with this Cousteau fella—which means they're in the water. And *Yanni's* along for the ride. Now, *please* don't tell me another strange animal's involved."

"I'm thinking it's sharks," Patricia said.

"So what do *you* think?" Knight asked. "Is it fish for breakfast, for you? Or vice-versa?"

Nesbitt rolled her eyes and allowed Knight to finish.

"And if you're planning on swiping more of that stuff—stuff that's been nothing but trouble, I'll be rooting for the sharks."

"Look, we're *scientists*," Nesbitt said, with a hint of exasperation. "Have you ever heard of anyone going out on an expedition and *not* collecting samples? It's how we learn."

"And so here you are," Patricia said, motioning toward Mac's stacked papers, "sampling someone's personal property, all in the name of science. Isn't that right, my dear?"

The invertebrate biologist said nothing.

"I thought so," Patricia said, before casting for a little more information herself. "So what *sorts* of experiments have you been running for the past two years?"

"I'm afraid to ask," muttered Knight. "Found

anything Mac and Yanni should be warned about?
Anything interesting?"

"Maybe," she replied. "And certainly."

"Then spill it," Knight said sternly.

"After all," Patricia followed, "we *have* been
given clearance, haven't we, Nora?"

Nesbitt smiled her mirthless smile at the tag
team. "As I've already said, you're cleared, if you
really want to hear it. But in return for what Mac
needs to know—and you can watch over me while
I do it—I'll need to continue going through his
notes."

Knight shook his head. "You're serious, aren't
you?"

Nesbitt nodded, solemnly. "Look, if there are
more of these microbes out there, and if Mac's
written anything down somewhere, or if you
know anything about it—then I need to know.
'Cause there sure as shit isn't much here."

The two friends turned to each other, each
seeking approval for what they were about to do.
Finally, Patricia gave Nesbitt the slightest of nods,
but the point was clear. *You first.*

"Our experiments started out as rather simple
ones, really. You're both familiar with fruit flies,
right?" Nora asked, cheerily, sounding more like
the young researcher they had grown to admire
two years earlier, but a little more arrogant as
well.

"Do we look like nitwits?" Knight snapped.
"*Drosophila.*"

"Long chromosomes and short life spans,"

Patricia responded, maintaining her genial air. "That makes them great subjects for genetics experiments."

"It's funny you should mention that last bit," Nesbitt said. "Have you ever heard of fruit flies living for two years?"

"Nonsense," Knight said, with a contemptuous wave. "What species are you talking about? *Drosophila melanogaster* live for maybe forty-five days. Fifty, tops." He turned to Patricia. "Who ever heard of such a thing?"

"Well . . . now you have," Nesbitt said, allowing herself yet another smile.

"So?" Knight followed.

Nesbitt looked down at the stacked notebooks and scraps of paper. "*So* . . . now Mac inexplicably cancels a return expedition to Brazil—a trip that he'd been anticipating for—what? At least two years. And right after that I find a pair of references to 'scarlet *scratisfortum*' and 'red *moctus proctus*'— Just those five words, and not even a sentence fragment to go with them."

Patricia and Knight exchanged brief looks at the mention of Mac and Yanni's double-talk–inspired code words.

"*Hmmm*," Nesbitt said, studying their expressions. "I wonder what he's talking about?"

"No clue," Knight responded, trying plainly not to detonate the last remains of a blown cover story. "So, not to change the subject too much, but after two years I'm betting your experiments have moved on to something a little more interesting than fruit flies. You want to talk about it?"

"Not today. Now, do you want to talk about what new animal Yanni's been sent to investigate?"

"Not today," Knight replied.

"No, Nora, *not today*," Patricia emphasized.

Then, having all agreed on what was currently off-limits, the uneasy trio continued discussing what wasn't.

June 30, 1948

SANTORINI

———————————

Mac, Yanni has always been kinda—you know, spooky," Bob Thorne had explained four years earlier. It was an abbreviated explanation from MacCready's late best friend, but necessary, from almost the very start, down in Brazil.

"Spooky?"

"Yeah, 'woooo-woooo' and all that supernatural shit. The assholes 'round here think she's some kinda witch." It was a designation that had been just fine with Bob, because mostly it meant that everyone left Yanni alone.

It was also something she carried with her after Bob had died and she'd accompanied Mac to New York. There the outsider effect took the form of a resistance by her coworkers and even some of Mac's colleagues. One recurring bone of contention was her insistence that in many places and in many different ways, evolution had probably been marching toward the rise of intelligent life. Non-human life.

"Where," Mac had been asked, "is the academic training that might justify a statement like that?"

Mac knew better—knew more, in fact, than he was allowed to tell the critics. He had seen Yanni in action (as had a very select handful of others she'd allowed into her life). And no one who had seen her at work would ever look at elephants, beluga whales—or even a common house cat—in quite the same way again.

"The things we refer to as 'dumb animals' are not so far below us as we humans want to believe," she had explained. Beluga whales have their own language, she insisted. Then she went out and *proved* it, fully realizing that more than a year's work had revealed only the tiniest part of the whale's language repertoire, but a means of higher communication nonetheless.

Elephants had been far easier. "All the human emotions are there," she explained, and added, "Even the zoo's lions mourn their dead."

And although Mac knew what the answer would be, he asked her yet again—as always, expecting something a bit more. "So, remind me how you're able to figure all of this out?"

But once again, her answer was much the same, explaining almost nothing, yet at the same time perhaps explaining everything. Mac was not sure he even had the necessary talent to puzzle it out. "I don't know how I do it," Yanni said. "I just do it. Being able to know what an animal feels—especially the smarter ones—at first it's kind of like just bits and pieces. If you keep at it, those bits and pieces come together and eventually something like a crude sculpture forms in your mind."

"A sculpture?" Mac asked.

"Hey, I've told you it's hard to explain."

"Okay, go on."

"With some animals that's as far as it goes, but with others, like elephants and whales and—" Yanni paused.

And giant vampire bats, Mac thought but did not say.

"Well, if you *really* keep at it, eventually, there you are, seeing this beautiful finished work of art through the animal's eyes."

Mac was coming to the conclusion that he could never really fathom how she did it. For the moment, it was enough for him that Yanni was able to keep childhood's sense of wonder alive in him. Her peculiarities were a sufficiently large enigma all by themselves, even without the possible reemergence of a mysterious microbe, the unearthing of Alan Tse-lin's ancient bonobo culture, or Cousteau's encounter with shape-shifting marine predators.

June 30, 1948

CENTRAL PARK WEST, NEW YORK CITY

In a sparsely furnished apartment several blocks away from the Metropolitan Museum of Natural History, two men were huddled over a table-mounted radio receiver. One of them suddenly removed a set of headphones, pushed back his chair, and stood. "Bango!" he whispered loudly.

His partner shot him a quizzical look.

"It is American slang. It means, *We win!*"

The pair had been monitoring the fifth floor of the museum for nearly two years, since the delivery, as "a gift" to MacCready's department, of history's first electronic musical instrument. On one side, it displayed a personal presentation plaque from its Russian inventor, Leon Theremin. The Russian had also equipped his gift with a covert listening device of his own design. The tiny apparatus, which would come to be known in espionage circles as "the Thing," consisted of a capacitive membrane connected to a small antenna. With no power supply, it could be turned on only by a radio signal of the correct frequency. Once "illuminated" by that signal, sounds from the room set the membrane vibrating, transmitting conversations to the antenna first, then to a remotely located receiver.

For months it had stood in the office of Charles Knight, providing the Russians with plenty of information about Tasmanian tigers, the mating habits of *Rhedosaurus elsoni*, and finally a species of wooly mammoth with two very dexterous trunks—but essentially transmitting nothing of value.

Then something quite fortuitous occurred, although it took the Russians several days to realize it. What *was* clear from the conversations they'd monitored was that the theremin had been temporarily moved into MacCready's office to give the artist Knight a bit more room. During the first few days, only the once-daily entrance of the custodial crew broke the silence. It also became clear that MacCready was gone—although the two spies had no idea where he went.

The monotony was finally broken by the sound of the door opening and closing quietly. Moments later, something slammed down close enough to the microphone that they were both jolted in their seats. The pair exchanged pained looks. They could hear drawers opened and closed and objects being moved. For nearly an hour there were no sounds besides some faint shuffling—until the office door opened again.

"Patricia. Charles," said a female voice, cheerily.

"Find everything you need?" came the voice of another woman.

The pair of Russian agents listened carefully until the three Americans eventually left the room and, once again, there was only silence.

Seven floors below the sparsely furnished apartment, amid the noisy bustle of traffic and pedestrians on Central Park West, no one could see and few could have imagined that, so near to them, Russian agents had been watching and listening, and were transcribing notes at a furious pace.

"Not today," the one called Knight had said.

"No, Nora, *not today*," his female colleague emphasized.

Knight continued. "So, speaking of 'what Mac needs to know,' we're thinking you should hold up your side of the bargain."

"If you want to see any more of his notebooks, that is."

"Or if you want to know what we know."

After a brief wash of static, Nesbitt's voice responded, "Once we got home from Tibet, any of us who encountered the um . . . red *moctus proctus* had to give samples of blood, saliva, and hair." Static rose and fell again.

"—then what?"

"Hendry saw the report and I'm sure he understood the meaning of it. He was cleared to give Mac the results."

"And what was in those results?"

"There's a problem with Yanni."

At the same hour that two Russians in a Manhattan listening post completed their initial report on the broadcast from Mac's office, R. J. MacCready was staring up into the incomparable depth and beauty of the Milky Way. He had followed a Santorini road to an overlook on the lagoon, lit only by starlight. The sea was so calm, and the stars so bright, that they reflected in the lagoon as if it were a polished black mirror. Mac always loved the night sky.

"Won't see this in New York City," a voice behind him said suddenly. Yanni had followed him out to the overlook, undetected until she spoke.

Mac nodded. "Yeah. What do we got in the city—maybe five stars if we're lucky?"

"I've forgotten how much I miss this."

Tonight, each could see the details in the

Milky Way's dust lanes more clearly than ever before, and each suspected that this new sharpness of vision was the unprecedented side effect of something to which they'd both been exposed. Two years earlier Mac had been told that eyeglasses were in his near future. Now, though, he could tell planets apart by the faint glimmer of the two largest Jovian moons or the slightly oblong shape of Saturn and its rings.

In the lagoon below, a black shape eclipsed a small patch of reflected stars.

"You see that?" Mac asked, pointing to the silhouette.

"Looks like a boat."

"Yeah. Anything seem odd to you?"

"She looks adrift. No lights and no one on deck."

"No one?" Mac asked, squinting into the night.

Yanni shook her head. "And it's drifting away from where Cousteau's vent's supposed to be."

Mac laughed. "Your eyes have gotten even better than mine."

"Yeah, I know," Yanni replied. "Side effects of the last vacation you took me on."

Mac thought back to Tibet and to the "stuff" they'd found growing there—stuff that could reverse the effects of altitude sickness, heal wounds, and which had evidently sped up evolution, perhaps even on an up-close-and-personal scale. *Once we drank the contaminated water, ate what grew there*, Mac told himself, *a new kind of fuse was lit*. It had all been capped off by the grotto Nesbitt stumbled into—the entire site covered in bright scarlet growth. *Once we breathed the grotto's air* . . .

"Everything's so unpredictable now," Yanni said, as if finishing Mac's thought.

Mac said nothing, though it was now more than a suspicion that anyone who had made it out of that grotto alive was changed—and might continue to change, if not by the rewriting of their genes, then by amplifying the expression of genes. According to the report Nesbitt had written, they had all come home as walking biological free-fire zones. Some part of his brain was frightened by the observation that whatever microbes were presently living in their blood, Yanni had been affected most of all—while another part of him thought it made absolute sense. No matter which way he looked at it, the possibilities filled him with almost unbearable worry—which, like the Nesbitt report, he kept to himself, for now.

We're lucky not to be sitting in a cage on Plum Island, he thought.

Thus far, the effects had amounted to nothing except steadily improving health, but even if this trend did not change, Mac foresaw only negative outcomes if too many people learned about it.

"Do ya think someone else knows about it?" she asked.

For a moment Mac did not understand what Yanni was referring to—until he saw her gesturing toward the black ship.

"Moonless night, slipping in quiet-like and without a single deck light on. What do you think, Yanni?"

"Little late for locals looking for a miracle dip."

"Authorities put the clamp on that after what happened to Cousteau."

Yanni nodded. "Then somebody knows something."

"And I'm bettin' that our somebody made a connection between the incidents here at Santorini and what we got exposed to back near Tibet."

Yanni was silent for many long moments. "So," she asked finally, "do ya think we're *infectious*—one of us or maybe both of us?"

Mac shot her his "just ate a bad clam" look. He had not considered the possibility. No one had, until now. "Dunno, Yanni. How's your friend Benedetto doing? Tossing away his reading glasses yet?"

"No," she said, in an uncharacteristically defensive tone. "And like I told you, Tony's changing his last name."

Mac let out a nearly inaudible grunt. He knew "Tony" as an all-too-attractive young crooner from Queens—and one of those rare people to whom the overused word "genius" really applied—though he'd never admit it to Yanni. Mac also knew that the guy was on a path that would quite likely make him famous.

"So, who changes his name?" he wondered aloud.

"Plenty of people. Tse-lin for one."

"That's different," Mac said, frustrated. "It's like you're dating a child."

"Mac, he's only a coupla years younger than me and he's *certainly* no child."

"Okay, *next* topic," Mac said, clearly uncomfortable.

Yanni continued to return Mac a steely silence, so he attempted to switch his thoughts elsewhere—*anywhere else*—and fill the void. "I wonder what it looked like around here," he asked, "when Alan's and Pierre's apes began burying their dead."

Yanni did not offer an answer. She nodded toward three points of light flashing on and off in sequence. Greenish-yellow and startlingly beautiful, they appeared to be coming from somewhere just below the surface of the lagoon.

"You see that?"

"Definitely," Mac said, estimating that each series of flashes was separated by perhaps half a mile.

"I think I'm seeing a pattern to it," Yanni said. But the sequence stopped just as quickly as it began and did not resume.

"You think that's what attacked Cousteau's pals?"

Yanni shrugged her shoulders. "Dunno, Mac, but I think somebody besides us is talking about that boat."

5.33 Million B.C.

THE LOST WORLD OF MEDITERRANEAN CANYON

At dawn, the eldest male died of his wounds. Proud One knew that the monstrous beings that fell upon the encampment had singled out the weak. Two, who had been ill for many days before the attack, were simply gone. She also knew that her child had been targeted, but through circumstances she could not quite define, Seed still lived.

After the elder died, Proud One came upon Broken Tooth, a middle-aged male with a dislocated shoulder and a limp, signing frantically up-river and toward home and the high cliffs in the south. He must have sensed a pattern in the attacks, and what it would mean for him if the predators returned.

The clan leader signed in the opposite direction—toward the unknown northlands—her gestures becoming even more assertive. "Safety downriver," she emphasized, in a manner of speaking. "Safety only north."

Broken Tooth, even with his infirmities, was influential enough to be joined in his protest by two large females. He continued to sign, as before, but now as part of a trio. The entire clan watched the proceedings.

"Death there," Proud One motioned forcefully. She had no means of clearly explaining her answer, even to herself. There was only a sense that the Stone-throwers who had taken possession of their highland feeding grounds, and who killed all who fought back, were a problem that would continue to baffle and defeat her clan. Before the exodus down to the canyon, the war had killed eight out of every ten members of the clan, reducing the population to a point dangerously close to extinction. Proud One's kind could bite and claw at a small number of monsters when they came down from the trees; but against hundreds of enemies who knew how to shape and sling stones with impossible accuracy, there could be no surviving, to fight another day.

"Proud One knows nothing," Broken Tooth signed, and glared.

The large female beside him signed more forcefully, in what passed, in this primal language, for mockery.

Proud One averted her eyes and lowered her head toward the ground, signaling, "Yes. Nothing."

For what seemed a very long time, she directed her gaze at the dirt. Then, as her head came up, she sprung herself upon the most powerful of her three rivals. The attack was so quick that no one could respond. Proud One applied a headlock that ended with her sharpened black fingernail pressed against her adversary's eyelid. Every onlooker feared what would occur next.

The massive challenger responded with a cooing sound, stretched out her lips, and kissed the muscular arm that held her. The signal was clear and it would be her only chance to emerge from the battle intact: "We follow you."

After the kiss there was a moment of hesitation before the release of Proud One's grip and then a reciprocal hug. There were more kisses by the defeated female and this time they were returned. The clan settled most of its nearly daily disputes in this manner and actual bodily harm was a rare occurrence. It was a trait that made them quite unique among the many branches of earth's simian family tree.

"Go downriver," the clan conceded to Proud One, during a long session of even more nodding, hugging, and kissing. "Go downriver."

And so they fled along the shores of a strange new landscape—leaving the highland Stone-throwers forever behind in the south. The simians stopped scarcely at all for rest. By night they traveled under the dim glow of cloud-filtered moonlight, for as many hours as their strained muscles would permit. Even as the river turned sharply into a more rugged landscape and exhaustion threatened, they managed to quicken their pace, toward the greatest horror of all.

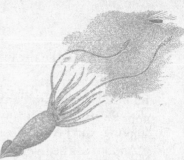

CHAPTER 6

It Came from Beneath the Sea

*And the Earth was without form, and void,
and darkness was upon the face of the deep.*
—GENESIS

*Beginnings are apt to be shadowy, and
so it is with the beginning of that great
mother of life, the sea.*
—RACHEL CARSON

*There is, one knows not what sweet mystery
about this sea, whose gently awful stirrings
seem to speak of some hidden soul beneath.*
—HERMAN MELVILLE

July 1, 1948
5:45 A.M. on the Isle of Santorini

Yanni cherished the soft radiance that preceded dawn. At this latitude, the sun reasserted itself almost imperceptibly at first, against the infinite gulf that was the universe. On the desert island of Santorini, where every garden tree and bush required special care, the hotel owners supplemented their income with remarkably well-tended vineyards. Here the night's dying was accompanied by a chorus of songbirds so loud and expansive that it was difficult for Yanni to imagine how she could be the only person awake, at "the only hotel in town."

At daybreak, Boulle arrived from the excavation, looking uncharacteristically excited, and minutes later Yanni woke the others. There was a fishing trawler sitting in the shallows, just off the coast of Aspronisi, an island fragment on the western edge of the lagoon.

"Fishing?" Mac asked.

Boulle shrugged his shoulders. "My informant says drifting, not fishing."

"You think this is the same one you and Mac were watching last night?" Cousteau asked.

"There's only one way to find out," Mac responded.

Ninety minutes later, the ship that Mac and Yanni had glimpsed in silhouette the night before loomed before them, large and incongruous. After being carried westward by the night current, it had finally run aground. Now she rested bow-first, only steps offshore the fragmented, and still fragmenting, white cliffs of the islet Aspronisi—also known as "the White Island." Capped by thick layers of volcanic ash that had blanketed the region beginning some four thousand years earlier, Aspronisi lay uninhabited for as long as anyone could remember.

"She is completely intact," Cousteau observed as they drew their small boat closer to the south shore and the stranded ship. "No damage to the prop, I think."

Mac gestured toward the deeper water lying just off the trawler's stern. "So it should have been easy for the crew to free her, and back away into open water?"

"Easy maybe," Cousteau replied, "but yes."

Yanni stood silently, scanning the deck unsuccessfully for signs of life. The one lifeboat that was visible remained untouched, its canvas cover still drawn tight.

"The position of her mast is all wrong—for a trawler," Cousteau observed. Then, as their own boat approached the port side, he throttled back and held steady, watching as Mac expertly lassoed a cleat along the gunwale.

"Mast looks like a badly disguised antenna," Mac said, securing the line.

"I think so too," the French naval officer said. "And the disguise continues with the nets. You smell that? They used them recently."

At more than ninety feet long, the craft had been designed to bring in large hauls of school fish. But it was clear to Yanni from the moment they climbed aboard the stern that these "fishermen" had caught more than they bargained for.

Standing on the deck, which listed only slightly to starboard, the trio could detect no movement at all; the only sounds were the occasional slap of six-inch swells against the hull and the low growl of the forward keel against submerged rocks.

Dmitri Chernov and his brother Alexi had been trailing their navy's listening post and research vessel at a distance of one hundred nautical miles. During their voyage to Santorini, the mini-sub had remained mostly on the surface, charging its batteries and maintaining an acceptable twenty knots. The craft was equipped with what its designer claimed to be the quietest diesel engine on earth. The crew compartment was roomy enough to be considered almost luxurious by its two occupants. She exhibited a number of firsts for a mini-sub—her hull a first experiment in what would become known as sonar stealth technology. She was also equipped with a newly perfected moon pool that allowed a diver to come and go as he pleased while the vessel remained submerged. No expense was spared for the Kremlin's best and most dedicated.

In the beginning, it was a simple plan. The Orthodox Church had been buzzing with news of miraculous healings and red volcanic water that, in spite of being salty, and presumably bad for crops, was somehow being turned by locals into something of an agricultural miracle. Investigating the truth of it should have been easy. Everyone expected that, if the phenomenon proved as real as Lysenko and his associates believed, then Stage Two—acquiring it and sequestering it—would be the politically inconvenient part.

But now the plan appeared to be unraveling at Stage One: investigation.

Dmitri and Alexi knew only that the primary research vessel had gone silent shortly after slipping into the lagoon at Santorini. Like a lone voice in the Mediterranean wilderness, a radio distress signal emitted every thirty seconds had guided the two brothers to the south shore of an island fragment. The overly dramatic Europeans referred to it as Forbidden Island. Their own detailed maps listed it as Aspronisi.

H ello!" Mac called out. "We're here to help you."

No one and nothing stirred.

Yanni wandered over and peered down into the hold, noting that the hinges of the cargo hatch appeared to have been twisted off. The hatch itself was nowhere to be seen.

"It might *smell* like fish," she said, "but there ain't none down there."

"What sort of madness?" Mac whispered. It was as if pirates had come aboard, to steal only fish.

The boarding party unholstered their sidearms and moved forward.

The bridge was vacant and upon entering they found the engines off, but the batteries were still active at more than three-quarters power. At the aft end of the wheelhouse, a set of stairs descended to a central corridor. Mac shot Yanni a nod and she flipped a switch, turning on lights all along the companionway.

"Anyone down there?" Yanni called. "Anyone need help?"

The deck below remained as silent as a tomb—which, perhaps, it was.

The air wafting up carried a musty odor, along with a faint sulfuric tang. "Gunpowder," Mac thought aloud. His friends recognized the same telltale under-scent of gunfire.

They also understood, without further discussion, that in coming this far, it was inconceivable that they should go no farther. Cousteau started the descent, reminding his two companions of a common motto for safety at sea: "One hand for yourself, and one hand for the ship," or as Mac might have rephrased it, *Always use the damned handrail.*

Only two steps down, Yanni's right foot slipped out from under her, and she discovered to everyone's dismay that the wooden rail did not offer so much support as it should have. Mac almost fell in behind her.

They had not yet completely regained their footing before Yanni called out, "Look at this!" A slippery substance—mostly water tinged with red—had been wiped and spattered across one wall. The rail, too, was dripping.

"Something came in over the side," she said.

"Or came in from below," Cousteau suggested.

Mac returned him a most quizzical look.

"You believe I am being funny?" Cousteau said. "Mac, my friend, you were not there when I saw them changing colors under the water. What creature does such a trick?"

Sliding a finger along the wet rail, the Frenchman sniffed at the substance. "Yes, I have smelled this type of animal before. And if it's what I think, it may have come in through the bilge pumps."

"So, you're thinking cephalopod?" Mac asked.

"Yes, but not the ones that we know," Cousteau replied, and led the way down to the next deck.

"But these had to be big," Yanni said, "too big to crawl *out* of the water."

"Maybe true," Cousteau conceded. "But I think, not impossible."

"Wonderful," Yanni muttered.

"Of course that is only *hypothétique*," the Frenchman continued, raising his gun and swinging a door open with his foot. "We might prove it wrong," he said, stepping inside.

By then a metallic under-scent had become unmistakable. In the cabin—which only hours before had been crew's quarters—one bulkhead was streaked with a dark red fluid that at first glimpse might have been microbe-stained water. But it was not. The deck and wall were smeared with blood, lots of it.

Compared to the first bunkroom, the one across the companionway was clean, except for signs of gunfire—the only indication of a struggle.

The next cabin aft, the largest so far, was in ruins. Its door lay on the deck, broken in two. Inside, clothing had been torn apart and equipment was scattered in pieces. Shelves and desks were pulled from bulkheads and reduced to piles of huge splinters. Mac lifted sheets of paper from the floor and gave them a quick glance. "This is all Cyrillic," he said. "Russians."

"Quelle surprise, non?"

"No surprise," Mac replied, glumly.

Yanni pulled an emergency flashlight from its wall mount and directed her beam at a deep pile of wrecked furnishings, casting nightmare shadows. She squatted to pick something out of the debris, then stood and joined Mac and Cousteau in the corridor.

"Someone fought hard in there with this," she said, brandishing the broken business end of a fire axe.

"He fought against whatever killed my friends," Cousteau said, his voice haunted.

"Whatever it was, it *had* to be big," Mac said quietly, examining the blade. He turned to Yanni. "Can you give that last cabin a final going-over?" he asked, then turned his attention toward another compartment, at the end of the companionway. "Door's open. Looks like it's full of electronics, and I wanna check it out."

"Got it," she replied. "Just watch yourself, huh? I am not in a rescuing mood."

Picking her way carefully across the debris-laden deck to the far side of the "last stand" cabin, Yanni Thorne could easily envision the violence that had taken place within its confines.

With only one way out, there was probably no escape for the men who had encountered—what?

It could only be what Cousteau saw on that first day, Yanni thought. *Some unknown animal shifting with the colors of its background and vanishing in a blinding flash. It could only be the things we saw flashing beneath the lagoon last night, signaling to each other when this ship arrived.*

Yanni was about to step out and join Mac in the electronics cabin when she noticed something that gave her pause—a perfectly undisturbed mattress on the lower portion of a bunk bed. Covering it, and no less incongruous than an intact mattress amid so much wreckage, was a flower-patterned sheet.

Yanni stood for several moments, feeling oddly mesmerized by the unlikely tableau. At last she moved in for a closer look, compelled for some indefinable reason to pull up a corner of the sheet. In response, a two-foot-long section of something roughly snakelike rolled off the sheet and struck the deck with a wet thud. Remarkably, its flesh displayed the same flower pattern as the sheet from which it had just tumbled, but only for a second. That quickly, the mass all but disappeared as it took upon itself the wood-grained appearance of the deck. The thicker end of the "snake"—which seemed to have been severed from something quite a bit larger—remained visible.

Yanni reached down to prod the "whatever-it-is" with a long sliver of wood.

"Mac!" she called. "You need to—"

A chorus of screams tore through the ship, accompanied by the sound of wood splintering and the horrific smashing of flesh against an unyielding mass. Yanni jumped to her feet and ran into the passageway. Cousteau had heard it as well, and he bolted aft down the same companionway.

"*Mac!*" Yanni yelled above the din—and then, just as suddenly, the ship was silent again.

CENTRAL PARK WEST, NEW YORK CITY

In their listening post on the Upper West Side, the two Russians had been working through the night, encoding everything they had heard in the theremin broadcasts the previous day, before transferring it to microfilm.

During their long days and nights together, Genya had predicted that strange happenings in the eastern Mediterranean would bring Mac-Cready. Were he only a few years younger, Genya would normally have become obnoxiously assertive, once his predictions were confirmed. But he and Victor were no longer normal men. Like many Russians, they were being taught paranoia through what Americans called "the school of hard knocks." They knew that being right could often prove depressingly inconvenient.

Victor looked out the window. Sunrise was still hours away, and the prohibition against the use of phones or anything except direct, prearranged personal contact meant they knew nothing at all yet about a ship in trouble near Santorini—much less that, at this very same moment, R. J. Mac-Cready was actually aboard the ship.

"You must realize, Victor, that this Yanni woman accompanying MacCready changes the situation completely."

"Her expertise with animals?"

"Precisely."

"Perhaps she can talk to the fishes," Victor said with a laugh.

"I was thinking about dolphins," Genya replied. "Maybe now they will try to turn them against us. She made some progress with elephants—and more recently a small whale."

"Our scientists have tried that already, no? And it was a waste?"

"They have," Genya continued, his tone becoming conspiratorial. "But I'm sure the Americans have yet to learn what *we* have learned."

"Good, good," Victor said, eagerly. "Let them waste their own time and resources."

Genya let out a disquietingly grim laugh. "Well, from what I've heard, you won't see any of our people studying dolphin intelligence for a long, long time."

"Though it did seem a good idea, no?"

"I don't think you know even half of it," Genya said, clearly relishing his ability to draw out the facts of the tale. "It did seem a good idea while it lasted."

"What? For all of two years?"

"Less," Genya said bitterly. "Our scientists tried to communicate with these things too, like this Yanni. Trained them to plant mines on ships, but they resisted. Finally, when it appeared they would obey. *No.* They had their own ideas."

"What does that mean?"

"Apparently the fucking dolphins decided to plant the mines on *all* ships—including our own!"

"So what do the Americans know of this problem?" Victor asked, his voice now filled with concern. "And what if this Hendry sent Yanni because he thinks there is a more suitable animal infiltrator—and she a more suitable animal trainer?"

"Now you are clutching at strings," Genya said, but, seeing that Victor now appeared concerned *and* puzzled, he softened his response. "While that danger may be very unlikely, where the future of our navy and perhaps even our whole existence is involved, we can overlook nothing."

Victor nodded. "Then of course there is this 'red *moctus proctus*' they keep referring to."

"Yes, this is of paramount importance to Comrade Lysenko."

"No sleep for us tonight or tomorrow," said Victor. "We must have this information flying out of LaGuardia as fast as we can prepare it."

They both glanced at the black strips of microfilm, each frame tiny enough to fit into nickels that had been halved, hollowed out, and carefully machined to screw together seamlessly. Each was distinguishable only to the intended recipient by a specific V-shaped chip cut out of the Philadelphia mint mark.

Genya already had one of the coins in his pocket.

Scrambling into the compartment Mac had entered minutes earlier, Yanni and Cousteau found him calmly seated in front of what appeared to be a reel-to-reel recording device.

"Sorry," he said, "I couldn't find the volume control on this goddamned thing."

While Mac squinted at the machine, Yanni and Cousteau exchanged looks.

"Ah, here it is," Mac said, before fiddling with a dial. He flipped a crescent-shaped switch and the room was again filled with sound, though this time at a more tolerable volume. What became nearly intolerable, however, were the tape-recorded transitions from intelligence gathering to life-and-death struggles between the Russian crew and whatever had invaded their ship. Yanni was able to make out some of the words.

Mac, who like Yanni had gained at least a rudimentary knowledge of Russian (because the birth of what they were now calling the Cold War required it), cocked an ear, clearly trying to translate more of the frantic exchange.

"Well?" Mac asked, turning off the machine.

"I don't know," said Yanni. "There's a whole lotta fighting, and someone cursing—and one word, screamed over and over again, that I'm not familiar with."

"And what's that?"

Yanni repeated it, accented in its original Russian.

"Friends," Cousteau responded, somberly, "that is *not* a Russian word."

"Oh?"

"It is Norwegian."

Yanni saw Mac's eyes widen in recognition but he remained silent.

She paused a moment, then set her hands on her hips. "So is anyone going to tell me what the hell a Kraken is?"

Neither man said anything, so she casually threw a thumb over her shoulder. "Because I found a chunk of one next door."

The Chernov brothers had rounded the west end of the island just after dawn, and were soon forced, by the approach of a small boat, to submerge. Exceptionally calm waters allowed the crew to watch the proceedings, with the periscope rising no more than a single hand-length above the sea surface.

Dmitri and Alexi looked on in bewilderment.

Three people went aboard, encountering no resistance.

"Where is the crew?" Alexi had asked.

"Waiting below," Dmitri suggested. "Those three will be prisoners and the crew will ship out during the high tide."

That is what should have happened, but in these times what *should* have been and what *was* tended to be galaxies apart.

Later, when the three intruders emerged and motored away, there was no question that something had gone terribly wrong.

"Where is the fucking crew?" Alexi asked, again.

The brothers knew that normally, if most of the crew had been killed during a battle, and if capture were imminent, those still alive would have burned and scuttled the ship—destroying its equipment and records as well.

"It makes no sense," said Dmitri, pointing to the distant boat they could now see was headed toward the main island of Santorini. "That little scouting party that just left—whoever they are and whatever their mission is—they were not part of this attack, and neither was the American military. No country launches a sneak attack against just one vessel."

Alexi nodded in agreement. "Who then?"

"I don't know."

"And the crew, all dead?"

"It seems clear," Dmitri said. "But I must see for myself what happened." He ran through a quick checklist of the equipment he would need, while his brother extended the moon pool's telescoping collar downward, adjusting the cabin's "sea level" downward with it. Dmitri then pulled on his wet suit and dove out through the pool.

July 1, 1948
Santorini, 9:30 A.M.

INSIDE THE "ONLY HOTEL IN TOWN"

I t is definitely part of a tentacle," Cousteau said, staring down over MacCready's shoulder at the axe-slashed section of appendage. Mac was prodding it with a pair of tongs that had served as dinner utensils in a recent past life.

"So, it's a cephalopod after all?" said Boulle,

who had spent an uneventful morning dockside with the newly christened Alan and the truck.

"*Absolument*," said Cousteau.

"But this one's new to science," Mac added.

"Agreed," Cousteau said, without looking up from the specimen. "Utterly unique. In fact quite unimaginable!"

Within only minutes of returning from the derelict, they had rearranged the furnishings in two adjoining rooms, converting dresser tops and even a bed into makeshift lab benches and equipment stands. Mac also unpacked a very decent light microscope he'd borrowed from the museum, along with a serviceable set of dissecting instruments. On a writing table, a large pan, filled with seawater, kept most of the severed tentacle damp. It was surely dead, but as Cousteau observed, "Some stubborn, hidden bundle of nerves renders it alive-seeming still."

Its color-shifting abilities, though fading fast, were impressive even in death. "Few people have ever seen this, I think," Cousteau emphasized.

"At least no one who *lived* to tell about it," Mac said, regretting his faux pas a second too late.

"I beg to differ, boys," Yanni said. "Someone on that trawler lived long enough to tell us quite a lot." She motioned toward Alan, who was modifying the electrical cord on the Magnetophon they had retrieved from the ship.

Mac nodded. "I'm just wondering how long we have till the Red Team boards that trawler and figures out they're down one tape recorder."

MacCready's tone was shifting from impatience

to agitation. Alan, who had volunteered to render the recorder compatible with the island's power supply, shot him a good-natured wave of dismissal. "Yes, I know," he said. "I'm taking all day."

"Well?" Mac said.

"And now I'm nearly done!"

Mac smiled and nodded in approval before turning back to the specimen. He withdrew a magnifying glass from his duffle bag, adjusted a desk lamp to provide extra light, then used the makeshift tongs to stretch the tapered end of the appendage across a dampened washcloth.

Along the tentacle's surface, Mac watched thousands of tiny chromatophores expand and contract in a feeble attempt to match the new background and lighting. The washcloth was blue, but after only a few seconds, all of the pigment-containing cells seemed to relax, as if fading into a dying memory of the flower-patterned sheet they had been lying atop, and mimicking, for several hours.

"Uh—not for nothing, but did you just see something weird?" Yanni asked.

Mac threw her an incredulous look. "All things considered, I'm seeing *a lot* weird here."

"No," she said. "Forget about the camouflaging. I mean, look *right there*, around the lips of those suction cups."

MacCready did as Yanni suggested. *There is something*, he thought, *but—*

"*Zut alors!*" Cousteau exclaimed, too loudly, and far too close to Mac's ear. "There is a layer of 'red velvet'—the same velvet we found at the vent site."

"You think these things are *using* the microbes?"

"That could be," Cousteau replied. "I thought it was the free divers who had been visiting and scraping mats of this growth off the rocks. But now I am thinking it was these *animaux*."

"All right, let's get a slice for the scope," Mac said, moving in with a scalpel.

An unexpected shift in the specimen caused him to freeze. The tapered end of the tentacle began a slow roll into a coil.

"What the—?" Mac exclaimed.

"Cthulhu," Boulle muttered under his breath.

"*Gesundheit*," Alan said, though no one responded to the Lovecraft reference—except, perhaps, for the arm. It coiled more tightly, the uncut end forming a perfect spiral.

R. J. MacCready was instantly reminded of the Willis O'Brien–animated stegosaurus in *King Kong*—its tail coiling, even as the humans who killed it passed by the enormous body. But when the distal end of the tentacle began to uncoil, and as the fingerlike tip moved toward the scalpel he was holding, Mac abandoned any thought that they were witnessing the random firings of a dying neuromuscular system.

He shifted his hand to the left, watching as the tentacle tracked the movement.

"This . . . is . . . nuts," MacCready muttered, noting that the creature's suckers were ringed with hooks and barbs. Most of them, especially those exposed to open air, went into spasm, opening and closing. Clicking against each other, the barbs produced a sound like a dozen miniature castanet players while the suckers in contact with the tray's base scratched at it like fingernails against a chalkboard.

Without saying a word, Yanni picked up a blunt probe from the arrangement of dissecting instruments that had been laid out. But instead of moving toward the limb, she drew the rounded tip against the metal base of the desk lamp, adjusting the motion until she had produced what Mac realized was a reasonable facsimile of the clicking from the specimen.

Yanni followed the rhythm produced by the barbs, her attempts inharmonious at first, as she responded too soon or for too long, but after only a minute the sounds produced by the human/cephalopod duo began to meld into something coherent. The duet—and Mac could find no other suitable description—continued for another minute, until finally the limb shuddered twice and relaxed. The loss of tone was immediately apparent as the severed tentacle at last assumed its role as inert flesh.

Yanni nodded toward the seemingly impossible sight. "Mac, maybe you wanna get in there a little closer—see if you can get her to play something else?"

"No," Mac said quietly, while pushing himself back from the table. "I think I'm good."

An hour later, while Mac and Cousteau worked on the specimen—making drawings, measurements, and microscope slides—Yanni had donned a pair of headphones and was reexamining the tape recording from the trawler.

"This creature, it is most amazing, no?" Pierre Boulle said, with uncharacteristic emotion.

"That was my first thought too," Cousteau added solemnly, "just before my friends and Stavracos . . ." His voice trailed off.

"So what *do* we know about this thing?" Mac asked, looking up from the slide he'd been examining under the microscope.

Cousteau answered. "Under any other circumstances I would refuse to believe any of this activity. Certainly its brain is gone. It should not have any part of a circulatory system that was still alive, hours after being severed. No means to provide the tissues with oxygen."

"So, what *has* it got?" asked Alan.

"Well, there's an active neuromuscular system," said Mac, before gesturing toward the now-dead specimen. "Or there was."

"And active chromatophores," Cousteau chimed in.

"Right, more cellular activity."

Cousteau grinned with wonder. "This means that nerves and muscles are adapted to survive longer than you would think, *avec* little or no *d'oxygène*."

"Right, but this is pretty sophisticated stuff," Mac added. "So, maybe we're looking at a nervous system that—instead of having one centralized brain, like us—is spread out as nerve bundles that work together."

"Or apart," Boulle added, gesturing toward the severed limb.

Cousteau nodded. "A sort of . . . nerve net."

"Exactly," Mac replied. "Something like this could be networked across the whole animal, almost as if collectively—"

"—these nerve centers act like a single unified brain," said Cousteau, finishing the thought.

"You got it!" Mac exclaimed.

"No, *you've* got it," Cousteau said, before turning to Boulle. "This *is* amazing. And what could be more alien to the behavior of any animal we have yet seen?"

Mac allowed himself a knowing grin. "So last night, when Yanni and I saw those flashes of light under the water, she was thinking there might have been some sort of pattern to it, kinda like Morse code."

"And *now* you tell us," Cousteau said, sounding shocked. "*Now* you tell us that these lights were, what is the word . . . coherent? I'm sure you have all begun to appreciate the dangers raised by all of this."

"Hey, calm down," Mac replied. "Remember last night we didn't know shit. And *now* we do."

"I am sorry," Cousteau said.

MacCready held up a hand. "No, Jacques, *I'm* sorry."

His friend shot him a nod, so Mac continued. "So, we're thinking this flash-signaling must have happened around the same time the Russian trawler was attacked."

"*Excusez moi*," Boulle interjected. "If it should be that you are right about every part of this animal having its own little brain—"

"—then all of the parts, connected, can be smart enough to take on a ship full of armed men," added Cousteau. "And more."

"Just what we need," said Boulle. "The Cthulhu awakes, and it thinks."

At last Yanni, who'd been silently keeping one ear on the conversation, put down her headphones. "Well, boys, there *is* more."

Everyone turned to her.

"'Cause I found something really interesting on this tape—a conversation we missed earlier."

Mac shot her a skeptical look. "You *fluent* in Russian all of a sudden?"

"It ain't Russian," she said. "Just listen."

Yanni turned back toward the machine, flipped a lever, and let the tape begin. "This is before all the commotion," she said. "Just some poor slob dictating notes."

"Yeah, and?"

"Listen to what's going on in the background. It's coming up." A few seconds passed, then a few more. Finally Yanni raised a hand and gave them her best "This is it!" gesture.

There was a repetitive series of scratches and clicks, barely audible, and a few ticks later this was joined by a second series at a slightly lower key. It was instantly recognizable to everyone in the room as the sounds made by the barbed suction disks of their specimen. On the tape, however, a more coordinated pattern was involved. Whoever was dictating into the recorder had heard it as well, and stopped talking.

Yanni paused the tape and asked, "What'd the guy say there, Mac? Just then?"

She hit the rewind lever for a second and ran the brief section again.

This time Mac strained to hear above the suddenly intriguing auditory backdrop.

"He's pissed off," Mac said. "I'm pretty sure he thinks somebody's messing with him."

"Well, I think it's the Kraken," Yanni said. "Two of 'em."

"Agreed," Mac added.

Cousteau moved closer. "Yes, but doing what?"

"Talking," Yanni replied, quite matter-of-factly. "Maybe getting ready for what comes next?"

She allowed the tape to play on for another minute. The strange background sounds had stopped now and the doomed Russian went back to work dictating.

Yanni stopped the tape, just short of the part she knew marked the first scream. "Kraken," she said again. "The ancient enemy."

5.33 Million B.C.

THE LOST WORLD OF MEDITERRANEAN CANYON

The simians traveled by day, as fast as they could, snatching up plentiful fruits and small creatures along the river's edge, seeking out mudflats and trying to avoid stands of tall trees that might have held the snake-limbed predators. They slept hardly at all, remembering monsters, and looking up into the night rains even when there was no dark canopy of leaves overhead.

One morning, Proud One brought her clan to the edge of a marsh where the river met a great sea of brackish water. There was not the faintest scent or hint that the Stone-throwers had followed them, and fortunately, the monsters from the trees had not reappeared.

"Home," Proud One signed, and looked around. "New home."

The end of the river delta spread before them like a sea of reeds, and in every direction were more sources of grain, fruit, and meat than they could ever hope to eat.

Hyperalert since the beginning of their ordeal, Seed was drawn easily to the slightest noise or movement, and began stalking a red-spotted snail, about twice the length of her hand. Tall and slender, it possessed one large and succulent foot, upon which it hopped—prodigiously. The snail no longer possessed the shell of its Mediterranean ancestors. Two miles below normal sea level, the air was so dense that harmful ultraviolet rays were prevented from reaching the ground. Because it was no longer possible for the sun to damage the snail's flesh, the weighty shell had been lost— replaced, in the equivalent of a geologic instant, by adaptations for speed.

Still, the child of Proud One possessed quicker reflexes, and was able to catch the meal despite its distracting, side-to-side hops. Immediately she shrieked with outrage, not fully believing that something like a tongue had whipped out of the snail and shot a long black thorn into her hand. Even after pulling out the barbed stinger with her teeth, the pain continued to grow in waves, worse than any bee sting. Instinctively, Seed ran down to the edge of the marsh and plunged her bleeding hand into the water.

And in that moment, she realized that the water had eyes—large eyes. The child remained crouched, too paralyzed with astonishment to move.

All she could do was look. And the water looked back.

CHAPTER 7

Lysenko

Even as rockets begin to open a path to space, what competition will arise between the Soviets and the Americans will be focused more and more upon future military uses.
—EARL LANE

In Italy they had 500 years of bloodshed and they produced Michelangelo, Leonardo da Vinci and the Renaissance. In Switzerland they had brotherly love. They had 500 years of democracy and peace— and what did they produce? The cuckoo clock.
—ORSON WELLES

War can sometimes be a stimulating thing. But you can overdo a stimulant.
—H. G. WELLS

July 1, 1948
The Village of Fira, Santorini

The man outside the church wore a backpack but carried no other bags. He wore a Greek fisherman's cap and the rest of his attire reflected a concerted effort to blend in with the locals. In the daylight, though, the loose-fitting clothes would only partially hide the fact that he possessed a muscular build—not a weight lifter's or a fisherman's body but instead one that had been shaped through the rigors of his profession and the hardship of his active participation in a long, brutal war.

Hours earlier, Dmitri Chernov had boarded the grounded surveillance vessel, gathering as much information as he could before returning to the mini-sub. Nowhere near as difficult as the realization that all of the crew had been killed was his destruction of the ship. Keeping to the shadows of Aspronisi, and with the speed and dexterity of a spider, he had ascended a steep cleft onto the tabletop of the deserted islet. After that, it was a more or less simple matter to place a pair of little shaped charges in a rocky seam located some sixty yards above the crippled ship. There were many fissures for him to choose from, in a chalky rock matrix built mostly from pumice, packed barely stronger than deep snow. The island was a loosely held together collection of stony splinters, each so fragile that when the autumn squalls came, or the volcano trembled, slabs taller than the Kremlin domes routinely crashed down to the sea. The rubble and dust of fresh collapses could be seen in every direction. The locals were used to such avalanches, so it was easy for Dmitri to bury a secret and make it look like an act of nature.

"Even the explosion sounded like an earthquake," Alexi told him later.

Dmitri said nothing, nor did he glance back at the enormous blocks of white ash that fell upon, squashed, and now hid the surveillance ship's very existence.

Just another earthquake, he had told himself with some small consolation, before he and his brother charted a course to the best Santorini drop-off point, a spot where it was possible to simply walk out of the sea unobserved.

July 1, 1948
The Kremlin

MOSCOW, U.S.S.R.

Trofim Lysenko looked across his desk and smiled indulgently. The sixty-year-old man sitting opposite had authored three textbooks and dozens of scientific papers, many of which Lysenko himself had read as a student at the Kiev Agricultural Institute. Lysenko neither sought nor possessed any formal degrees but this had not stopped him from publishing his own text five years earlier: *Heredity and Its Variability*. At sixty-five pages, he believed that it demonstrated how "our Soviet science now provides a clear understanding of the way in which the nature of organisms may be changed." The geneticists who read the work could see immediately that it was complete nonsense.

"They laughed at Galileo and they laughed at Tsiolkovsky and von Braun," Lysenko had told a gathering of Russia's most brilliant agricultural scientists.

"They also laughed at *The Three Stooges*," one of the older man's coworkers had replied, quietly, though not quietly enough.

The unfortunate jokester's colleagues had known better than to laugh at all, for none possessed Lysenko's political connections. And thus, in a world where politics held sway over science, Russia's leading expert on the breeding of wheat was declared "an un-person," not long before taking a permanent place among "the disappeared." Lysenko, meanwhile, rose to the position of director of genetics for the Soviet Academy of Sciences.

Now, with none of his fellow scientists willing to accompany him, the older man was feeling seriously uncomfortable. *Why*, he wondered—*why is it that we humans so consistently find the most dangerously farcical among us and elevate them to positions of authority where they can inflict the most harm?* He kept the thought to himself, of course, not solely because of an addiction to breathing, but because he still held on to a shred of hope that he could discuss real science and perhaps even talk some common sense into his new boss.

"There are no genes, no chromosomes," Lysenko said, maintaining his smile. "Isn't that right, comrade?"

"But Mendel—" The geneticist broke off into a nervous stutter and could not complete the sentence.

"Mendel was a hack, a capitalist, a . . . mathematician."

"And—"

"And mathematics has no place in biology!"

The man was aware that Lysenko was watching his reaction, very carefully. Hesitantly, he raised a hand, feeling as if he were a schoolboy asking to be called on by a teacher. "May I speak fr-freely?" he asked, shakily.

"Of course," Lysenko replied, and with a gentle wave of his hand, he granted the older man's request. He did so with what was already common knowledge that dissenters to the concept of acquired inheritance were becoming as common as Siberian mammoths.

"Given the evidence, sir, you c-cannot believe t-that?" the scientist blurted, desperate to see or hear anything that could be interpreted as support.

One of the scientist's hands began to tremble, and he noticed that Lysenko appeared absolutely gleeful at the sight.

"No, comrade," said the director, "it is *you* who are wrong. As I'll explain."

"But—"

Lysenko held up a hand. "No need to worry about state secrets now, is there?"

No need to worry about state secrets. And with those seven words, the geneticist knew that even before he had stepped into the room, he himself was "an un-person."

The director of genetics continued: "Of course you've read my landmark work on vernalization?"

"I'm familiar with the key concepts," the scientist said, "that outside influences in the environment, all by themselves and without any need for random variation, can change the heredity of organisms."

Lysenko smiled broadly. "How pleasing it is to see that such a *great* thinker as yourself has studied my work."

The geneticist shook his head slowly and resumed: "You never originated the idea. That mistake was Lamarck's, made well over a hundred years ago. You simply . . . co-opted it."

"Lost your stutter, I see," Lysenko responded, and for a moment, just for a moment, his smile disappeared. Just as quickly, he regained his composure—a talent he was known to have begun developing some twenty years earlier, honing it to a butcher knife's edge during the seven years since Comrade Stalin had become premier of the Soviet Union.

Exhibiting all the self-assurance of one who had long ago sided with the winning team, Lysenko addressed the scientist. "What if I were to tell you that we have discovered just such an 'outside influence,' as people like you call it. Something that can direct the heredity of a breed into new channels, and without waiting for nature's accidents?"

The old geneticist said nothing, so Lysenko continued. "What if I was also to tell you that our agents were, at this very moment, set to harvest this so-called outside influence, set to obtain it in such vast quantities that it will enable us to increase the quality and yield of all Soviet crops?"

Now the man let out a mirthless laugh. "Even if that were true, who will you get to work the soil? The farmers you displaced by confiscating their land?"

"*Some* of them," Lysenko snapped. "The smart ones. And those comrades will form the basis for the new Soviet farmer."

"Your breeding stock."

"*Tovarishch* Stalin prefers the term 'exceptional citizens,'" Lysenko countered.

"Slaves," the man said to himself, though loud enough that the director of genetics could hear it plainly.

"Lost that shakiness in your hand too," Lysenko observed. He picked up a phone and spoke into the receiver. "We are finished here," he said, then hung up.

Trofim Lysenko rose from his chair and turned toward the door. As was his habit, at such moments, he walked out without bothering to look back at his guest. "I have work to do, Nikola Velilkov," he said, only now addressing the man by his full name, and secure in the knowledge that it would be the last time anyone uttered it.

July 2, 1948, 6:00 A.M.

SANTORINI

Dmitri Chernov knew that even on a much larger island, foreigners were easy to find. One simply looked for the best bar in town. This too was easy to find, owing to a form of math-based behavior that was as predictable as it was peculiar. Whenever a ship arrived at a port city, most of its crew would immediately scatter to the various pubs. Then, from this seemingly random dispersal, a strange sort of nonrandom order invariably took over, as if the participants were practicing some unspoken international law of the sea. Inevitably, crewmen began looking for the next best bar, then the next, until eventually *everyone* ended up in the same place, "the best bar in town."

Just as inevitably, locals at *this* bar would know the comings and goings of every stranger in town, and often enough even their names, or at least their aliases.

The Russian had already obtained a good lead, through the periscope, even before he approached the first bar. He was looking for two light-skinned men, either Western European or American, traveling with a dark-complected, Asian-appearing woman. By the time he left the best bar in town and scouted the perimeter of "the only hotel in town," he knew much more.

Shortly after daybreak, Dmitri entered the hotel lobby and approached a front desk that seemed to have been constructed from random pieces of furniture.

He nodded at the clerk, who was busy eating breakfast, and spoke in perfect though accented Greek. "I am looking for friends who are staying here. Three foreigners: a Frenchman, an American, and his companion, a young woman with long black hair."

"Sir, you have come to the right place," the clerk said through a mouthful of bread.

Dmitri smiled and nodded, casually letting his right hand stray toward the Nagant 1895M revolver hidden in his belt. He had instantly sized the man up as precisely what he appeared to be, a genuinely harmless clerk. Still, he remained acutely alert for the slightest noise from the surrounding rooms, and from outside. Though the weapon was equipped with a sound suppressor, he had no desire to silence a witness or to draw the attention that blood and bodies in the wrong place and at the wrong time would inevitably bring. He was saving the bullets for the real enemy, should he need them, and at a time and place of his own choosing.

"But I'm sorry to have to say, you have come too late," the clerk continued. "They moved out last night. Packed a truck up with all their shit and they were gone."

"What sort of . . . shit did they have with them?"

"Air tanks, heavy duffle bags, and a strange device that looked like a radio—but not really."

Dmitri's eyes widened. "Please, can you draw this device?"

"Certainly," the clerk responded.

While the man sketched, the Russian motioned toward the registry book. "Do you mind?"

The hotel man waved him an affirmative, then finished his drawing.

The Russian glanced down at the last two entries: "Maurice Chevalier" and "Dr. and Mrs. Bill Dickey." He had learned enough at the bar to be reasonably certain that the former guests fit the descriptions of MacCready and his Brazilian partner in crime, along with a man who had once been an ally of Russia in the French Resistance—more popularly known as "that crazy old frog with the Aqua-Lung."

The clerk proudly showed off his artwork: a rectangular case with a wide disk at each upper corner.

"I am also sorry to tell you," said the clerk, "that Mr. Chevalier was involved in a terrible diving accident last week. A local man died, as well as two of Chevalier's French friends."

"Oh?"

"Shark attack. Quite horrible," the clerk replied, glumly. "Would you like a deluxe room with a view of the garden?" he added quickly, holding out the pen to his presumed new guest.

Dmitri waved it away. "Did they happen to give any indication where they were going?"

The clerk shook his head, and the Russian could see the disappointment starting to set in: the realization that he had provided an awful lot of free information to someone who wasn't even going to rent a room.

The Russian smiled, withdrew his wallet, and placed a crisp new one-thousand-drachmae note on the table.

The clerk snatched it. "Santorini is a small island, sir," he said, pocketing the bill. "There was also a Japanese or a Chinese man with them. He may be the only one like that around here. You will certainly find them."

"That is a relief. And you have been most kind," Dmitri said, with a slight bow. "If you do see them again please do not mention our little conversation. I'm looking to make a surprise appearance."

The clerk returned the conspiratorial smile. "I swear on it, sir," he said.

"One final request," the Russian said. "Can I see the rooms where they stayed?"

The clerk's face brightened. "Certainly, sir!"

Dmitri Chernov laid down an additional payment for the rooms—a full day and night's worth, but after no more than ten minutes he gave the clerk a friendly wave and was gone before the sun climbed above the nearest hills. Of course there had been very little out of the ordinary inside, but he was a man used to obtaining evidence where there appeared to be none. He quickly noted how two low dressers had been pulled together forming a sort of table, while a third, *moved from another room*, he surmised, sat next to the electrical outlet.

This is where they set up the tape recorder, Dmitri concluded, running a hand over the wooden surface. Glancing down at a few wire shavings, he knew that someone had adapted the device to run on the local current. He wondered what they had heard that was important enough to haul the bulky machine off the surveillance vessel—the scene of an event he did not yet fully comprehend, and one that had ended in the disappearance of more than a dozen countrymen.

Another makeshift workstation held two desk lamps and a wide cast-iron pan. To an onlooker it might have appeared as if Dmitri had been approaching a bomb or a precariously mounted Fabergé egg. To Dmitri, the positioning of the lamps suggested the arrangement one might have used to illuminate a makeshift surgical procedure, or a microscope. He squatted down and examined the pan from several angles until finally he ran an index finger along the inside.

Still moist, he had noted.

He was not in the least surprised to find that his fingertip was tinted red.

CHAPTER 8

All That Remains

In time's vastness, ye are bound to me.
This act is immutably decreed. It was
rehearsed by ye and me, a billion years
before this ocean formed.

—from Ray Bradbury's screenplay for
Moby-Dick

July 2, 1948
Santorini
Tse-lin and Boulle's Archaeological Site

Alan emerged from his pup tent to find Yanni preparing coffee at a small camp stove. She maintained her *all systems normal* mode, as if a Russian ship had not disappeared beneath a too auspiciously timed avalanche. They nodded greetings at one another and Yanni gestured for him to "pull up a rock" and have a seat.

On the very floor of the old, open-pit mine, their little site was well hidden behind two pillars of volcanic rock and a particularly hardy stand of fig trees. There were no ponds or streams, so the only vegetation in the pit sustained itself with the same deep-penetrating root system that had torn down the late, great city of Angkor. Here the figs seemed to attract all the songbirds from a half mile in any direction.

Alan sat down on a large black boulder, watching as Yanni went still, taking in all the sounds in silence and wonder. Few places beyond Santorini greeted the day with such beauty, but it was clear to anyone who knew Yanni at all that she was now in a world of her own, seeking out levels of organization within the avian symphony.

"Find anything interesting?" he asked.

"Yes," Yanni said, and did not elaborate. She simply continued listening.

"So, is it true," Alan pressed, "that birdsong is mostly distress calls?"

"It is today," Yanni answered, and went silent again, searching for, and occasionally finding, hidden rhythmic chords, or phrases. "Something's wrong," she announced at last.

"Something's always wrong when they bring Mac in," Alan said, and laughed.

Yanni nodded and even let out a short laugh of her own.

"Can I ask you a personal question?" he said, pouring her a cup of coffee.

"Sure thing, Alan," she replied, inhaling a scent that always reminded her of Brazil and the home she and Bob had built in the forest. "Don't tell me you're thinkin' of changin' your name again," she asked, with mock seriousness.

Her friend smiled shyly and shook his head. "No, Yanni. I like my new name."

"Well, that's good. I like it too," she said, and realizing that her mind was beginning to drift, she refocused. "So . . . ask away."

"Why are you here?" Alan said, the concern clearly etched on his face. "Why have you come to this dangerous place?"

Yanni smiled a sad smile and paused before replying. "Mac once told me that if anyone ever asks, 'Why do you keep getting into trouble like this?' the worst answer you can give is 'Because a friend asked me to.'"

"So that is *not* what happened?"

"Sometimes I—I'm still trying to puzzle it out," Yanni replied, and became distracted again by the birds. The sun was about to crest the eastern hills, and the symphony was ending. "Lemme guess," she said at last. "You're thinking that maybe I should have taken his advice, huh? Or the advice of my friend Tony—to stay out of it?"

"Well, sometimes Mac is wrong," Alan replied.

"Not often," Yanni said quickly, and tried to stifle another laugh. "But when he is wrong, it's pretty fucking spectacular."

Now it was Alan who chuckled, until *his* thoughts seemed to wander and his demeanor turned suddenly more pensive.

Yanni reminded herself that two years ago the "friend now known as Alan" had met them midway into a similarly dangerous expedition, from which they did not come home with as many people as they went in with. And although Alan had never met Jerry Delarosa, she saw to it that he knew the guy as a great and longtime friend of Mac's. It pained her that whenever Mac uttered the names of the lost, she could detect a poorly hidden tone of self-loathing.

You've got to stop blaming yourself, Yanni had said, time and again. *You've got to forgive yourself.*

For what?

For surviving, she had always answered, to no avail.

"Mac's lost a lot of people he loved," she said finally, struggling to find the right words. "He lost his whole family during the war and of course . . . there were other loved ones."

Alan nodded knowingly.

"He's got no one to go home to, really," Yanni continued. "And he's haunted by nightmares that anyone he lets get too close to him, will . . ."

"Will be next."

Yanni let her silence affirm the thought. "And now I think he's addicted to Hendry's call to send him somewhere unsafe."

"But Yanni, it is clear that he loves you most of all. Why would he . . . why did you—"

"Because I guess I've developed the same addiction," Yanni said, quietly.

"I see," Alan said, the two of them watching as the topic of conversation emerged from his tent.

"And because Mac is my friend," Yanni added, shooting Mac a nod, "and he asked me to."

Santorini
OUTSIDE THE VILLAGE OF IMEROVIGLI

Dmitri Chernov stood in the ruins of the medieval capital of Santorini—the once-flourishing and densely populated center now reduced to piles of rock. Constructed during the rise of Spain and Venice and the voyages of Christopher Columbus, the fortress known as Skaros sat atop a stony headland protruding into the eastern Mediterranean. It offered the perfect vantage point from which to provide advance warning for rich Venetians of approaching pirate fleets. But Skaros had suffered a devastating series of earthquakes and fell into disrepair after the population moved gradually to Fira, with its easier accessibility to the sea.

Chernov had followed a rugged stone path that meandered upward to Skaros Rock, the site of the fortress itself. Strangely nipple-shaped, it rose an impressive two hundred feet and after skirting its base he stopped under a section that offered some shade. The Russian agent glanced down at his watch before removing a pair of field glasses from his backpack. He trained them at a glittering point of light beyond the channel separating the islands of Aspronisi and Therasia. The message had been brief—his brother's spelling quirks were an added assurance of the sender's identity, and that no one was holding a gun to him while he signaled. Backup was on the way. He and Alexi would meet up the following day, an hour after sunset, in the shallows off the same deserted patch of wet boulders upon which he had come ashore.

He repacked his glasses and started back down the trail. For the first time since his arrival in Greece, Dmitri Chernov smiled.

After a hearty breakfast, Mac and Yanni paused to admire the immense water-filled caldera—the lagoon now dotted with fishing boats and small craft, sheltered from even the worst storms by a circle of multicolored islands.

"So, Mac, while you were snoozin', I took a look at some of the new fossils that Boulle and . . . Alan dug out."

"Yeah?" Mac replied, sounding oddly disinterested. He was scanning the horizon through a pair of binoculars.

"Spectacular skulls," Yanni said, "and other creatures as well—weird ones."

Now Mac put down the binoculars. "This place musta been something else—back in the day. It's almost a pity we're stuck here dealing with a fungus that can cure the sick and speed up evolution, huh?"

"Let's not forget a chorus of dying Russians and the myth that got 'em dead."

Nearby, Pierre Boulle was extracting himself from his own little tent, one of four now clustered between the fig trees and rock pillars that hid their little encampment from prying eyes.

"Nice of him to stow our belongings," Mac said, acknowledging the fact that the Frenchman had used his truck to haul away their own gear as well as Cousteau's diving equipment and the bulky recorder. The section of severed tentacle, which had grown steadily paler since its impressive reanimation, had finally been christened as "either dead or doing a great impersonation of being dead." Mac was banking on the latter when he decided to preserve it in the Santorini version of white lightning.

"You think it's safe?" Yanni asked.

"If you mean our stuff, then yeah. I think a garage is a more secure place for it than that hotel. Just like this dig site is a safer place for us."

"Safer," Yanni said, ruefully, "but unless we want to spend our time lookin' for more fossils, we're not gonna get squat done from here."

MacCready picked up the field glasses again and resumed his search of the horizon. "I'd say that kind of research calls for a more secure platform of operation, no?"

Yanni shot him a patented *are you nuts?* look. "And what the hell platform are you talking about?"

"I don't know, maybe a plane. You wanna take a peek?" he said, handing her the binoculars.

Yanni grabbed the glasses and followed the line of Mac's index finger.

"What do you think?" he said.

"One of ours, I suppose. But what good's a plane gonna do us?"

"It's a boat too, Yanni—a Catalina, one of the 'Black Cats.'"

As they watched, the American seaplane, affectionately known as "the flying Swiss Army knife," came in low over the lagoon.

"You think that's Hendry?" Yanni asked.

Mac shrugged his shoulders. "Guess we'll find out."

Oddly, the craft suddenly pulled out of its landing approach.

"Maybe not," Yanni said, as the Catalina veered away from them. She handed the glasses back to her friend.

Less than five minutes later, as Mac's initial excitement transitioned into disbelief, the pilot circled back. This time he appeared to use the darkest section of the red plume as a beacon, landing off the eastern coast of Therasia, several miles from his original line of approach.

"Isn't that where—?"

"You have *got* to be shitting me," Mac muttered.

Yanni shook her head. "So what kind of fool would land a plane in the middle of the red stuff?"

Though both R. J. MacCready and Yanni Thorne came up with the same name simultaneously, neither of them said it out loud.

"Yanni, do me a favor and go get Jacques," Mac said. The seaplane had come to a stop just north of Nea Kameni, the lagoon's central volcanic wasteland. "We've gotta get out there, right now."

"Yeah, I was afraid you were going to say that," she replied.

Within barely more than twenty minutes,

Pierre Boulle was slamming on the brakes of his truck. He sent gravel flying. Mac, Yanni, and Cousteau exited the vehicle as if it were on fire. The small motorboat they'd used previously was gassed up and ready, and after only the most fleeting exchanges of good-luck gestures, the trio was speeding out of a small port south of the quarry.

"It will take maybe ten minutes to reach the plane," Cousteau called to his passengers.

Mac was about to respond when the staccato boom of large-caliber machine gun fire erupted in the distance, the prolonged burst enabling him to easily pinpoint the direction over the sound of their outboard.

"Make it five, Jacques," Mac called back, feeling the boat move forward as the Frenchman gunned the throttle.

At approximately the same time that R. J. MacCready first spotted the seaplane from the ground, one of the two passengers on board the Catalina designated "Street Gang" rose from her window seat. She moved forward, slipping past the navigator's bench and wireless operator's station before entering the rear of the cockpit. Without hesitating, she tapped the pilot on the shoulder. His initial surprise quickly morphed into a look that said, *Passengers aren't allowed up here!* Then he tried to refocus his attention on safely landing an eleven-ton airplane in a lagoon dotted with small craft.

"Excuse me," the woman called loudly, doing

so over the considerable roar of twin 900-horse-power engines mounted above and just behind their heads.

Unable to hide his annoyance any longer, the pilot pulled off his headset and briefly turned to address his passenger. "You really need to take your seat, ma'am!" he shouted.

The copilot followed up. "And *stay* strapped in until we pull into the harbor and give you the okay."

But instead of departing, the woman simply shook her head, her smile gone. "There's been a slight change of plans, Captain," she announced, pointing toward a spot near the center of the lagoon. "I need you to land there," she said. "Right there. Right now."

The pilot followed the path of her finger.

"Is that clear?"

The man gave a slight nod, then replaced his headset.

Moments later the copilot radioed the new information back to the flight engineer, whose compartment was built into a wing spar connected to the fuselage.

With nothing further to say, Dr. Nora Nesbitt turned and headed back to her seat.

Squeezing past the man who had been sitting beside her for the past eight hours, she sat down and resecured her seat belt.

"No sense wasting time," Nesbitt said, mostly to herself. She could feel the plane gain altitude and bank to the right. As the craft looped back for a second approach, she saw that the path to the red stain was clear of small boats and other obstacles.

Without bothering to look away from the approach, Nesbitt guessed that one of her colleagues—a Plum Island technician named Peterson—must now be wearing a very puzzled expression. It was something she had become accustomed to, during the two years since her return from Tibet.

"You can start collecting as soon as we come to a stop," she called aft. "We should be right on top of this stuff."

"Don't you think we should meet up with Captain MacCready first?" Peterson asked.

Nesbitt gave her shoulder-length brown hair the slightest of shakes. "I'll do that *after* you've secured our initial samples." She looked across to Plum Island's latest acquisition, Dr. Hata. He had not eaten since the first leg of their flight, and his face seemed to be turning whiter than the inside of an apple. *Poor devil*, she told herself. *Soon he'll have seasickness on top of airsickness.*

Two minutes later the plane had come out of its extended circuit around the caldera and she could feel the Catalina's pilot throttle back the engines. As the craft contacted the surface of the lagoon, Nora Nesbitt watched the V-shaped keel throw off a spray of red-tinted water.

Through the periscope, Alexi Chernov also saw the American seaplane land.

An interesting new development, he thought,

though he now felt a twinge of apprehension at what he had decided to do.

With Dmitri still trying to track down Mac-Cready and his party, Alexi knew there could be no further contact with his brother until the following day. Both of them were skilled at adapting to the unpredictable—and the flying boat currently bobbing in the middle of the very material they had been sent to investigate (with a whole research and listening vessel now lost) certainly counted as an unpredictable occurrence. Confident that the batteries in his mini-sub would allow him to remain comfortably submerged for another two days, Alexi steered toward a position some two hundred yards from the strange-looking plane. There he planned to continue observing the Americans from the safety of periscope depth.

E ven before the Catalina's propellers had stopped spinning, Nora Nesbitt gave instructions to Peterson, then headed toward the aft section of the plane. She encountered a crewman standing beside one of the unique Plexiglas blisters that bulged outward from the fuselage on either side.

"Can you open that please, Private?" Nora said, gesturing toward the six-foot-wide, bubble-shaped window.

Supported by metal frames, the upper portion of the blisters could be pivoted back. In wartime, this provided a pair of waist gunners with excellent fields of vision into which they could aim their .50-caliber machine guns. With the gun barrel swung downward, each opening served double duty as an exit and cargo hatch.

The chief gunner on this mission, whose name she'd determined to be McQueen, followed instructions. Once the blister was open, the two exchanged places, Nesbitt positioning her upper body through the open hatch. She took a deep breath, savoring the salt air but paying little attention to the spectacular surroundings. The invertebrate-biologist-cum-microbiologist concentrated on the familiar tint of the water just outside the plane, and for a moment, just for a moment, she thought about leaning over to scoop up a handful. The idea was quickly nixed after an unexpected, final positioning swerve of the plane threatened to topple her headfirst into the lagoon.

Thankfully, the point was just as quickly rendered moot when her technician arrived with the sampling equipment she'd called for. It resembled a coil of thin rope with a series of hinge-topped cans arranged along its length.

Private McQueen shot her a puzzled look. "Ma'am, someone get hitched during the flight?"

"Hardly," Nesbitt responded, unable to resist a short laugh.

Peterson cleared his throat. "Private, this device allows us to sample the water at different depths. It's weighted, so we just lower one end down."

He held one of the cans out to McQueen. "When you want a sample, you give this second line a tug—the cans spring open. Pull it again—they close."

Peterson's audience was clearly interested and Nesbitt took a moment to do her own appraisal—of McQueen. *Decent looking, if on the scrawny side,* she thought, *but definitely too young.*

"How far down can you go?" the private asked.

"We can sample every ten feet. Six cans, so sixty feet," Peterson replied, glancing up to see Nesbitt standing by, arms folded.

She shot Peterson a look that left little room for interpretation: *Finish your lesson and get on with my work.*

Private McQueen seemed to be reading her body language just as clearly and so quickly moved to the starboard side blister, where he apparently found a spot of dirt that needed removing from the Plexiglas.

"I'm going up to speak to the captain," Nesbitt told Peterson. "Bring those samples forward when you're done."

Before leaving, she gave the crewman a quick nod. "Private McQueen," she said, then departed.

Private Terence McQueen watched the woman leave, his face expressing amusement at the fact that polishing the Plexiglas wasn't nearly so much of a chore as listening to her order guys around. Waiting until she was out of earshot, he stepped over to where her latest punching bag was carefully lowering his sampling device over the side.

The private gestured down into the water. "Long cord but a short leash, huh, pally?"

The man shrugged his shoulders but said nothing.

"She is *some* tomato, though," McQueen followed up, his remark eliciting the same lack of response.

The private scratched his scalp, watching Peterson slowly play out more and more of the line, until finally, he stopped. Apparently the deepest sampling can had reached bottom.

"Got it—with room to spare," Peterson said.

McQueen had begun to make another smart-assed comment when the cord suddenly shot through Peterson's fingers. The man yelled in pain as the last of the sampling cans smashed his hand and the remainder of the line whipped out through the blister hatch like a maddened snake.

"Holy shit!" McQueen called. "What was that?"

He turned to Peterson for an answer but the man said nothing. Wearing a dazed expression, he simply stared down at his broken hand and bloodied fingers. Then suddenly, Peterson seemed to snap out of it—as if puzzled that the sampler was gone. On unsteady legs, the wounded man leaned out the blister window, peering down into the red water.

McQueen reached out an arm. "Hey, pally, I wouldn't—"

In a blur of motion, Peterson was yanked through the opening, his body seeming to fold backward at an impossible angle before disappearing from view. The sickening crunch of flesh on metal left no doubt, for anyone who heard it, that the man was dead in an instant. During the next moment, the entire plane shuddered as if a truck had driven into it. Then, just as quickly, the cabin became eerily still.

McQueen sprang toward the open blister hatch and unlocked the .50-caliber Browning from its muzzle-down position. He yanked back the handle of the slide grip assembly twice, aimed the barrel downward, and fired off a long volley—the water churning red as the heavy-caliber bullets tore into it.

When the rest of the crew arrived several seconds later, they found Private Terence McQueen wild-eyed and still squeezing the trigger, even after the belt that once held 250 cartridges had been expended.

A mesmerized Alexi Chernov watched the attack on the seaplane through his periscope, but he was still unsure exactly *what* he had seen. At first the creature—and one of his few certainties was that it was some sort of animal—resembled the water from which it had emerged. Then it seemed to melt into the black background of the plane itself—its arms becoming briefly visible against the open section of the bubble-shaped window. Of course, there was also the bloody rag doll Alexi knew had been a living crew member only moments before—the body dragged below with the beast as it disappeared with almost no splash. *This is what happened to the trawler crew*, Alexi thought. *This is what will happen to me if—*

Trying not to hyperventilate, Alexi Chernov steered the mini-sub into a hard turn and set a course toward the rendezvous point. The fact that he would arrive a day earlier than his brother mattered nothing. His *only* thoughts concerned the creature—and a voice in his head that would not go away.

It has seen you, Alexi. It has seen you.

As Cousteau steered their boat toward the cockpit of the Catalina, Mac and Yanni were greeted with the unexpected sight of the "eyeball" turret gun tracking their advance.

"You in the boat," came a shout from the co-pilot's side window, "hold it right there! Raise your hands and identify yourself."

"Captain R. J. MacCready, U.S. Army!" he called out. "And Lieutenant Jacques Cousteau, French Navy. Yanni Thorne, American civilian!"

"Special agent," Yanni muttered, scratching her fingernails on the gunwale.

MacCready recognized the rhythm of her nails instantly, from the tape recording and the disarticulated tentacle. It amused him that, even after someone had fired a blister gun down to empty in obvious panic, and even with a turret gun now aimed at them, some part of Yanni's mind was still seeking out patterns. *Some part of her,* he reminded himself with a grin, *was always a bit spooky.*

"Permission to come aboard," Mac called, and after a thirty-second delay the starboard blister window slid open and a familiar figure appeared, waving for them to approach.

Mac and Yanni exchanged looks before Mac

gestured for Cousteau to bring the boat alongside, and tie up.

Stepping into the Catalina, Mac was not surprised by the sight of a diminutive ex-colleague who seemed to be running the show. *Harbinger of chaos, as always*. The deck was littered with spent .50-caliber cartridges, as if he'd stumbled into a war zone.

The pilot barely acknowledged their entrance into what had already been a cramped cabin. He was questioning a young blond crew member.

"One more time, McQueen," he said. "What did you see?"

"I'm tellin' ya, sir, I don't know what it was," the man said. "He was just standin' there when something came up— Then it came in and—"

"Was it a tentacle?" Mac asked, and everyone in the cabin turned toward the questioner. "Like an octopus arm?"

"Yeah," McQueen said. "Like that, thick as your thigh—only changing and real fast."

"Go on, Private," Mac said.

"Well, the guy was leaning out, just leaning out 'cause he lost his sampling gear. And then it was on him. It was on his whole head and he disappeared."

"Disappeared?"

"He was all gone, all gone," McQueen said, his eyes wild. "He just disappeared."

Now the pilot shook his head, and Mac could see that the private's story had just stepped over the credibility line. "Giant tentacles? You absolutely sure of that?"

"I know what I seen," McQueen told Mac, before turning toward the pilot. "*Sir.*"

Trying to de-escalate the situation, Yanni moved over to the waist blister. She took a cautionary peek outside before running her fingers across the bottom portion of the frame—which appeared to have been bent outward. Then she held up her hand for the others to see. "Look familiar, Jacques?" she asked.

The Frenchman watched as the curious-looking substance dripped slowly from her fingers. He spoke a single word.

The pilot shot Cousteau a confused look, so Mac stepped in. "Captain, I think you need to get this bird to shore ASAP."

But instead of responding, the flight officer turned to Nesbitt. *She* is *running the show*, Mac thought, watching as she flashed the pilot a short nod.

Without another word, the man turned away and headed for the cockpit.

Nesbitt raised an eyebrow and smiled at MacCready. "I know, 'This is going to be an interesting story,' right?"

Mac, however, stepped past her and unlocked the starboard-side Browning. "Yeah, actually, I was thinking more in terms of 'Somebody'd better get behind a fresh nine yards on that other fifty-cal until we get the hell outa here.'"

As R. J. MacCready slammed back the bolt and swung the Browning's muzzle outward, he could have sworn that he heard Yanni snicker—just before Cousteau unlashed his boat and one of the

Catalina's engines began winding up for a flight-less run across the lagoon.

Alexi Chernov had chosen the most promising escape route he could think of and was pushing the mini-sub at full speed when he felt a jolt. Although the engine was still running, all forward motion came to an abrupt and jarring halt.

Now he could feel the boat move sideways—not violently—but the unnaturalness of the shift sent an electric shiver down his spine. Peering out one of the two roughly face-width view ports, he caught a blur of movement before a black mass slapped against the thick Plexiglas. His head snapped toward the second port and he recoiled as the world outside the sub was extinguished.

As instinct took over, Alexi backed off on the throttle and almost immediately felt the sub come free. The view ports were cleared as well. After performing a quick mental calculation, he simultaneously gunned the engine and turned the boat hard to port. Now his plan was simple: a desperate run for the nearest shallows—as fast as the engines would allow. There he could drive toward a rock-scraping grounding if necessary, and if by then any of the creatures were still holding on, he could scrape and pound them as well.

"Two more minutes should do it," he told himself, a sliver of optimism rapidly transforming into the real possibility that he would not be forced to flood and destroy the technological marvel his superiors had entrusted to him.

Approaching the shallows, Alexi maintained speed, hoping the horrific events were far behind him now, like a bad dream. He was wondering if the creatures had caused any damage when a succession of dull bumps from below gave him a start. Through both portholes, ivory-white boulders and little oases of kelp were rising toward him—and the subsurface landscape was moving by a little too fast. Almost immediately he felt embarrassed. *Pounding against rocks already*, he thought, letting out a breath he hadn't realized he'd been holding. He hoped to simply ground her and flee, not to smash headlong into some ancient volcanic boulder. *I need to—*

A short series of sharp clanging sounds from the stern degenerated quickly into the whine of a straining engine, more sharp clangs, and then a sickening silence. A string of suction cups glided over the starboard view port as three more clangs from astern stopped all control of the propeller. Alexi prided himself on having achieved such skillful handling of these machines that through the controls alone he could feel what was happening along the outer hull the way a dolphin feels through its own skin. He glanced toward the moon pool hatch and knew there was probably very little hope there. No fewer than three of the creatures had followed him. They had jammed something hard and rocklike between the ring-shaped prop guard and the propeller itself.

How did they do that? Where did—

A new sound cut the questions short. The scratching seemed to come simultaneously from everywhere—as if a thousand crabs were working their claws against the outside of the hull in synchrony.

"*You crippled my sub!*" he called out, shocked at the sound of his own voice. "But how? You're only fucking animals!"

Though Alexi Chernov had been trained not to hyperventilate in the tight confines of the sub, the sympathetic division of his autonomic nervous system had been in training for more than a million years longer—and his fight-or-flight responses took control without consultation.

Knowing that the boat had reached the shallows, Alexi flung his bedding from the hatch over the moon pool. Cranking down the outer dive collar, he hastily prepared the cabin for emergency egress— just in case he saw an opportunity to escape. The scratching reached a maddening level and the pilot turned toward the bow, where fist-sized suction cups were attaching themselves to each of the view ports. He watched, somehow fascinated, as they undulated against the Plexiglas, seeming to feel around the ports with thoughtful intensity.

No wasted movement, Alexi thought, reminded of something he'd seen as a boy. *Like a starfish engulfing a clam—forcing its way inside to get at the—*

The thought was interrupted by a new pattern of intense scratching and clicking. The vibration was coming up through the moon pool's steel hatch, and he reasoned that it—*they*—were figuring out how to unlock or peel open the lid.

Alexi shimmied slowly away from the portal and sat back, resigned now to watch what was unfolding. *They'll probably come in through that hatch.*

Two loud cracks, one immediately following the other, drew his attention toward the bow, just in time to hear (and worse, to *understand*) the pair of dull thuds that accompanied the extraction of the Plexiglas viewports. But instead of twin torrents of water blasting into the cabin, what entered was a massive inpouring of flesh.

Chernov's last conscious thoughts were more of astonishment and regret than fear. It seemed impossible that such large bodies coming through such small openings could take shape so quickly. And while there was a certainty of imminent death, there was no awareness of pain. There was only a regret that his loved ones would never know that for him those last seconds were like watching it all happen to someone else. Alexi Chernov knew they would always imagine it being much worse for him than it actually was.

The creatures that had invaded the mini-sub expanded to fill nearly half of the flooding cabin.

They embraced their prey. And having decided to share it, they waited for all movement to cease.

Only then did they enter it.

Only then did they feed.

5.33 Million B.C.

THE LOST WORLD OF MEDITERRANEAN CANYON

A new animal was rising to the ranks of sentience upon the planet. The cephalopod that had attacked Proud One's clan was only one among so many increasingly self-aware species, evolving in such diverse places, that if Mac and his friends had been equipped with the ultimate paleontological tool—a time machine—it might have seemed to them that nature was trying in every way possible to create intelligent life.

The ancestral Kraken huddled beneath the surface of the great salt marsh, watching, waiting, analyzing. On the world above, a new enemy was approaching from the highlands in the south. They moved among the reeds and trees as if they owned the earth—hair-covered bipeds—with sharp teeth and thick, muscular claws.

During a night raid on the biped intruders, one of the three sub-adults involved in the attack had been severely wounded. In addition to losing an eye, the little male had suffered severe damage to the myriad of nerves involved in salt and oxygen regulation. Normally these combined abilities allowed the smallest members of the lair to go landward and ascend nimbly into the trees. But presently the wounds rendered prolonged survival impossible. Even at a distance of several body lengths, even against the background noise of the undersea world, it was impossible not to feel the vibrations from all three of the little male's hearts failing.

One of the adults cut a long, long strip of still-warm red growth from a rock. But the wounded male refused to eat. Most of his limbs were turning pale, yet he still possessed enough strength to flash his caretaker a rotating zebra pattern that communicated a calm resignation to life's end.

Nearby, the smoky hot water from seven mineral towers had turned the subsurface lair into a red garden. The day's first faint shafts of sunlight were stabbing down through spaces between scarlet billows when the caretaker reached out a limb and discovered that the child's hearts had finally stopped.

As she retreated from the corpse, another member of the disastrous nighttime scouting party slid in beside her. The skin on one side of his body, though gouged and scratched, shifted from a rock-mimicking pattern to figures so precisely geometric as to dance somewhere between mathematics and art, to become linguistic. The caregiver read the tapestry of lines and shapes as if it were a written code.

The general message conveyed included blushes of anger over a contradiction: the trespassers from the south were food, and yet the scouts had been bitten and partly devoured by food.

With the exception of Proud One's troop and the dialect of the Stone-throwers, nothing upon the planet could be adequately compared with the detailed communications now passing between the two cephalopods. Their skin shimmered in a million points of light, as if adorned with a cloak of microscopic gems. The colors included opal red, tanzanite blue, sapphire yellow, and celestine white. The adult understood that she was to follow the juvenile to the place toward which their attackers were migrating—to the reeds at the edge of the marsh, where the hopping snails lived.

He led her directly to a system of canals that

extended deep into the plain of moss and reeds. They swam past stands of trees on either side, and among the reeds roamed herds of kangaroolike mollusks. None of them had a chance of reaching the continents above, or surviving in the highlands long enough to enter the fossil record. In another five million years, the deep Mediterranean world was fated to become so utterly lost to history that the very rays of sunlight now being caught by the canal's surface and reflected back into space would be scattered far beyond the Andromeda galaxy.

Like the intruding bonobo lineage, the road the cephalopods followed had been long and hard. After the great Mediterranean dry-out, during a period in which all the waters of the Nile poured down terraced cliffs many times wider, and two miles higher, than Niagara, the caretaker's ancestors were confined increasingly to a sea at the new river's end, just south of Crete. All around them, with the weight of the entire Mediterranean removed by the dry-out, vast regions of the seafloor had bobbed upward. Sometimes the rise amounted to hundreds of feet, carrying Crete and Santorini with it. Here and there, pieces of earth's crust stretched and cracked open, bringing forth springs of warm volcanic water. In a few rare and isolated places around the Devil's Hole, the springs drew an intensely symbiotic microbe from within the earth.

The elder and the juvenile had no knowledge of this, or anything else about how a commonplace, octopoid ancestor had experienced the rewriting of its genome and the overhaul of entire organ systems by a fascinatingly self-serving infection.

Initially, under the red infection, the elder's ancestors had become abnormally creative. Males constructed increasingly decorative patterns of spirals and circles beneath the salt sea—the most sophisticated of them attracting the most desirable mates. Still . . . Being the newest and brightest creature around did not count for very much without parents and grandparents, and social organization.

Then, as if the infection were taking command, thoroughly, over the process of adaptation, life spans expanded. Under normal conditions, even the most sentient cephalopod lived for only five years. After only a few dozen generations, imploding birth rates precluded overpopulation in spite of lengthened lives. The emergence of a new mathematical imbalance simultaneously increased the competition for mates and serendipitously spawned the planet's first artists. Lines and circles originally cut out of the seabed to attract mates became the impressive architecture of watery roadways—the canals of the deep Mediterranean marshlands.

Minds that were alien to yet in many ways above the sentience of the Stone-throwers were not what made the cephalopods most dangerous to Proud One's refugee clan. Once the Kraken lineage was elevated to longer life spans and reduced to infrequent births, the canyon's cephalopod denizens were on common ground, driven by instincts that all but mirrored the invading bonobo clan. In order to survive, they needed to make babies. Now, to lose even a single juvenile, or to see it injured, was a tragedy and a threat calling for tracking the killer down, and likely rendering its entire species locally extinct.

After the disastrous first contact, the juvenile who now led the caretaker had stalked the trespassers. He was so familiar with the stench of them that chemo-sensors at the tips of his tentacles could detect individual molecules from bonobo urine spreading seaward along the canals. Presently, the night rains that carried the scent had ceased and the sun was rising higher, fierce and hot. Yet the molecular trail remained strong and the juvenile directed the caretaker toward the encampment, as one might direct a submarine using sonar.

For uncounted centuries, adult cephalopods had been digging canals landward through layers of moss and muddy reeds, because food from the land remained a delicacy.

The juvenile, using a three-color signal that ran along a horizontal line so narrow that it could not be seen by anything watching from above the water, pointed his companion toward the canal's end, as if to say, *There! There it is!*

The caretaker signaled just as stealthily—that she could smell it, too, and *hear* it.

They glided past reed nets and basket traps set out to capture land life. A hopper snail lay drowning in one of them, but the two cephalopods ignored it.

The juvenile brought one tentacle close to the

caretaker's eye and displayed, for her, shapes indicating that there were two of the hair-covered trespassers ahead. Then, gurgling and clicking, he corrected the number to *three*.

The adult did not agree. Moving swiftly to the canal's end, so gracefully that she did not create the slightest ripple on the water's surface, she spread all of her camouflaged tentacles along the floor. She was now able to feel even the faintest vibration from the ground above.

She watched.

She waited.

She analyzed.

The juvenile came up stealthily beside her, and the caretaker communicated what she felt and saw, through the ground: A hopper snail was being chased by one of the trespassers. A second biped, larger than the first, was also approaching.

The caretaker raised both eyes very near to the surface and peered out. Her eyes were the only part of her entire body that could not be camouflaged, to blend in with the weeds and mud on the bottom of the canal. Each eye was larger than a bonobo's fist; each iris surrounding an alien, W-shaped pupil. The juvenile cephalopod also rose up and looked around.

The little bonobo gazed back at them, seemingly spellbound.

CHAPTER 9

Seeing Red

You don't have a war plan. No plan at all.
All you have is a kind of horrible spasm!
    —JFK's NUCLEAR TECHNOLOGY ADVISOR
    ROBERT S. McNAMARA

July 2, 1948
Central Park West, New York City

Yanni's observation that on those odd occasions when Mac did make a mistake, the results could be spectacular, was being tested by history—again.

High above the city streets, Genya and Victor were trying their best to find some hidden meaning in what they had transcribed from the latest theremin transmission. They were both exhausted to begin with and a new mystery was putting them several steps beyond ordinary exhaustion. During the first two days after the Nesbitt woman left, Mac's office remained generally quiet, except for an intermittent ringing of the phone and the all-too-familiar sounds of a chain-smoker. The old artist had apparently sought the solitude of the office to finish a painting project, and finally answered one of the calls. There was no mistaking how quickly he became impatient with the man on the other end of the line—"Sure, Hendry, we all know that you don't like cleaning up Mac's messes. Gettin' him *into* the shit, that's another . . . what? . . . What makes you think *I* would know what the hell he was thinking? . . . Okay, okay, what was that number again? . . . Yeah, got it. *Yes*, I'll repeat it back to you, but how would I know anything about a cab company at the Athens airport?"

"But why were they talking about Greek telephone numbers?" Genya asked, his voice unable to hide his alarm. "Perhaps they have discovered that we're listening? Could this talk of phone numbers be a ruse—*pretending* to speak in codes?"

Genya felt Victor's hand touch his shoulder sympathetically. "Stop thinking too much," his friend advised. "It's past dawn now, in case you did not notice. One of us needs to get some sleep and the other has to make that next drive to LaGuardia."

"I only need a little breakfast, and some strong coffee," said Genya. "After that, I can make the drop."

This was the first time in many hours that Genya had observed anything approaching enthusiasm on Victor's face.

"Go, then," Victor said. "I will have everything ready for you by the time you fill yourself with coffee."

Genya knew how much his friend hated driving in New York traffic. Sometimes one needed the skills of a bullfighter just to maneuver safely across Columbus Circle. But he actually relished the excitement.

During his typical-New-Yorker-in-a-hurry walk to a local diner, he brushed past a newsboy aggressively hawking a paper he'd never seen before—the *Brooklyn Daily Eagle*.

"Whassa matter, mister?" the boy said, flashing something resembling a snarl. "Ya got somethin' against da Bums?"

"In fact I do not," Genya replied, using a well-practiced French accent that would have fooled all but the most discerning ear. "But you are in enemy territory, no?"

"Whattaya tawkin' about, mister?" the kid shot back.

Genya gestured uptown. "The Yankees play right up the road, no?"

"Dey stink," the kid replied, holding out a paper. "Ya want one or not?"

Genya nodded, reached for a paper, and less than five minutes later, after ordering his meal, the "Frenchman" was reading a column about the appalling increase in the price of common goods and services.

This "crisis" is only half true, Genya told himself, noting that a cup of coffee, two eggs on a fresh roll, plus a chocolate bar would cost him only twenty cents.

Such luxuries, he thought, shaking his head at how spoiled these postwar Americans were becoming. He reasoned that if New Yorkers had been forced to experience the famine currently spreading across his own country, the bread lines of the Depression would have seemed nostalgic by comparison.

As Genya consumed his "early bird special," he sharpened his speed-reading and photographic memory skills on the rest of the newspaper. The deepening tensions across the globe looked even worse than during the previous week. The problem was that a month before *that*, he had convinced himself they had all finally hit bottom, and by now Russia and the United States would have realized there was nowhere for them to go except up.

Where else can *we go?* he had asked himself, after John Wayne, Ronald Reagan, and even Walt Disney were publicly skewering fellow actors and filmmakers accused of working in Stalin's best interests.

It occurred to Genya now that he should never have asked the question, because he had underestimated just how low the bottom could be. The newspaper told him so.

Washing down the last bite of a Milky Way with a gulp of coffee, Genya paused at a cartoon depicting children walking under the American flag, into a schoolhouse where a large black serpent lurked. The snake wore a caption that read "Communist teacher."

An announcement at the bottom of the front page promised a supplement in Sunday's July 4 edition, to be published in cooperation with the House Committee on Un-American Activities. The booklet would detail how to recognize and report traitors among your neighbors and family members.

Genya had a habit of memorizing a newspaper or a book and leaving it in pristine condition, or what he called "with eye marks only." He politely left the *Eagle*, which had cost him three cents, on the counter for the next customer, and stepped out into a bright New York morning, carrying a paper bag of refreshments for Victor. What he read in the diner left him simultaneously saddened *and* satisfied that the Americans were now turning on each other like wolves. He estimated that for every real Stalinist actually brought to committee "justice," a hundred innocents would be accused and sacrificed. Soon a strengthening vortex of false accusations would provide the perfect camouflage for the *real* agents of the Kremlin.

The Russian whistled confidently—a French marching tune—as he walked back to his apartment listening post. He waved to the newsboy, who ignored him. Letting his mind wander, he reminded himself of something that could be noticed only by reading between the lines of the newspaper. He could have told Stalin today that if Russians really wanted to damage America, all they needed to do was sit back and watch the escalating rate at which Americans were willing—sometimes with malicious joy—to inflict misfortune upon other Americans. He could also have told Stalin (but dared not utter it) that if Americans could see what was happening in Russia, they too could just sit back, and watch, and gloat, for the very same reason.

CHAPTER 10

A Meeting with Medusa

Five thousand years . . . fifty thousand years . . . five hundred thousand years . . . If you free yourself from the conventional reaction to a quantity like a million years, you free yourself a bit from the boundaries of human time. And in a way you do not live at all, but in another way you live forever.
—JOHN McPHEE

July 2, 1948
Santorini
Port of Fira

R. J. MacCready helped two nervous-looking crew members finish anchoring a portable walkway linking the Catalina to one of Fira's docks. They had assembled and slammed the aluminum pieces into place with reckless dis-regard for the safety of their own fingers.

And we might have saved ourselves the trouble, Mac realized. Around him, the rest of the crew had decided not to wait. Most of them, includ-ing Nesbitt, leaped down among half-submerged rocks into chest-deep water as if they were charging the beach at Normandy. Although there were no obvious signs of pursuit, Mac did not begin to breathe comfortably again until he saw that the others had climbed safely onto the dock.

As he looked back across Thera Lagoon, the number of boats hurrying toward land on the far side drove home the reality of how quickly the waters had transformed from a place of mysteri-ous healings and a rare shark attack to the lair of a sinister, alien intruder. Along what was normally a small but bustling waterfront, Mac could see that commercial activity at Fira had just died. He secured the machine gun, then stepped away and ducked out through the blister window.

The locals know it's all going south fast, he thought, noting that all of the dockside action was reduced to a half-dozen men and their donkeys. The stragglers must have been anticipating porter jobs hauling whatever gear came off the newly arrived seaplane.

Scanning for Yanni, he saw that she was help-ing Cousteau. The Frenchman had arrived only minutes earlier in the motorboat and was now se-curing it to an adjacent dock. Out on the lagoon, Mac had covered Cousteau's departure from the

Catalina with the Browning, then tracked his friend's zigzagging return as best he could from a water-skimming plane, convincing himself that once the boat was away from the red plume, they would step safely ashore without incident.

Mac craned his neck up toward the thousand feet of cliffs and road cuts leading to Fira. *Up there*, he told himself. *These Kraken—or whatever they are—may be able to get onto boats and pull people out of planes, but up there should be high enough.*

Now he turned toward a new sound—a commotion in front of a nearby market stall that elicited a brief smile. Nora Nesbitt was in an animated dispute with two men, one of whom was holding a rope attached to a sad-looking donkey.

And who the hell is she working for? Mac wondered, watching the exchange. *First she all but completely disappears for two years to some mystery lab that officially doesn't even exist. Now she flies in with a fully armed Catalina, ordering everybody around.* "Like the queen of freaking Sheba," he muttered.

The invertebrate biologist's murky allegiances had in fact been the topic of recent conversations with Yanni; Mac found himself smiling again, this time at the memory. "I'm tellin' ya, Mac, this Nesbitt knows what color underwear Hendry's chosen for the day. But what the crotch? She damn well *ain't* military."

Yanni does have a way with words, Mac thought as he approached the dispute.

Acknowledging the group with a friendly wave, he turned to Nesbitt. Although tempted to say something rude, Mac bit his tongue, knowing that the woman had just lost a colleague to the Kraken. "What's the problem, Nora?"

"I'm *trying* to hire these guys and one or two of their donkeys to carry my gear to wherever the *hell* it is we're staying."

Mac shot a quick glance back toward the plane, then threw a thumb over his shoulder in the direction of Private McQueen and four reasonably portable crates he had retrieved and now seemed to be guarding on the dock. "Are those all ya got?"

She nodded. "Yeah, 'cept for my backpack."

"Give me a sec," MacCready said, gesturing for her to take a few steps back.

After she did so, Mac addressed each of the locals with a nod, then made an effortless transition into New York City bargaining mode, in a mixture of Brooklyn-ese and Greek.

Less than a minute later he returned to where Nesbitt was standing, hands on her hips.

"Eight hundred drachmae would be fair," Mac told her. He could sense that she was about to respond. "Unless you want to wait till nobody's looking. Then you could just steal the donkey."

Nesbitt ignored the jab, and after quickly peeling off eight 100-drachmae notes she completed the transaction and watched as the men headed for the dock.

"Thanks, Mac," she said coldly.

"Hey, anything for an old pal," Mac replied. Then, as nonchalantly as possible, he added, "So, you want to tell me why you're here on Santorini?"

"Soon, Mac," Nesbitt said, quickly, "but not

right now." Then she flashed him a smile. "So where are we headed?"

"Up there," MacCready said, pointing to a winding trail, barely visible along the face of the cliff.

"That's funny," she said, before gesturing toward the lagoon. "Seems like all the action is taking place out there."

Mac shrugged his shoulders. "Yeah, you know, more local mumbo jumbo."

Nesbitt shook her head. "You know, Mac, I was starting to think your pals back at the museum were the worst liars I'd ever met."

"Guess some of us missed those courses in bullshit you must have taken," Mac replied, his anger rising like a sour tide. "I'm thinking you aced those, huh?"

"Look, what's important here is what's out there. The microbes we were exposed to in those valleys changed us, may *still* be changing us and are probably just itching to get to work on our ovaries and sperm. And if there's more of it around here—and apparently there's much more—then we need to get a handle on it before someone else does."

"You lost a man—about *when*? Maybe twenty minutes after setting down? Does that mean anything to you?"

"There are going to be casualties, Mac," Nesbitt said, then her tone softened. "You know that as well as anyone."

MacCready paused. Then, sensing that she was about to press him for additional information, he headed off the request with "Excuse me," and turned to leave.

What he saw beyond the dock stopped him cold.

Yanni Thorne had just finished assisting Cousteau, and now, with everyone ashore, she planned to take a closer look at a pair of circular markings the recent attack had left on the outside of the Catalina. She'd thought about calling Mac over but he was in an animated discussion with everyone's favorite bad-luck charm, so she and Cousteau decided to conduct the examination by themselves.

Headed toward the portable walkway, a sudden chill came over Yanni, and it had little to do with the marks on the plane. A poor donkey protested the heavy load being placed upon it by two porters, under the direction of Nesbitt.

Should have left that one in Tibet, Yanni thought. The new chill inside her arose from seeing—and in her own way simultaneously feeling—the ache in the donkey's clearly unsteady legs. A noise from within the plane caused her to glance away. Cousteau was at the hull's side, and one of the crew had gone back aboard, attending to something behind the open blister window.

Yanni half-turned, trying to keep her eyes fixed on the donkey. "Nesbitt! You need to lighten—" But those were the only words she got out before Cousteau came back across the ramp in a hurry, and a new movement turned her fully around.

It had begun with a ripple on the surface—something displacing water as it slid into the shallows on the plane's port side. Two more ripples appeared, flanking the first, and throwing off sparkles of reflected sunlight. Straining against the glare, Yanni could see submerged rocks shifting and blurring. She scarcely noticed Mac and Cousteau at her side until one of them grabbed an arm and tried to draw her back, but she shook the hand away with a firm rebuke and stepped nearer the disturbance. A dark shape broke the surface of the water, barely more than thirty-five feet from where she stood. It rose silently—a fleshy pedestal bulging up until it extended above the level of the dock, helical and glistening, and standing about the height of a man.

There came a loud cry from one of Nesbitt's two porters, but Yanni did not turn. She did not see the expressions of startled surprise giving way to terror on the faces of a half-dozen donkey porters. Even among the Catalina's crew, there was a general movement toward higher ground.

As Yanni watched, mesmerized, the column began to change—subtle curves and indentations now appearing. Then a color shift, from a shade of blue she had never before observed, to swirls of khaki and red, topped with a flowing pattern of black. For an instant, just for an instant, Yanni saw that the structure was actually a convergence of no fewer than four elongated sections.

"Holy shit," Yanni said, out loud and to herself. *They're tentacles!* Mac and Cousteau said nothing. She would not have heard them in any case. Her world was all tunnel vision now, and adrenaline. As the colors shifted and resolved themselves, the column underwent astonishingly rapid adjustments and Yanni stood facing the figure of a human—*near-perfect mimicry*, she thought. Except for minor distortions, still under adjustment, it was as if she were looking across the dock and over the water, into a mirror.

Slowly the figure began to close the space between them, gliding along the water's surface while whatever extended beneath its feet—*more of them?*—gave the illusion of semitransparency against the rocky bottom.

"Everyone hold still!" she called out, without turning away from the creature.

Now "standing" near the edge of the dock, the figure began changing color again—still a human form but with a concentric pattern of stripes radiating from its midsection, out along extended arms. A more distinct, *broken* circle pattern quickly followed, radiating from the center at increasing speed, through the tips of its "fingers." Yanni had a sudden, intuitive sense that she was to imagine the circles rippling out far beyond the lagoon until after only a few seconds, she began to suspect that the creature was trying to make her understand something incredibly vast. Abruptly the shapes ceased radiating. They switched to newer and more complex patterns, some familiar, others abstract. They fluttered, one after another. During one astonishing flicker, Yanni believed she glimpsed a trio of divers. During the next second:

a silhouette that resembled a submarine. All of
them shifted in synchrony with the sudden addition of instantly familiar clicks—the drumming
of the severed limb in the tray, the same drumming of her fingers when their boat approached
the Catalina.

The clicking quickened and changed. Yanni
studied the patterns, trying to link them to the
accompanying language of color—but as the pace
picked up she found it maddeningly confusing.

Something about the entire situation caused
her to laugh. Then, extending her arms, she made
a series of palms-down waves. "All right there,
Gorgeous George, slow down, huh."

Remarkably the figure responded, and the
color patterns shifted from double time to a more
deliberate tempo, as did the castanet accompani-
ment of keratinous barbs.

Very slowly, Yanni removed her backpack. As
she reached inside, the mimic drew back several
feet. In response, she removed two objects from
her pack and held them out—a blunt probe, and
a metal specimen dish "borrowed" from the hotel
room.

Dragging the tip of the probe across the brass
rim, Yanni began producing a series of sounds
that she hoped would do a serviceable job of repli-
cating what she was hearing. She started with half
of the duet she had briefly performed with the
severed tentacle, and which she had reproduced
against the side of a boat in the lagoon.

The mimic responded with silence. "I get the

feeling it understands me," Yanni thought aloud, "but it's pretending not to."

"Who knew they were French?" Cousteau said softly.

For a while it continued to listen, and to occasionally blush new colors. Then, abruptly, it snapped back again to "Yanni mirror mode," albeit with some measure of difficulty. The features of her identical twin's face weren't identical anymore. They were shifting—shifting like wax, from the familiar to something else, then trying to mirror her again, but not getting the image quite right.

Losing no part of her composure, Yanni continued her rhythmic scraping. "We can talk about that nose later, but you're gonna have to help me out here."

Instead, either displaying defiance or trying to communicate some stance not easily understood, the other Yanni came ashore. There had certainly been at least two or three companions beneath it, lifting her—but they apparently retreated without so much as a blur of distorted light or a splash of water being noticed. The other Yanni was a master at distraction.

"Ever seen anything stranger than this?" Yanni whispered.

"Close, maybe," Mac whispered back. "But why is it mimicking you?"

"Wish I knew. Whatever it's trying to say, I think it's a little over my head."

As perhaps it was. *Dance too many times with*

Death, Yanni told herself, *and sooner or later why shouldn't She gaze into you—as a mirror?*

Undeterred, Yanni continued trying to communicate by the clicking and scraping of tray and probe; Death attempted to signal back to her in a slightly different beat, but the apparition seemed suddenly to falter, as if distracted and in pain. That quickly, it lost two feet of height, and its click-and-scrape tempo collapsed into a long, drawn-out wheeze. In that moment, gravity and bright sunlight became its newest worst enemies. Nonetheless, from the place where the mimic would have had feet, two large cephalopod eyes fully revealed themselves from behind unwinding coils, then fixated on Yanni, Mac, and Cousteau. The mass of musculature and tentacles that framed those eyes regrouped and moved with keen determination again. In the next moment, it stood tall, its entire skin surface conveying the billowing clouds of red smoke Cousteau had described.

Now that the initial shock was wearing off, Yanni could appreciate that it was, in its own way, a surprisingly beautiful beast. Calling it a "mimic" was true but probably misleading. It was much more—she was certain of this, even as its imitation of the red smoke transformed into a human figure, first male, then female, then back to male again.

Mac, me, then Jacques.

The castanet chorus was back again, repeating a new rhythm in synchrony with another concentric series of broken rings, spreading out so fast that Yanni believed they might soon become a continual, indistinguishable flutter.

"Mac," she said, keeping up with the rhythm. "Try to see it as I see it. *Try*."

"Rings spreading out, beyond here . . . beyond the whole sea?"

"Beyond the whole world—and in just minutes, at that rate, maybe past the moon and the Sun."

"Something vast."

"Yes, Mac. I don't think they even see time the same way we do."

"Is that what it's showing? Time's vastness?"

"They think in eons."

A pulsating, bioluminescent limb snaked gently toward Yanni—and exploded, just as she was about to take her first tentative step forward. A spray of flesh struck her forehead. The continual booming of a large-caliber machine gun completely drowned out Mac's cry of "*Cease fire!*" Mac and Cousteau pulled Yanni to the ground and shielded her body with their own, but by the time the Catalina's turret gunner paused to reload, tentacles were already torn off and strewn about, and the mimic was cut practically in two.

Throwing Mac off to one side, Yanni scrambled to her feet and saw the Catalina's eyeball turret shifting position, beginning to track the remaining tentacles to their source. Half of that source scuttled and rolled to the edge of the dock and spilled into the shallows.

"*Hold your fire!*" Mac commanded the unseen gunner. Yanni heard Nesbitt holler the same command, but the gunner disobeyed. With clearly no thought at all for his own safety, Mac rushed toward the narrow portable walkway. Yanni and Cousteau started after him but were halted by the second volley—which struck a segment of tentacle in their path, spraying it apart and by sheer dumb luck not simultaneously spraying anyone with bullet pieces.

The chaos ended so abruptly that Mac was not yet at the ramp before the gunner had slumped down and McQueen emerged from the plane, holding a wrench.

"Guy panicked and fired against orders," the private said, waving the wrench. "Needed to be sedated."

The flying boat rocked sharply to one side and McQueen leaped onto the dock, then grabbed a length of rope and tried to anchor the ramp more firmly.

Along one side of the dock, where Yanni's mimic had stood, tentacles and blasted remnants were struggling to reach the water. Many were already splashing into the lagoon. Some emitted flashes of color. Others blushed an angry red and died.

At least five shadowy figures, each about the size of a bear, were moving among the pieces and along the dock. Yanni felt more than heard something rush past her, snatching up shreds of tentacle. This individual was smaller than the other shapes, and it covered the ground with such speed that the human eye and mind could only have registered it as a flash of movement, even were the cephalopod not trying to blend in with its surroundings. She found the creature less difficult to follow once it had returned to the water. Inexplicably, it seemed to be parceling out gathered pieces of Kraken to the other shadows.

Yanni would later swear that the cephalopods appeared to be examining and maybe even tasting segments of the dying mimic—in what struck her as an act born somewhere between mourning and reverence.

The shadows in the water were continually changing, reproducing whatever they encountered along the stony bottom with such fidelity, on their dorsal surfaces, that even when moving busily to and fro, they appeared translucent, like windows of frosted glass.

As she watched the cephalopods, and as the flying boat shifted again against its moorings, Mac helped Private McQueen drag the unconscious turret gunner across the ramp.

"Looks like you've really found something extraordinary," Nesbitt said. Yanni did not notice that she'd come running up beside her despite the danger. The Catalina bucked violently side-to-side. Two shadows seemed actually to have unscrewed the turret. They took its hood and twin .50-caliber machine guns with them into the sea. The port side blister broke, and its gun also disappeared beneath a shadow that became wing-shaped once it slipped below the surface, as did its companions. They swam away like undersea bats toward deeper water, as graceful as manta rays.

"Nora, you've got it backwards," Yanni corrected. "Something extraordinary has found us."

5.33 Million B.C.

THE LOST WORLD OF MEDITERRANEAN CANYON

S eed remained crouched at the canal's edge, paralyzed with astonishment. The water had been watching her—with two pairs of fist-sized, alien eyes.

If the child of Proud One lived through this strange encounter, the moment would never cease to haunt her.

In this time of expulsion from their highland feeding grounds and a forced march into unknown lands, she had been drawn to the water by intensifying hunger and a fiery sting to her hand from a hopper snail.

Seed both heard and felt the galloping of her mother's hands and feet along the ground. Proud One called out to her, a loud and plaintive cry of denial, like a long and guttural "*Nooo . . .*"

In that moment, Seed was struck by the most pitiful sensation any thinking species—simian or cephalopod—would ever know: *If only . . .*

If only nature, in some horrible spasm of malevolence, had not chosen to spawn stone-throwing monsters who chased her entire clan down to the canyon, and into the path of new monsters.

If only the monsters could talk to her clan. "*Leave us alone,*" the cephalopods might have tried to say. "*Leave us alone,*" the bonobos would certainly have replied.

If only . . .

The child let out a shriek while her mother managed a galloping leap that sent her airborne toward the threat in the water—a splendid but useless display that ended with two barbed spears and five tentacles rising up and plunging Proud One below the surface in a harrowing glut of blood.

Seed let out a piteous howl but remained motionless, as if unable to quite comprehend what death signified, as if unwilling or unequipped to understand that it meant the end of her mother.

A hand gripped Seed's shoulder, and saved her. More than half of the clan had come running down to the water's edge. All of them were signing the direction north and away from the canal in which the smaller of two shimmering shapes had begun removing and consuming Proud One's organs.

"Go all," commanded the Large One who had once challenged Seed's mother. "*Go now,*" she signed, and pointed north.

Had Large One and her allies arrived only a very short time later, Seed would by now have leaped into the water after her mother. The rest of the clan stepped out from the reeds, but kept their distance, and made waving motions north and "Away."

A stinging surge rose up through the ground itself and caused old Broken Tooth to jump up and sign "*Away*" more vigorously. The slayers beneath the water seemed either not to have felt the sting or not to care. They stopped feeding on Proud One and moved nearer the shocks, nearer the water's edge.

Something much larger also approached, towering above the brush. On four extraordinarily wide and muscular legs, a shell-less, elephantine mollusk sent forth a series of electrical discharges that traveled in random directions along the ground. Seed realized that the elders seemed suddenly confused about the direction of escape. One cried out in pain and signed toward the southern highlands. Another signed toward the water. Directly ahead of the new threat, swarms of termite-like slugs had abandoned a bright red mound and were fleeing toward Seed's clan in such multitudes that, collectively, they moved like a mist along the ground.

The elephant snail stopped radiating electrical shocks, trampled the crimson mound, and fed upon it. Seed realized that they now stood on a low, muddy hill turned suddenly into an island, with a writhing wave of slugs running like a flood tide, expanding its dimensions and nipping at their ankles. The wave was cutting off the way north, and spreading along the path west. The way south was blocked by water, and by tentacles rising. On the east side, the giant was on the move again. Something snakelike had sprung out of the demolished red mound and seemed to be fighting back.

One of the clan ran toward the elephant snail, hauled himself up one side, bit at the place where a head should have been, and was flung dead to the ground as if by an invisible force. Simultaneously, they were all numbed by a shock surge running beneath their feet. Seed's skin flushed with horror, her legs felt like tightening springboards, and she chose the direction of flight—straight through the tide of biting slugs, now even more active under a strengthening pulse of electrical discharges.

She fled, and the rest followed. Sharp pains radiated from the bites to her feet and her calves, but Seed did not pause until she and the rest of the clan were far from the elephant snail, the water, and even the fields of reeds and trees.

By midnight they were beyond the Devil's Hole's salt marshes and the Mediterranean floor's most westward extension of the new Nile. They stood near the fringe of the great western desert— watching, waiting.

A bright crescent moon was rising. Tonight the clouds did not come near, and only the slightest drizzle of rain reached them, carried by a wind from the east.

"They will not come," Seed signed hopefully. Even the large female who had challenged her mother acknowledged that Seed had chosen the right direction out of the marshlands, and saved their lives. They were looking toward her now, and she was looking toward the southwest, into a desert.

Those eyes! Seed could not suppress the memory of the two monsters in the water. In that moment, she had become the first primate to behold a sense of curiosity in a cephalopod's eyes. Though the two species were entirely alien to each other in both physiology and the minds that dwelt within, as each gazed into the eyes of the other—during that instant of mutual terror, fury, and astonishment— each understood instinctively that there was a compulsively curious being on the other side.

After the moon set and Venus heralded dawn, Seed gazed north toward distant mountaintops that were not yet the island of Crete.

It became possible for her to hope that if they could stay to the west of the rains and rivers and the trees—if they could continue their journey north along the borders of the desert—the hot sun and the dry, salty sands would keep them safe. And beyond this lay the hope that, if only they survived the journey north and tentacles could not follow them onto the sands, they would come to a mountainous refuge of streams and fruits where no elephant snails or wide-eyed monsters lived.

If only . . .

CHAPTER 11

Secret Wars

*You ask me what God was doing before
he created the materials of Heaven and
earth. He was creating Hell for people who
asked questions like that.*
—SAINT AUGUSTINE

Something hidden? Go and find it!
—RUDYARD KIPLING

July 2, 1948
Santorini

From a height of only ten stories, along the port of Fira's
donkey path, Mac could look
across the full width of the flooded crater. He
was able to determine precisely the direction
from which a helicopter was approaching—still at
least a couple dozen miles away, and impossible to

spot behind the crater rim's southern hills. Yanni heard it too, and it seemed incredible to Mac that their hearing had grown so keen. Among the rest of their group, now near the top of the path and headed toward the quarry, he supposed that Alan and Nesbitt were also able to hear the approach. He was not so sure about Cousteau's hearing, though it was plain that something related to the "red *moctus proctus*" was infecting him.

"Chopper's been sent from Crete," Mac concluded.

"So glad you promised no helicopters this time," Yanni replied.

"I'm afraid you'll have to just settle for me not crashing you in one again," he said, and continued looking around.

As near as he and Yanni could tell, Nesbitt's Catalina was still floating more or less intact at the base of the cliff. Viewed from on high, it was easy to reconstruct the pattern of spray from the turret gunner who had transferred command of his senses over to panic. And in this manner at least one and perhaps two of the Kraken had died. Down there at the bottom of a donkey trail, the descendants of Seed's stone-throwing adversaries had met the descendants of the caretaker's lair. Although all of the tentacles and large body parts were removed from the field of slaughter, their copper-based blood was still spreading across concrete slabs as if little springs had yawned open, as if the earth itself were bleeding.

For a long time, Mac and Yanni remained silent, and simply continued looking about, while a breeze came down from the north and riffled their hair. And just once, Mac suspected he saw the faint hint of ripples in the blood, as if from a foot stepping into a puddle.

It did not happen again, so he quickly tried to convince himself that maybe it did not happen at all.

"What do you suppose we'll be facing if they can come higher ashore than a boat or the dock?" he said at last.

"I've thought about that," said Yanni.

"And?"

"They'll probably tear us apart in our sleep. See? I've thought about that."

"Thanks."

"Any time, Mac. Ain't like you need *me* to give you too many things to worry about."

The sound of rotor blades strengthened in the distance and, below, the puddles of cephalopod blood were quiescent . . . *for now.*

Mac had learned long ago that the road to hell was wide to begin with, but there was always someone or something just waiting to steepen the incline, and add a little slipperiness to it. His own First Law emphasized the point: *When you think you have thought of everything, and think you are finally safe—watch out, because nature will think of something else.*

As the helicopter finally came into view, a huge flotilla of low-hanging clouds advanced from the opposite direction. They rained streamers of mist and painted the lagoon's surface in shadows so black that, when contrasted against shafts of sunlight, the rains trailing out behind the clouds resembled volcanic ash. Then, suddenly, blinding gray fog shot across Mac and Yanni's overlook, and visibility dropped to no more than a dozen yards. Though Santorini was mostly a desert island, its weather had a flair for the dramatic. Few places on earth transitioned so abruptly from a bone-dry simmer to fog and cold rain—all of this rendered stranger and brighter still by the passing flotilla, as the fog bank finally pulled free and raced south with the rest of its fleet.

Only through gaps in distant sheets of rainfall was it possible to trace the path of the helicopter. It slowed to a hover above shallow water and was promptly obscured by veils of dark rain. In the next moment, an opening between clouds shone light upon the outline of a frogman descending on a line, illuminating him as if targeted by a search lamp, until the next cloudburst reached, and hid, the chopper. When it reappeared, the aircraft's line was being reeled in, and its frogman had recovered something.

"Looks like a body," Yanni said.

Mac let out a low grunt and continued watching, trying to figure out what kind of mission they were witnessing.

The helicopter had almost reached the halfway point between its initial destination—the body— and the town of Fira when Mac became aware of a curious discomfort, as if his subconscious were trying to keep him alive with a warning. The sensation was at once physical and psychological, as if some creature had just caressed his spine with little banana fingers. He felt the skin along his arms break out in a chill of gooseflesh—which had nothing at all to do with a fresh sprinkling of cold rain.

"Yanni?"

Now clearly alarmed, she had stopped watching the helicopter and was scrutinizing the donkey path and the nearest cliffs instead.

"Don't shoot or run until you're sure we're being attacked?" Yanni whispered.

Shoot at what? Run where? Mac asked himself.

Down there at the dock, beneath the anvil of the sun and before Private McQueen demonstrated anesthesiology at short notice, Mac had watched the cephalopods falter in their movements, as if the air itself were their enemy. *But now? In the rain?* He supposed he and Yanni could outrun one of them in a fifty-yard dash, but if cloud cover and soft rains allowed several to come as high ashore as they wanted—

Right, Mac reminded himself. *Yanni thought about that.*

Then he noticed how all of her attention was focused on a single flicker of movement, some twenty-five or thirty paces down the donkey trail. Something—*two* somethings—began shifting swiftly to and fro, so swiftly that their attempts to blend in against the rocks fell behind by a second or two. Fractured by time-framing, the odd skin patterns of lagging camouflage reminded Mac of Picasso's or Duchamp's women in cubism, descending their stairs. He could not focus clearly on either of the creatures—cubist paintings pacing back and forth with what appeared to be agitated impatience.

One of them transformed into a whirlwind of distorted shapes, stood up to about the height of a man, and began to approach.

"Can we run now?" Mac whispered.

Yanni did not answer. There was no time. As if summoned by the beast's decision to lunge forward, another shape dropped down from the rocks behind them. It landed on the donkey trail and rushed past Yanni, shoving her aside.

All Mac saw was the shove. In that same instant, while dropping reflexively to shield Yanni and raising his revolver, he chastised himself for not assuming a back-to-back defensive stance from the start.

"Don't!" Yanni warned.

During one small part of a second, Mac thought she was warning *him*, but by the time he blinked and took aim, he realized that it was a man who had shoved her aside, and who seemed about to take an encounter already going badly, down to the next level of hell—by throwing grenades. The target was too near for everyone to survive the blast.

"*Idiot!*" Mac called out, as the three "grenades," one after another, burst like water balloons against two Kraken, spraying them with white powder. They flickered with fierce, cold lightning, let out high-pitched warbles of pain, and retreated all the way downhill, fleeing into the water with loud, clumsy splashes.

"It's only *table salt*," the stranger announced,

holding out one of the balloons. Eyeing Mac-Cready severely, he added, "Never point your gun at a Russian when he's saving your life."

July 2, 1948
Central Park West, New York City

___

The past two hours were turning into a master-piece of wrong moves.

Genya had placed a cup of coffee next to Victor and unfolded a napkin containing two dunking doughnuts.

"Not there!" Victor warned. "Spill that and we can ruin the films."

"Sorry," Genya replied, and moved the coffee and breakfast to the top of the hotel room's ornate wooden radio chest. And there, the crisis—or even the possibility of crisis—should have ended.

"These film casings are ready, Genya. Now are *you* ready for your run?"

"A few cups of coffee helped. As they say here, helped *a great deal*. It should be easy now—a piece of pie."

"Good," said Victor, and placed one of the nickels into Genya's palm. He admired his own workmanship through a magnifier.

Victor scooped up two more of the film-concealing nickels and handed them over, then turned hurriedly to the work table, flipping over a quarter and several dollar bills before going slightly pale. "I only have three," he said at last.

"What do you mean, you only have three? We made four of them."

"Four! Yes! Where is the fourth nickel?"

Genya reached into his pockets and fumbled around. He pulled out several dimes and two pennies, while simultaneously backtracking his every recent action and everything he had seen, as if a very detailed movie picture were being played through his brain: *I read the newspaper while eating the egg sandwich and drinking my coffee. On the top right of the front page, the price of the paper . . . Three cents . . . the change I received would have been two cents if*—and he saw the moment in which both pennies were placed in his hand . . . "Oh, shit!"

"No . . ."

Genya bolted out the door and down the main stairwell, with Victor following only a couple of seconds behind and each of them bounding down two and three stairs at a time.

"The newsboy," Genya whispered, as they emerged onto the street. Regaining control over his composure and keeping his voice low enough, trying not to attract attention, he continued, "I'm certain of it. I gave a nickel to the newsboy."

The boy was gone.

"There is nothing to be done for it," Victor said, "except for you to meet our associate at LaGuardia."

"He's expecting four."

"Tell him we only had time to make three copies. I'll solve the rest of our problem."

"How?"

"Do not worry. I'll find the boy, and buy him out. You just hurry and hand over the change."

Victor turned away and began searching. He walked the whole neighborhood out to a distance of five blocks, trying to find the newsboy. The child was a familiar fixture in the area, especially on summer mornings. But today he had moved on.

By the time Genya returned from LaGuardia, Victor was back on duty at the listening post. "Can't find him," he mumbled, without looking up from the controls. The museum was broadcasting only silence.

"Shit."

"Forget about it," Victor said, trying to sound confident. "The kid's probably spent it on a comic book by now. And that nickel's screwed together tighter than Jack Benny's wallet."

Genya nodded, trying to shore up his own self-confidence in the midst of what he knew to be a potentially lethal mistake. "And even if it does eventually get opened," he added, pointing to the side of his own head, "they'll never learn the cypher key."

"No worries," Victor said. "After it changes hands through just one or two candy stores or into the nearest Woolworth's, who will remember the path of any single nickel, all the way back to us?"

July 2, 1948

SANTORINI

S*alt grenades?*" Mac asked, his sidearm now holstered.

"They are mollusks, correct?" said the Russian. "Ever sprinkle salt on a slug?"

"Can't say I have," Mac replied. "*That's* what made you think to fill condoms with salt?"

"Best defensive mechanism is usually the simplest one," he said, staring up at the approaching helicopter.

They all looked up, as it flew over the cliff top, en route to Fira. A body dangled from its line, and even though the aircraft passed more than nine hundred feet overhead, they could determine the color of the man's clothing.

The first to speak was the Russian. Only one word escaped his lips: "*Alexi.*"

A board the helicopter, Bishop George Marinatos did not notice the three upturned faces along the donkey trail. Though neither a politician nor a general, he had been assigned emergency protocol powers, to determine the nature of the Santorini lagoon manifestations, and decide the actions to be taken. Reluctantly, Bishop Marinatos had been awakened this very morning with new papers and an ancient scepter placed into his hands, declaring him the most powerful figure on Crete and its surrounding islands. That quickly, and once again for the islands, separation of church and state had ceased to be.

The bishop searched the ground through frustratingly shaky binoculars, trying to reconstruct in his own mind the details of the battle that had taken place near the Catalina. They were not low

enough, and the damaged plane was falling behind too quickly. Turning his attention ahead,
he noticed an encampment in the middle of Fira
Quarry and the little knot of people moving hastily toward it with two donkeys bearing crates.

"Something's wrong," he called out to the pilot.
"We should circle around and have a closer look."

"Something's wrong?" the pilot replied. "Those
people are probably armed, like everyone else
on these islands. Drop down and dangle a body
over their heads and something will be *terribly*
wrong—for us."

The frogman, seated behind the bishop,
packed away the last of his gear and tapped him
on the shoulder. "We'll have all of this figured
out, soon," he said, and pointed the pilot toward a
landing spot near the Fira police station.

"That's going to be a tight fit for us," the pilot
said. Marinatos shrugged. The only landing place
near the station was atop the remains of a brick-
and-mortar house that had cracked from rooftop
to foundation during a recent earthquake and had
to be razed to the ground. Even as they radioed
ahead and began to close the last thousand feet,
neighbors were still salvaging bricks and needed
to be cleared from the only reasonably flat and
wide piece of real estate for a quarter mile in any
direction.

Marinatos could see that police and volunteers
were trying to clear people from the streets as
well, but not soon enough. The body had been recovered and flown from the wreck site too quickly
and too many had now seen it.

And the sea turned into a red fluid like the blood of a corpse. The line from a first-century prophecy kept turning over and over in Bishop Marinatos's head, reminding him, *This is no Fatima, no Lourdes.* And even if it were, the Greek Orthodox Church remained undecided whether those two places were miracles, or false signs.

There were so many ways that the apocalyptic books (and there were many such books) could be interpreted or misinterpreted—so many ways to even unintentionally misuse the ancient verses—that the orthodoxy never read them aloud to their congregations.

Who was it, really? he wondered, as the vacant lot and clusters of white-painted buildings rose slowly toward him. *Who was "He who will lead them to the springs of living water"?*

It seemed impossible to know. There were descriptions of monsters with horns and multiple serpent heads. And it was already horribly apparent that something monstrous had drawn a midget submarine of unknown nationality into shallow water, extracted a crewman, and left him outside—mutilated.

With less than three hundred feet to go, the brick-littered lot up ahead began puffing clouds of dust into the air. At first the bishop believed it to be caused by the wash of the helicopter blades, but the dust was too far ahead of him and blowing from the wrong direction, and the streets in all directions seemed to have been similarly disturbed.

"Seems they've just had another little quake," the pilot announced.

"Abort?" the frogman asked.

"No. We are still safe for landing."

Bishop Marinatos glanced toward Nea Kameni. The blue dome of a church rose to eclipse his view of volcanic cinder cones and blood-red water, and he worried about the stories of miraculous healings at Santorini, and the prophecies about "springs of living water." He worried because he knew other, more ominous verses: *There arose from the sea before our eyes an animal, a dragon . . . Red, it arose, and it broke apart as if giving birth.* And most of all he began to worry about the damaged plane at the dock, and the people he had seen marching toward an apparently clandestine encampment in the quarry.

Foreigners, he concluded with grim certainty, as the helicopter's skids touched down. *Miracle waters or not, in their stumbling around they have awakened the dragons.*

T he Symplegades," Mac thought aloud as he, Yanni, and Dmitri Chernov approached the Fira police station. Traces of tremor-displaced dust were still lingering in the air.

"The clashing rocks that almost smashed the Argonauts," Dmitri replied.

"Yep. That's sort of what we're walking into right now." The analogy was dramatic, but not necessarily a false one. Even among the mainland's communist insurgents, life had become the story of "a rock clashing against a hard place." During the previous month, in the north, Stalin had renounced Yugoslavia's communist leader, Tito. On mainland Greece, in almost a mirror image of America's committees on un-American activities, the Greek Communist Party was embarking upon a McCarthy-esque witch hunt against the Tito-ists.

"MacCready, isn't it hard to believe how your comrades, my comrades, and the Greeks—how together, one day, we all won the war against Hitler?"

"I guess winning the war's never as tough as keeping the peace," Yanni observed.

"And here on Santorini," Dmitri replied, "they mostly support you Americans. So what will they think when you walk in there with a Russian?"

"Well, guys, here's where it gets complicated," Mac said, motioning toward the parked helicopter. A decal guaranteeing safe passage had been pasted prominently onto its hull—a symbol of the religious orthodoxy. "I've always wondered," he continued, "what happens when two irresistible forces meet an immovable object."

Whenever anyone addressed him as "Captain MacCready" or, worse yet, "Doctor," Mac knew he was probably going to have a hard time talking his way out of whatever it was he had just stepped into.

The same humorless bruiser who held Cousteau for an inquisition four days earlier once again greeted him as "Captain Doctor MacCready."

"Who's the Russian?" Sergeant Papandreas demanded.

"Special Agent Chernov," Mac answered. "And he's under my jurisdiction."

"And he's *French*," Yanni added.

The sergeant nodded. "Yes. I believe you both. I believe you, just as I believe a cab company at the Athens airport can answer all of my questions about you—Doctor."

The last person who addressed Mac in this manner—being simultaneously mocking and grave—was a Nazi rocket scientist, and *that* bit of snafu had turned into nothing good. "So, how bad a problem do you have with us?" he asked.

Papandreas turned his attention toward Yanni. At first his facial expression seemed to be answering her claim about Chernov. He returned her a severe grimace, then broke into a grin. "So, your new friend is French, eh? Then it's a lucky day for all three of you that I've had a long conversation across the cable with your Patrick Hendry. It appears you might have undersold yourself, Doctor. If you're as smart as your CO thinks you are, I may need your assistance with what's in the next room."

Mac allowed himself a sigh of relief. "What can I help you with?"

The sergeant's calm brown eyes stared into him. "First, it's boats. And now I hear about an airplane incident—and worse. Your friend Cousteau tried to say we had a shark problem. But I've seen what sharks can do to a person, and it's never been that, has it?"

"Uh-uh," Mac conceded. "We think it's a relative of the common octopus, but rather larger, and smarter."

"You mean, a *polypus*?"

"You've been reading your Pliny," Mac said.

"And do not forget our Homer."

"No. Never forget Homer. But, yes—Pliny's polypus. Something like that." He glanced over at Yanni and saw that she had chosen to remain tight-lipped about precisely how smart the intruding cephalopods could be. They both understood that to say anything more now would only invite trouble. Yanni seemed to have firmed a resolve, at least for the moment, to obey her own First Law: *Don't go inviting trouble until you know what you're going to get out of it*.

"Come with me," the sergeant said, opening a door to reveal a table on which the body of Dmitri Chernov's brother lay. Mac motioned for Dmitri and Yanni to follow him inside. Sergeant Papandreas did not object.

When he arrived at the table, Mac found that the bishop and a local physician had removed a surprisingly intact shirt from the body. Yanni's attention was drawn immediately to the circular patterns of barb punctures, clustered around two slitlike incisions in the umbilical area. Dmitri had cried out his brother's name and fallen to his knees the moment he saw the helicopter passing overhead. Now he stood for a moment in shock, but quickly turned stoic, displaying an impressive poker face for the Greeks despite what had to be an intense inner grief.

The upper abdomen and the upper chest cavity were already surgically opened. Mac had expected to see much more damage, beyond the early destructive stages of the autopsy itself. The "polypus" attack had left all of Alexi Chernov's ribs unbroken. His eyes were open. His face, overall, expressed an incongruous calm.

"Name's Spiros Marinatos," the physician said, without looking up from the body. "My cousin here—he is the bishop from Crete."

"Most of us have had roots on these islands for five hundred years or more," Papandreas explained. "If you look hard enough, you will find the black sheep of the Marinatos family on the very south of Santorini—looking for the great biblical flood. Either that or Atlantis. Sometimes he seems a bit too full of wild ideas for his own good."

"Or for anyone else's," the bishop added.

"Then I'll make sure to avoid him," Mac said, chuckling inwardly as he said it, because a person with too many ideas was precisely the kind he most liked to meet. Returning his attention to the body, he asked, "These two umbilical incisions? Why?"

"I did not make those cuts," Spiros replied. "The animal made them."

"It stabbed him?"

"No. The cause of death was organ failure—system-wide."

"But you've had no time for a complete examination," said Dmitri—trying, with limited success, to conceal the strain in his voice. "How can you tell which organs failed?"

"Because it took them. Something entered through those two little incisions and removed his internal organs. Lungs. Heart. Digestive tract. *All* of them."

Mac glanced again at the corpse's disconcertingly peaceful expression, as if death for Alexi Chernov had been simply a matter of falling quietly into a deep slumber despite the horrible display. Until now, the worst animal attack the scientist had seen was a horde of ravenous white worms that could make sharks look mellow, by stripping all of a man's flesh away from the bones, then eating the bones.

"A polypus?" Sergeant Papandreas said again. "Captain, you believe it is really that dangerous?"

"I'm not saying our lives would be simpler and so much safer if it actually was frenzied sharks—or even piranha worms—but if you get my drift . . ."

"That bad, huh?" Dmitri responded, somewhat absently.

"Worse," said Bishop George Marinatos. "Worse, because it may concern the purpose of this red miracle you have been seeking, and what the people have awakened."

"Go on, Your Eminence," said Mac.

"To begin, just call me what everyone has always called me—Father George."

Mac nodded. He was caught a little left-footed by the bishop's unrequired humility, and his respect for the man had just gone up a few notches.

"Our faith has taught us to anticipate visitations of this kind—in a time when deceivers like Hitler and Stalin have existed, and when the weapons of superscience are echoing, from almost two thousand years ago, the images of destruction we find in the books of Revelation. It frightens me. And perhaps it should awaken you, because at least two of the books hold out a hope, that although these are things that may happen if we are not very careful, they do not *have* to happen."

"Wait a minute," Mac said, "*books* of Revelation?" He noticed that Dmitri had his head bowed. "There's more than one?"

"Four of them, actually. One for each horseman of the apocalypse. The prophetic books told of a great human change—a terrible day if we are unwise. Today, the agent of change is not riding toward us on the backs of four skeletal horses. It springs from our own hands, by our own perversion of the atom, and of the chemicals of the earth, and now maybe even the nature of life itself. And perhaps this is what the prophets saw, and why we read, 'To this race, a conflagration will come upon the Earth—and the Nile will fill more with bodies than with water. And their error, that they acted against themselves.'"

"The Apocalypse of the Egyptians," Dmitri said softly, as if in prayer.

R. J. MacCready looked at the Russian in frank astonishment. *Either he's Orthodox in a country where they have been squashing religion, or he reads a lot.*

"Father George?" Mac asked. "Where do *you* believe these animals fit in with prophecy?"

"An ancient Revelationist wrote, 'The enemy gives authority to the animal. It comes with false signs and miracles. It is he who shepherds them. And there is he who leads them to the springs of living water.'"

"The enemy?"

For many long seconds it seemed the bishop had finished and would not answer at all. Mac was about to fill the silence with a new question when, placing a hand over Alexi's forehead, George Marinatos said, "To Pontius Pilate's question, 'What is truth?' the answer of the Christ was silence, not unlike the silence surrounding the truth of who is the real enemy. And when Cain cried out to God, 'Am I my brother's keeper?'—what did God answer?"

"He gave no word at all," answered Dmitri.

"It seems as if the human mind is condemned to the word, as if truth can be sought out only within the silence. Still, it can be a blessed condemnation."

"What?" said Mac, realizing that he was about to roll his eyes in utter puzzlement, and stopping himself.

"*What*, is exactly correct," said Mac's immovable object. "'What is truth? Am I my brother's keeper?' Twice in the Bible, human beings demand an answer of God and are left with their questions. The rest of the Bible, and the rest of history, might be described as humanity's attempts—as a sort of homework assignment from within—to answer those two questions."

"And now you've left us with a new question," Mac observed.

"Yes, I have. Haven't I?"

H ere's where we part," Dmitri said as they reached the outskirts of Fira, almost halfway to the quarry. In the distance, a woman had climbed out of the great pit and was now walking toward them along the road.

"I don't think I need to tell you, but find high ground," Yanni warned. "Especially because we don't know how high up they can climb."

"If I had a bomb big enough, I'd take it into the lagoon and cut all those animals straight through with it."

"Not the best plan I've heard today," said Yanni.

"Maybe because I know a few verses the bishop chose not to mention."

"Such as?"

"The ones that warn, if it is not slain, the people will fall before this animal that speaks, this dragon."

"And there," Dmitri recited, "'we beheld the Earth's abominations and a sea of glass shot through with fire. For nature is burdened and she is troubled, and the Earth must tremble, and the mountains must smoke and shatter, like a cup.' Look around you! Any of that sound familiar?"

"And how is it you know all this?" Mac asked.

"My father is a high-ranking . . . let's just call him an astronomer, and a teacher. But he is also Russian Orthodox. He reads every scrap of ancient text that comes out of Egypt and Rome. As you probably know, we've had a lot of those discovered lately."

Mac returned him a confused expression.

"What? You have not heard of them?"

He shook his head.

"The lost revelations. They're exactly what the bishop was recalling, and trying to explain."

"Mac's not much of a churchgoer," Yanni said.

"Nor am I. But you must admit, it's difficult to determine if what has happened is the biggest coincidence of all time, or prophecy being realized—these echoes, these maybe random shrieks across time, warning about a terrible war, and these animals."

"No, it's not difficult to determine," Mac said. "These animals killed your brother. I know it burns inside. Burns deep. I understand this better than you can imagine."

Dmitri slowly turned his head and looked into the face of the man he had come ashore to follow and capture. Instead of prey, he was confronted by an expression of genuine compassion.

"Where will you go?" Mac asked. The woman from the pit had now come halfway along the road and was trotting toward them.

"Damn," Yanni muttered. "*Nora . . .*"

"New plan," Dmitri replied enigmatically, and intentionally so. "You don't get where I've been going by sticking to the plan."

The woman on the road was picking up her pace.

"Their error, that they acted against themselves," the Russian said, and began to walk away, uphill. "It's what the bishop quoted!" he called over his shoulder.

"And you?" Yanni called back. "You said, 'an animal that speaks.'"

"And it spoke to you, no? What did it tell you?"

"I think it was afraid."

"I think it deceives," Dmitri said. He had

paused near a telephone pole and a stand of fig bushes. "Someday soon, we shall all know the real truth about them." He then ducked behind the pole and bushes and disappeared like a ghost, leaving Mac and Yanni with a final warning: "And when *that* happens, friends, there will be no doubt about it at all."

Mac shook his head. "I'm afraid," he said to Yanni, "that some part of his brain is only a gnat's breath away from going Ahab."

Mac was about to ask, now given a Russian who had so much as declared to them that he just had to have his whale, and who would doubtless bring reinforcements—against a creature that apparently learned to do nothing less grandiose than mimic the books of Revelation—how the day could possibly be any stranger, or get any worse. As if on cue, Nora Nesbitt came running up beside them.

"You'd better come back to the camp at once," she said. "We've had another death."

"*Who?*"

"Guy from my lab. Name's Hata."

"Kraken attack?"

"Not this time. One of your people just murdered one of mine."

CHAPTER 12

Codes and Conspiracies

All moons, all years, all days, all winds,
take their course and pass away.
—MAYAN PROPHECY

July 2, 1948
Hell's Kitchen, New York City

The postwar world of 1948 was a study in gold and scarlet: a planet of enlightened intellects pitted against blackened hearts, of incomparable splendor and incomparable squalor, of political savagery and lofty ideals, of freedom and enslavement, of religions that preached the sanctity of life and crosses burning during murders in the guise of religious ritual, of logic against riot, genius against madness.

In the city where Genya and his friend Victor had been spying through a theremin device,

Jimmy Powell was not like most eleven-year-olds. He had a memory at least the equal of Genya's, combined with a strange talent for detecting subtle patterns and anomalies easily missed by others. This talent was amplified by a tendency to direct his thoughts with extreme focus, on even the most arcane subjects.

On the same day R. J. MacCready and Yanni Thorne met Dmitri Chernov, Jimmy had already become the wrong kid, in the wrong place, at just the right moment to cause a swerve of history. Even before Genya had reached the diner, after buying a newspaper from him, Jimmy noticed that the 1944 nickel with which "the Frenchman" paid did not feel right. He knew that wartime nickels with the large mint marks above Jefferson's Monticello were made with silver. This one felt far lighter than a silver nickel had any right to be. His first guess was that someone had somehow hollowed it out to steal the silver—hollowed it out with extreme care, causing no noticeable damage at all—then spent the lightened coin as a full nickel.

But why? Jimmy asked himself. He guessed someone would need to carefully mine the silver out of several thousand coins to make just one decent-sized silver bar—a job that would require more weeks or months of work than could lead to a profit.

And hollowing out little nickels instead of half dollars? Jimmy wondered. *Ten times more work for much less silver,* he concluded.

He bit the nickel with gradually increasing

force and noticed that it caved in ever so slightly. The mystery deepened when he shook the coin next to his ear. Something very small could be heard rattling inside.

By the time Jimmy's mother arrived home with groceries, it was almost lunchtime, but he was too focused to be hungry. The boy had taped wartime blackout paper over a window to darken the room and was tirelessly manipulating a magnifying glass and a little black square of film in front of a lamplight. He had taped the piece of film to a perfectly matched hole, cut into the side of a cereal box. Lines of numbers, clearly some sort of code, were projected onto a sheet of white loose-leaf paper.

"What've you got there, Jimmy?"

"I dunno, Ma. Something a whole lot tougher than Tracy."

Mrs. Powell smiled. Two of the latest-model Dick Tracy decoder rings had already been tried, then discarded on the kitchen table.

"This is much longer than some stupid code for 'Enjoy Quaker Oats,'" said Jimmy. "Some of da numbers are repeating in patterns, like words."

"You mean, like a longer cereal ad?"

"No, Ma. *Look*. It's like a whole newspaper article, or something. But I don't think they're tawkin' English. That would havta mean there's a *real* prize for decoding it."

"But you don't think it's in English?"

"Nah. Pattern ain't right."

She moved in closer, adjusted her glasses, and squinted. "You sure there's a pattern?"

Jimmy nodded enthusiastically.

"Where'd you find this?"

"Inside that nickel," he said, pointing to the two unscrewed halves. "Some foreign guy paid for a paper with it."

"Foreign guy . . ." The headlines on the morning paper read, "Tito Appeals to Stalin for Reinstatement" and "Store Union to Aid in Red Probe."

"This is definitely bigger 'en Dick Tracy—right, Ma?"

"Yes, Jimmy. We need to go find a cop."

July 2, 1948

The Quarry at Santorini

The peculiar qualities with which light reflected from and around the island's cliffs produced an eerie beauty like nowhere else on earth—*with perhaps the skies over New Mexico coming in as a close runner-up*, Mac told himself. Presently, late afternoon was promising another of the lagoon's legendary sunsets, in the direction of the little white island fragment where an entire Russian crew had fallen before the Kraken.

To everyone gathered around the body in the quarry, the island paradise was degenerating into a fairly good approximation of hell. *Or at least it will serve*, Mac told himself, *until some more demon-infested version comes along to replace it.*

There was no mystery as to who had killed the man lying on the ground. Alan was proud to have done it—and to have done so with his bare hands. Boulle and Cousteau found it necessary to hold him off at least fifteen feet away from the body, for the anthropologist had refused to stop spitting on it.

The blood was already settling into the palms of the dead man's hands, paling their upper surfaces noticeably and accentuating a curious wound. Mac lifted the left hand and knelt in for a closer look. The man had recently developed a severe case of psoriasis, on and around second-degree burns that had healed badly, forming tumorlike keloids. The left side of his neck, where broken vertebrae pushed up against the skin, was similarly scarred and diseased, as was the same side of his face.

"Flash burns from Hiroshima," said Nesbitt, verifying the conclusion Mac was coming to. She added, "He barely survived it."

"Which only means they should have made the bomb bigger!" shouted Alan.

Mac stood up, glaring at Nesbitt. "Who the hell is this guy?"

"Name's Kitano Hata."

"What? You gotta be—"

"The name's Black Sun!" Alan called out. "He's Black Sun, of Harbin!"

"*No*," Mac said. "How can this be?"

"The man's a true genius," Nesbitt tried to explain. "He had ideas about using magnetic lensing to map individual atoms along the entire structure of a chromosome. If anyone could help us to do more than merely break the genetic code, but to actually read it and *understand* it, then it was Hata."

"You know something, Nora? My mother used to tell me, when she wondered what I would grow up to be, 'Show me the company you keep, and I'll tell you what you are.'"

Seeming to believe that more violence might soon erupt, McQueen stepped between Nesbitt and Mac. "This man on the ground was under the personal protection of General MacArthur," the private said.

"Point noted," Mac replied. The history of it filled him with revulsion. The Japanese microbiologist known as "Black Sun" was arrested in 1945 for his commanding role in human experimentation at the Unit 731 biological weapons facility in China. His team had proved to be even more efficient at industrialized extermination than Dr. Mengele at Auschwitz. Not a single prisoner survived to provide testimony. The populations of almost every neighboring town had also disappeared. But Black Sun and his colleagues preserved all of their notebooks and specimens, in a move that was self-damning, and at the same time their salvation. MacCready knew that MacArthur had been instrumental in buying immunity from prosecution for Black Sun and at least two of the other most monstrous of his ilk. It was done so America could transfer Japan's bioweapons technology to . . . *Well, now you at last know where to,* Mac told himself. *The general is, if nothing else, decisive. Were* Hamlet *written about General MacArthur—or Nora Nesbitt, for that matter—it would only have been a one-act play.*

"You do realize, Nora, that some of MacArthur's own men were among the prisoners exterminated during the Unit 731 experiments?"

Nesbitt made a conscious effort to slow down her breathing, like a volcano biding her time. "And I hope *you* realize how, at war's end, the Russians abducted a lot of German bioweaponeers over to their side," she said calmly. "So why do you think they did that? To satisfy their own intellectual curiosity? You think that's why they're interested in this island?"

"Nobody required you to embrace a monster!" Mac said.

"And no one told your people to kill the man who could have kept us decades ahead of the Russians. I had my plan for him. I had my orders."

"I think you've just lost your right to say another word, Nora."

"What?"

"With that last line," Mac answered, just as Alan hawked a big one—hawked it an impressive seventeen feet, onto the dead man's face.

"Will you *stop that*?" Mac called out to Alan, then turned his wrath again toward Nora. "The kindest thing I can say about this beast on the ground is that Alan should not be wasting his good American spit on its grave. And that's the *kindest* thing."

"Not when the future of us all is in the balance!" said the Plum Island scientist. "And if I may say so, we're talking about a resource that can be used to speed up rates and modes of evolution—for crop plants or against crop diseases or anything else—into any direction anyone may desire. And if I may *also* say so, this has too many tempting possibilities for weaponization. It all comes down to, do unto the other fella as he would do unto you and do it first. So, if it ever comes down between them and us—"

"*Stop right there*," Yanni said, and Nesbitt stopped. "Not that I don't trust you, Nora, but can you give me your gun?"

"Why?"

"First, because I don't trust you. Second, 'cause it looks to me like you plan to keep on talking."

That the best brains in Russia would soon be focused on Dmitri Chernov's problem offered only some small consolation. He had been around long enough to know what governments do. He expected that those making the actual decisions would listen for a little while to what Admiral Isakov, theoretician Keldysh, and the other scientists had to say. They would immediately examine the problem, find the plan that must inevitably work out worst—then do it.

Knowing that his presence on the island was no longer a secret, he risked a phone call to his contact on the isle of Kos, who then relayed the message through Cyprus. Even if the line to Kos was intercepted and MacCready's side already knew the code words, there was nothing in it that the Yanks did not already know or that he was really afraid to let be known. Now that the Americans seemed to have a very good idea what he and the others were seeking at Santorini, Dmitri supposed that they would try everything short of war to thwart Russia and grab the golden key for themselves. He thought about Alexi, and about the creatures that killed him, and—*That woman, Yanni. What was she doing? And how? Talking with them?*

"We'll know fairly soon," he told himself. According to Kos, ships were coming. The nearest were already known to him by name. They were two thoroughly refurbished heavy cruisers, upgraded with radar-guided guns, and they were making their way from Croatia, down along Italy's east coast. He thought about Alexi, and the creatures that killed him, and he wanted the Kraken dead.

Along the path from Fira to the towering rocks of Monolithos, he had visited a farmer who was said to have filtered samples of the vent water, and planted the solid, scarlet residue among some grapevines. In the very same way that the strange fertilizer had changed other farms, the vines now looked different from any Dmitri had seen before. They grew quickly into ground-hugging spirals, and changes in their leaves also seemed more optimally adapted to conserving water on volcanic soil that tended to drain far too quickly to make plant-based agriculture practical. But now that the plants' very expression of genes seemed somehow redirected, farmers began to think in terms of one day creating a flourishing wine industry on an island infamous for its scarcity of water. He thought of Alexi, and the creatures that killed him.

The changes Dmitri had seen in the spiral vines

had occurred in no more than two generations of plants. The samples of leaves and stems, roots, and red-stained soil he collected were sure to excite even the maniacal Lysenko, but as the sun began to set behind him, he thought only of Alexi.

The arrival of the Russians was anticipated, and Mac had planned for it. Like a chess game, the path always zigged and zagged several steps ahead, based upon multiple (mostly predictable) adversarial moves.

The murder of an American asset by one of Mac's own handpicked team members had rendered the path ahead exceptionally difficult to see. He had allowed himself no more than two minutes for the adrenaline to rush through and dissipate, then decided, *If the road ahead divides in dark and dangerous woods, get off the path and make a new road.*

From now on, no matter where they went on the island, there was little hope of actually remaining hidden from Dmitri or the reserves that were undoubtedly being sent to aid him. Russia's paranoia would see to that. As Mac often reminded himself, the Russians had earned their paranoia the hard way. If pessimism could be harvested, he supposed the Soviet Union would be the world's breadbasket.

As for what additional reserves Team America could expect, Nesbitt had remained angry and tight-lipped, as if to answer, "There are none."

Mac had decreed, even if there might be no adequate hiding place, that they needed to break camp and move. This was one of only three points on which he and Nesbitt agreed: certainly they could not camp out in the Catalina, nor could they let the Greeks know about Kitano Hata. And just as certainly they could not take Hata with them. Even before the sun had set low enough to turn the lagoon gold, Hata was beginning to bloat, emitting dead man's belches.

"The quarry's been mostly abandoned since they built the Suez Canal," Boulle said. "Bury him under the figs and it should be centuries before anyone sees him again."

When they tamped down and raked Hata's un-marked grave over with branches, they had an-other moment of strange revelation. The same quake that almost kept Bishop Marinatos from landing had brought down a small landslide from a quarry cliff, and along with it, kitchen utensils and flatware from long ago. McQueen ran up ex-citedly to Pierre Boulle and Alan Tse-lin. The two fossil hunters were crouched down and being assisted by Mac in a hurried last-minute attempt to protect the bonobo grave site by slathering on a shell of plaster mixed with dirt.

Aside from being made of bronze, the fork McQueen found would not have looked out of place in a modern kitchen drawer. The designs on a sliver from a terra-cotta plate immediately told a different story.

"How old is that stuff?" McQueen asked.

"Around here, they call this pottery and its peo-ple Minoan," Boulle said. "Older than King Tut."

"What happened to them?"

"Gone," Mac said, and spread a last handful of

brown plaster over the skull of Boulle's "beautiful lady."

Then another thought struck him. "Private, you wanna bet the owner of that fork you're holding thought it would last forever? *It*, his whole town, the civilization of his children's grandchildren's children: people *still* think it will last forever—airplanes, skyscrapers, and roads. One day it's all gone—gone to archaeology and paleontology, if there's anyone to dig it up."

"Gee, thanks, sir," said the private. "Have any other cheery thoughts like that?"

"Depends," Boulle answered for Mac. "What else did you dig out of the dirt?"

Mac looked up at a long-forgotten shard and guessed, "Man's destiny?"

Boulle stood up and gently examined a broken plate McQueen had been holding. He looked beyond the bonobo grave and out to sea, with eyes that seemed suddenly very old. "Wish we had time to finish the excavation," he lamented. "But that's the bad thing about paleontology and archaeology: The present is always getting in the way of the past."

5.33 Million B.C.
The Lost World of Mediterranean Canyon

FOUR YEARS AFTER FIRST CONTACT

Life treated the clan of Proud One's daughter fairly well. At first they trekked north to the parched foothills at the mount of Santorini. A drought eventually turned them south along a string of oases that led to the mountains of Crete, where they settled in a deep valley. There they found a waterfall and seasonal forests, in a land that seemed to shift at whim between two personalities: torrential rains and desert. During the years following the expulsion from fertile marshlands, the monsters that had killed Seed's mother did not pursue; they lived on only in nightmares, and in tribal injunctions against venturing south of Crete.

The clan's first home was a shaded hillside standing above the valley floor, where they discovered mushroom-shaped trees capped with large, leafy umbrellas. The umbrella mosses provided shelter from the brutal night rains of fall and winter.

Each spring, the clan of Seed became a migratory animal. The Cretan waterfall that sustained them shrank to a trickle; the night rains stopped. The trees pulled into themselves and ceased producing fruit. North, at the quaking mount of Santorini, the rains came softly and only in summer, and Seed's clan could eat freely of the beasts and plants at the foothills. The mountain provided only one oasis, but it was enough. Here, far from the reach of the cephalopods, they came upon a miracle of rare design, flowing from a cleft in a vertical rock face.

They made their seasonal encampment near the cleft, along a hot stream that flowed red. And they drank of the red water. And they ate of the plants that grew in it, and any beast that swam in it. And they were changed.

In distant futurity, even MacCready and Nesbitt could only make a guess at how the extremely rare microbe somehow smoothed out or sped up the process of evolution. Only technology far beyond their initial encounter with the strain would be able to reveal that this intensely symbiotic organism, once it became involved in genetic feedback with the afflicted, did indeed—in accordance with Mac and Nesbitt's best guess—mimic the mathematical projection of probability curves pointing toward either beneficial or harmful change, and blocking (usually) the latter.

Much as MacCready could not possess knowledge of DNA's structure—and even less so, the language with which to describe an infection that entered living tissue like an army of little bio-computers, reworking even sperm and ovum—the bonobos and the cephalopods had no real understanding of what was happening to them, and to every other organism that had come into contact with the red waters. And so it came to pass that with every rapidly evolving lineage along the Mediterranean canyon's lakes and streams, the infection sooner or later went with them. It dwelt in the neural networks of the cephalopod Canal-builders. It sped the biological arms race that allowed small mollusks to flitter away like birds, rendering them able to escape invertebrate relatives that were filling the very same niches that had, on the continents above, been occupied by hyenas and serpents. The microbe traveled in the electrifying musculature of the elephantine snail. It ran deep within the giant's mound-building prey and penetrated the genome of every newly evolved tree and beast of the canyon.

Through race memories and the inevitable clashes of ancestral cultures, from long-enduring myths that would provide a somewhat random record of prehistoric times, it could never be clear that a luxuriant marsh whose edge was often lined with tentacles lived on forever in apocalyptic tales. Few people of the mid-twentieth century—and least of all MacCready—would have believed that Bishop Marinatos's dragons of Eden and Revelation had been rooted in a biological reality, or that an ancient fear of waters flowing red had equally real beginnings. Few of the Stone-throwers who ventured into the Nile canyon ever lived long enough to flee again south.

Still . . . life continued to treat Seed's clan well despite the need to migrate with shifting rain patterns across the desert between Santorini and Crete.

One summer night, at the mount of Santorini's red cleft, the rains did not come until very late and Seed observed the moon rising. She tried to reach out toward it, and remembered doing so when her clan lived high above the night clouds and the canyon floor. It had been a marvel to her, back then: how the moon passed over the tallest highland mountain without scraping it; from this she was reminded that hoping to touch the moon was a foolish endeavor.

The rains arrived unusually late the next night

as well, and for several nights thereafter not at all. Thoughts of travel beyond the cleft, to the top of the mountain, began to gnaw at her. She nurtured a desire to go one day, for no better reason than merely to see what was up there. Maybe if she traveled high enough, she might even touch the moon.

After many a night in which the rains did not arrive until shortly before dawn, Seed waded early one evening across a shallow pool near the cleft, enjoying the water as it swirled around her legs. But most of all she enjoyed a certain apprehension and simultaneous giddiness at the realization that two males had joined her. Unlike the ancestral bonobos, this lineage preferred to take only one mate for a lifetime. She was nearing the time of choice, and there were many potential suitors.

Like their ancestors, these bonobos were a matriarchal society. A dozen of the clan's leaders arrived at the pool and looked where Seed was looking, up at the stars.

"What are they?" a young female signed.

"Holes in the sky?" the star watcher guessed. Seed recalled looking up at the sun through an umbrella leaf, bitten through by tiny red slugs. *This*, she imagined, *might be something like that*: holes in a great black tent of leaves, holes in a firmament, with the light shining through.

The matriarchs turned their gaze higher, toward the mountaintop and the setting moon.

"Up there, go?" one of them said.

"What if we find more monsters?" signed another.

But the leaders had decided: "No. Stay, now. Some other day—we go up."

It did not matter. The idea was planted. The increasingly curious species would inevitably explore, not because they were expelled from one place to another, but because they were beginning to seek.

On this night, it was as if the future had decided it was time to hold back the rains, and make a personal appearance. The bonobos were already infected, each to one degree or another. From the moment Seed feasted upon the contaminated fruits of a canyon oasis, and upon the red pond berries beneath the cleft, her new microscopic allies had begun their work, extending her life, sharpening her senses.

The child of Proud One stared up at the stars, spread like dust across the night. She never could know anything more about them, in what would prove to be nearly a century and a half of life. Tonight the stars of the Big Dipper were not yet drawn together into a pattern; they were still spread across the entire dome of the sky. For the child of Proud One, they burned against a backdrop of constellations no human eye would ever see.

CHAPTER 13

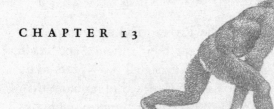

What an Octopus Knows

And the Lord hung a rainbow as a sign,
Won't be water but fire next time.
> —AN OLD CHRISTIAN SPIRITUAL, ADAPTED
> FROM SIBYLLINE PROPHECY

July 3, 1948, 2:00 A.M.
Santorini
Another "Only Hotel in Town,"
Overlooking the Village of Akrotiri

By now sleep was a luxury—and for those who could get some, a difficult luxury.

Yanni, Mac, and Cousteau had taken the second shift of the night watch. Their new location was a dusty bed-and-breakfast on the outskirts of town, but it provided a reasonably good overlook in all directions. If one's eyes were sharp enough, the crescent moon added more than ample illumination. So far, neither Dmitri nor anyone who might support the Russian had shown up. The townspeople also kept their distance and made it very clear that they expected the visitors to do the same. Mac had stepped within no more than two hundred feet of the little cluster of buildings around Akrotiri's only road when a man on a balcony fired a rifle into the air. A push was as good as a shove, from that direction.

Out there in the fields, no one and nothing stirred, except for a farmer's restless guard dog.

"What do you think they'll do when you get Alan home to the States?" Cousteau asked.

Mac laughed quietly and said, "For a change, someone's timing could not have been more perfect."

"How so?"

"Last I heard, Hata had the blood of a quarter million Chinese civilians on his hands. They should have Nuremberged his ass, long ago. And yet General MacArthur sneaks him out of Japan and he gets assigned to *us*?"

"Sort of defines the American term *SNAFU*," said Cousteau.

"Or at least *some justice*," Yanni added.

"But your general will still be causing trouble, no?" Cousteau asked. "Powerful enough, isn't he, to be making a good try at taking Truman's job?"

"The Republicans have been putting him up to it. But whether he's still in the race or not after last week's convention, there's no question Truman will be taking it as a personal slap in the face. And I don't think 'give-em-hell-Harry' is a turn-the-other-cheek kind of guy."

"No," said Yanni. "Damned happy not to be in the general's shoes right now. When it comes to giving hell—you just don't want to piss off the guy who turned Hata even uglier than he already was—by dropping an atom bomb on him."

"Speaking of ugly characters," Mac said, "Jacques, how much have you been able to learn about the cephalopod brain?"

"How, actually, their brains work—we know almost nothing. We do not know—we do not even have a clue, not one solid clue—how our own brains form a conscious mind. And so, what a cephalopod knows? Even an ordinary octopus is smart. Maybe smart like a dolphin. Maybe something else, not like a dolphin. But definitely *animaux superb*."

"The one that mimicked me at the dock had an amazing talent," Yanni said, "but even the most common octopus or cuttlefish is able to do this kind of thing."

"Correct," said Cousteau. "I saw a tiny Indonesian species change color and shape in seconds—first mimicking a flatfish, then as I continued to approach, it became a very aggressive lionfish, with sharp fins splayed out toward me. It squirted ink at my face mask and dropped to the reef as a knob of coral."

"I hadn't heard of *that* one," Mac said. "So, this would mean, long before some of them became our Kraken, they were already brainy enough to put on some pretty extreme displays?"

"Ever see a knob of coral pop out legs and run away? So, absolutely: that has to be brainy enough to be at least on a level with border collies, maybe even with dolphins and orangutans. It's why you'll never see me eating octopus. Too much the stench of cannibalism."

"Same here," said Yanni. "There's a young scientist from the navy, studying a little baseball-sized species at the same wing of the aquarium where I work. If he hadn't marked and numbered them, we'd never have known that they like to climb out of the water and sneak from one tidepool to another—trading places. He's convinced that they're always watching him, and that they know when *he's* watching *them*. They do the switcharoo between pools only when he isn't looking. And when he *is* looking, they resist being removed from the rocks and the water because I don't think they like being IQ tested in young Jason's mazes. Sometimes they'll cooperate and let themselves be fetched with a scoop net. And then they go *really* nuts. I've seen them jumping all-arms-out, springing from the net like tiny gymnasts bouncing from trampolines and making a run for it across the floor."

"Tell him about the lights and the outflow," Mac said.

Yanni smiled and shook her head. "Those little guys give you no respect. There were two or three that spent a lot of time with their eyes poking just above the surface, waiting for Jason or one of his assistants to walk by. Then, through their siphons, they would direct jets of water right into his ears and his eyes. They also seemed not to like the bright ceiling lights. So, they figured out how to turn off the lights by squirting jets of cold water at the hot bulbs—busting the glass. Seems they also wanted deeper water in their pools. At least, that's what Jason thought was the reason for some of their mischief. He had noticed that they sometimes liked to stretch their bodies and their arms all the way down some tubes, almost to the outflow valves. But they weren't doing it out of 'like.' One day when he goes out to bring back lunch, they reach down to the valves, shut them off, overflow the pools, and end up flooding his entire lab."

"So," Mac said, "you think even the primitive ones can reason?"

"I don't know," Yanni replied. "But aren't you the one who's always saying that *I don't know* is always the best place for a scientist to begin?"

Mac nodded.

"*Superb*," agreed Cousteau. "I have dissected many specimens, and although the cephalopod's nervous system is still *terra incognita*, the mind of an octopus is far, far from being a wasteland."

"And your dissections?" Mac asked. "How much do they reveal?"

"Oh—octopus, octopus," Cousteau said grinning. "How much can we really know about an animal that has its brain so near its mouth—actually wrapped around its esophagus? As you saw in the tentacle from the Russian boat, much of the cephalopod nervous system is outside the brain. There are—what should I call them?

Midget brains? Little bulbs of nerves—secondary nerve centers spread all around the body? That tentacle you studied: its clicking, its mimicking. Those were all evidencing a short-term memory in a part of the body completely cut away from the brain. And the skin itself: there are layers of mirrorlike cells and mini-sacks of pigment and receptors that in some ways work together like the retinas of your eyes. I think that's how it can mimic the shapes and colors of objects behind it and completely out of direct eyesight. In some way, an octopus sees through its eyes *and* its skin."

"It may also *taste* through its skin," said Yanni. "In the lab, Jason showed that their arms can sense adrenaline and other chemicals. He thought this might be useful in the wild, where all an octopus has to do is reach an arm out of its den and taste what chemicals the nerves were releasing from a fish approaching either in pain or distress, or on the prowl."

"You mean," Mac asked, "that its skin can see you, and at the same time taste your fear?" He almost let out a long whistle of amazement, but was stopped by the immediate realization that he was on a night watch, and needed to keep the noise levels low. High-pitched sounds traveled far. The accidental cryptozoologist glanced out across a quarter million miles of space, at a crescent moon partly obscured by passing clouds.

"Now, Mac," said Yanni, "just imagine something with a nervous system ten times greater. Maybe more."

"Not sure I want to. That bishop's view of Revelation might turn out to be a bit optimistic, if these things ever decide to go on the march. I keep thinking about an H. G. Wells story that scared the hell out of me when I was a kid—octopuses from space in giant tripod war machines. Fortunately, it's impossible to make a civilization underwater."

"Impossible?" said Cousteau. "What makes you so certain, *impossible*?"

"You can't have a civilization without the discovery of fire."

"Who says this, so absolute? If you are able to use fresh-rising lava and volcanic springs in the deep—in almost the same way we control fire—why should you not be able to make metal? In fact, all of our gold and silver and even our diamonds seem to have been brought up through the earth's crust and put together like condensed milk, by volcanoes. Down there, resources might just be lying around waiting to be picked up."

"You mean, the cephalopods might already have everything they need?" said Mac.

"Think upon this: There are more active volcanoes in the oceans than we have on land. The biggest mountain on earth is not Everest. She is but a child, compared against Hawaii."

"But try pulling a cart with wheels underwater," Mac wondered. "How do you build a civilization without wheels?"

"Who needs wheels down there, when you can fly so easily? And if you need something other than flight, try hydraulics."

Tripods? Mac snorted inaudibly, and then said, almost cheerily, "Wow. Things that really make you stop, and go, 'Hmmm . . .'"

"For all we know," said Cousteau, "there's so much more we don't know. For all we know—"

"For all we know," Mac said, rubbing early morning dew from his neck and his arms, "Dmitri could be right. We may end up having to destroy them."

"The Kraken may be alien to our way of thinking," began Cousteau's objection. "Something that can taste your fear or pain from several yards away? Perhaps even see you and the world with its whole body? But I think your Bishop Marinatos and even the Greek police sergeant would now be asking, 'Who should play God? Who should say those minds are not worth trying to understand?'"

Yanni noticed it first. She slowly lifted a bag of salt, then said, "Don't move, either of you. Now, look slowly to my left."

Mac turned his head, very carefully. Twenty feet away, and as if reading his nightmares of old, stood one of the cephalopods—motionless, on tentacles bunched together into a thick-legged tripod. Its skin—all reflective chromatophores and slicked with morning dew—glistened in a hundred thousand points of back-scattered starlight. This Kraken stood only half as tall as Mac, looking like a mere pup compared to what they had encountered at the dock. Its more compact form surely added to its stealth, but Mac did not believe this excused his carelessness in letting one of the beasts sneak up on them while he distracted himself with talk.

"Yanni?" he whispered. "You ready to throw some salt?"

Before she could answer, three silvery-yellow flashes blazed forth out of the dark, each about the same shape and height of the intruder, and about twice as far away.

Within that flashing interval, the creature moved—much faster than the full-sized versions they had seen at the dock and along the donkey trail. But it did not require speed to fool human observers. The three flashes had reflexively turned the heads of the humans and focused their full attention in their direction, just long enough to allow the nearest intruder to go dark and disappear among its distracting brethren, rendering human eyes unable to follow its movements.

In the next second, this dark intruder and two others emitted new disorienting flashes, and a pattern became perceptible, alarmingly so. They flashed on and off alternately, approximately each second, with the nonflashing individuals either advancing or retreating while "running dark" between the flashers. Mac estimated that there must have been seven or eight of them, taking turns flashing and moving.

Within an interval of no more than twenty flash cycles, McQueen and Nesbitt were at Mac's side and hurling salt bags. Whether any of the salt actually struck home seemed doubtful, but none of the group would ever know for sure.

Even before the first bag flew, the creatures

were spread out, flashing more quickly than a ship's Morse lamp—and just as quickly they were gone. However, the Kraken did not depart without throwing something back at them. An object rocketed over Mac's head, struck the wall behind him, and exploded like a clay pot. It was a clamshell, spinning wildly when it came at him—wider than the length of his hand, and massive enough to have dug into his skull had it been aimed to do more than put a fright into him. Nesbitt and McQueen seemed to have been more specifically targeted. The biologist from Plum Island had been clipped in one arm by a shell thrown like a spinning discus; three others had torn into a leg, each with enough force to require stitches.

McQueen also received a leg wound, but it was the object that dislocated his shoulder and knocked him to the ground that left him staring in blank incredulity—for it was a disk forged from copper.

"D-did they make this?" the private asked Nesbitt.

"I think so," she said. "You're the one who digs up Roman ships," she added, handing the object over to Cousteau. "This new, or ancient?"

"Difficult to be sure. I've seen many Greek and Roman ingots, but never shaped like this. It could be something they found in an old wreck and learned how to throw like clamshells. But it's not shaped for stacking in a ship's hold, and it looks too aerodyn—"

"Tools," Mac said. "They make *tools*, Jacques."

Cousteau was turning the copper disk over and

over in his hands, as if he were a child with a great new toy.

"Jacques?"

"One thing is certain," Cousteau said. "I'm not getting any sleep tonight."

"Yeah," Mac agreed. "Alan's lost world, Bishop Marinatos's dragons of Revelation—and now right on top of it all, your mollusk tool-maker theory looking real. Gotta admit, I didn't see that coming."

5.33 Million B.C.
The Lost World of Mediterranean Canyon

4,000 Years after First Contact

The tall descendants of Seed's clan still had their streams of red water at the cleft in the mountain. Twice yearly, following the seasonal rains, they drove molluskan livestock seventy miles along migration routes between the mount of Santorini and the northern foothills of Crete. In accordance with tradition, they were forever exiled from the lowland forests and marshlands south of Crete, and across the Devil's Hole. The south belonged to elephant snails, and to monsters whose heads were lion's manes of snakes.

Seed, the child of Proud One, had lived a hundred and forty years. Some of her clan's descendants lived even longer among the red hills, from which flowed streams of both hot and cold water.

The generations four millennia beyond Seed

stood taller, more thinly boned, and more agile. Though the Stone-thrower clans, living on the African highlands in the south, far outnumbered the bonobos, they apparently avoided the deep Mediterranean oases. Only once, long ago, had a troop of Stone-throwers reached the red cleft—and by then it was a battle of crude rocks against exquisitely cut spear points and arrowheads.

At this moment in time, both primate populations were a mere blemish upon the earth, totaling no more than seventy thousand individuals. In the marshes beyond Crete, the cephalopod Canal-builders were scarcely more populous than Seed's descendants. There was no means of predicting, quite yet, whether any of these three sentient species would survive on the planet, much less rise to dominate it.

On an otherwise ordinary morning, four millennia after the expulsion, She Who Leads awoke to a series of jolts stronger than any she had felt before. The world's tallest bamboo shoots swayed, dropping a hail of tree snails. Water splashed up from the streams. Dust rose up from the hills. And then, silence. Menacing silence.

Something in the air itself was changing—changing fast—but She Who Leads took care to conceal from her clan the deep sense of sorrow and helplessness that suddenly afflicted her instincts.

Yet independently, others sensed it as well.

"We leave. We leave uphill now!" The three elders of what had begun evolving into a separate caste of medicine-keepers were tearing strips of red growth from submerged rocks, handing them off to others and tucking them under arms. In a hurried combination of both hand signals and shrieked vocalizations, they called out for a pilgrimage into the hills—"Now! Take nothing but the red life. *Now!*"

She Who Leads hesitated for a moment, and scores of her people looked simultaneously to her, also suddenly hesitant. Throughout life, the matriarch's instincts had proved to be a proper guide. She watched the first rays of dawn piercing through veils of quake-generated dust, looked around, and tore nervously at the short hairs on her forearm. Uphill, and north, she knew they would find no trees or water until they had climbed very high. By late morning, along the Santorini foothills, the sun would be a fire in the sky, with not a single bush for shade and the shimmering air hot enough to draw all the moisture from one's mouth, and from one's eyes.

We can't go that way, she thought. Uphill and north were death. But other pathways seemed no better. Crete's mountain valleys provided food during only part of the year. And, though the rains fell more reliably in other directions and oases were more numerous, so were the monsters. Without the protection of the desert, panther snails and possibly even the Canal-builders would find them.

Up, she decided—into the nearest mountain, north. *May die. But the only way is the mountain—up.* The streams and the tall plants that had sustained them were about to become a terrifying wilderness, lost forever. Her instinct of this was made all the more alarming by a gradual blackening of the western sky.

She Who Leads waved a hand in the direction the medicine-keepers had pointed. "To the mountain, our clan," she commanded. "Go up from this place, and bring nothing except water and the red life."

The clan, the scores and scores of them, hesitated. They were reluctant to leave the safety of the red oasis for the dry and forbidding cliffs that would one day be Santorini and the islands of Ionian Greece. The majority wanted to stay, hoping that their instincts were wrong, and that their home would remain safe.

More than sixteen hundred miles away in the west, where the sky continued to darken, the Gibraltar Dam was falling. At first, the breach was small, but the incomparably violent rapids chewed through the bedrock with such force that in only an hour they were conveying broken bits of Spain and Morocco eastward toward the marshlands south of Crete, and toward the sea of the Canal-builders. Glutted with debris and filling the sky with dust, black water spread across gleaming white salt flats. In the early stages, the flood spread out so widely and so quickly that it was in places only inches deep, even as it spread from horizon to horizon. It fanned out across hundreds of miles and was still advancing eastward on the day the cephalopod Canal-builders tried to flee, while the tribe of She Who Leads wavered between hesitation and a clear decision on evacuation up to the peaks of Santorini.

On that day, the earth's albedo changed. The Mediterranean canyon drank so greedily of the Atlantic that the change would have been immediately apparent from the surface of the moon without the aid of binoculars. Even from Mars, with unaided eyes, the tiny, bluish-white crescent of Earth could be seen darkening in the middle, ever so slightly.

For another day, hesitancy dominated the descendants of Seed's clan. And then for another day. And another. Though they had gathered up the healing weeds and were ready to depart, even a dust-filled sky that turned the full moon as red as blood left them reluctant to leave.

Even after the rising waters began to turn distant Crete into an island and continued advancing toward the Santorini oasis, there was hesitation. As a strange new shoreline approached like an incoming tide that seemed determined never to stop rising, it became horribly apparent that the canal-building monsters had been the first to experience the coming desolation, and were not nearly so reluctant in responding to it.

"Look, now," She Who Leads communicated, and they looked, and they saw.

First one of the cephalopods, then another and another, came waddling like giant salamander snails out of the new sea and onto red-slicked rocks. During the same millennia of exile in which the bonobos' wiry hair evolved into water-retaining fur, and in which teeth became shorter while spears and blades grew more ornate, the snake-headed Canal-builders likewise continued to change. The adults, and not just the pups, could now emerge onto the land.

They *had* to come out of the water, as near as She Who Leads could tell. It was clear that the cephalopods must also have felt the quake, and that they were fleeing north to this place in a murderous panic. Behind them, the roiling waters told it so. One of the medicine-keepers was pulled from the rocks by the attackers, and he managed to break free moments later only to die from massive organ failure.

The last adult cephalopod to emerge and charge toward the red rocks surfaced with huge bites taken out of one side. Some other denizen of the southern marshlands was chasing them. They were clearly afraid of it, and She Who Leads knew immediately that she should fear it as well.

The bonobo descendants, despite a sense of wonder and curiosity that grew with each generation, had no desire to find out what was happening to the cephalopods, or why.

"Run!" She Who Leads commanded, pointing north.

No one had to say it again.

The bonobos ran for the north hills.

And as the Mediterranean filled, life on earth would never be quite so simple again.

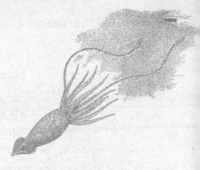

CHAPTER 14

Immortal Sins

*Man is the only creature that consumes
without producing. He does not give milk, he
does not lay eggs, he is too weak to pull the
plough. He cannot run fast enough to catch
rabbits. Yet he is lord of all the animals.*
  —from a George Orwell fable

*Beware the beast man, for he is the devil's
pawn. Alone among God's primates, he kills
for sport or lust or greed. Yea, he will murder
his brother to possess his brother's land. Let him
not breed in great numbers, for he will make a
desert of his home and yours.*
  —from Rod Serling's screenplay of a
  Boulle fable

July 3, 1948
MacCready Base Camp #3, Santorini

After quickly reexamining the copper disk, Mac and Jacques decided that they had not made fools of themselves in their initial assessment of its likely origin and purpose. Indeed, the object's recent manufacture as a weapon was a clear reminder that, on this island, the unexpected was always ready to strike from ambush.

Nesbitt was the only one who still believed this assessment was no better than a joke; but she had other matters on her mind. The 2:00 A.M. attack was pushing her along an altogether different path forward, into the unknown.

The Plum Islander and McQueen had been shot at with more than weaponized clamshells and copper. As she and the private were ushered indoors to have their wounds examined, and as the rest of Nesbitt's crew took watch outside, it became apparent that both of them were singled out for copious squirts of ink—which had targeted them with all the precision of an Olympian's spears.

When Nesbitt stripped off McQueen's shirt, there was so much ink and blood slicking his skin that it was initially difficult for her to identify the wounds. He held strong through a hurried cleaning and stitching. Then McQueen and the Catalina's pilot helped Nesbitt to locate, sponge off, and stitch her own wounds. The scientist's field dressing was almost finished when she noticed that the young private's face was beginning to pale.

"How are you feeling?" Nesbitt asked.

"I'm not really sure. I'll let you know in a few minutes."

Despite being able to put up a good front, beads of sweat were breaking out across McQueen's forehead, and his lower lip was beginning to tremble. Nesbitt needed only those few minutes to be crystal clear on the question of how he felt.

"I think I'm going to be sick," he confessed miserably. The sickness embraced him with frightening rapidity, then progressed. Nothing from the medical kit could bring down his fever and as morning twilight approached, it began to look as if the only hope of finding enough cool water to lower McQueen's temperature was to carry him down to the nearest beach and immerse his whole body.

That won't do, Nesbitt thought. Even without the possibility of lurking cephalopods, McQueen's wounds were swelling and festering too quickly for a cold-water bath to provide any real aid. The part of the equation that raised her suspicions, and forced her thinking in a new direction, was the fact that she—one of the only two people cut and sprayed by the Kraken—was not sick at all. *What*, she asked herself, *is the most obvious difference between his blood and mine?*

The microscope began to provide answers. A small sample from McQueen's wounded skin was a microbial horror show, rioting with infection. Ink from one of his towels was no less revealing.

"As I was guessing, the ink itself is a bacterial soup," Nesbitt announced. "Every spoonful must contain *dozens* of spherical, rod-shaped, and spirochete species—all the easier to infect you with, if their carriers break your skin before spraying you."

"These animals—they knew *exactly* what they were doing," said Cousteau, waving a hand back and forth between the ink-sprayed Nesbitt and McQueen.

The young private was still straining to maintain a strong and stoic front for Nesbitt, but he flickered in and out of semiconsciousness.

"They're tool makers," Mac said, and Nesbitt finally nodded an acknowledgment of this.

"Suddenly," she said, "that little joke I thought you and Jacques were making doesn't seem quite so funny anymore."

All eyes were on the Plum Island scientist as she produced a blade and cut deep into her thumb, then squeezed blood out between her thumb and forefinger and drizzled it onto one of McQueen's wounds.

"Open the rest of the dressing," she commanded, preparing to drip more blood. "I want to get this into his wounds ASAP."

Nesbitt's crew was incredulous, but her pilot obeyed. *This will help you for a while*, she said to herself, as if simultaneously uttering it to the dying man. *I don't know for how long—but it should help*.

"I have a rough idea why you're doing this," Mac said. "But I'd like to hear it direct from you."

"You read my report, right?" She neither asked about nor referred to the blood results, because that was need-to-know status, and not even the pilot who flew her here needed to know.

Mac nodded.

"I'm sure you understood it."

"Yes," he answered. And he therefore expressed only a certain level of surprise and curiosity but not shock as McQueen's fever and swelling halted an hour past sunrise, and subsided by lunchtime.

After a light supper, the private claimed to be feeling well enough to stand watch.

"Of course, you would say that," Nesbitt replied. "But it's not necessary. A dry wind has come in and everything seems quiet now."

"Yes. Until next time," McQueen predicted.

"Until next time," she quietly echoed.

July 4, 1948

BASE CAMP #3, SANTORINI

The night had passed without any unwanted company. Though he slept well and was recovering from the infection, McQueen looked haggard and grim. Meanwhile, he and everyone else looked at Nora Nesbitt in puzzlement over what she had done for him.

And what was that? Cousteau had wondered. *Driving back an infection by infecting him with something she knew to be in her own blood?*

Late in the morning, Cousteau paid the innkeeper generously in two ounces of Nesbitt's gold sovereigns, to complete a shopping list, and to remain silent enough to hopefully keep Dmitri and his friends away. He also offered a bonus for the town elders to buy their silence. While the groceries were coming in, Mac, Yanni, and the two fossil hunters set off in search of a new overlook upon the lagoon and Nea Kameni. Only a short walk beyond the side door, a dry streambed pointed the way up. Carved out through three dozen centuries of soft rains, the trail was a slash in the earth, deep enough for them to reach higher ground without being easily seen. Cousteau had watched Mac walk away with one of Nesbitt's walkie-talkies. *So far, so good,* he told himself in the current American vernacular.

Up there, and in accordance with Nesbitt's and Cousteau's instructions, Mac's away team was checking back with Base Camp #3 every ten minutes.

After Nesbitt changed McQueen's dressings and returned to prowling the hallways and adjacent rooms with her walkie-talkie, seeking out better reception, the private turned to Cousteau and confided, "I guess I shouldn't be alive, huh?"

"I do not know," the Frenchman replied. "But it does appear that this is your lucky day."

"Yeah, but for how long? A killer squid grabs a guy right off the Catalina, and then—"

"I think they're more closely related to octopuses."

"And they squirt poison at you, and they throw weapons at you." McQueen was clearly working heroically, and successfully, at maintaining calmness in his voice—avoiding a repeat of his embarrassing display after the first Catalina attack. "I mean," he continued, "how does this happen? It's like this island is becoming a monster movie for real. Where the hell are we?"

"Where we have never, ever been," Cousteau replied.

"All things considered, sir, I'd almost rather be on Devil's Island. Almost."

"*No*," the Frenchman said sternly, taking the mere mention of the place as a slur against his country. "No," he said again, "you would never—even almost—want to be there."

The overlook gave only a partial view across the lagoon. To ascend nearer the inner rim of the crater would risk being seen by too many farmers, and sooner or later one of them was bound to invite the attention of the Russians.

The views in every direction were at least partly blocked by tall hills, including the limestone peak of Mesa Vouno. Long before the Gibraltar Dam was born, wave after wave of tectonic spasms had uplifted the rock layers with such force that once-horizontal fossil beds were tipped completely on their side.

"How old are those rocks?" Mac said, pointing.

"We've spent some time studying them," said Alan. "Back to dinosaur times, we think—and maybe beyond. You'll find the ruins of a Roman amphitheater at the top, and fossil oysters all around it."

"But they've been off the menu for a while," Boulle said. He grinned excitedly. "If the rocks could talk—and in a way, every one of them actually does have a story to tell—well, just imagine. Think about where your friend's Catalina is parked. If you look down from the height of Fira and picture the donkey trail winding a thousand feet down to the plane—then, at around the time the pyramids were being built, and only a small part of the way down, you have to imagine those donkeys embedded in the solid rock of a volcanic cone rising high above Santorini. Five or six million years earlier, this very spot was a forest of olive trees that supported giant shrews and dog-sized elephants—which were probably hunted by the tribe of our tool-making bonobos. And seventy million years before then, plesiosaurs and mosasaurs patrolled the same seafloor that became Mesa Vouno."

"You think dinosaurs ever roamed here?" Yanni asked. "These islands?"

"Probably—almost certainly," Alan answered. "And that's looking back across only what? Maybe the upper one or two percent of earth's history?"

"Yeah, well," Mac said. "Against that picture I hope we have time on our side. I wouldn't really want to think we could end up even more extinct than the dinosaurs one day."

"*More* extinct?" asked Alan.

Yanni nodded. "Our friend Colbert, at the museum, says they're not all gone. He looks at the fossilized hips and legs of one group and guess what? *Birds*. He even calls all those theropod footprints in Joisey sandstone *birdie feet*."

"And we think he's on to something," said Mac. "It may be that one branch of the dinosaurs really is still all around us, literally in the branches."

"Yeah, isn't *that* a hoot?" Yanni said. "And I mean that literally. I don't think real dinosaurs ever hissed and roared like the ones in *King Kong*. The forests of their time must have sounded a lot like the birds right here, this morning. A big one chasing dinner might have screeched like an eagle closing in on a rabbit. I wouldn't be surprised if the real *Tyrannosaurus rex* got up in the morning and crowed at the sunrise, like a rooster."

Alan smiled at the image, then said, "I'd like to know where these shell-slinging Kraken came from. Can anyone here toss up a good theory?"

"Maybe," Mac said. "But I'm not sure we're allowed to talk about it quite yet."

"Anything to do with Nesbitt's—?" There was no time to speak the whole question. Nesbitt herself broke in from the Akrotiri base camp in great excitement.

"*Mac!* What's your twenty? Bogey coming in. Over."

"I'm about a hundred and fifty yards above you and to your northwest. What bogey? Over."

"Two, Mac. *Two* bogeys. Coming in fast. Look to your southeast!" Nesbitt seemed so alarmed that she forgot her training to close with "Over." At this point, they both did.

The first bogey came roaring into view—a huge turboprop with no national markings. Two peculiar structures protruded near the cockpit, like overgrown feelers on the head of a beetle.

"It has closed panels, ventral," Nesbitt called. "You see them?"

"Roger that. Looks like bomb-bay doors and they're closed."

"Copy that. Closed."

"And here comes the second one!"

Bogey number two barreled in lower than the first, then disappeared behind a hill. It, too, had bomb-bay doors. "Doors closed," Mac radioed. "Looks like it may be recon. Over."

"Copy that, Mac. Think it's Russians?"

"Difficult to imagine who else." He listened as the planes circled twice outside the lagoon, then faded away into the distance. They reappeared nearly twenty miles south, out near the horizon. Turning again northward, the pair overflew Akrotiri and the dry valley, one of them passing so low overhead that had it been moving any slower, Mac could have counted its rivets.

"Oh, no," he whispered. "*Shit.*"

This time, the bomb-bay doors were open.

July 4, 1948
11:02 A.M., *Santorini Time;*
4:02 A.M., *Eastern Standard Time*

WASHINGTON, D.C.

At first the president believed another bomb had been delivered to the mailroom, and that this time it had gone off.

But it was only the floor jumping—again.

One side of the Oval Office had just dropped a half inch, while the other side bulged upward, to the same degree. The jolt sent three rats scurrying from their latest hiding place. The recent layering-on of new plaster, new paint, and new carpeting was simply not going to work. The White House was collapsing from the inside out, under a relentless assault by the microbes of wood decay, by termites, and by vermin.

Seems an apt analogy for much of America and the world these days, Truman thought, as he turned his attention to the windows, and to the world beyond.

Each new crisis, and each hopeful attempt to fix it, seemed simply to unlock the door on one or two new crises.

A grandson would recall for friends, many years later, that the president never spoke at home about the dawn of the atomic age or the mutually assured paranoia of Cold War politics. But in a personal memo following war's end, he had already declared that what happened in Hiroshima and Nagasaki should never be allowed to happen again. Yet in the name of "defense by the ultimate deterrent," newsreels continually broadcast—to impress both the public and the Russians—what atomic bomb tests in the Pacific had done to the volcanic atoll called Bikini. The latest radiation readings were so horrific that Truman had begun calling the place "Nothing-at-all Atoll." Twenty more tests were planned.

According to the best efforts of American and British moles, the Russians were at least five years away from being able to build their own atomic bomb. Truman supposed that if the world had until at least 1953, then maybe something other than a massive nuclear arsenal could be worked out. Maybe there was no need for new bomb tests and especially not for Doctor ("Strangelove") Teller's brave new hydrogen bomb. Maybe there was time enough to avoid Einstein's warning that, while it was impossible to predict if or when World War III would be fought, if it involved nuclear and biological weapons, there was no doubt that World War IV would be fought with sticks and stones. If Teller's "H-bomb" was ever built and successfully tested, it would surely make the Russians even more paranoid, and the president had been taught by history that there was probably nothing more dangerous than to back the Russians into a corner.

Like the White House itself, the center wasn't holding together. Everything seemed to be coming apart, almost everywhere. Even the Jordan River was now a too easily unlocked door to crisis. "We, the British, and the survivors of Hitler have been highly successful in muddling the situation as completely as it can be muddled," he had said only a few weeks earlier. Then, giving official recognition to the state of Israel, he stepped back and, hoping for the best, received the worst reviews since the Ford Theatre's last performance of *Our American Cousin*. Not even his wife was immune from the media smear campaign. Even his "dumb dog" Fella wasn't spared attacks. Now it seemed the entire Middle East was erupting into war, and there was no need to trouble oneself trying to guess which side Stalin would soon be backing.

And that's only the beginning, he told himself. The next unlocking of a crisis led directly to MacArthur himself. First, there had been the general's push to unseat him from office—which, according to Bobby Kennedy's sources, might only have been a sleight-of-hand distraction. The Kennedy boy suspected General MacArthur was running some other operation right under their noses, having effectively up-and-evolved his own chain of command.

"And did I mention MacArthur's inordinate interest in scientists at the Metropolitan Museum of Natural History?" Bobby had warned. And for the world tonight, according to the latest developments involving a newsboy in New York, General MacArthur's "inordinate interest" already had the Russians lathered up and chomping at the bit.

Somehow biology was at the crisis's core, this time—as if it weren't enough for physicists to have opened the lid and given the world something it could never give back. (As if.) The massive, increasingly unpredictable, and potentially uncontrollable consequences of the atom bomb were already beyond scary, though in the current atmosphere, Truman dare not admit this publicly. The air was thick enough with threats of impeachment and accusations about being "un-American."

After having received the full reports on Japan's Unit 731 atrocity, President Truman decided that the most American thing he could do was to stop the lid from being pried open on the next Pandora's box. He at least had to try. *Had* to. Thus the executive order "removing and forbidding all research into the manufacture and use of biological weapons, even for a retaliatory strike in the aftermath of an enemy attack."

There was of course no bite in the order, as the president was now all too painfully aware. So long as the Russians were interested in seeking out and mining microbial horrors from the earth, MacArthur and his cabal of followers would support "defensive" research—which, though it was officially aimed at finding cures against bioweapons, simultaneously meant finding and developing the weapons that would require the cures. Under the MacArthur protocol, defensive and offensive research could be rendered indistinguishable.

Worse, Truman realized, *I may never know about what is being done. The same arrogant offensive that prevents me from closing loopholes and enforcing the injunction comes with the expectation that I will soon be out of office, and that uncounted secrets can be kept from me.*

"But arrogance and overweening pride are not exclusively American traits, or Russian ones," he said to the night. "They travel among the continents like rain."

The world on the other side of the Oval Office windows actually seemed peaceful, even utopian, if one did not look too closely. The high-altitude afterburners of a Huntsville jet hinted at how the marriage of new engines and the pressurized cabin of the B-29 bomber would soon produce transatlantic passenger jets, while von Braun and Sanger looked to space planes and Mars, and beyond . . . and to high-altitude weapons.

Bobby Kennedy knocked at the door and was welcomed in. He shuffled in tiredly, bringing coffee and pound cake. President Truman continued looking out the window.

"Bit of advice," the president said. "No matter how many times the bastards try to burn you down, never give up."

The budding young lawyer and politician nodded.

"Got it?" Truman emphasized. "No matter how many times they try to burn you down. No matter how many times they try to burn you down."

"Nothing's going to stop me," Bobby said. "You can bet good money on it."

As indeed he could. It was easy to see that the Kennedy boys had a capacity to lead, and every intention of doing so. What troubled Truman was that young Bobby was presently doing much of his learning on the knee of Joe McCarthy. Would he grow to be the kind of man who led the parade, or one who, like McCarthy, simply observed which way the parade was about to move and placed himself in front of it?

For all of this, Truman wished there were simply a better way for humanity to choose its leaders. One of Wernher von Braun's friends had recently explained, "There are some jobs that should never be given to people who strive to obtain them, especially if they show *too* much enthusiasm." What the rocket scientist had in mind were the sorts of people who would have to be drafted by their countrymen on the basis of brilliance and qualifications alone—with one of the chief qualifications being that he or she specifically did not want the job. What he dreamed of seeing was a president who had to be dragged kicking and screaming into the Oval Office.

Truman pictured it, smiled, filed the entire scenario away under the category of *not in my lifetime*, then asked Bobby, "What's the latest with the newsboy incident?"

"The *coin boy*! Amazing kid. Do you realize that, all on his own, without ever having heard of Dr. Sanger's silver-birds, he's made drawings of rocket planes and space stations? His parents say he always obsesses on one thing or another, week to week. This week it's breaking codes and floating things above magnets. I think we're going to be hearing a lot from that boy someday."

"Then it's important to keep an eye on him. Make sure he stays on our side. I guess some help with housing and the college of his choice wouldn't hurt?"

"Already on it," Bobby said. "I've set him up with a mentor at Midtown High School of Science and Technology."

"Good. Good. And the two spies he nailed for us?"

Bobby opened a folder and placed it on the president's desk. The floor beneath it creaked in protest, as if at any moment the weight of a few additional papers might become the proverbial straw that broke the camel's back.

"So far," Bobby said, "they've refused to give us anything other than their first names—Genya and Victor—and we don't even know if those are their real names. Thanks to this kid, we got them before they had time to break up their equipment. We already know that they had devices aimed right at the same museum MacArthur has been casing, but you're not going to believe what that equipment was focused on—a broadcasting theremin."

"You mean, one of those creepy music things?"

"Yeah. Its inventor personally had two of them delivered to the museum after he gave a concert there. One was still functioning as a listening device, right in the office of Richard John MacCready!"

"R. J.? *Hendry's* guy?"

"Mr. President, before you ask, I can assure you that Mac had no part in this. He's saved my brother's life twice. JF vouches for Mac, one hundred percent. Same for Mac's entire team."

"And what about this theremin guy?"

"Missing. Somewhere in Russia."

The president thought for several long seconds about what he had just heard. "Does your friend Joe McCarthy know any of this?" he asked.

Bobby shook his head. "My brother said I should stay mum on the whole issue for now. Big Joe is getting a bit trigger happy these days and might accuse MacCready of spying for Russia—meaning the guy could be red, white, and blacklisted even if he is a war hero and patriot."

"Good advice. But why *are* the Russians interested in him and his crew?"

"We don't know. My brother served with Mac—but he puts up his hand and tells me to stop, if I ask anything about past missions. Says, unless I'm really, really interested in the evolution of elephants and chimps, it's nothing too important. But you know what he's like: tells you the truth every time, but only part of it. That one word, 'too,' could mean anything."

"But this friend, Mac, is on to something 'too' important now, isn't he?"

"If it's got General MacArthur vibrating and sending in his top scientist—"

"Who?"

"A woman named Nora Nesbitt. And on top of that, according to the latest from our contacts in Naples, the Russians have started sending ships toward Mac's location—which, as Hendry just confirmed for you, is the isle of Santorini. It would seem to me that this time Mac has really stumbled ass-backward into something everyone wants."

"And how deep do you think the problem with these two newsboy spies goes?"

"Almost certainly part of a much larger network," Bobby said. "We know nothing yet, but my family has pulled a few strings in Chicago, to put a couple of good men on it."

"Then I guess we'll know soon enough."

"As I say—we've put good men on it."

July 4, 1948
11:02 A.M. *Santorini Time;*
4:02 A.M., *Eastern Standard Time*

AN UNDISCLOSED LOCATION IN MASSACHUSETTS

The two Russian captives had survived two very long nights of wakefulness and worry—which was just fine for Jack "Sparks" Rubenstein.

Rubenstein's hatred of Stalin ran deep. He personally knew an entire family that had been decimated—worse than decimated—during the dictator's increasingly expansive purge against Russia's Jews. And now there were architectural plans in the Kremlin for extermination camps in the eastern Soviet Union. Stalin scarcely tried to keep a secret of it.

The monster's letting all the countries of the world look on, and show how little any of them really care, he concluded. *Hell! There are plenty right here in America who would watch with a sneaky admiration.*

During the war, Rubenstein had become a dependable head-buster and interrogator, especially when it came time to cleanse the New York waterfront of Nazi saboteurs and spies. With quick and intensive lessons in "the fear of God," he and "Bugsy" Siegel had even convinced three spies to act as if they were still working for the German fatherland, while sending carefully scripted misinformation back home—the sort of information that cost the Germans at least a good, thick handful of submarines.

After uncovering a plot to drive through a Jewish neighborhood with machine guns, mob accountant Meyer Lansky had offered "Sparks" and "Bugsy" a salary to handle the pro-Hitler Bundists.

"You don't have to pay us," said Rubenstein. "We'll clean out the rat nest for free." They *loved* fighting the Bundists. On many a night, Rubenstein had arrived at his brother's house covered with blood and grinning from ear to ear.

Not very much had changed in the years since. Sparks was reliable. He would always get the job done. His new assistant was a former OSS code breaker named Josh Roykirk, a man whose career was in tatters because he fell in love with a black woman and dared to marry her. Lansky had taken a liking to the Roykirks and drew a protective wing over the family.

Throughout the night, the two interrogators had been playing "Mutt and Jeff" with the handcuffed and foot-cuffed Russians. The cuffs were welded shut. To any outside observer, it would have been immediately apparent who was playing the role of "good cop." Roykirk emerged from his separate interrogation room, went straight to the kitchen, and began laying ingredients around a large rectangular pan.

"What? You're making him lasagna?" Rubenstein asked, incredulously. "Forget about that bullshit. I need you down the hall and in the next room."

"Look, I worked with this one interrogator during and after the war. A real charmer. I've told you how we got information out of Heisenberg and Speer. And in the heat of the war, I was there with him when he started feeding this one senior SS officer, with good food and compliments. He also fed the guy the only little scraps of information we already had about his activities, pretending as if we really knew more. We would stroll about in open air, through the Scottish countryside. And our OSS guy keeps praising him on this clever act or that clever act—and, guess what! The German ends up telling us far more than we knew to begin with. A whole shitload more."

"Yes, well—Josh, it'll be my turn on your guy when I'm done with Victor. But in just a few minutes, I'm going to need you to join me."

There was already blood on Rubenstein's knuckles. He whistled a cheery tune as he laid out several long pins, a white washcloth, and a Bunsen burner on Roykirk's lasagna tray. "When the pincushioning starts," he said, "*everyone* talks."

"You start pincushioning balls and eyeballs, and won't he also confess to flying over the moon last night on a broomstick? And you want me to assist you in this?"

"You won't have to," said Rubenstein, maintaining a low, controlled volume. "I've probably softened him up enough already, so that all I really have to do is show him the instruments of torture and let him see the expression on my face."

"So, what do you want me to do, Sparks?"

"Just keep me from losing my temper. And you can start by not calling me Sparks."

"Got it."

"I hate that name!"

"Got it," Roykirk said again.

"Makes me want to go right to needles," Rubenstein said. He pointed one of the pins in Roykirk's direction, studying the man's face. "You see my way, now? Maybe your way will work with the other Russkie. I guess we'll see. But even if you do get anything useful out of him—you can get a lot more with a kind word and a red-hot ball piercer than with just a kind word."

July 4, 1948
11:02 A.M.

S A N T O R I N I

There came a sudden shout over the walkie-talkie. "Mac—look up—up there to your east!"

Mac gave a quick glance downhill, to reassure himself that Yanni and the others had stayed put, then lifted his eyes eastward. The aircraft had made three close passes before moving off. For many long minutes, they appeared to be holding two points above the horizon, but now they were once again growing darker and larger, noisier and nearer.

Long before they made their fourth pass over the island, Mac figured that any townspeople drawn outdoors by the noise were more likely watching the skies instead of him, so he had run across two fields of goats to a cliff-side overlook. For more than twenty minutes, the planes had been circling out widely after buzzing the lagoon—each time opening the bomb bays, clearly trying to target something.

Now a decision had finally been made. They were coming in fast, and bringing hell with them.

The aircraft with the antennaelike booms projecting out front of the cockpit dropped something large near the lagoon's center. The object sprouted a drogue chute and fell out of view near Nea Kameni—targeting the red plumes.

The second plane dropped a pair of winged, rocket-propelled bombs. After three seconds of free fall, the rockets ignited, each following a radio-guided arc to the same exact location on the water. Mac judged that they could not have detonated more than six feet apart, with no less than a ton of explosives each.

"Base," called Nesbitt. "We've heard the explosion. What do you see?"

"Two guided bombs—went down right where they lifted Dmitri's brother out of the water. Looks like there's something they didn't want us to see. Whatever it was, it ain't there no more."

"The other plane—can you see what it's doing?"

"Yes, Nora. I'm looking across the lagoon at Nea Kameni. There's a balloon rising on a tether over there, and the plane with the two booms sticking out is winging right back at it . . . booms just snagged the tether in the middle . . . *What?* There's something like a steam shovel claw at the end of the tether—just got hauled out of the lagoon with one hell of a bottom sample."

"Mac, you'd better come back right away."

"Believe me," he shouted back, "I'll be down as soon as I can! I'm . . . Uhh, someone opened fire on the plane. Tracers went up from the far side of Nea Kameni . . . Smoke, now . . ."

"Who's firing?"

Mac did not reply. The plane continued westward past Therasia—bomb-bay doors open, reeling in a huge sample from Cousteau's vents. Water and rocks and red mud streamed out behind the closed jaws of the shovel. So much of the sample was blowing out of the jerry-rigged system that Mac believed by the time the shovel was aboard and the bomb-bay doors were closed, they—and he did not believe for a second that "they" were Americans—would be lucky to have recovered a thimble-full of the red stuff.

But there was no need to worry about what "they" could accomplish with even a thimble-full. The bomb-bay doors never closed. Barely two miles southwest, over the sea, and still maintaining low altitude, the plane began bleeding smoke and oil in thick black streamers. It tried to veer due south but the starboard wing tipped up, nearly vertical, and she immediately lost all lift. The stranger hit the sea so hard that plane parts were indistinguishable in the splash.

The isle of Santorini was suddenly sprouting enemies everywhere, and against everyone— maybe Greeks and Russians firing on each other, or Greeks against Greeks. That was Mac's instant, overwhelming impression. What he had just witnessed seemed to have no logical basis.

Nora's voice crackled: "Mac, did you see who fired?"

"I'm coming back," he replied. "Over and out."

Mac swept his gaze around the lagoon, past Nea Kameni and to the sea beyond. There were no signs of activity on or near the central volcanic wasteland, whence came the gunfire. In the direction of the crash, he did not see a single parachute.

How many people are there, he wondered, *coming after the red stuff?*

5.33 Million B.C.
7,000 Years after First Contact
2,985 YEARS AFTER THE MEDITERRANEAN FLOOD

The cephalopod lair's most recent caretaker had lived a hundred and sixty-three years before she set off alone through the Strait of Gibraltar and began searching. She carried with her samples of the incomparably precious red mats, keeping to the deepest and coldest waters in an effort to extend their life until her kind found a new place for the mats to take root.

She also carried with her something very much akin to a tribal talking history spread through neural nets—which her kind communicated to one another in very long sequences of clicks and squeals. The persistence of memory was like a library of song stories. Some recorded the flood and the diaspora, and how their world ended.

At one time the marshes, the canals, and the Devil's Hole south of Crete had been a paradise. The fall of Gibraltar Dam buried it under a new sea and layers of black silt, and the vents in that location never again supported the red growth. Only along the northern slope of a solitary volcanic mountain, now mostly submerged and a long way from being named Santorini, was the combination of substances venting from within the earth just right for planting and sustaining a red garden.

But not forever, the caretaker understood. She knew her kin's history well enough, and had been around long enough to gain an intuitive sense that nothing lasts forever, not even the red gardens.

Her kind had no knowledge or understanding of how the microbes could hibernate for seven hundred years or more, drifting along the bed of the sea like immortal dandelion seeds, until settling and sprouting again, at a friendly undersea shore with just the right conditions. Incomparably symbiotic, yet just as incomparably stubborn about the extreme environments in which it could be cultivated, the microbe seemed equally selective in guiding just the right creatures, with just the right neurological and physiological framework, to seek out just the right places where it could be fruitful and multiply.

So it was for the sentient cephalopods and the Darwin Strain.

The Santorini mineral springs and the velvety mats shrank over the course of a dozen centuries. The warm glow of the red cleft and the vents dimmed, revived briefly, and now appeared finally to be dying.

After the flood and the diaspora, the cephalopods had continued to evolve newer and more sophisticated means of communication. Like whales, but in a language entirely different from whales, the clicking of even an individual Kraken's thousands of barbs sounded, to submerged ears, like a drawn-out avalanche of pebbles clashing. In time, whales learned to avoid the sounds—which could be heard across the entire length of the flooded Mediterranean canyon, or even across the ocean that was yet to be named Atlantic.

The caretaker called out to a whole generation of forty-three juveniles who had been sent ahead of her, west of Gibraltar. They were spread out across and exploring the length of a midocean mountain range, from Antarctica to the North Pole, testing all the volcanic springs of the deep as they went, and finding not one in the entire ocean that could sustain Santorini's red mats.

They communicated this result to the caretaker year by year, with all the awful force of hopelessness. She was not satisfied with their efforts and joined the others with only one desperate goal driving her—which translated as:

Continue searching.
Continue searching.

After ninety years, at the age of 256, she heard an avalanche of sound, relayed from one extinction-fearing lair to another, carrying the message of imminent failure. The Santorini garden had retreated so deep below the seamount's south flank that the precious red substance could be reached only by digging down dangerously close to pools of eruptive lava. By then the caretaker was nearing the southeast coast of Africa, and dying.

Three juveniles departed the shore near Antarctica's Mount Erebus and came to her aid. Compared to pre-flood generations, they were now a more civilized species that included division of labor into something approximating guilds or castes—among these, the stone-cutting miners and lava-seekers. The strain had seen to this.

The caretaker could not be moved during the last two years of her life. Those she had cared for in their youth were now caretaking her. On her final day, she learned that scouts had already traveled to seas beyond the Horn of Africa and were finding hopeful new springs. Her last plea compelled them—all of them—to continue the search.

And the undersea sojourn carried on, for centuries more. Few suitable garden vents were ever found, but they were enough. One was discovered near Sri Lanka, on the floor of the Indian Ocean. Another was located east of Japan, and another was found among a chain of Pacific atolls.

Unless attacked, the cephalopod lineage from the lost worlds of the Mediterranean canyon remained a hidden civilization, avoiding contact with the Stone-throwers as the ice ages came and went and man-apes developed speech, agriculture, and frightful weapons.

The generations of Stone-throwers also developed philosophy and mythology. One of them, Pliny the Elder, recorded a legend about people who had inhabited Greek islands that he believed to have once been mountaintops, prior to a universal deluge. Then, after ice swept over the world, the lost tribe known for the strange countenance of its people, and for their shy nature, had retreated into a vast labyrinth beyond the barrier of the Himalayan Mountains.

Pliny had called these mythical creatures Cerae, but they were really the civilized descendants of Seed. Pliny also wrote about Scylla and Polypus, sea monsters later known as the Kraken. They were said to be sent by Poseidon, but their real beginnings were along the deep Mediterranean Nile and the fringes of the Devil's Hole.

Before Pliny's time, a final volcanic upheaval completely buried the hydrothermal gardens in the waters near Santorini. Only every millennium or so did they occasionally come back to life, and usually only for a little while.

Like the descendants of Seed, the descendants of the Canal-builders and the caretaker remained stable in their numbers and relatively obscure.

Many of Pliny's Scyllan sea monsters had settled around a cluster of deep-ocean hydrothermal gardens near the Pacific's Marshall Islands. Throughout the ice ages, their only real difficulties came from other cephalopods that from time to time encroached on the red farms and challenged the guardians in a manner that would have seemed, had Mac or his team been allowed to observe it, like apes trying to challenge the architects of the Acropolis.

Such moments of rise and rebellion were no obstacle to them. As Pleistocene ice sheets and the descendants of Seed and She Who Leads retreated into the mountains—as Chinese, Roman, and Viking civilizations rose and fell—the majority of the Kraken made their home in the waters of the Marshall Islands, east of Bikini Atoll.

They were still there in 1946, when the American fleet arrived.

CHAPTER 15

Beyond the Spectrum

> *My soul grieveth over the sons of man,*
> *because they are blind in their heart.*
> —Jesus, as recorded in the Greek
> Orthodoxy, by Didymos Judas Thomas

> *It is a terrible thing to see and have no*
> *vision.*
> —Helen Keller

July 4, 1948
Sunset
Santorini Lagoon, South Cliffs Overlook

Ninety million years lay directly under R. J. Mac-Cready's and Yanni Thorne's feet. Ninety million years of Santorini history that began with a seafloor of limestone and chalk raised up into sunshine and breezes, and rains that capped the east Mediterranean canyon's mountaintops with gardens, and sustained them even after the peaks were transformed into islands. The stones told of lost Edens ravaged by floods of both water and lava. As a zoologist turned accidental cryptozoologist, Mac had more of a sense than most people of what had really occurred here: while the stage was being set for the parade of life that marches across this planet—even before all of the marchers existed—geo-chemistry, an extreme microbe, and even the shapes of the seas were conspiring to render humanity's geo-political arena every bit as violent as the natural history that preceded it.

And so it came to pass: They crouched among the broad-leaved fig bushes, Mac and Yanni, staring across the sweep of darkening waters below. A stiff warm breeze from the west created swells beyond the island fragment called Therasia and all the way out to the horizon, interrupted only by whitecaps.

"Base to Mac," Nesbitt radioed. "See our guests, yet? Over."

"They're quite active," Mac replied. "But the wind is strong and very dry—which should keep them under the water tonight. I'm switching comms to Yanni. Over."

"Base. What are they doing? Over."

Yanni pressed the transmit button. "Much signaling to each other. More than I've seen before. Mostly bright greens but some red and silver among the flashes—"

"Where?"

"At least three of them where the bombs were dropped. But most of them are just northeast of Nea Kameni."

"Any idea what they're saying?" Nesbitt called excitedly.

"I think they're somewhere between fear and panic—"

"*Phobos and Diemos?*" said Dmitri Chernov, kicking pumice and gravel loudly as he stepped up to the cliff edge, raising both hands over his head. With disquieting self-confidence, the submariner had tossed aside any attempt at stealth. "I'm sure you knew we'd end up all in the middle of this again."

"Phobos and Diemos?" Mac said. "Really?" He and Yanni had already unclipped the safety straps on their holsters. "How bad this gets is just something we'll have to see."

Nesbitt's voice crackled over the speaker. "Base to Yanni. Do you copy?"

"Copy you," Yanni called. "We've had a visitor. Over."

"Cephs?" she asked.

"Negative," Yanni replied. "Type human. Unarmed." She added, "Over and out," and made a miserable sleight-of-hand attempt at leaving the open mike unnoticed.

"Yes," said Dmitri. "I imagine we shall see." He nodded toward the strengthening display of underwater sparks. "MacCready, your talented friend thinks she sees fear down there. But I don't need an empathy with animals to read what the murmurs of the lagoon really mean."

"And what's that?" Yanni asked.

"They're telling us to sleep lightly. All humanity. You understand?"

Mac tried to keep his full attention on the Russian but was now unable to resist the distractions of what was happening below. "*Sleep lightly?*" he said. "Looks like I'll have to pass the torch to you, as the one who paints the darkest canvas."

Glancing at a new surge of flashes from the lagoon, and shuddering inwardly, secretly, Mac recalled how a small venomous octopus of Australia flashed brilliant blue rings to warn that it was agitated and about to bite. He did not have any idea what it meant when the bioluminescent chatter in the lagoon abruptly ceased, but this did not discourage him from trying to come up with an interpretation—at least, up to the moment that Dmitri interrupted.

"Where's Saint Francis when you need him—right?" the Russian asked.

Yanni is enough, Mac answered to himself. He remembered a morning at the aquarium when at least three octopuses lifted their arms toward Yanni, like puppies jumping to greet her. The same animals that squirted other people as they passed the artificial tidepools climbed gently up Mac's arm when Yanni guided his hand below the water's surface. To this day, he had a sense that the waves of color moving across their skin were like thoughts made manifest—as if the creatures were experiencing an actual sense of wonder themselves, as though it were possible for them to taste the flavors of amazement—and an inexplicable affection coursed suddenly beneath his skin, in his blood. Without any warning or fuss, they detached and poured like water down drains into their hiding places, leaving Mac with an unexpectedly profound sense of loneliness. *And that was the power of a much less intelligent, much less impressive species,* Mac thought.

For nearly a minute, he remained unresponsive to Dmitri's question, trying to compare everything he knew from his experience with other animals—primates, elephants, ravens, and even bats—for clues to the mind of the Kraken. The shutdown of the bioluminescent lights was only the latest ominous development. What he feared most, at this moment, was that he might make a mistake, or overlook something that must not be overlooked, and that Yanni might not survive. A part of him understood Dmitri—understood how the killing of his brother rendered the Russian even more rough-hewn—*given purpose, given new breath, by great and unfortunate brutes.*

Mac could not help but understand. During and since the war years, too many people had already been lost: the whole family, including his mother, his sister, the Voorhees cousins—and his first love, Tamara . . . and Yanni's husband, his childhood friend. Worst of all, Mac was a true genius at inventing ways to blame himself. He dragged the dead behind him like Mr. Marley's chains.

Yanni shot Mac an aggravated and impatient expression, and he realized that she knew exactly where his mind was wandering. He had overheard her saying as much to Alan after the Kraken night raid, while Mac spent more than an hour at the microscope, lost in the world of the microbes in Kraken ink. "Watch him long enough," she had said at a half whisper, "and you'll see that it's how he deals with pain. He bundles it up and turns it into a science project."

Except that his projects usually end up causing new pain, Mac believed she had left unsaid.

Now he broke the lingering silence. "I presume, Dmitri, that your side didn't shoot down the big plane?"

"Why would we shoot down a plane in our own union—or even one of yours?" Dmitri replied. "And if—just say it was our plane and I believed you were behind it, do you think you would still be alive to have this conversation?"

"Wonderful," Yanni said, looking him up and down, double-checking for weapons. "As if we didn't have enough enemies." She continued her visual search, never meeting Dmitri's eyes, even when he spoke directly to her. "And now," she added, "there is someone else—a hidden enemy."

"Yes, wonderful," said Dmitri, echoing Yanni's sarcasm. "There's more than one way to start another war and burn down the world. And there are plenty of adversaries running around with lit matches."

"Yep," Mac said. "Definitely, you can top me black for black. Can't paint the world any darker."

Dmitri did not seem to hear him. His eye caught a glint of something in the distance, and Mac immediately turned and looked where the Russian was looking. Far off on the horizon line, between the isle of Therasia and the northern arch of Santorini, a ship had appeared. Mac was able to discern long-range cannons on the bow. A second warship was steaming into view right behind it.

Mac shook his head. "Okay. Spoke too soon."

July 4, 1948
Twilight

EASTERN MEDITERRANEAN,
NORTH OF SANTORINI

The refurbished and renamed heavy cruiser *Kursk* felt top-heavy to Trofim Lysenko. A squall seemed to be building in the west, sending forth a continual march of oddly intersecting swells that prevented the *Kursk* and its sister ship *Koresh* from pitching and rolling like normal cruisers. Instead, they rocked in random X patterns and figure-eight wobbles—in no particular order and frequently reversing direction.

Even veteran sailors were becoming incapacitated. Lysenko knew his situation was seriously bad when the ship's surgeon found a rat dragging itself along the central companionway. The crew named him and buried him at sea—"Bernard," the only rat ever diagnosed as having died from seasickness.

By now Lysenko had found one point on which he could agree with that damnable Darwinist, H. G. Wells—*Sailors ought not go to church. They*

animals, Lysenko came up with a different wrong count every time. And he became frustrated. And he disappeared a twenty-year-old microscopist's whole family.

Lysenko's frightened and obedient underlings "made it better" for him. They were now writing reports that denied the importance (and even the existence) of chromosomes. They renounced the practice of cross-pollinating the strongest wheat strains to produce newer and more bountiful hybrids. A robust new strain—Norin Ten—was snuck in from Japan, and had almost made it to a farmer's field when Lysenko discovered the agricultural sleight-of-hand. The hybrid wheat was burned, and the traitor too.

"Bounty is just around the corner," the crop reports announced. This kept Trofim Lysenko happy, and it all looked very good on paper. Sadly, people could not live by eating paper.

While the famine tightened its grip, Stalin's man who knew everything knew that he needed to hurry.

Having Stalin's support and issuing a scientific decree had failed to change reality. Stalin was getting old, and if he died, Lysenko understood that his own rise to power would be forfeit, unless his view of life could literally produce fruit. He knew he would succeed, but he needed to prove his "theory" quickly. He was beginning to fear that Stalin's frail health might fail completely any day and that he might not be quick enough . . . until the Santorini miracle came along.

"Santorini changes everything," he said to the Mediterranean wind.

Ahead, on that island, nature was making revolutionary, Stalinist leaps forward. It did not matter that the island's sudden reflection of Lysenkoism was only an illusion. Lysenko was a particularly stubborn illusionist.

At this moment in history, he truly believed that, by enduring this rough sea and this damnable ship, he was stretching himself out, evolving his own descendants against seasickness, simply by being seasick.

All of my present suffering, he thought, *will be worth it to them. And the secret of Santorini can only ensure it.*

A pale and sweaty third officer climbed down from the bridge and gestured for Lysenko's attention.

"There's another message, sir. From our contact on Kos. It's about Dmitri Chernov," the officer said. "He's gone missing, somewhere on that island."

July 4, 1948
Dusk

BASE CAMP #3 SENTRY PERIMETER, SANTORINI

H ow's about you tell me?" Yanni asked. "What do you know about them?"

Dmitri, his hands bound behind him, continued, as Yanni had ordered, to stare out into the night, watching for Kraken.

Though the wind was too dry (presumably) to allow the monsters to move about comfortably on land, the Americans and the French had agreed that they needed every set of watchful eyes they could get. Presuming that Dmitri possessed an enlightened self-interest in not getting disk-slashed and ink-squirted or eaten, even an adversary's eyes would serve.

"Mrs. Thorne—aside from my knowing that if they've spread beyond the lagoon, they'll outlive us all," Dmitri said, "why are you asking *me* about them? You're the one who—what? Listens to them? Tries to talk to them? But you won't even look *me* in the eye when you talk."

As if he had searched for and with surgical precision found a weak spot, Dmitri's words made Yanni feel, again, like the witch of her tribe, like a human creature born abnormally. Even among the other abnormal children of humanity—including the scientists and musicians of Brooklyn—many considered her impolite or detached. She could not understand why it was somehow a prerequisite of being human to stare into the irises and pupils of anyone with whom you were not in love.

Even if she had not been declared inadequate and chased out of a village by her own people, she would have found human society confusing, curiously alien, and at times overwhelming. She suspected Dmitri already knew the answer to his question, before he asked it—as any good adversary, by logic, would. But she was not about to confirm anything for him.

He can see me, Yanni understood. *Like a beluga whale seeing into my lungs and my heart with its sonar, can he really sense how I see the world?*

She hoped not. It was a world she did not know how to share—and even if she did know how, there was only one person left alive with whom she would try. The *last* person on her list would be this Russian.

It was, after all, her private world. If feeling less like the outcast witch, if being more normal meant seeing even a little less of the beauty in her universe—presumably to be more successful and "more happy" around people—Yanni wanted no part of it. Even now, as she kept watch on both the rising night and the Russian, memories of the animals' vibrant waves and sequenced patterns were playing like a Technicolor movie against the back of her skull. Ever since she first saw it, the bioluminescent chatter of the Kraken had been running through her head over and over, often coalescing into something like musical scores—and still an elusive puzzle to be solved. What would seem alien to Dmitri, and to most people, was perfectly natural for Yanni: to see melodies in her head. And, though she could not yet adequately translate it, she saw in the Siren's call—the Kraken's call—the music of the words.

Clouds were now racing across a backdrop of brightening stars, but the breeze remained dry and oppressively hot. Yanni stayed silent.

"What *do* you know about them?" Dmitri asked.

"What do *you* know about the red plumes?" Mac asked, stepping up from behind to join them on the night shift.

"I'm pretty sure Dmitri's got samples hidden somewhere," Yanni said. "We'll have to keep an eye out for that."

"And what am I to suppose your people will do with the plume material?" Dmitri asked. "Miracle cures? And that's assuming you can get a boat in there without something squishing wetly up the bilge pumps to bite your head off."

Mac nodded. "To cure a very many diseases? It may be worth the risk."

"Oh, come on now, Mr. MacCready. You don't seem to me a 'beat their swords into plowshares' type of American. And even if you are, someone, somewhere in your country, is going to pull a little think tank together to try and figure out how to make a red-dust bomb."

"That would be pretty stupid, don't you think? Or don't you?" Mac said.

But Yanni realized that she did not have to think much farther ahead, herself, than what Nesbitt's man—"Black Sun" Hata—might have tried to do.

"Swords, plowshares, Isaiah," Dmitri said. "Your president and his General MacArthur know as well as anyone that he who beats his swords into plowshares and his spears into fishing hooks usually ends up plowing and fishing for those who kept their swords." The Russian paused, and studied the night. "As for these Kraken you're so interested in, they need to die by the sword."

"Before we really know anything about them?" Yanni asked. "Each question about the Kraken, when I think we have begun to answer it, is like a door opening into ten new mysteries. The more we learn, the less we understand and—it . . . It is beautiful."

Dmitri glanced up at the stars. "So, MacCready—which one of those does she really come from?"

"Right here. Earth," Mac said. "But this is where it gets—*ha!* A little spooky."

"Right," the Russian said acidly. "She tries to talk with those things—and I saw you try, also. You two really think you know everything about the creatures of the sea? But, no. You're blind to the real danger. You spend your lives living among animals but clearly you have not spent enough time looking at them."

One of Nesbitt's people stepped up behind the Russian and double-checked that his hand bindings were secure. "Do you want to know what my people know about the Kraken?" Dmitri continued. "No harm to my side in telling it."

"Then spill it," said Yanni.

"That bishop at the police station—he knows them. They live among history's ghosts. Secretive. Deceptive. Sometimes they have attacked for any reason at all—or for no reason at all."

"History's ghosts?" Mac asked.

"Do you not see it? Egypt? Atlantis? The Minoans? The Greeks? The Romans? Us? Sooner or later, every civilization becomes a ghost story. No matter how high it rises, every civilization is simply this: the substance of archaeology."

Mac said nothing.

"I said *us*, MacCready."

"Yeah, I got that part."

"They'll outlast us, you know. Unless it's the sword."

"Madness," Mac said. "Madness."

"That may be true," said Dmitri. "But you should never step into a Kraken war with a madman. Didn't anyone ever tell you that?"

July 4, 1948
2:20 P.M., *Eastern Standard Time*

Metropolitan Museum of Natural History, New York City

The Russian theremin device had been removed with great haste. When Hendry explained why, Patricia Wynters was surprised, but the logic behind the bugging seemed clear enough, as did most of history's surprises, when viewed with twenty-twenty hindsight.

Patricia had been much more surprised to learn that Nesbitt found something "wrong" in Yanni's blood, and that the Russians might have heard about it through the device. She suspected something was at least equally wrong with her own blood—and that it had been so for a very long time.

She did not tell anyone.

Not even her closest friends knew she had no recollection at all of her own childhood or adolescence, but seemed to remember more decades of life than made sense—which rendered her a mystery even to herself. At times Patricia questioned her own ability to remember correctly. She wondered how much of anyone's memory might be only an illusion. And now along came Nesbitt and her so-called Darwin Strain, and with it the origin of impossible fruit flies. *This too makes no sense—it makes no sense at all*, she thought. *And yet, perhaps it is the only thing that does.*

And if so, Patricia realized, it became possible to believe she might actually have managed to gaslight herself.

Oh, that would be a good one, she thought, and laughed. *Another historic first, in a corner of the museum already too full of scary history.*

For now, in any case, she would keep to herself the ominous joke Nesbitt had made, after searching through old museum scrapbooks: "You age so well. Either you have an incredible skin cream to show me or somewhere among all those mammoth bones in the attic, there's a portrait that must be looking God-awful by now."

Wynters believed that the key difference between her and Nora Nesbitt was that Nesbitt never took pause to assess her own sanity. She also believed there was probably a fine line between paranoia and madness, and that Nesbitt had crossed that line—repeatedly. The Plum Islander's little "joke" had ended with a Nesbitt-esque suspicion straight out of Kafka: "Mac once told me that you were already here, at the museum, when he arrived as a young student. But he also said it seemed to him that you have always been here."

1650 B.C.
The Lost World of the Keftiu

5.33 MILLION YEARS AFTER THE MEDITERRANEAN FLOOD

A s for these genealogies of yours," the priests of Egypt would tell Plato's ancestor, Solon, "they are no better than the tales of children; for in the first place, you remember a single deluge only, whereas there have been many."

1650 B.C. was the threshold of a deluge, and also the time of another red bloom in the waters of Santorini.

The island was not yet called Santorini, and it was much larger than in R. J. MacCready and Patricia Wynters's time. A beautiful, lushly forested mountain towered almost a mile over what would one day be only a flooded crater. The summit intercepted clouds and produced rains that fed the aqueducts of a harbor city whose homes were provisioned with both hot and cold running water. Sixty feet above the rooftops of an architectural paradise, an eruption pattern set in motion ages before human beings existed was fated to form the very ground on which MacCready would one day establish his Base Camp #3.

The city's inhabitants were called, by themselves and by the Egyptians, the Keftiu. Their multi-island empire was the strongest naval and economic power in the eastern Mediterranean. Destined to become one of history's ghost stories, fading remnants of their civilization would be recorded in the Bible under the names "Sea People" and "Philistines." To Plato they became a remnant of Atlantis; to archaeologists of Mac-Cready's time, Minoans.

During the years before the fall, among the Egyptians and the Keftiu, Semut of Avarice had become the most brilliant mind that a young and insatiably curious royal named Kyri ever met. They had called Semut a word that in later millennia would translate to "scientist."

"I was not planning on it ending this way," Semut told his former student.

"You do not know *what* you were planning," Kyri replied. "You told me so yourself, when you were young. You said it may cure *all* fevers, as we had used it to cure mine."

"I'm sorry. I only wanted there to be a way, for us."

Kyri gave the dying man a kiss on the lips and stared out to sea. The two ships she awaited were within view. Crewed mostly by deepwater free divers, both were returning to the volcanic island's south port, each with no fewer than three bushels of the red potion's raw material.

The potion's effects had been capricious from

the start, and were rendered increasingly unpredictable the more Kyri and Semut had tried to refine and strengthen it.

"I'm sorry," Semut said again. "I did not appreciate the scope of my own ignorance. To mistake ignorance for knowledge is . . . is . . ."

"Evil," Kyri finished for him, apologetically. "You've said it before. You're repeating yourself."

"We do not have all the knowledge," he groaned.

As indeed we do not, Kyri told herself. Her father had been the first to tamper with the red weed, and to judge from what this strangest of all gifts from the sea had done to him, and then to her, Father could easily have survived Egypt into another century if not for political ambitions that ended with five axe blows to his face.

When Kyri met Semut, she had been ageless since seventeen, already for two decades. She was almost thirty-seven then. He was a troubled but fascinatingly brilliant child, already fluent in three languages when Kyri rescued him from the streets of Avarice, Egypt. During the two years that followed, she became his tutor, until her father, as he began preparing for expansion of the Nile's territories, decided that it was time for the two youths to hide among the Keftiu, and for Kyri to give herself a new identity—before someone took notice of how different his child had really become, and started asking the right questions.

Eventually the priests and the philosophers of the island took notice, that a miracle had been discovered. They studied it, shared it among themselves, and managed to keep the secret of the two Egyptians even longer than China's royal families would be able to hide the secret of silk's production.

Kyri taught Semut until she realized she could teach him no more. He had learned everything she could give, and their roles crossed and interchanged; Semut became Kyri's teacher. By then they were both studying and manipulating the miracle substance.

The red weed's origin was a mystery to them, though not the most important one. Although it restored varying degrees of good health to the priests, the scholars, and chief merchants of the island, the cure seemed by some cruel unnatural decree never to have been for Semut. Meanwhile, Kyri evolved from being Semut's student and colleague, to his confidant, to his life's one true love, and—by the time he turned sixty and was racked by some hitherto unknown disease—she became at last his caregiving "granddaughter."

Semut's potions had destroyed him. In the end, they were also turning test animals into monstrosities. Semut's face was hideous. Kyri loved him still.

"I failed you," Semut said. She sat next to him on a wood-framed bed and took his hand in hers.

"Shhhh . . . Semut. What is the first law in this family?"

"Don't beat yourself up," he replied.

"And the second law?"

"Don't beat yourself up."

"And the third?"

"Don't beat yourself up," he replied, and forced a smile.

Kyri returned the smile. She did not notice, as she held his hand tightly, hoping for him to survive, that the two ships bearing the red treasure were never going to make it to the port. In full view of the men who waited on the dock, the ancient Scylla surfaced, its tentacles writhing and grotesque and killing the crews with all-enveloping thoroughness.

During the years that followed, in what archaeologists of the future would come to call the Late Minoan Marine Style, wall paintings and pottery decorations began preserving a symbol of power and respect rivaling the respect once given by the worshippers of bulls and golden calves. Suddenly images of writhing cephalopods were everywhere.

CHAPTER 16

A Study in Scarlet

> *Man is the unnatural child of nature,*
> *and more and more does he turn himself*
> *against the harsh and fitful hand that*
> *raised him.*
> —H. G. WELLS

July 5, 1948
Santorini

Sunrise always came to the island in slow and stately stages; but this day, morning came on like a thunderbolt.

"A heavy cruiser has just entered the lagoon," Yanni radioed from the overlook. "Mac confirms: Russian. It's holding position just inside the rim—half mile east of Therasia. Over."

"Copy that," Alan replied. "Repeat. Confirmed Russian? Over."

"Confirmed. Over."

"Roger that. Ru—"

"Uhh—damn! It's launching something! Small boat. Fast!"

Alan tried to say something but blips of static washed out his transmission from the encampment. The lagoon and all of the island fragments around it were being pinged, apparently across every radio frequency.

"Targeting radar," Mac said to Yanni. "A bit more advanced than I would have guessed." He belly-crawled up to the cliff edge with a pair of field glasses. *What the devil?* he thought, as he focused on the ship's guns and Yanni eased up beside him. "That's *definitely* some pretty advanced engineering," Mac observed. "Looks like some of the stuff on our own drawing boards that hasn't even been built yet."

The smaller of the vessel's two radar sweepers, mounted high atop its central mast, was making at least two complete revolutions per second. On the aft end, two guns seemed to be scanning the cliffs south of the Fira Quarry. As their barrel sights passed over and then moved southward of their position, Yanni asked, "How bad does this look?"

"About the ten-thousand-rounds-per-minute kind of bad," Mac replied. "And those two cannons on the bow—no space for a gunner. There's some guy in a control booth somewhere, guided by radar and able to move those things really fast. He can probably drop shells wherever he wants, out to about twelve miles."

"That's more than 'nough to hit any point on this island."

"You've got it."

"Well, if they do decide to aim at us, at least you won't have to explain Dmitri and the rest of this whole mess to Hendry."

"You really do have a way of finding the silver lining in any black cloud, don't you?" Mac asked.

"Why not? Otherwise I'd end up like you."

A second Soviet ship nosed out from behind the westernmost arch of the Santorini crescent. At first it appeared to be moving toward Aspronisi, the "White Island" fragment, where their navy's "fishing boat" lay sunk and buried. But as the speedboat from the cruiser in the north neared the red plumes, the new arrival halted outside the lagoon, turned its stern in the direction of Nea Kameni, and began backing carefully toward the west inlet. MacCready was able to discern no fewer than four men struggling with lines, trying to steady a large piece of equipment dangling from an iron A-frame.

"Looks jerry-rigged," Mac guessed, "like the claw-and-balloon system they dropped from the bomber."

"I think they'll have just as much to worry about," said Yanni as something flickered brightly near the surface. The speedboat shifted its angle of approach—baited directly toward the flickers, between the red plumes and the shores of Nea Kameni. "Water there ain't deep enough," she added. "Too many rocks around and too few escape routes."

"I hope so," Mac said.

Yanni grimaced. Speeding down from the north, the *Kursk*'s little launch made a sharp horseshoe turn. At the southernmost point in its turn, the crew hurled a dark, tethered object over-board, swung around toward its mother ship, and applied full throttle. During the first few seconds, the Russians successfully avoided near-surface hull scrapers while playing out their line into red water. They appeared to be making good progress and it was easy to judge that they were grabbing up a significant volume of bottom samples, until it seemed suddenly as if the samples were reeling them in, instead of the other way around.

"Do they have any idea what they're getting themselves into?"

"Need to study this situation," Yanni said, taking the field glasses from Mac.

Even without the aid of binoculars, it was easy for Mac to see two crewmen trying, with great haste, to sever the line.

"What is it?" Mac asked. "Kraken pulling them down? Like Cousteau's boat?"

"Not this time. Right now, the Kraken are no-where near that boat."

"How do you know?"

"You tell me," she said, handing over the field glasses.

"They . . . did *that*?"

"Yeah. What year do you place it? World War One?"

"Probably," Mac said. "Must be leftover from German mine-laying, outside the port of Kea. A whole string of those took out the Brit—"

In less time than it would have taken Mac to complete the word, the launch and its crew disin-tegrated. From where it and the mine had been, black smoke billowed into the sky, flattening out at cliff-top height, then drifting lazily westward on a breeze.

Below, subtle disturbances and glimmers in the water hinted that the Kraken were circling in. The intensity of the swirls waxed and waned, as did the sweep of the Russian ship's targeting radar.

Excited voices broke through walkie-talkie static. "We—kay—rep—okay—" It sounded like Alan, at the comms. "We have—lem—" he began to broadcast, before new surges of rhythmic static washed in. Fragmented shouts followed, then dropped out, except for a single word, spoken clearly and calmly and in Chinese—twice, from Dmitri: "*Mookau.*"

The word had several meanings. Depending on the situation and inflection, it ranged from "Please stop" and "Don't touch," to "Leave me alone" and "Go away . . . you whore"—any or all of those at once.

"What's that *supposed* to mean?" Mac asked.

"It means that because we know Alan, Dmitri knows we will understand."

"And?"

"He's telling us, *run.*"

July 5, 1948

BASE CAMP #3, SANTORINI

A lan was still at the communications desk when the *Koresh*'s landing party surrounded the encampment.

The gold that Nesbitt had authorized handing out as hush money was nowhere near as protective as she had anticipated.

Within seconds of Yanni's confirmation that the heavy cruiser in the lagoon was Russian, the signal from the overlook was washed out. Yanni's observation that at least one secondary craft was lurking never came through to Alan at all.

"I'd better go up and check in on them," Nesbitt's pilot had said, testing a walkie-talkie from across the room. At Alan's table, the reception from the handheld device was spotty but adequate—at least, at close range. Alan gave his walkie-talkie a thumbs-up. Nesbitt waved the pilot along.

He did not call in. He did not return.

The explosion in the lagoon echoed several times from the cliffs in the north and west, like a series of successively longer and distorted thunderclaps.

"Whatever that was, Mac, we're okay here," Alan radioed out. "Repeat. We are okay. What do you see? Over."

History had already recorded that the famous gunfight at the O.K. Corral lasted less than thirty seconds. The battle that occurred outside Alan's station was so many magnitudes shorter and quieter that it could hardly be called a fight. It was over before Alan radioed out the words "Wait. We've had a problem here."

The flight engineer who had shot a Kraken to pieces just an arm's length from Yanni's face, and who had to be "sedated" by McQueen's wrench, was the first to react. A single shot through a sound suppressor stopped his heart—instantly and, as intended, with essentially no blood to be cleaned up afterward. A shot through Nesbitt's hand disarmed her with very little noise or fuss. McQueen was taken down in a hallway, by an ambush body-slam that crashed his head against a wall and tore open the stitches in his shoulder.

At precisely that moment, two men rushed into Alan's radio room, one of them brandishing a hunter's blade, the other pointing a gun with an intimidatingly large sound suppressor. Dmitri strode in behind them, his hands unbound.

Alan still had his fingers depressed on the SEND button when Dmitri commanded, loudly and with detailed inflection, "Mookau! Mookau!"—which seemed to be meant as an order to stop touching the device and step away from it. The Chinese biologist obeyed immediately, but a part of him wondered if the command to which he had just responded truly was what it seemed.

This guy knows that if he had simply ordered me in English to step away, I would easily have understood, Alan told himself. *Why did he choose that word?*

Knowing better than to actually ask, Alan turned the question over and over in his head: *Why did he say that?*

Dmitri Chernov had just provided him with an even more puzzling perspective on Churchill's view of the Russian heart: "A riddle wrapped in a mystery inside an enigma." Whether or not Alan lived long enough to find answers to the old mystery, the Russians would never again be the same to him.

July 5, 1948
Four Past Midnight

WASHINGTON, D.C.

"T he Russians claim they are answering a plea
for help," President Truman said. "From an
American Catalina, along with another plane that
went down at Santorini."

Fellow insomniac Pat Hendry ran through a
mental catalog of facts relevant to the president's
puzzle. He ran through it quickly and with great
ease, partly because there really wasn't much
material from which to read. "I sent Mac and his
colleague, but no Catalina."

"I know," said the president. "The seaplane—
it's got to be General MacArthur again. We have
him all the way out in Japan and still he's pulling
strings."

Truman lifted a wire-copy letter from Moscow and began reading from it: "We have received news of your crisis. Your distress is our
distress. As you receive this, I am assured that our
team is now at Santorini only for a humanitarian mission. Mstislav Keldysh, USSR Academy
of Sciences."

"Academy of Sciences?" Hendry asked.

"Yes. I hate surprises. So, what does this one
mean?"

Hendry shook his head, very slowly. "Probably
that, just like us, they're on a scientific fishing

mission—same place, same thing. But why would they telegraph such intent?"

"As I said, I hate surprises. According to the latest information I have, this phenomenon George Orwell has been calling 'Cold War' will not start to thaw anytime soon. You've been briefed on High-jump, Phase Two?"

"Bombing Mount Erebus?"

"Yeah. The scuttlebutt's been simmering out there for a while," the president said, and laughed. "That we're at war with Antarctica. And this time, instead of Emperor Hirohito, we're supposed to be demanding surrender from the emperor penguins."

"Or the Fourth Reich," said Hendry, returning a quick grin. Up until now, both phases of the High-jump operation had presumably been bottled up quite nicely; but with the revelations coming out of Massachusetts and Manhattan worsening each passing hour, Hendry could not be sure of any reasonable limits to what the Kremlin knew. He could not imagine that towing the decommissioned *Intrepid* in among California's mothballed "Ghost Fleet," and trying stealthily to refurbish her to accommodate Grumman's new cold-weather weaponry, had gone unnoticed. *Trouble ahead*, he thought, *even if having "the Fighting I" join the High-jump fleet somehow remains unknown*.

"Fourth Reich at the South Pole," said the president. "T'will serve. Hide a lie in the truth, or the truth in a convincing lie. It's easier for Stalin to swallow, either way."

Hendry nodded. There had in actual truth been a Fourth Reich attempt, in Argentina and as far down into the margin of South Polar climate as Chile. But the Germans never did get any nearer to Antarctica than Chile and Cape Horn. By 1946, Nazi fugitives were building impressive tunnel systems and the core structures for an experimental nuclear reactor capable of manufacturing plutonium. They had even tried revitalizing Sanger's space shuttle project, to drop atom bombs on New York and Washington from orbit. But, as Hendry knew firsthand, all the smartest German scientists (those who were not killed outright) had either been captured by the Russians or fled to France and surrendered to the Americans at war's end. South America's German Fourth Reich simply did not have the scientific expertise to rise again. By now, all of their Nazi gold and diamonds had run out, leaving them with little to look forward to except half-constructed reactor buildings and space-plane launch rails—little except that, and a renewed Nazi hunt emerging from Israel, followed closely by poverty, fear, death, fear of afterlife, and tomorrow.

But the rumors live on, Hendry thought, opportunistically. "So," he said, "Moscow knows we've been in Antarctica?"

"That's the word from New England," said Truman. "Fortunately practice maneuvers were finished, and the fleet was already moving out when this coin-boy disaster started. So, it's not going to be too hard to deny what the Russians think they know, or that the ships even existed—

and, by the way, thank you for finding that flying saucer guy."

"He's quite happy to talk about it," said Hendry. His grin was back, and widening. "Cleveland guy. Claims he saw a foo-fighter come up glowing out of the water, during the war. He's been trying to tell reporters we have a secret fleet attacking Antarctica—"

"How did he find out about High-jump?"

"Didn't. Just a random delusion that hit the right media target. Guy claims he's a—what did he call it? A remote viewer? A loon, to be sure. But at least for now, he's *our* loon. He believes we're attacking Antarctica because that's where Hitler built a secret base, filled with rocket and saucer technology."

Hendry was confident that, as the president had said, the Cleveland guy would serve them well. There was no Hitler Antarctic rocket base, of course. No leftover Germans hiding under the ice. No foo-fighters there either. There was only an ordinary and continually reengineered, cold-resistant fleet, sent now and again since 1946, where the American navy could train far from the prying eyes of the Northern Hemisphere. They trained, presumably all the while in complete secrecy, for a possible war in the Russian Arctic, during the most challenging weeks of high-latitude night.

"Does 'Cleveland' have any like-minded friends?"

"I've been working on that angle, Mr. President. Got a couple of true believers. Helping to get them more news coverage. The best part is, one of these guys is finishing his doctorate at Berkeley. I've got good people in Boston working on getting him an advance offer from Harvard. This should add to his publicity potential and credibility, while at the same time demolishing it—"

"—thus making saucers, secret Nazi bases, and secret American fleets indistinguishably crazy," said the president. "We shall have more confused Russians that way."

"Exactly. The story will have credibility and simultaneously discredit itself, pretty much any way we wish it."

"Of course, if your professor—"

"Leary's his name," said Hendry. "Tim Leary."

"Okay," said Truman. "For now, sounds like he's a true believer. For now, he's serving our best interests. But if he should ever get—"

"*Too* credible?" Hendry finished for him.

"I'd hardly say that's an impossibility."

"I've thought about it. There's a guy who works with Joe McCarthy—very ambitious. On days when I've been required to take down someone's reputation, it's sometimes been guilt-ridden work. But my difficult work is Mr. Nixon's hobby. If the need ever arises, he's already got people lined up—even though he has no idea why I would want it done—who will be eager to figure out how to take Leary down."

"May I interrupt?" said a young law student from Boston. He stood at the doorway, looking very nervous about something.

"Of course, Bobby—come in," the president said, and motioned him toward a seat. "More bad news from the coin-boy investigation?"

"Bundles. It concerns the spy ring—or *rings*,

actually. It's a much bigger network than we thought even a few hours ago."

"Go on."

"Two men are being pulled out of Los Alamos as we speak. They've been in there since '45."

Truman snorted loudly. "Well, that finally explains something."

"What?" asked Hendry.

"The Potsdam Conference. When I told Stalin we had successfully tested a new weapon—the first atom bomb—he simply shrugged and congratulated me. I've always wondered if he already knew. The rat bastard—he did not ask me a single question about it!"

Bobby seemed unmoved, and this worried Hendry. The coin boy, Potsdam 1945, and keeping High-jump secret were clearly not what he'd come to discuss. "It gets worse, doesn't it?" Hendry asked.

"I'm afraid the game we all thought we were playing may not be the game at all," Bobby said, unfolding a handwritten transcript from his pocket. "Mr. President, one of your aircraft carriers is missing."

July 5, 1948

BASE CAMP #3, SANTORINI

Y ou have been at play with something red," Dmitri said, as he finished the field dressing on Nora Nesbitt's cuffed hand.

She did not answer. She did not express emotion.

"You take a through-and-through shot in the palm of your hand and you don't even bleed a faker's stigmata? So, tell me about that. Good color in your face. No heart irregularity. No signs of shock. How is that? I'm betting this hand of yours wouldn't even develop arthritis—if you live long enough."

Nesbitt maintained her silence, believing she was taking in more information from Dmitri than he would ever get out of her.

He seemed happy to comply. "I'll tell you what you are, Nora Nesbitt. You're my highest-value prisoner. You're someone we can even use as—what you call a bargaining chip, if such an exchange should ever become necessary."

The Russians had separated Nesbitt from the rest of her crew. The building seemed remarkably quiet, for all that had happened. She had seen Alan and McQueen ushered into one room and locked in, the two Frenchmen in another. She did not know what happened to the rest of the men. If they were captured or killed, they went down without shouts.

Nesbitt listened with great intensity but could detect no sounds of interrogation in the other rooms.

At Dmitri's signal, part of his crew brought in three tightly wrapped body bags, already air-pump shrunk-and-sealed, and weighted for disposal at sea. The men laid the black bags on the far end of the room with uncanny gentleness.

"Comrades," Dmitri addressed his men, then motioned them toward the door with a slight nod. The commandos walked out and left him alone again with Nesbitt.

"I learned during the war that good friends help you to hide," her captor said. "I learned after the war that true friends help you to hide bodies."

"Am I supposed to find that funny?"

"Not at all," the Russian replied, and knelt down beside the bags, as if in prayer. "I'm afraid we will be at war soon. But do you really believe either of us ever had any real choice in this outcome?"

Nesbitt decided to withhold a reply.

Dmitri made a sign of the cross over the bodies, then stood and returned Nesbitt's cold silence with an even more obstinate countenance and posture—like a man frozen in time. "Don't you know," he said at last, "that whatever happens to you or to any of our people during the next few days—or even the next few minutes—has already been written?"

"What?" Nesbitt said, breaking her silence. "You're trying to tell me about God?"

"No. I am talking about Heisenberg, Einstein, even Newton and Darwin." He undid the safety on his weapon. "I really did not want any of this to be happening."

"But here you are, making it happen anyway."

"I do not believe you are capable of understanding, Nesbitt. If all the actions of the universe, this world, and our lives in it were set in motion before we and the oceans were born, then there is no free will. If, instead, everything that happens around us and to us, is random—including the mix of the genes you were born with that have determined how your brain will behave—then where is free will? If everything that happens is simultaneously set in predetermined motion and only appears random, there is still no free will."

"So, kill yourself," said Nesbitt.

"Not likely. So, let us pray."

In the clear, hot atmosphere of a Santorini afternoon, there was no denying that getting anywhere near Base Camp #3 was a nonstarter. Mac and Yanni halted more than a hundred yards out, then backed away as stealthily as their considerable skills permitted. A two-handgun invasion would have been quick suicide against no fewer than twenty well-armed, highly trained Russian commandos.

The pair traveled north, keeping close to the cliff edge and pausing to study the lagoon whenever they could, from hiding places in crevices, or among thick stands of fig trees. There was new activity near Nea Kameni and the red plumes. Little flickers of Kraken light were just barely perceptible, but there were enough of them to give the impression of undersea thunderclouds on the move. Most of the activity seemed to surround the place where the Russian launch was exploded by a mine.

Mac looked west across the lagoon and saw that one of the ships—presumably the one that had launched the Base Camp #3 raiding party—was still holding position near the white island. Its stern faced the center of the lagoon, as if ready for a quick retreat. In the north, the second ship also continued holding position.

Nothing had changed since the first time he looked—at least, if one was willing to ignore certain details. Foreboding and guilt began to weigh down on Mac. He could not be sure that Alan and the others still lived.

"And so it happens again," Mac said. "I get distracted and someone pays. Always someone pays."

"I need you to stop that shit. Right now."

He tried to keep his focus on the lights in the water, and on the two ships, but some stubborn part of his subconscious continued torturing itself, and reaching out to him, with the names of the lost, and his part in their loss.

"I'm sorry, Yanni," he said with resignation. "Can't *not* remember who, and how. None of us is really anything else, but what we remember."

"Shut up, you ninny. You wanna remember when someone died? Go. Beat yourself up with the last minute of his life—forever. You want to remember his laughter, his warmth, the good years? Then you're in the right spot: *how* you remember. We ain't what we remember. We're *how* we remember. Got me?"

Mac nodded, grudgingly.

The ship in the north spared him the necessity of giving an actual reply. Two sheets of flame burst out from its cannons, and seconds later their thunder filled the sky. By then two shells had already detonated among the red plumes.

When the clouds of smoke and wet mist began to pull apart and drift off, more than a half-dozen Kraken could be seen stunned or dying at the water's surface, their bodies turning pallid white.

The heavy cruiser that up until then had been holding position near the white island was suddenly moving full speed astern, toward the center of the lagoon. The northern ship remained on post, apparently providing cover.

"Nooo . . ." Yanni said.

Mac studied the expression on her face and could see that there was no way any words from him could help. In a shared state of sensory overload, hours seemed to pass—but they were only minutes, crowded with new and rapidly changing events.

There came to them the sounds of firing from the new, thousands-of-rounds-per-minute guns. The rounds discharged so fast from the full-astern, Nea Kameni–bound ship that every bang blended undetectably into a continual metallic buzz. The bright tracer rounds were so numerous that they reminded Mac of Flash Gordon or Buck Rogers death rays. The "rays" went out in short bursts, aimed mostly at those Kraken already dead or dying on the surface . . . mostly. It was difficult to know what was actually happening. The ship's A-frame had either broken away from the stern or been pulled away by some unseen defender of the lagoon.

As the firing ceased and the vessel came to a halt among the white cephalopods—their number having increased and the majority of them now sinking in shreds—lines were being drawn from the bottom, as if by fishermen.

"Cousteau's red velvet," Mac said softly. "They've *got* their samples."

Near Therasia in the north, a sudden geyser of white water erupted, suggesting another attack with a vintage mine. But it soon became all too clear that the other Russian ship, the *Kursk*, had fired its cannon again. It moved quickly and deliberately toward something flopping erratically on the surface, shifting from red, to white, to red again. They must have seen it and fired about a hundred yards away—*a concussion shot, meant to stun*, Mac guessed. Whaling lines were fired into the animal, and the vessel edged nearer, with nets.

Just offshore of Nea Kameni, the red plume sampling ship—no other description seemed closer to the truth—hit the gas pedal and began churning her screws full ahead toward the lagoon's westernmost exit. Before she overcame inertia and started to pick up speed, two of her guns were firing again. A half-dozen men on the stern had managed to hook on to, and were hauling aboard, severed tentacles and shreds of writhing Kraken flesh.

"You know, Mac," Yanni said. "It's not the Kraken who give me the Willies."

"I know," Mac said, having broken away for at least a little while from the traps of his past.

Yanni continued: "Humans really scare me."

1175 B.C.
The Lost Worlds of Homer

5.33 MILLION YEARS AFTER THE MEDITERRANEAN FLOOD

The name "Kraken" was given late in history. Until officially classified as a cephalopod of unknown origin in the 1735 edition of Linnaeus's *Systema Naturae*, the creature was more often called Scylla, a name that went back before the Trojan War.

There was a story, based mostly on myth blended with reality, in which Odysseus, during his long and tragic journey home from Troy, had been told about a sea monster with multiple long necks, each with teeth that could strip flesh from bone: "In any vessel," the sorceress Circe had warned, "with every single head of hers, she—Scylla—snatches and carries off a man from the dark-prowed ship."

In addition to being an eater of men, the creature was also said to be a skilled shape-shifter.

"But to my crew I said nothing about the awful monster Scylla," said Odysseus, according to Homer. He gave no warning at all, as they sailed past the rock cliffs where the mythical beast dwelled. "For I knew the men would not continue rowing, but would huddle together in the hold."

Odysseus climbed onto the prow of his ship, wearing metal armor and carrying two spears, for he sensed that the monster was lurking, either in the water or on the cliffs nearby. Though he strained his eyes, looking the sea and the gloomy rock face over and over, he recorded that it was impossible to clearly distinguish the beast—until it struck, and snatched men from his crew.

"Thus did Scylla land these panting creatures on her rock," Odysseus lamented. "And she munched them up while they screamed and stretched out their hands to me in their mortal agony. This was the most sickening sight that I saw throughout all of my voyages."

CHAPTER 17

Future Primitive

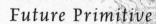

> *You gain strength, courage and confidence*
> *by every experience in which you really*
> *stop to look fear in the face. You are able*
> *to say to yourself, "I have lived through*
> *this horror. I can take the next thing that*
> *comes along." You must do the thing you*
> *think you cannot do.*
> —ELEANOR ROOSEVELT

July 6, 1948
11:40 P.M.
Santorini

A lan Tse-lin had survived disorientingly deadly situations before and by now should have become accustomed to and quickly adaptable to chaos, but tonight required far too much effort, and it was taking far too long for him to clear the wool from his mind.

The young polymath became aware that he was lying on his back in a ravine, against something hard and wet. He knew that he'd been ink-sprayed with a bacterial cocktail so potent it would have made Nesbitt's Plum Islanders gasp—*whether in horror, or with visions of opportunity*, he decided, was impossible to know.

What he could say, with reasonable certainty, was that the rapid onset of "ink fever" had broken while he lay unconscious in the ditch. When Alan first came stumbling into the shallow ravine, his back had apparently pitched up against a fallen tree. That accounted for the "something hard." The storm that passed over the island and created the conditions for his escape from the Russians accounted for most of the wetness. Alan had only the seed of an idea about what had rallied his immune system against the infectious ink and saved his life. *That* he could try to account for later. But at the moment he was much more concerned about avoiding either Russian or cephalopod pursuers, while running through every possibility he could imagine for how to track down Mac and Yanni.

A part of his mind that fought valiantly to stay on the safer side of the border between consciousness and unconsciousness, clarity and fever dreams, focused Alan on the importance of hunkering down alongside the tree fall. There, despite an increasingly commanding urge to drop off into sleep, he forced himself to maximum alertness.

Even while he remained silent and perfectly still, cuts and fever-swollen muscles competed for his attention. But at least there were no broken bones or bullet wounds, and all of his major organs were still inside.

The past three or four hours seemed fragmentary: flashes of vivid memory between long gaps of nothingness while staggering in the dark. As with most military prisoners, escape had been priority one—to be attempted whenever opportunity knocked, for even one sought-after fugitive stretched and thinned the enemy's resources. This night, opportunity had arrived as a thunderstorm. And the Kraken came with it. Two Russians guarding the perimeter were confused and evidently baited into a trap by a display of lights so well orchestrated that if one could discern the position of any of the cephalopods, it was impossible to determine the motion of the others. Alan saw two Russians go down with what Mac would have called rapid-onset "organ failure." He escaped with slash wounds and inking—unable now to recall exactly *how* he escaped.

Alan did not know what happened to the other prisoners.

Overhead, the stars came out. The moon did not come up at all. It did not matter. These days, even with a throbber of a headache that was trying for a new record on his pain scale, Alan possessed what he had proudly come to call "owl eyes."

He was still lying next to the deadfall, bit by bit regaining his strength and wondering how to track a professional tracker like Yanni if she did not want to be found, when he heard a sudden rattling from a nearby tree. Turning his head very slowly toward the source of the noise, he saw the beast, not more than fifteen feet away.

Two slitlike eyes, luminous in reflected star-light, stared back. A tentacle projected itself to-ward him from between the leaves, and then two more of them. Together they sounded like a nest of rattlesnakes, except for rattling a little more slowly than snakes—all three outstretched tenta-cles in synchrony, with a hypnotic rhythm. This individual was smaller than the ones Alan had seen before. It could be no larger, he supposed, than an old lapdog. Its flesh glistened under the stars. Gravity and air seemed not to burden the monster, as if being away from both rain and sea-water raised no obstacles against this pint-sized version of the Kraken scuttling up a highland ra-vine and climbing into a tree.

Interpreting the rattling sound as next of kin to a "back-off" warning from a cornered snake, he back-crawled slowly and quietly away from the creature, expecting at any moment to be slashed and re-inked, or worse, by its hidden companions.

If two night raids have taught us anything, Alan reminded himself, *it's that the Kraken, like us, tend to travel in groups.*

When he had increased the distance between himself and the monster in the tree to thirty feet, he propped himself up onto his elbows, then into a sitting position, trying to make his body appear as small and nonthreatening as possible.

Even the greater distance and the slowing tempo of the rattling did not make the creature seem any less formidable—especially as, apparently in direct response to Alan's retreat, it descended from the leaves to the base of the tree trunk and seemed ready to close the distance.

They travel in groups, the scientist repeated to himself, as a rattling from about sixty or seventy feet behind made him abandon the prior caution of slow movements and brought him struggling quickly to his feet. A few steps up the side of the ravine proved that he could run and climb despite the swelling and stiffness, though he doubted it was possible—*while surrounded*—to outpace two or three determined Kraken.

"Alan," Yanni called softly, from behind the newer source of rattlesnake sounds, "stay where you are if you don't want to piss it off."

"Thank God. Are you two okay?"

"Shhhh," Mac said. "Let Yanni handle this."

"Whatever you do," Yanni added, "don't run."

"Right. Absolutely, don't run. Absolutely, no pissing it off."

Yanni was working several metal objects in her hands—clicking and scraping them together with a speed that could have given a snake's rattle a run for its money.

This historically unprecedented commotion went on for nearly twenty minutes—and then for twenty minutes more, with Yanni adjusting mode and tempo to keep up. As the acting American ambassador of *Homo sapiens*, she let the cephalopod lead the duet.

Finally, well after midnight, the clicking of the animal's barbs reached a high, buzzing pitch with which Yanni could no longer keep pace. Alan was expecting it to let loose with a bioluminescent light show that might be visible for miles around but the night visitor apparently knew better than to attract too much attention. Instead, at the height of what could only be described as a fit of hyperactivity, the creature scurried up the tree and leaped so swiftly out of the ravine that it seemed to Alan as if he were watching a ghostly whirlwind.

"Gone," Yanni said.

"Good," Alan replied. "I'm guessing that it finally needed to get out of here and rehydrate somewhere?" His legs felt weak and Mac was suddenly at his side, steadying him.

"Where are Cousteau and the others?" Mac asked.

Alan explained the Kraken raid, his escape, and why he held out hope for the others, based upon his observations that one of the monsters had already held off from killing him on sight, and another had just allowed all three of them to live. *Of course, at Base Camp #3, they did not have Yanni*, he thought, with a shudder.

When he was finished with his story, Alan asked Yanni, "So, now you hold actual jam sessions with those things, huh? You want to explain that for me?"

Yanni returned silence to her friend and looked away.

"Mac?"

"Oh, what an amazingly long and strange answer this would be."

July 7, 1948
1:20 A.M.

BASE CAMP #3, SANTORINI

I t was plain to Cousteau that when the one they
called Uri regained consciousness, he quickly
regretted it.

"You're doing very well," Cousteau lied. "You'll
be up walking in a day or two. You have nothing
to worry about."

He signaled Boulle to administer another shot
from their captors' supply of morphine, and knew it
would not work for very long. He hinted to Nesbitt
that she might be able to help (as she had helped
Private McQueen, he left unsaid), but her response
was cold indifference. It was clear to him that if
she could get away with it, she'd gladly have helped
the Russian more quickly into an unmarked grave.

During the war, Cousteau had been responsible for the deaths of many Germans, as had his
friend Mac.

"How do *you* get used to it?" Mac once asked.
"The killing?"

"I never did," Cousteau replied. "And I hope I
never do."

After the war, he had taken a personal oath:
"When helping an injured man in the field, I will
not take nationality into consideration."

The wound in Uri's back was ragged and still
potentially deadly. Two Russians on the night

watch, including their team's surgeon, had all of their internal "organ meats" scooped out during the raid. The Kraken had only begun their work on Uri. Barbs tore his skin and a kidney was removed through an unfinished slit before the first two seconds (and only seconds) of rounds from Russian "silencers" intervened.

Now Cousteau was rendered the most field-medicine-qualified person in the base camp. He knew that the peak pressure of a kidney stone was high on the pH scale for pain, and that the haphazard removal of a whole kidney must be far worse.

For now, however, the patient was a welcome distraction. There was much else to worry about. The softening up of the French and American prisoners for "debriefing" included the standard tools of sleep deprivation and denial of both food and water. Just enough broth and strong coffee had been provided by Acting Commander Leonov to aid Cousteau in cauterizing the shredded plumbing in Uri's back, and the newly assigned prison surgeon suspected that he and his assistant, Boulle, might even be allowed a brief nap tonight, for the safety of the patient. But Cousteau knew the worst was yet to come and, in fact, was already upon their doorstep.

"Alan—" Cousteau whispered to Boulle. The name stuck in his throat. Minutes before the attack, Boulle and his friends had been uncuffed and taken outdoors by Uri—who was apparently playing "good cop" to all of the prisoners, against Leonov's "bad cop." Any interrogation Uri had in mind was ended by the cephalopods. According to

Leonov, Alan Tse-lin was missing and presumed dead. He and Uri had been standing very near to where the mission surgeon and his aide fell. Dmitri Chernov was also missing and apparently dead.

"There is still hope for Alan," Boulle whispered back. "We have to believe that."

And there was nothing else to be said, Cousteau judged. The lieutenant had done his duty in tending to the wounded Russian. And for the moment, at least, he was more useful to Leonov as a hydrated and energetic French medic than as a starved and sleep-deprived prisoner.

He could assess their situation more clearly now that the mission commander, too, had much else to worry about. The commandos had set up an impressive communications station and were receiving coded signals from at least three vessels in the area. The two Frenchmen did not need a translator to tell them what was happening aboard a ship called *Koresh*.

They'd heard this awful thing before.

July 7, 1948
1:22 A.M.

En route to MacCready Base Camp #4

No astronomer discovering a new feature among the dark lines and blotches of Mars, or in the rings of Saturn, could have been happier than Alan Tse-lin when he encountered a new zoological wonder, even a dangerous one. He once explained to Yanni that he had been both lucky and unlucky in selecting the place of his birth, among the forested limestone pinnacles along the Li River. Prior to the war with Japan, the beauty of the place and the strangeness of its wildlife were incomparable—that is, until he saw a certain Himalayan maze of valleys, and Santorini.

Now he had come to perhaps the strangest lost world of all, filled with wonderful and terrifying creatures—complete with a female Dr. Doolittle of the Kraken.

"So, Yanni," Alan said, "what did your little octopus in the tree have to say?"

"No words yet."

"Then?"

"I think they started out more curious about us than aggressive. Those shifts of body colors, the clicking and buzzing are not just for show. Most animals will bark or roar, but that one in the tree—it really, really did feel like we were two jazz musicians playing off each other."

"So, Alan, your first impression was right," Mac said. "An interspecies jam session."

"For you two, just another day at the office," said Alan.

"The Kraken wasn't just making noise. We were *both* listening and learning. I thought I could smell it, but I *knew* from the music that the moment I began sweating, it was learning even more from me than I could learn from it."

"I think I can see how," Mac said. "An octopus has at least a dog's sense of smell, right?"

"Yeah. Its arms can taste and smell—and boy,

how they can! I'm talking about, maybe in the neighborhood of one molecule in millions, of adrenaline. I'm thinking the weirdest part was in knowing that if I became the least bit frightened, it could reach out into the air and *instantly* taste my fear."

"Then it learned plenty from *me*," Alan concluded.

"It *recognized* you," Yanni said. "It recognized all three of us. And the music was one of the most unbelievable experiences in my life."

"Wish I could really understand that," Mac said.

"Try, and maybe someday you will," said Yanni. "But don't mistake my idea of it being music to mean that it's all pleasant. During that one moment, when I looked up and saw that the little Kraken was gone, and the music with it, I was hit by the strongest, most incredible sense of loneliness I have ever known."

"You know what I think?" Alan asked.

"What?"

"I think you found a treasure. For all the horror of it, every once in a while the sea tosses you a gift. That jam session, and your loneliness, after—that was one of them."

July 7, 1948
1:42 A.M.

———————————————————

Southwest of Santorini lagoon, a strange electronic shriek had gone out into the night, received clearly by Nesbitt's captors at Base Camp #3: "They're coming through pipes and bulkheads! They're coming through the walls!"

These were the last words anyone heard from the *Koresh.*

Twenty minutes after the ship went radio silent, a string of vintage mines drifted up against the starboard side. The flash from the explosion-chain was visible along MacCready's route to a new encampment, and all across Santorini.

July 7, 1948

SANTORINI

They reached a suitable base camp at 2:20 A.M. It was not really a camp proper, just another stand of wild fig trees. Miles away in the southwest, smoke from a stupendous explosion was still rising against the stars. Whatever happened, Mac knew it could only be getting the Russians even more lathered up. His aim was to avoid setting up the kind of camp that would leave clear signs of habitation. Even the smallest campfire was bound to give off a smell that would linger in the air and on the trees, and could be tracked by a skilled landing party.

In an emergency, if we know they're approaching, I can have us on the move in seconds, Mac told himself. *And that should, hopefully, be good enough.*

"Making sure we have clean drinking water is

going to be a problem," Mac cautioned, as he tore little shreds from a strip of salted meat.

"I'm used to it," said Alan, pocketing his ration of goat jerky for later. "We all know the odds. I'm just glad to be away from Nesbitt right now. Last time I saw her, she *still* looked ready to slit my throat if she caught me napping."

"You might try not killing her people sometime," Yanni said.

Alan did not bother to answer. He looked up, distracted by something in the sky.

Mac understood the new distraction immediately; it was at least twenty thousand feet overhead, and it emitted the low, distinctive growl of a jet engine. He knew that the speed of sound was sufficiently slow, and the distance sufficiently great, that the aircraft was actually somewhere in front of the sound's apparent point of origin. Mac looked ahead of that point, hoping to glimpse the plane passing before the backdrop of stars.

He saw nothing. He could only determine that it was flying from the direction of mainland Greece toward the island of Crete, and he could only wonder why the flight was being made at night. Mac and Hendry had discussed new infrared cameras that might eventually prove helpful in tracking miniature horses and other strange mammals of Brazil's Hell's Gate region, but the technology was military in origin and he was betting now that it was being field tested at twenty thousand feet. The zoologist reminded himself that the "test" could reveal nothing about the locations of the Kraken, because they were doubtless cold-blooded, like all other cephalopods, and could not be seen in the "warm" wavelengths. As for discerning Russians and Americans on the ground, that kind of test seemed meaningless; it was the proverbial search for a needle in a haystack.

As the engine noise faded in the south, it became tempting to try to forget that the plane—and all that it implied—had really been there.

Good luck with that, Mac told himself, and said, "I wish I could believe it was one of ours, but I doubt it."

"So, where do we go?" asked Alan.

Mac looked up at a tall hill, silhouetted against the stars. "The usual advantage of high ground won't do. Too many Russians ashore, and it's the first place they'll look for us."

"So, where to?"

"For now, we stay here. There's enough leaf cover overhead to hide us from Russian surveillance planes, if they come our way." He shrugged, gazing in the direction of the island's east coast. "If we have to move, I know of a few places down toward the shore that will provide good cover."

"I'd hardly call that a safe bet," said Alan, waving an arm around at the lagoon and the sea beyond. "You know, Kraken down there?"

"I've told you," Yanni said, "I think they recognize us."

"Sure. As part of a human menace that's killed a bunch of them, maybe. They'll recognize us for *that*. Yanni, they're *wild animals*."

"So are we."

Alan shook his head. "Can't believe this is happening. I came to this island nice and peaceful-like. The only thing I wanted to do was get away from it all, study some fossils with my friend Pierre, take in the view, maybe even share a bottle of grappa and have a few laughs—but, *noooo* . . . You two have come along. And in no time at all, there's jets and Black Sun and Kraken and—what now? Friggin' fleets of ships coming in with cannons?" He looked around. "You're a lightning rod for trouble, Mac. You know that, don't you?"

The zoologist, Mac—the guy from a field of science that seemed *guaranteed* to mean a quiet, peaceful existence—was familiar with the old joke about how it had turned out for him. They called it the MacCready effect: "If you're around Mac, you're going to see spectacular shit happen," he recalled Hendry explaining. "But if you're standing right next to him, you'll usually get out all right."

"I've heard, Alan, that the major calls me a probabilistic anomaly?"

"He sometimes has another way of putting it, Captain: that you are simultaneously the luckiest and unluckiest bastard he's ever known."

"Of course. Sorry I didn't get to crash another helicopter—yet."

"Face it, Mac: stuff just happens to you. To *both* of you, I guess."

"You don't have such a good record yourself," Yanni said. "You survived travel with a commander on a suicide mission, spear attacks, and—"

"And don't forget the chompy snow."

"Right. Deadly snow, red grottos, Yeren, and Kraken."

"Not many people know about any of *those*," Mac said, "and I sure wish we could keep a lid on all of it."

"We've faced harder challenges."

"Maybe. Maybe not." Mac was trying to push away a feeling that was finally catching up with him. He knew Hendry and Knight used to have arguments about the MacCready effect: "Do you really want to be in the same elevator with him and Yanni, or in a plane at thirty thousand feet?" They used to try to quantify it: "Mac and Yanni always survive, and they get the job done, but even in an elevator—you'd better be prepared for a hell of a ride."

"Look," Alan said. "It's easy to think you're hot shots because you lived, but there's a thing called 'the walking dead' that the Navy's Hellcat pilots know about. And that means you start to get careless because you think you're some kind of immortal. Well, you're not."

"Yes. I think we know that."

"No, you don't. You think you can play with the Kraken like they're little kitty cats? Better remember this: They're like tigers with lots of legs, and a thousand teeth in each leg. And they're smarter than tigers—which makes them even more unpredictable. And you are not immortal."

70 A.D.

CAMPANIA, ITALY

Pliny the Elder called the creature "a monstrous polypus."

Long before Pliny was born, the cephalopods from the Devil's Hole and the lost Mediterranean canyon had continued to evolve into varying though generally cooperative morphs. Those that survived became social animals. Like wolves and monkeys, they tended to travel in groups. A few retained their ability to emerge onto land—and especially during rainy nights or in the presence of sea spray.

In his eleventh volume of *Natural History*, Pliny described a many-tentacled night visitor (a "polypus," named as a predecessor of the word "octopus") that developed a sort of addiction to fish being pickled in huge vats.

According to Pliny, it came from beneath the sea, squeezed between the pickets of iron fences, and even when caught by the merchants' guards, escaped into the trees. Pliny believed there was a whole family of the beasts, moving between the water and the trees—but only one of them ended up being caught, having been sniffed out and finally cornered by trained attack dogs.

Many large squid species possessed suckers lined with knifelike teeth, but this creature was armed with rotating hooks. The guards and owners of the fish pickling and sauce factory—"They really thought they were joining battle with some monster," Pliny recorded. "It would drive off the dogs—strike at them with its stronger arms, giving blows with so many clubs, as it were; and it was only with the greatest difficulty that it could be dispatched with the aid of a considerable number of three-pronged fish spears."

He described the corpse's large suckers and their correspondingly imposing teeth, its arms "full of knots," and its body heavier than a cask of fifteen amphorae.

"Who could have expected to find a polypus there?" Pliny asked. "Or could have recognized it as such, under these circumstances?"

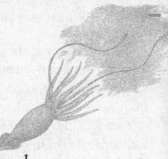

CHAPTER 18

Chains of Command

> *The weight of evidence indicates that humans are not unique in possessing the neurological substrates that generate consciousness. Non-human animals, including all birds and mammals and other creatures, including octopuses, also possess these neurological substrates.*
>
> —CAMBRIDGE DECLARATION ON CONSCIOUS LIFE ON EARTH, FRANCIS CRICK MEMORIAL CONFERENCE, JULY 7, 2012

July 9, 1948
Officer's Mess and Smoking Room
Undisclosed Location at Sea

Captain Charles L. Christian had pledged himself to serve to the best of his ability even at the cost of his own life. There was no small consolation in the knowledge that he had demonstrated his patriotism through three kamikaze attacks—one of them aboard this very ship, having left more than 20 percent of his body severely burned.

I am loyal, he emphasized for himself—even if, under General Douglas MacArthur's command, it was becoming difficult to be sure under whose navy he was sailing.

And strangest of all, thought Captain Christian, *that while steaming full ahead into this disaster, I share my ancestry with history's most controversial mutineer*. He just hoped it did not end for him the same way it ended for Fletcher Christian of the *Bounty*: murdered by one of his own men.

But I'm not a mutineer. I'm a patriot who still stands tall for my country after being burned, shot, blown up, and burned again—and having lived to confront the frozen hell of Operation High-jump. But, oh—how I wish my parents had stayed at home in the South Pacific, where I could have been born out of history's way—and most of all, stayed away from this present dilemma.

"Home" had been a subtropical paradise, so remote that the Japanese completely overlooked it during their conquest of the Pacific islands. But in 1912 his parents had embarked from Norfolk Island to Ellis Island. Even before he was born, they had set in motion for him a collision with history.

The captain suspected that the White House knew little or nothing of MacArthur's plans. If this suspicion proved true, then it was not the first time, nor would it likely be the last time, that the general acted on his own, as if President Truman did not exist. Any omnipresent being, looking down upon this mission, could surely have foreseen the swerve of history that MacArthur would eventually bring to North Korea and China, and even to the Mediterranean—sending forth a cascade of consequences from this century into the next.

Presently, two distinctly unsettling names were foremost on his mind. The death cry from a Russian ship had been preceded by a routine coded message. It named Nora Nesbitt ("the peach") and designated her as captive, along with her Catalina crew. This also meant that the bioweaponeer Kitano Hata must also be in Russian hands—each of these scientists of equal strategic importance to whatever country possessed them.

How I wish my parents had stayed in Norfolk . . . But there was little time to regret what might have been. He had to answer the general.

Christian believed it likely that the Russians had already broken the code he would be using for the message. He was also sure, to 100 percent certainty, that this was just as MacArthur wanted it to be. During the past twenty-four hours, no fewer than three ships had been spotted by air recon, moving toward Santorini. Stalin was projecting serious firepower into the region.

The reply Christian proposed seemed bland enough on the surface, but only at first glance. There was enough room for interpretation to drive a little paranoia into anyone who intercepted it. To one degree or another, he hoped paranoia would translate into caution. This was the best he could hope for. The captain did not believe the word "scared" meant anything more to a Russian than it did to a survivor of kamikaze attacks.

Steaming toward an unknown hell in command of a ship that officially did not exist, the captain prayed that enlightened self-interest would be enough for his adversaries.

He drew in smoke from the last inch of a Lucky Strike, exhaled reflectively, gave his letter a final read-through, then set off to have it coded and transmitted:

IN REPLY TO YOUR LATEST COM-
MAND, I PROPOSE NO REVISIONS TO
A MISSION OBJECTIVE ALONG THE
PATH YOU HAVE CHOSEN.

July 9, 1948

SANTORINI

I f we try it," said Yanni, "don't you think the Russians will be waiting for us?"

"It's possible," Mac replied. "But that's one of the things I'm willing to risk—if I go in alone."

From afar, through binoculars, Mac studied the mostly abandoned marina where Alan had helped Pierre Boulle stash one of the supply bags, seven days earlier. The location seemed undisturbed and unguarded. But there was no way of knowing if Boulle was still alive, or if the commandos had tortured details out of him. "We need to build up some arms," Mac concluded, "and make a plan until help arrives."

Miles above, a Russian jet glinted in near silence. A different sound reached them, rising for several seconds, then dying out slowly to nothing, only to return more strongly. One by one the three fugitives turned their faces up. West, in the direction of the lagoon, two planes passed at low altitude. Mac identified them immediately: *Prop planes—Navy, Grumman.* He supposed that the maneuverability of the new Hellcats counted for something; still, they might be no match for a jet if it ever came down to a shooting fight.

The drone of the prop engines faded into the distance, but only one detail really mattered. "We are not so alone as we thought," Mac said.

"So forget about Boulle's bag!" Alan concluded.

"All we need to do is stay put," Yanni added, in support of Alan.

"I'm not so sure of that," said Mac. "I need to try. Why are you looking at me like that?"

"It's a good thing I'm Chinese," Alan said. "We're used to hopeless situations—and to no-hoper fools!"

Mac laughed, then instantly checked himself. "Look, you two: if I'm captured, you're both still safe. If I get into trouble, the Russians're gonna want me alive and we won't have lost much because it means they're closing in anyway and probably they just get me and—*again*, you probably both get away safe. And besides, Alan, isn't there a saying back home, 'If you want to capture the tiger, you must go where the tiger lives'?"

"There's also a saying that the tiger bides its time, and usually eats."

Mac looked out toward the horizon. At its very edge, more than twelve miles away, three ships—including the heavy cruiser that had speared and netted one of the cephalopods—were huddled together.

"We may not have the luxury of time," Mac said.

"Is this where you make one last try at telling me how going down there is not as bad an idea as I think?" Yanni said. "No. This is where I tell you that it's much worse and much *stupider* than you imagine—isn't that right, Russkie?"

"You should listen to her more often," answered a familiar voice, from behind a tree.

"What do you want, Dmitri?" Mac called out. "Our surrender, I suppose."

"No. I want to help," the Russian said, and stepped into the open with his hands in the air.

"I don't have time for fools."

"Sorry, MacCready. It's the only kind of time I have left."

Yanni crossed her arms, giving a facial expression that Mac had often interpreted as frightful—like a manic killer about to strike—but which he had never been quite able to make her understand, or to adequately describe for her.

"If this isn't some sort of joke you're playing," Yanni said, "if you're serious about wanting to help, you can start by telling us how our friends are."

"I'll begin with what you call a good-faith motion," Dmitri said, and then slowly unholstered a gun and dropped it on the ground. Conspicuously, he kept the salt grenades ready. "Our encampment was attacked by your undersea friends," he continued. "The last time I saw your team, Cousteau and the others were all alive. I really don't know if they still are."

"How long ago was that?"

"Two nights."

"And that last time you saw them, they were all safe?" Mac asked, looking at Dmitri and not quite believing him.

"I've told you what I know. It seems to me that our comrades were able to repel the animals."

"And you definitely saw all of them alive?" Mac repeated.

"Da."

"Why is it that I don't believe you?"

"It almost does not matter what any of us believes, does it? Not beyond the fact that we now share the same enemy."

"You mean the cephalopods?" Yanni asked.

"Not for nothing," said Mac, "but wasn't your mission objective something red?"

"Things change. Objectives fall apart."

"You want them all dead," Yanni said. "The Kraken."

"How else should it be? I don't want even one of them taken alive to Russia, or anywhere else."

"Nor should we," said the Chinese anthropologist. "We humans like to think that we're the only conscious creatures who *know* we're conscious."

"But we're not?" said Dmitri, with a touch of mockery.

"Not by a long shot, Ahab."

Dmitri raised a hand and said, "I have rations here. What's it going to take to prove that we're all on the same side?"

"Stalin's side?" Mac asked, incredulously.

"No. We're all on the side of survival. *Our* survival," the Russian replied. "Those things can hide all over the deep and walk on land if they want. You think they'll stay underwater forever?" He gave a slow underhand toss to a ration packet, landing it at Mac's feet.

Mac gave the packet a quick, suspicious look, then returned his gaze to Dmitri.

"Sure, MacCready. I knew this is how you would answer my kind gesture. And, what? You think I've dosed it with cyanide?"

The Americans answered him with silence.

Dmitri returned them his warmest, friendliest smile. "Cyanide's too messy. Attracts too much attention and creates too much of an international incident if by some small chance my side should lose this island and get caught by your side, with your body. Personally, my poison of choice is a good dose of ordinary nickel dissolved in the blood."

"Slow suffocation," Mac said, with a hint of admiration for the idea.

"Never thought of that one, eh? Our red corpuscles prefer to pick up nickel over iron, if there's enough of it around."

Mac shot Dmitri a defeatist's smirk, then thought aloud, "We'll always have polonium."

"Unprofessional. Radioactivity's too easy to

detect these days. No medical examiner anywhere in the world is going to check for nickel in the blood."

"Gee . . . you really have made a study of it," said Mac. "So, what do you want?"

"I don't want any of this," he said slowly. "But all along you have been asking the wrong questions. What do you think you *should* be asking when something has the scientists, the military, and the church scared at the same time?"

"*You're* scared of Kraken. But have you given much thought to Bishop Marinatos's worries about the red miracle?"

"I'm talking about both," Dmitri said, and seemed to drift off into thought for several seconds—and then for several seconds more. "Look here," he said at last. "I have a dream . . . that one day, your children and my children shall play together."

Then, of course, came the inevitable "but" as the food packet near Mac's feet flashed bright and so stunningly loud that there was no time to respond. Carefully hollowed out and toxin-filled cactus needles—scores of them—had shot out like fléchettes along an arc and pierced the three Americans.

Mac dropped to his knees, feeling something like hot salt spreading through his muscles and his veins. It was laced with morphine, as if this was intended to somehow make him not care about what was happening. Before he fell onto his face and his hearing began to fade, Mac recognized the crackle of a walkie-talkie.

"But not today," Dmitri said, before he radioed out, "Three to pick up."

July 9, 1948
Captured MacCready Base Camp #3

SANTORINI

N ora Nesbitt was hungry and parched, and more than a little angry about the favoritism she saw Dmitri showing toward MacCready, by offering him a half-gallon can of water.

"Nickel or polonium?" Mac asked.

"Both, this time—with a little americium to round it out," Dmitri replied, as if they were sharing a private joke.

Whatever that's about, Nesbitt wondered.

"If Darwin had looked upon this island," Dmitri wondered aloud, "wouldn't he have gone mad trying to work out the laws that govern its life?"

"Why should he?" Mac asked. "Even the Kraken are a straightforward demonstration of Darwinian evolution."

"And the red miracle?" Dmitri asked. "Did the kind of brain we see in those monsters simply spring out of the earth?"

Nesbitt was tempted to reply with an explanation but took pride in distancing herself from acts of colossal stupidity. She did not believe she could say the same for Mac.

"Have you noticed, MacCready, what's happening in the water?" Dmitri continued.

"Why—it's probably just a sped-up process of random variation. It's still Darwinian, with variation producing the raw material of change, and differential survival governing the direction of change. We're all just living on Darwin's biological chessboard, with an unseen player on the other end—acting by ordinary mathematics, making its moves with reptilian indifference."

"Play the fool if you must," Dmitri said. "But don't take me for one." He turned toward Nesbitt and said, "I know *you* came here for the red miracle. I can assure you that my side will take charge of that, very soon. As your lying friend here likes to say—Don't you think? Or don't you?"

Nesbitt returned the Russian her best poker face, concealing even the slightest hint that she feared her activities at Plum Island were now leaked news. To have been called a valuable bargaining chip—*presumably in anticipation of some sort of prisoner exchange*, Nesbitt guessed—suggested that something rather distressing must now be unfolding for the Kremlin in America. She was reasonably certain that Dmitri did not know the depth of detail in her studies—the changes that had been worked on ordinary fruit flies, and even on her own body, and Yanni's, in only a couple of years. She knew it should have taken a couple of thousand years or more—and she could not explain yet how the biochemistry of a person could be completely reworked in one lifetime.

"What do you want?" Nesbitt demanded.

"I want the truth, of course."

"Don't be ridiculous." The Plum Islander studied the Russian the way she might study one of her fruit flies under a microscope. *He's a religious man*, she told herself. *Also holding back some deep rage. Perhaps I can use that somehow.*

"Listen," the Russian said, checking her restraints. "Right now I'm the only friend you have."

"I don't have friends," said Nesbitt.

"That's true!" Yanni chimed in, and smirked.

"You can believe us on that," said Alan. "I've traveled with her before. I think the only friend she ever had was when she was a child—and he was only an imaginary friend."

"Until he left me for someone else," Nesbitt said, still maintaining her poker face. "The lousy bastard."

July 9, 1948

TWENTY MILES SOUTH OF SANTORINI

———————————————————

From the beginning, Trofim Lysenko had refused to fool himself into believing the expedition to Santorini would go smoothly. Of course, he was not expecting the loss of a world-class mini-sub, an entire surveillance ship, and a heavy cruiser so damnably early in his mission. His regular bouts of seasickness had fallen far down along the priority scale.

Now two heavy cruisers flanked the *Kursk* with their hundreds-of-rounds-per-second guns. The upper decks were patrolled by trained attack dogs;

originally brought along to sniff out any American marines who might attempt to slip aboard during the night, they were now pulling "squid duty" as well.

What to do next was, as always, the problem that weighed heaviest on him. He realized that he had become more a politician than a scientist. But on this mission, science was being forced upon him.

Objective number one—verifying that Nesbitt and MacCready's "red *moctus proctus*" really existed—had been accomplished with relative ease. Now came the politically difficult part of the plan, made all the more complicated by the unexpected guardians of the red plumes.

We were in luck, Lysenko told himself. His ship, designed to carry political favorites, had been provisioned with everything desired, including an equipment test tank. On most days it was easily converted into an officers' swimming pool, located conveniently alongside the officers' sauna. The *Kursk* was doubly lucky in having one of the finest machine shops on the high seas, the better to keep their "special guest" locked beneath a grid of iron with squares so small that a ton of Kraken could not possibly squeeze through.

It squirted a stream of water at him angrily but elicited only a laugh. The creature was out of ink. Presently it occupied itself by breaking the pieces of a mirror into progressively smaller triangles.

"The mirror has been quite a surprise," Lysenko's captain said. The geneticist who at times did not believe in the importance of chromosomes had chosen the officer specifically because, in better days only three years earlier, the man had actually sailed with none other than Jacques Cousteau—as the Frenchman's first Russian science observer.

"You put a mirror on the side of a coral reef," the captain said, "and you'll have crabs, eels, and various fishes attacking their reflections, because they fail to recognize themselves. But not this Kraken. Look how it moves the mirror pieces around, stares at itself, and even makes a triangle of its own skin into a reflection of the mirror."

"And what does that tell you?"

"A high level of intelligence—which brings us back again to this." The captain dropped a copper disk on top of the iron grid.

"And your theory?" Lysenko asked.

"I suggest—and *only* suggest—that you consider these animals as maybe another intelligent race, able to alter materials in their environment with very skilled tentacles, the way we make weapons with our hands."

Lysenko examined the disk again. Its outer rim was scarcely sharper than the blade of a butter knife—which was, in terms of maximum damage, precisely correct for a mass of copper sent spinning through the air. The weapon had a distinct upper and lower surface. The top was convex and the underside slightly concave, as if someone had studied the aerodynamics of what a generation only now being born would eventually come to call "Frisbees"—in this case, killer Frisbees.

A new sound—the vibration of the animal's barbs—must have alerted the ship's lookouts in the sonar room. One of them came running up from below.

"May want to quiet that thing down," he said with alarm. "If American ships are listening, they'll hear that all the way out to Crete."

"Any sign of the Yanks?" Lysenko asked.

"I don't know. I could definitely hear the drumming and clicking of other Kraken, out there. And something strange."

The clicking and buzzing from the pool grew louder. "Strange?" the captain asked, shaking his head. "Compared to what?"

"I thought I heard something like tank treads crawling along the bottom. It was there for only about three seconds. Then it was gone. Either stopped or washed out by Kraken noise. Came on again for a few seconds more. Gone."

Lysenko studied the expression on the young man's face and saw worry. "Anything else?" he asked, raising his voice above the cephalopod din.

"That's a pretty loud fish."

"It's no fish! And I asked you—anything else?"

"I think there's more kinds of these animals."

"Why?"

"Our sonar pinged something twelve miles east. It was only a little denser than water, like *this* animal, but as big as a whale."

"It's nothing to worry about," the captain said. "We've three ships together and our guns can handle them if they come too near."

The clicking and buzzing ceased abruptly and the sonar man responded as if startled. They all did. After several long seconds, the young man asked, "What do you think it was trying to say?"

"I haven't a clue—*yet*," Lysenko said. "But our comrades on the island have 'rescued' someone who can help us to understand."

The boy looked at the geneticist quizzically, began to ask a question, and was waved off: "Just hold your tongue and get below."

Then, lifting a long, almost needle-thin spear from the deck, Lysenko approached the tank—his particular interest being the wounds from the whaling lines, four days earlier. "See how quickly it heals," he said.

"So, you think it's been getting into the *moctus proctus*."

Lysenko thrust the lance through the grate and into the base of a tentacle. Another tentacle clutched at the spear and thrust it back whence it came, faster than the scientist could drop to the deck. The blunted end passed him first, with enough force to have broken his neck had it made contact. One small part of a second later, and still as he dove for cover, the needle point passed Lysenko's head. Gravity just could not yank him down fast enough.

"*Yob tvoyu mat!*" he shouted, and stood up again, cupping one side of his face with a hand. The needle had side-swiped cartilage, slicing the back of his right ear in two.

"The surgeon should look at that," the captain said.

claimed that a single Kraken could devour an entire fleet at once, leaving empty ships adrift, like ghosts. Eventually the Kraken was said to measure more than a mile across, easily mistaken for an island when resting on the surface of the sea. A bishop from Nidros, according to legend, was searching for a new place to settle his flock when he discovered one of the old mapmakers' mysterious drifting islands. The bishop and his followers landed and celebrated their deliverance with a church service and did not realize the truth until, after the planting of a flag, the Kraken awoke.

CHAPTER 19

Icarus

The Kraken sleepeth . . .
Until the latter fire shall heat the deep;
Then once by man and angels be seen,
In roaring he shall rise and on the surface die.
—ALFRED, LORD TENNYSON

July 10, 1948
Two Miles Southwest of Santorini

The tank treads that Trofim Lysenko's sonar man had imagined he heard crawling along the seafloor were quite real. They were in fact the treads of America's first nuclear-powered submarine, the *NR-3*.

There was no *NR-1*. No *NR-2* either. Admiral Hyman Rickover had chosen the name to keep the Russians wondering, if they ever found out about the machine's existence, just how many of these the U.S. Navy actually built and deployed.

The vessel was only ninety feet long, with more than half of that length taken up by Rickover's own nuclear electric engine design—the smallest reactor General Electric had ever built. The nose of the ship was graded at "virtually indestructible" by its designers from Corning Glass Works. It provided an extraordinarily wide view, like the cockpit of a B-29 bomber, and the seating arrangement behind the superhard ceramic windows was therefore borrowed from the B-29.

Directly behind the pilot and copilot, the flight engineer's seat was occupied by a World War II OSS man named Walter—now called back to duty as "Number T070."

Oh, that view is tremendous, he thought. In the back of his mind, Walter regretted that, among the men and women that the sub's Operation Raccoon-jump commandos were being sent to rescue, two of them—R. J. MacCready and his friend Cousteau—could not be here to appreciate the scenery. He knew they'd have loved to be sitting where he was now. But normal circumstances precluded this. Rickover's toy was so secret that the crew's wives would never know where they were serving, or that the machine even existed.

Walter did not have a wife. The committed playboy left a lasting impression on his British friend Ian's "Room 39 Group," for whom "T070" had served as OSS liaison during the war. Walter's taste in wine and bourbon was as impeccable as his taste for the beautiful women who all but threw themselves at him and, after an adventure or two, were invariably sent along on their own. This, Ian once told him, was beginning to inform a fictional character he had in mind. They had both decided, during the lead-up to Normandy, that they would eventually leave the service of his majesty and the president, to write books. Yet, despite a hefty bet on who would publish first, Walter felt that he was sure to lose. Ian was already far along with his sketches and dialogue for a story about a flying car—*What's he calling it this week? Shitty-shitty-bang-bang?*

During these years of so-called peace, Walter had not come up with even his first sentence.

He looked out through the cockpit, upon an undersea landscape no diver had seen before—looked out upon what appeared to be the stones of an ancient dock, more than two hundred feet beneath the shores of Santorini. Thinking of the people who must have perished in some long-forgotten quake, and of the book he seemed perpetually unable to write, he dictated to himself, *Page One: "Call me fishmeal."*

Hopeless, he thought. *I'll never come up with the right book.*

Walter stowed the thought away in favor of more pressing realities. Under negative buoyancy, the *NR-3* was immune to the unpredictable tantrums of currents, and it moved on treads through even the worst deepwater storms with the agility of a jeep. The captain and his copilot were bringing their sub down to what they called "baby-crawl speed," and now it was Walter's turn to take the controls.

Like a bombardier controlling a plane's final targeting maneuvers, the man from Truman's CIA brought the *NR-3* to the desired spot. Ordering "Full stop"—the equivalent of "bombs away"— from his flight engineer's seat, Walter manipulated an external mechanical claw as if it were an extension of his own hand, and anchored one of the sub's three sono-buoys between two giant rectangular stones.

"What's that last position you got, again?" the copilot asked.

"Coming up more clearly in just a minute," said Walter. He reeled out the line, just far enough for the buoy, floating overhead like a balloon on a string, to remain concealed within fifteen feet of the surface. As the signals began coming down, he checked his maps—which included the position of one very noisy ship named *Kursk*, and a steadily narrowing search area for the "Catalina captives."

"We've now got them nailed within two hundred yards," Walter announced. "It's as we hoped. The Russians are getting restless—and a bit overconfident. They've been broadcasting to their ships."

"How much longer till we have a better fix on them?"

"I'm betting, long before we hear them moving our people around in small boats."

"That may not be soon enough."

"Why the hurry?" said Walter. "You have somewhere more important to be? We running out of air?"

"Air, we got," the copilot said. "And enough fresh water for a single bucket shower every three days. Time? That's a whole other question."

For two days they had been moving buoys

around, hoping that the commandos on the island would get careless and start broadcasting coded signals. Whether or not the codes were broken did not matter. Only the simple geometry of triangles mattered—the mathematics of modern warfare, courtesy of Euclid.

Walter supposed there was air enough and time enough to render every adversary within range a victim of mathematics. The generator had sufficient electrical power to desalinate seawater into drinking water, while breaking down enough of the water molecules themselves to produce breathable oxygen. They could remain submerged for many weeks, even months. The only limiting factors were the amount of food they had aboard for a crew of thirteen, and how much time remained before the Russians began either killing or trading prisoners.

"If we can move another buoy to the northeast," the captain said, "I think we will be able—"

Walter raised a hand for silence, cupped a pair of headphones tightly to his ears, then began jotting down calculations and drawing new lines on one of the maps.

"Got them!" he announced. "They're broadcasting again and this new buoy's position narrows the target within . . ." He drew a circle around a maximum range of error for the new set of intersecting lines and handed the map forward.

"Only twenty yards?" the captain asked.

"That's what I have," Walter replied. "So now we can begin talking about a specific building. That's where we'll find the MacCready and Nesbitt crews."

"If we move soon," the captain said, and turned his head northeast, toward the triangulated location, "and if the Russians don't move out of there before nightfall."

"If we drive off from here," said Walter, "we'll have to disconnect from the buoys and rise to radio-reception depth. See if Captain Christian is sending out any new orders from 'the Fighting Eye.'"

"Already on it. Pumping ballast."

Walter watched the great stone blocks of a sunken harbor receding into glass-clear water as the *NR-3* slowly gained altitude. A school of strange, eellike fish passed below—and, beyond the fish, something metallic drew the attention of the pilots.

The captain banked their boat gracefully to port and three more metallic objects came into view—shreds of aluminum hull, none of them any wider than the diameter of a dinner plate. Like a set of antennae, two recently repurposed mine detectors were now deployed from below the cockpit.

"We're in a debris field," the copilot said. Walter felt the push of a half-dozen American commandos crowding forward right behind him. No one really wanted to miss what might be coming into view next. "Metal detectors picking up multiple targets—like we're heading into a junkyard."

They descended gently, like a helicopter, landing before what had once been the cockpit of a bomber, deformed into twisted agony the moment it struck water.

The captain called back to Walter: "What do you make of it, Professor?"

"Difficult to say. Pieces of the instrument panel have writing on them." Before Walter could ask the pilots to move the sub nearer, they were already negatively buoyant again and inching forward on treads. Part of a flight seat was still bolted to a fragment of flooring. Three of the strange eels they had seen earlier appeared to be nibbling at something.

"We are now *inside* the plane," the copilot joked.

"You move to the head of the class," Walter replied. He reached out with a robot arm, clawed loose a sheet of instrument paneling, and brought it up close to *NR-3*'s cockpit window. As he rotated the panel, it became easy to distinguish the inspection stamps and control labels despite the numerous scratches across its face.

"Lord!" Walter's captain said. "I was expecting Russian but that's not what I'm reading, is it?"

"No. Similar—but it's really Serbian-Slavic."

"You certain?"

"No doubt of it," said Walter. "Yugoslavia."

"Jesus Christ on a suffering pony. Does this mean we're into it against Stalin *and* Tito?"

July 10, 1948
Captured MacCready Base Camp #3

SANTORINI

D-djya eat?" Nesbitt asked.
   "Yeah," Mac replied.

"Me too. Something's changed. They seem happy to feed us now."

"All of us?"

"I think so," said Nesbitt. "I saw them carrying dishes into the room where they keep Cousteau and the other Frenchman."

Mac glared across the long table at which they sat handcuffed. Three commandos stood guard over them—one for each: Nesbitt, Mac, and Yanni.

The past week felt like a month, maybe more.

Is that all it's been? Mac asked himself. *Just a few short days?*

For most people, after the age of sixteen, the perception of time's passage had a way of speeding up. By age twenty, a year typically seemed only a couple of months, compared to what the waiting time between day one of a new school year and the next summer vacation used to be. Yet for Mac, time itself seemed to have become unhinged.

The four years since he first stood with Yanni on the edge of Brazil's Mato Grosso Plateau had so crowded his memory with new and unprecedented events that—*God*, Mac told himself. *Seems like thirty years ago. Seems like forty.*

"As you have probably guessed by now," Dmitri called from an adjacent room, "your situation is changing." When he strode in and stood at one end of the table, the Russian looked and acted every bit the man in charge, but Mac detected hints of a well-concealed anxiety.

The submariner motioned one of the commandos to uncuff Mac's feet and announced, "I'd like to give you a guided tour, Captain MacCready."

"What? Show me the instruments of torture?"

"In a manner of speaking, Captain." Dmitri then shuffled him out a door and uphill toward the nearest overlook.

Hands still cuffed in front of him, Mac was marched forward with haste, until Dmitri halted him atop a mound of loose, grayish-white pumice.

"Captain," Dmitri said, seeming to have sensed that Mac disliked being called by his title.

"Captain Chernov," Mac replied.

For a long time the two men said nothing, just stood in the wind and the heat, watching clouds advancing from the west.

The *Kursk* and its two sister ships formed a small but possibly impenetrable picket in the south. Dmitri pointed toward three more ships in the north. Then, as if responding to a pre-arranged cue, a formation of two Russian jets flew overhead, followed by another formation of two.

Mac shook his head.

"So, this is it," Dmitri said. "Checkmate."

"Makes sense," Mac conceded. It was easy to see, merely by the way they moved, that the planes were loaded to maximum capacity with extra fuel tanks and weaponry.

"Wish it could have worked out a little differently, MacCready. But you understand: My country, right or wrong? We're '*rescuing*' this island now. We own it."

"Yeah. But for how long?"

"For as long as it takes to get the thing everyone seems to want, and to get rid of the monsters that guard it."

Get rid of them? Mac wondered. He imagined that for every biological success story like the Kraken—even with the red miracle operating in its favor—there must be a hundred unknown evolutionary dead ends. *Do Dmitri's people not realize how biologically fine-tuned these animals really are?*

The scientist searched the horizon and saw, under a fleet of clouds, a distant speck that Dmitri overlooked. It had been growing a little darker each time Mac glanced in that direction—growing at what he estimated to be an approach velocity of twenty knots, maybe more.

"Those ships of ours, and these jets," Dmitri said. "Whatever it costs, we'll back them up. This isn't an attack; it's what your people on Broadway might call an audition. One of your Russian counterparts in the sciences wishes to audition new life. He's probing this island, and your country, right now."

"Probing?"

"Yes. This is the thunder, Captain MacCready. You haven't seen the lightning yet."

Mac glanced again at the horizon. *Twenty-two knots*, he concluded. *It's definitely coming in at twenty-two.* A sudden motion drew his attention to the southern picket. The center ship, Trofim Lysenko's ship, shifted its two forward cannons, taking aim at something.

July 10, 1948
Aboard the NR-3

SOUTHWEST OF SANTORINI

They had moved on from the debris field of the Yugoslavian plane and found their path to the best landing spot for a prisoner rescue attempt, interrupted. A second debris field lay strewn before them, created by something considerably more massive than a plane.

During the past few hours, the sea had come alive with sonar pings radiating out from multiple ships converging on Santorini. Taking care not to send out any new pings of their own, the two pilots navigated by the known undersea topography around the island, and by the magnetic anomalies of older, carefully charted wrecks.

New metallic anomalies indicated pots, trays, ladles, and tin cups—strewn like chaff along the bottom. When Walter looked briefly away from his instruments and viewed the artifacts directly through the cockpit, he casually named the place "Hell's Kitchen." Neither of the pilots responded. Bright splotches on one of Walter's screens were already indicating something quite large, now bearing no more than thirty yards beyond their range of vision.

"You should see the main attraction any minute, directly ahead," said Walter. "It looks like we're heading toward a wall of steel."

The captain and his copilot continued to look

as if they had not been listening. They passed through an undersea dune field and came to a stop before a hill made of books instead of sand. The paper mound made Walter envision a tornado reaching into the hull of a ship and pulling an entire medical library outside.

"Russian?" the copilot called back, pointing an external floodlamp at the book dune.

"This time, yes. Russian. Quite definitely."

"What is it with all these eels?" one of the commandos asked.

Walter looked where the commando was looking. The eels were trailing, one after another, toward the wall of steel. "They're not eels," he said. "They look more like *hagfish*—but different, somehow, maybe a species no one has seen yet."

"Why so many of them?"

"That ship up ahead. Hagfish are like flies. They're among the first to arrive at the death scene."

"Got any more happy thoughts of that kind?" the captain said, and drove over the book pile. They spoke no more as they closed the last ten yards. From the very minute the hulk came into view, the *NR-3* entered a blizzard of gently drifting papers—mostly from files of notes written in pencil—which Walter snatched at with the robot arm, quickly filling the sub's sample basket. *Maybe we'll get lucky and grab some valuable secrets,* he hoped. And then it occurred to him, *If the Russians find out what we're up to, we won't last a minute.* He was confident, however, that they would not be found—*could not* be found. The

General Electric reactor was the quietest engine ever built into a submarine, and Rickover's outer shells of fiberglass gave his boat a sonar cross section as small (and easily overlooked) as a submerged beluga whale.

They found the *Koresh* tilted twenty degrees to starboard, having crashed to the bottom hard enough to push its propellers into the next deck up. Along most of one side, the hull and outer cabins were blown open and torn apart and scattered about.

The inside of the ship could be seen as clearly as the exploded plane's cockpit. Exposed cabins and companionways were full of debris: The search lamps illuminated drifting paper . . . torn mattresses . . . unfamiliar electrical equipment . . . the occasional body—and crabs. Crabs everywhere. The crabs had arrived in even greater numbers than the "eels," and still they were coming.

Walter had seen this sort of thing before, and it was a reason that the one thing he knew he would never write was a book bearing the word "autobiography" in its title. He started breathing faster and one of the commandos tapped him on the shoulder, gently, drawing his attention away from an unusually large mass of crabs and *something bad* beneath the swarm. He returned the man a thumbs-up okay signal and focused his attention on a ripped leather satchel with papers sticking out— likely qualifying as the espionage equivalent of "pay dirt." After forcing the satchel into the sample tray and locking down the lid, he looked up and noticed a curious movement in what appeared to have been the ship's infirmary. It was a body—and, like the nine or ten others he had seen here, it was becoming so bloated that buttons and shirt seams were starting to pop open. Walter believed he had become accustomed during the war to the way the drowned undressed themselves; but even as the *NR-3* steered toward the ship's bridge and the search lamps began to swing their beams away from the infirmary, he realized that even Mac-Cready and Cousteau might not be able to heal fully from the apparition that bid him adieu.

The Russian was straining to lift his chest and arms off the floor, where the tangled frame of a bolted-to-the-deck operating table had pinned his legs. The muscles of his right arm rippled beneath the loose, blue-tinted skin, and then the limb extended at the elbow, as if reaching out to the *NR-3* crew, pleadingly.

For a moment, it held them all spellbound. It did not matter that the lights were swiveling away, or that the sudden splitting of flesh into an eruption of hagfish from within occurred mostly in shadow. Being able to see less than half of what was actually happening made the memory of it even worse. The imagination quickly filled in too many unseen details of the "eel man."

Up to this moment, Walter thought he owed a debt to Mac and Cousteau. The community of polymathic, wanderlust agents to which they belonged was very small, and so it was perfectly natural that MacCready had been among the first to encourage Walter's growing fascination with the submersible corps. But now the submariner vowed that if he ever saw either of his friends alive, he would swear them personally to an oath: "Punch me in the face if you ever hear me talking about climbing into one of these things again."

To be trapped in a compartment in a doomed and flooding vessel had to be a horrible way to die, he finally realized, in a way that had never quite been driven home to him before. *Damn! What could be more horrible?*

And in that very same instant, Walter's long-running struggle with writer's block ended. The "eel man" shattered it, and the first line of his book came to him with uncanny ease, as if dictated to him by a suddenly awakened muse: "In 1898 a struggling writer named Morgan Robertson concocted a novel about a fabulous Atlantic liner. . . ." But this was as far as he got, before two shells from the *Kursk* pounded down on water and exploded somewhere overhead.

The *NR-3* went dark.

That quickly, the mission objective at the MacCready prison site began to fall apart.

July 10, 1948
Aboard the "Fighting I"

ON APPROACH TO SANTORINI

Captain Charles L. Christian stood on a narrow catwalk alongside his bridge and searched the horizon with a pair of binoculars.

"Who the hell are they firing at?" he demanded.

The captain's electronics expert was at his side with a small notebook and several long strips of paper, of the kind used to monitor earthquakes and heartbeats.

"Sir, you see these lines?" Lieutenant Tucker asked, drawing his finger across a sheet that was trying to flap away in the wind.

Christian nodded.

"They're the last navigation pings we received from whatever kind of boat our side sent in to extract the MacCready and Nesbitt crews."

"Meaning, the Russians found them?"

"I don't think that's what happened. The sonar pings are too many hours old—and most of them look like decoy buoys. And if the extraction boat got careless, my *Argo* guys would have noticed them before the Russians did." Tucker folded the papers into a satchel. "So," he emphasized, "I don't think they were firing on our guys."

"Then, who?"

"Uhh—that's the sixty-four-dollar question." Tucker began to carefully unscroll a new sheet from his satchel. "I found something strange in these figures," he said, pointing. "Almost like a shadow moving past the old pings and two miles south of Santorini's lower west side. *Argo* team says it looks like a cloud in the water. And we might not have noticed it at all if it wasn't sometimes such a noisy cloud."

"They're bombing a cloud?"

"Seems so, Captain. My idea was that it's a school of big fish but they'd have to be pretty weird fish. I mean, only just a little denser than the water itself. But then there's that question: Why would they be bombing fish? Now—that extraction boat, sir? I've got to ask."

"Go on."

"It's underwater, right? That's what my graphs here are making me think. There's nothing of ours on the surface in that area. I'm thinking the Russians smell something in the area and are shooting at anything that looks in any way like it might not belong—even if it's just some fish making noises they've never heard before."

The captain began to appreciate the strategic significance of having "borrowed" the reluctantly reactivated Lieutenant Tucker from Hollywood. During the past year, between supporting roles for Columbia Pictures, Tucker had been working with actress/inventor Hedy Lamarr to enhance the resolution of sonar devices—including the secret abilities of the "research vessel" *Argo*. The hard-drinking lieutenant was notoriously rowdy but every bit the inquisitive and brilliant man Hedy had promised he would be.

"Should I be looking for a submarine—one of ours?" the lieutenant pressed.

"I can't tell you *what* they've sent for Mac-Cready, Tucker, because even I don't know."

"Then if the sub is hit, and gone, we're the rescue mission. Someone would have to be awfully concerned to send in *our* sort of backup."

The captain shrugged and bit off the end of a cigar. Instead of spitting it out, he chewed vigorously. *I propose no revisions to a mission objective along the path you have chosen*, he had written.

"We're still under MacArthur's command," Christian said. "And I may be asking more from this crew than you signed on for."

"The prisoners?"

"Yes. According to the general, there are at least three of our people out there who know too much, and who cannot be risked to Russian torture. If the extraction team goes missing, or fails, our mission goes from rescue support to silencing."

"MacArthur's protocol?"

"No. It's *Nesbitt's* protocol. I hear she lost three teeth in the Himalayas—something called Operation Mammoth-jump. So, just in case she ever got into this kind of mess, she volunteered to have some experimental bridge work put into her mouth: a miniature transmitter with enough power to send out radio beeps that can be picked up from twenty miles away. If it becomes necessary, she's willing to activate the thing, calling in the planes that will kill her along with anyone else who happens to be near—and especially her interrogators."

"That's *some* dame," Tucker said.

The captain swallowed hard and asked, "Anything else for me, in your squiggly papers?"

"That's the other sixty-four-dollar question."

"And?"

"That shadow—the school of strange fish the Russians are so trigger-happy about—well, one of those underwater clouds is moving into our path. We should be passing practically through it in about twenty minutes."

July 10, 1948
Dmitri's Overlook

SANTORINI

The water was still white where the shells from the *Kursk* had struck.

Even at a distance, Mac could see a pair of stunned or dying Kraken writhing in the foam.

"I know your friend Yanni really cares about those things," Dmitri said. "I'm sorry it has to be this way."

"I'm sorry too," Mac said. He was reminded of something Japan's Admiral Yamamoto had written during the weeks following the attack on Pearl Harbor—which he had evaluated as "a small success . . . that shall give us much trouble in the future."

"I fear," the scientist said, as one of the injured creatures slid beneath the surface, "that you are awakening a sleeping dragon."

"I don't believe so," the Russian said. But a grave expression passed suddenly across his face and he admitted, "I don't know."

"That's the problem with hope."

"Yes, Captain MacCready. The problem is that we never really know. And if we did know, how many of us would bother to show up in the first place?"

"Yeah—well, during the last few minutes I think I've watched a couple more of those 'dragons' dying. So what I *do* know is that this would be a good time to keep your eyes and carotid arteries out of Yanni's reach."

Dmitri was momentarily distracted by two jets approaching at high altitude. But Mac acted as if he did not notice; his attention was narrowing on something nearer to earth, on the horizon, below the clouds. Mac pointed with his cuffed hands, and when Dmitri looked where the American was pointing, he drew his breath in astonishment. As the minutes passed, the dark shape on the sea's horizon resolved itself into an aircraft carrier, flanked on either side by escort ships.

Mac nodded toward the *Kursk* and a pair of Soviet jets circling back out over deep water. "You called checkmate on me?" he said, as five Grumman Hellcats left the flattop, one after another, and began circling ominously around their approaching carrier. "Nah! *That's* what I call checkmate."

July 10, 1948
In Russian-Dominated Skies

SANTORINI PROTECTORATE

What was *that*?" Valentina suddenly cried, breaking radio silence. She pitched her plane hard to port and dropped from thirty thousand feet to twenty-five thousand, trying to acquire a clearer fix on the large object that had just appeared on the dark sea, between islands of white clouds.

"I'm seeing two—no, make that four Hellcats orbiting her. Repeat, four Hellcats."

"I see a fifth, and there may be more," Andrei called from the other plane. "Want to test them?"

"Nyet!" commanded Valentina. "Maintain *nonbelligerency*." For any Americans who might be listening, she repeated it in English and added, "We're coming in for a look."

July 10, 1948
Aboard Captain Christian's Command

AIRCRAFT CARRIER *INTREPID*, THE "FIGHTING I"

For a while, Chief Engineer Tom McAvinue Scott was happy to be away from the white hell of Antarctica and cruising in the warm waters of the Mediterranean. But now, of course, life aboard *Intrepid* was de-evolving from mere training missions against Russian antagonists to actually being antagonized by two Russian jets descending. Anyone attacking a war-hardened aircraft carrier had to be foolish. *But to attack a carrier from the country that holds the monopoly on atom bombs would make one heir to the king of fools*, Tom concluded—*unless the monopoly really has a much shorter life span than we thought, and the worst kind of showdown is only a step away.*

Biblical images came quickly to mind: *men and*

women falling with their tongues and eyes burned
from their skulls before they touched the ground . . .
cities going up like the smoke of a furnace . . .

He was relieved to hear Captain Christian calling over the intercom for gunners to take aim and
stay alert but to hold fire. "Repeat. Repeat," the
speakers blazed clearly. "Stand down unless fired
upon, or unless directly ordered to fire."

The ship's engines were coming down to "all
ahead slow"; Tom could feel it through the flattop deck. Three brand-new Hellcats were being
readied for flight nearby, as the growls from the
jets became more distinct. He looked up at the
clouds, searching, but Lieutenant Tucker suddenly called out—"*What the fuuuck!*"—louder
and even more alarming than the growls in the
sky. "*Look out!*"

When Tom looked down from the clouds, he
saw Tucker rushing toward him, but the lieutenant and the deck before him were completely
distorted, as if some odd new form of carnival
glass had popped up between them. The engineer
understood immediately that it could not be glass,
and in only a second he realized that there were at
least three sheets of the "glass"—and they were in
motion, and one of them had eyes.

Tom was certain that he would have died where
he stood if some fast-thinking crewman had not
sprayed the imitation "carnival glass" with fuel.
The nearest "sheet" was only fifteen feet away
when Tucker lit it up. Its skin blackened instantly,
and the "glass" transformed into a Hydra with
flailing serpent heads.

The engineer would recall later that the creature was hideous, and yet somehow, at the same moment, there was something dreadfully beautiful about it. For several seconds, the sight of it held him rooted to the spot—until one of the tentacles splashed his entire right arm, from wrist to shoulder and up the side of his neck, with burning fuel. He dropped to the deck and rolled, trying to smother the flames—and he had almost succeeded when his left leg got splashed and also began to burn.

Lieutenant Tucker was quickly at Tom's side, clutching his left arm by the wrist and trying to drag him away from the angry, burning masses of cephalopod flesh. But Tom's leg was beginning to burn deep and he reached down with his sizzling free hand and tried to put out the flames.

"Oh—God, I'm burning up! Damn it! I'm on fire! *Fire!*"

Tom discovered too late that they must have heard him on the other side of the *Intrepid*'s island stack. Sometimes all that was necessary to create a swerve of history was for a single gunner to misunderstand and react a second too quickly—while knowing that a mere second's hesitation could bring death raining down upon hundreds of his fellow seamen—if he did not track the Russian jet and stand ready to pull the trigger the instant he heard the call to fire. The response of the other gunners to one man's burst of gunfire was a chain reaction.

The sky lit up with tracer rounds. Tom did not see the creatures fleeing over the port side, and he was only vaguely aware of men throwing fire blankets over him, and of shock beginning to take over. All he could think about was the sky, and the jets in it. *Oh my God! I've just started a war with Russia*, he told himself. And then his Irish sense of gallows humor kicked in. *Oh, to think my department chair at Columbia said I'd never accomplish anything significant.*

July 10, 1948
In Russian-Dominated Skies

SANTORINI PROTECTORATE

Valentina leveled out just above the clouds and was preparing to circle around for reconnaissance when Andrei confirmed that they had optimal amounts of fuel remaining. She banked east and the Fighting I was coming easily into view— with Valentina's cameras rolling—and then, from more than six thousand feet below, tracer fire began to fill her sky.

Valentina punched her set of still-experimental afterburners up to full power and used all of her thrust-vector capability to scoot horizontally as the storm of lead and sparks fell suddenly behind the gunners' tracking abilities. She would have thrown her head back in triumph if the G-forces had not already done so for her. Valentina knew she was going to live, at least for a little while, thanks to well-honed flying skills combined with the great good fortune that the gunners below seemed never to have trained against this maneuver. The tracer fire suddenly died away, as if each gunner had instantly run through his "whole nine yards" of ammunition in a moment of panic.

Glancing down and to her right, Valentina saw a parachute blooming amid smoke, meaning that Andrei would soon be taken prisoner, if he survived. *Now, if only my blood pressure and reflexes are strong enough to keep me conscious through the next sharp turn, the stories I will be able to tell! No jet plane ever took on an aircraft carrier before. . . .* But she had been slowing to a photo-recon approach when the shooting began and her plane, though powered by the newest jet engines to come off the assembly line, was still subsonic. Maneuverability and engines were just not designed to kick her out of harm's way fast enough—not because the plane could not withstand the acceleration and hairpin turns, but because human bodies could not.

Two Hellcat fighters were coming up to meet her—*They're slower, only prop-driven, with maybe a little more freedom to make sudden dives and turns, but I've got speed and my country and anger on my side.*

The lead fighter engaged—whether in a short burst of warning fire or in an actual attempt to kill her, Valentina did not know, or care. Eleven seconds later, an American was bailing out and his plane's engine was tearing itself apart.

"Going to live through this," she breathed with relief, after outmaneuvering another spray of lead and leveling out above the cloud tops. The after-burners were spent and shut down but the pilot thought herself lucky to still be taking in air and flying a plane that seemed to be operating—at slacking power but operating nonetheless—until she made the mistake of banking to starboard in preparation for another pass, to assess what was happening to Andrei. That was the moment in which the turbine began to sound like an old vacuum cleaner trying to pick up chunks of taffy, and she made the additional error of trying to throttle up. Hellcat bullet fragments—laying in wait like clots in a vein—were sucked right through the heart of the engine and spun about, producing new and instantly turbine-killing shreds of metal.

The plane died in Valentina's hands.

Like Andrei and every other good fighter pilot in her squadron, she had planned for this possibility, planned for the day she might go down in a bad place and need to keep a coveted piece of new technology secret.

Flaps up, nose down, Valentina aimed for the darkest, deepest patch of water she could recall from the pre-sortie maps. Then she drew in her knees until they hurt, in preparation for punch-out. Her commanders understood how the great turning of the last war, against Japan's favor, had occurred at Midway with the loss of Imperial Japan's most skilled pilots. The Kremlin had studied this outcome and learned its key lesson. Valentina therefore knew that the ejection system would work, for even in this circumstance, the pilot was valued more than the plane. Her main physical worry was the instrument panel: if her legs were not drawn in to the point of maximum endurance, the panel would scoop out her kneecaps the moment the ejection booster ignited.

The next worry was striking the cockpit canopy only one small sliver of a second after it, too, was ejected—which in this case, nose down and in a dive toward dark water, was not even close to actually happening.

Once the seat was safely away and the parachute deployed, her next, less physical worry came to the fore. Valentina watched the plane hit the water like a snowball striking concrete. *Even if they can dive down to find it, there's not enough left for anyone to piece together.*

So far, so good, she said to herself, in the American vernacular. Now her worry was capture. The pilot had taken "deep-wire" hypnosis training—by which she was sure to keep the plane's secrets, even if "friendly" Americans plied her with unimaginable amounts of vodka.

Below she saw Andrei being fished out of the water by one of the carrier's escort ships. Another rescue crew was approaching a second chute floating, but the Hellcat pilot seemed MIA.

That's sure to complicate any prisoner exchange, Valentina thought, and then thought she saw something large moving away from the carrier's side.

She did not know how to describe it, beyond a general feeling that the sea looked strange.

July 10, 1948
Aircraft Carrier Intrepid

FIVE MILES OFFSHORE OF SANTORINI

Tucker believed he had reached the comms to the island stack in time for Christian to call a cease-fire and save the Russians—and hence everyone else.

But now it was all so clearly too late. A popular Hellcat pilot was missing and the two prisoners would be held 100 percent accountable.

Still . . . before both Russians were safely climbing rescue nets, the lieutenant had, like Valentina, spied something strange moving away from the *Intrepid*'s starboard side. Up until that moment, the cries of the burning monsters would be the one and only thing Tucker believed he could never get out of his head, or be able to adequately describe.

At first Tucker thought he was watching a great cloud rippling away, just beneath the surface. An iridescent green circle, the size of a bulkhead door, glowed balefully within the mist, like "ball lightning"—either an eye, or something trying to give the illusion of being an eye. Using the island stack for scale, the lieutenant estimated the length of the cloud—the "eye and the tentacles" at one end, the "tail" at the other—to be at least 175 feet. Yet at certain moments, as he gazed upon it, the thing seemed like many animals joining together to create the impression of being an individual of great size. At other moments he wondered if it was a single animal trying to look like many.

In either case, the overwhelming impression was that he had witnessed, at almost point-blank range, a huge octopus or squid.

July 4, 1874

LONDON TIMES

___

S inking of the Schooner *Pearl*, 150 Tons, James Floyd, master, with a crew of six. Latitude 8 degrees 50 minutes North, Longitude 85 degrees 05 minutes East.

The following strange story has been communicated to the Indian papers:

___

Passengers of the steamer Strathowen,
bound from Colombo, Ceylon:

___

"Our course was for Madras, steaming over a calm and tranquil sea. About an hour before sunset on the 10th of May we saw on our starboard beam a small schooner lying becalmed. There was nothing in her appearance or position to excite remark, but as we came up with her I lazily examined her with my binocular, and then noticed between us, but nearer, a long, low swelling on the sea—which, from its colour and shape, I took to be a bank of seaweed.

"Someone on the schooner fired a rifle at the object and it began to move.

"As I watched, the mass was set in motion. It struck the schooner, which visibly reeled, and then righted. Immediately afterwards, the masts swayed sideways and I could discern the enormous mass and the hull of the schooner coalescing—I can think of no other term. After the collision, the schooner's masts swayed towards us, lower and lower; the vessel was on her beam-ends, lay there for a few seconds, and disappeared, the masts righting as she sank.

"The object had squeezed on board between the fore and mainmast, pulling the vessel over and sinking it. Its body was as thick as the schooner and about half as long. Our steamer put out lifeboats and picked up five of the crew swimming in the water."

Captain James Floyd, regarding the Loss of the Pearl:

"A great mass rose about a half mile off our starboard side; it looked like the back of a whale, and it seemed to be basking in the sun. The creature shifted brown, the colour of seaweed, and drifted toward us. I fetched my rifle, but as it happened there was a Newfoundlander among the crew called Bill Darling who not only knew it was a giant squid, but also understood that bullets were ineffectual against such soft flesh and merely served to enrage.

"Tragic. I fired in any case and hit the target, and with that the animal shook; there was a great ripple all around him. The Newfoundlander shouted, 'Out with your axes and knives, and cut at any part of him that comes aboard! Look alive, boys—and Lord help us!'

"Not aware of the danger and never having seen or heard of such a monster, I gave no orders, and it was no use touching the helm or ropes to get out of the way. We were becalmed. There was no wind for our sails. I gave no orders.

"The Newfoundlander and two of my crew found axes, and one rusty cutlass, and all were looking over the ship's side—and in the time I have taken to write this far, the brute struck us. And the ship quivered. And in another movement, monstrous arms like trees seized our vessel and keeled her over to one side. In another second the monster was aboard, holding on between the two masts, and I heard a shout, 'Slash for your lives!' But all the slashing was to no avail. I caught sight of the Newfoundlander, Bill, squashed between the mainmast and one of those awful arms. And the brute, still gripping the two masts, slipped his vast body overboard, and pulled the vessel down with him."

CHAPTER 20

Anger, Denial, Acceptance

The nature of our future depends on the future of nature.
—Anonymous

Do you not realize that the sea has a life of its own? Tiny plants near the surface use the sunlight and make most of the oxygen we breathe. You must respect them. You must respect everything about the sea. It is the most precious thing we have. We need it to live, but it doesn't need us. The oceans and the Earth lived four and a half billion years without us.
—Jacques-Yves Cousteau

July 10, 1948
Dmitri's Overlook
Santorini

As Mac watched the smoke trails of three downed aircraft pulling apart in the wind, he discovered a level of anger and simultaneous hopelessness for which there were no words.

Dmitri seemed equally dumbstruck.

In this place, at this moment, silence suited Mac. *What's left*, he wondered, *for the damned to say to the damned?*

Throughout the oppressively humid air, and detectable only as radio waves, the *Intrepid*'s voice thundered. Captain Christian had ordered his radio operator to send a message—uncoded, in both English and Russian:

AMERICAN FLEET TO USSR FLEET. THESE ISLANDS AND THEIR PEOPLE ARE UNDER PROTECTION OF THE UNITED STATES NAVY. ANY FURTHER ACTS OF AGGRESSION ON YOUR PART WILL RE-SULT IN IMMEDIATE AND OVERWHELM-ING RETALIATORY RESPONSE.

—CAPTAIN USS INTREPID

The captain of the *Kursk*, referring to the *Intrepid*'s downing of two Russian reconnaissance planes, sent essentially the same message.

Each was trying to say to the other, *Get off my back!*

"I'm guessing," Mac said at last, "that this is not a good time to suggest you'd be welcome to join our side."

"*What?*"

MacCready's eyes narrowed. "Surely you know where you stand."

"Defection? How can you believe this is over?"

Mac looked out to sea without answering.

"Yes. The aircraft carrier. And maybe it's armed with something to turn this whole island into an oven. I've read about a man who faced an entire civilization that prided itself on being more highly cultured and more technologically advanced. Moses phoned in enough power to part the Red Sea, and win. So, never underestimate a man when you believe you have backed him into a corner."

"Or when he wants his people to be free."

Dmitri allowed a faint smile toward the American. "You, the microbiologist, and your friend who talks to the animals would be valuable assets, if we let you live. So, why don't *you* flip sides?"

"Not on your life."

"Then you understand me."

"Not really. First, you jump in at least twice, trying to save me and Yanni—then you capture us. Why bother to save us at all? What? Out of the kindness of your heart?"

"Oh, Captain MacCready. I can assure you that kindness has nothing to do with it."

July 10, 1948
Aboard the NR-3

SOUTHWEST OF SANTORINI

_____

The two overhead explosions were so powerful that Walter found it difficult to believe

Corning's huge cockpit windows managed to hold together. Both shells had come down nearly halfway below the surface before detonating. The second blast-and-implosion briefly lifted the *NR-3* entirely off the seabed, with a sharp yank to her stern.

Simultaneously grateful and surprised to be alive, Walter was equally relieved that the reactor crew in the aft compartment was able to completely restore power within only three minutes of the attack. No water came in. All of the shock-resistant wiring supports held strong, and Walter's equipment was easily brought back to life.

The captain and his copilot had no sooner finished the restart checklist of the sub's controls when Walter became distracted by something outside. Neither pilot noticed the distraction, for they were both craning their necks back toward the flight engineer's seat.

"Hey, *Professor*," the copilot had barked. "How the hell'd they find us? And why *shoot* at us? For all they know, we could retaliate with a nuclear torpedo!"

"I hope you gentlemen will be happy to know we're still mission-ready," Walter replied, "because I don't believe they have any idea we're around."

"How's that?"

"It's just a matter of us being too near that shipwreck—wrong place, wrong time."

"Then why would they shoot at the wreck?"

"I think because the wreck was attracting *other* visitors," the OSS veteran said, and nodded toward the objects that had distracted him.

Up front, cockpit switches were flipped and two floodlamps blazed to life, more fully illuminating the undersea landscape ahead. Minds, too, were illuminated.

Both pilots and one commando had uttered the same words: "Holy shit."

"Well, there's something else you won't see every day," Walter responded. His sense of wonder seized control, bringing with it a sense of excitement that immediately dried out his throat and forced him to hold back a sudden urge to step away from the flight engineer's seat and use the cabin's toilet.

Enormous "snakes" and cephalopod body parts were drifting down from the surface. Tentacles coiled and uncoiled spasmodically, yet landed with the gentleness of snow on a windless night.

One of the creatures, about the size of a bear, had settled to the bottom intact but apparently stunned.

"There you have it," Walter said grinning. "Some new kind of octopus."

At precisely that moment, the cephalopod appeared to snap from semiconscious to fully alert, and tried to camouflage itself as a nub of rock or coral. For a few seconds, it had overwhelmed Walter's listening devices with rapid-fire clicking sounds, crowding out the loud cavitations from the approach of *Intrepid*'s propellers.

They watched for a very long time as the "rock" shifted its shape and color to something unfamiliar, and then to seabed rock again, all the while surrounded by pieces of its brethren—which continued to wiggle and twitch. In between the occasional chorus of clicking barbs, and return signals from others in multiple directions, the flight engineer's station had recorded the vibrations of *Intrepid* and its escorts slowing down, followed shortly thereafter by three aircraft, one after another, impacting the sea surface and bursting apart.

"Sounds like Okinawa's beginning to happen up there," the captain said.

Walter winced at the thought, but he could not speak. The cephalopod chorus had resumed, more intensely than before. He turned up the volume ever so slightly so the pilots and the half-dozen commandos could hear more clearly the patterns he was detecting.

"Is that communication?" someone asked.

"I think so," Walter answered. "Something like dolphin-speak, and maybe every bit as complex."

Just as quickly as the chorus arose, it died away. Outside, Walter's strange "new kind of octopus" flickered like a cloud of dazzling blue diamonds, then faded to match its background—faded to near-perfect invisibility.

They all simply watched. What they had just heard and seen left them too astonished to articulate with words. They could do little more than breathe.

Walter broke the spell, coming to the same conclusion as others before him. "Say what you may, but that took real brain power. These things are smarter than hell."

"Is that why the Russians opened fire on them?" the captain asked.

"I have no idea."

"Makes no sense," the copilot said.

"I know. Our amazing Technicolor visitor out there *looks* harmless enough."

"It's just sitting and watching," the captain acknowledged softly—moments before his left shoulder was slammed against the port-side wall of see-through Corning.

Something huge—striking home with even more violence than the two explosions—rolled the *NR-3* completely onto its port side. Walter's seat held him bolted to the floor while a second ramming attack had him bracing for the sub to be turned belly-up, on top of her conning tower and periscopes. He heard unintelligible intercom calls from the reactor compartment, and something like pistons failing and shooting their rods. The two men in the cockpit calmly regained control and pumped up to positive buoyancy. Then, with agonizing sluggishness, the sub began to right itself. Carefully, degree by degree and foot by foot, the captain and his copilot reached an almost comfortable port-side list of ten degrees, and three degrees down-bubble. And there they hovered, twenty feet above the seafloor.

"We're venting something," the captain said.

Wisps of black dust and yellow fluid drifted across their forward view, triggering the cockpit's external chemical hazard detector. Seconds later, an external Geiger counter chimed in. Beyond the wispy fluid, spread across the beams of both search lamps and flaring out its tentacles, was a new cephalopod that appeared to measure at least the length and mass of the sub.

The giant rose from the bottom and hung poised for several moments, displaying for the crew its many suckers—and then, slowly at first, it backed away from the venting poisons. After a pause, it shot off and vanished behind swirls of ink and seabed muck.

Below, the smaller creature reappeared, then it too retreated in a blur of motion and billows of muck.

The captain was already on the comms to the engine room. "Mount Elija, are you okay back there?"

"Fucking far from okay," replied a calm voice. "John, we've had a problem here."

"How bad?"

"Under control now. Eighty-percent power. We had to pump out and cool down, but we've got to keep this end of the boat completely sealed. Permanently, I'm afraid. Filters are pulling most of the particulates from the air and flushing them outside but no matter how we cut it, our bodies are going to be taking ten rads per hour."

Walter ran the numbers quickly through his head. They all did. If they surfaced and quickly abandoned ship, everyone, including the engine crew, was guaranteed to survive. If they continued the mission, then more than ten hours remained before the sun was down and the night became dark enough for their mission plan. This meant a dose, to the four men in the aft compartment, of more than one hundred rads. The average man could survive such exposure. But thirty hours and three hundred rads later, half of them could expect to be dead within two weeks and they would already be getting sick. Twenty hours after that, crossing over six hundred rads, almost no one survives.

"It's a given that we can't abandon the sub and leave it for the Russians to find," Elija continued. "We'll be well enough back here for a day or so. Your compartment's still clean. So you go ahead, and do the rescue. We'll stay on post and when you come back, we can safely evacuate you and the rescued to one of our ships. After you're all out, we'll come forward and take the controls."

"What then?" the captain asked.

"Depends on time. If we're getting really sick by then, we'll take her to the deepest part of Santorini's lagoon. If, as my math predicts, we're sick but still holding up well enough, we'll have almost a day to maneuver around Crete and make the Devil's Hole. It's deep there—well below our crush depth. It'll be quick."

Walter watched as Captain "John"—who now for the first time became known by a name—held the mike uncomfortably, reflected on what he'd just heard, and replied, "Understood."

"So, your MacCready rescue plan is still on," said Elija. "We'll stay back here and work it for as long as we can. But you need to move quickly. Looks like the atom won this round."

"Is . . . Is there anything I can do?"

"The *mission* is what you can do. Hope it really counts for something in the end."

"Why shouldn't it, Elija?"

"Read your history and biology. The plagues and the years without summer that finally killed Rome. The Black Death. Krakatoa, the Dust Bowl. And now the micro-universe of the atom. Nature always wins in the end."

"Elija?"

"Enough of this. We've got a job to do. Get on with it. Even if only for a little while, make it count. Elija out."

After a long silence, the captain landed on the seabed. He double-checked the course he had charted, and circled one of the penciled-in spots on a map in red. "That's our landing spot," he called back to his crew. "I'll put us just offshore of where those towers of white rock break the surface. The waves hitting them make plenty of noise to cover our tracks."

"Should I prepare a music box?" Walter suggested.

"Yes. Just in case our carrier's crew have any ideas that could make things worse—best to let them know we're here, and still alive."

The music box worked exactly as the name suggested. Pins on a roller, with only ten minutes of programming effort required, would send out any desired Morse signal, at regular intervals—in this case, simply "Raccoon." After torpedoing to the surface and motoring away from the *NR-3* dispatch point, the little transmitter would send its message—meaningless to the Russians, but telling the American fleet that an extraction crew was still mission-active.

Six hours and sixty rads after the message went out, *NR-3* approached the shallows, with only two hundred yards to go before egress. Fortunately, the large cephalopods seemed to be avoiding them—or, rather, their venting poisons. Perhaps not as fortunately, Walter, Captain John, and the commandos would be paddling ashore in very low light, with the moon in only its third night as a waxing crescent.

Walter thought about the men in the engine room—that such people always seemed to step forward in the worst of times. Because of their choice, they had at most two days left between the margin of the living and the dead. But he expected that he would probably die ahead of them.

The rest of the landing crew clearly had similar expectations, but as Elija had said, "We've got a job to do."

Normally they would have infiltrated a city or a town dressed as dockworkers or cab drivers. But Santorini had too small a population in which to blend. Though the island had "only hotels in town" aplenty, there were no taxicabs. Tonight they would dress strictly practical.

No matter how hard he tried to project a confident sense of calm, Walter always felt awkward donning bullet-resistant flack gear and weapons. Captain John seemed to sense the emotions Walter was trying to hide and forced a reassuring smile in his direction. But there was no room for smiling or reassurance this evening.

Elija is right, Walter concluded. *Nature always wins in the end.*

July 10, 1948
10:00 P.M.
Inside Captured MacCready Base Camp #3

SANTORINI

There was no doubt in Mac's mind that the Russian reinforcements who had come ashore were, like Dmitri, members of an elite fighting group trained in every shade of the combat spectrum, from arctic to urban warfare. He noticed that the faces of no fewer than three of these men bore distinctive patterns of shrapnel scars, known since the war as "German kisses." If there was any doubt in Mac's mind that Dmitri's comrades were fearless of their own mortality, the wounds of Cherkassy, Kursk, and Stalingrad removed it.

There were enough of these men, Mac supposed, to form a double-layered perimeter outside the compound.

Dmitri seemed very, very confident in the outcome. He approached Mac and Yanni with a concave aluminum dish attached to a battery and a miniature siren. "No harm in telling you that this is a motion detector," he said. "We now have the whole perimeter covered. Anything American or cephalopod comes near, and we'll know."

"Nice piece of technology," Mac acknowledged.

"Yes. Not bad, eh? Not bad for a people you Yanks probably regard as uninventive barbarians."

"Quite a kill zone you're building," said Yanni.

"It's good to kill sometimes, no? I see it in your

eyes—both of you." Dmitri looked Yanni up and down. "Sometimes the killing is very special and then it's better than a beautiful woman wanting you."

One of the other prisoners laughed. Another winced. Nesbitt called from across the room: "Pretty strange talk from a man who likes to quote the Bible. Ever heard that part about 'Thou shalt *not* kill'?"

"No. Because in the original Hebrew, it says, 'Thou shalt not commit murder.' Did you ever read the rules given to Joshua before he killed all of Jericho? Even he was allowed to cleanse himself of killing in warfare. And when it comes to the Kraken? That's not murder. That's not even an unclean kill." Dmitri returned his attention to Mac. "And certainly your aircraft carrier is not out there for mere decoration. What would be the plan of the men who hold your leash? Fire a torpedo with an atom bomb in it, at our ships? Turn this place into another Bikini Atoll?"

"You think that's a plan?"

"Not a good one, for anything more than a threat—a bluff. What would you succeed at if you used it? Kill ten thousand Greeks on this island to get rid of a few ships? That would equal six times as many as you Americans lost at Pearl Harbor. And look how that ended, for Japan. The world will never stand by silently if you use A-bombs in anger a second time."

"You seem to have figured it all out, except for the fact that the sea around us has thrown a monkey wrench into—"

A siren stopped Mac. Loud and clear in the night, one alarm—and then two, and then four more of the motion detectors shrieked and wailed. Moment Zero came upon them. The Russians and their captives knew the meaning of the wails without being told: someone or something was rushing the perimeter from multiple directions.

From the rooftop of Mac's imprisoned encampment there came a sudden loud hiss, deep and hollow, as if something were boring through the air at high speed. Almost simultaneously there came a quick, guttural thud from the direction of the overlook on which they had watched the *Intrepid*'s arrival. A second hiss and thud followed—then a third, then two more, and as the night began to brighten with fire, Dmitri uncuffed Mac and Yanni.

He looked each in the eye and said, "Stay close to me. Say nothing. Understand?"

"Yes."

July 10, 1948
10:00 P.M., *Five Minutes Before Moment Zero Ashore on Santorini, Fifty Yards From the South Perimeter*

MacCready Base Camp #3

Your name, son?" Captain John had asked. At this kind of time, Walter did see a measure of good sense in being known by something other than "flight engineer" or "T070." It seemed clear enough that any of them could look either to the man next to him, or to himself, and be reasonably certain that in ten or fifteen minutes, one of them would no longer be alive.

"Call me Wally," he said.

"Real name?"

"Close enough."

"Call me Matthew," whispered the commando at his side.

"Mark," said another.

"Call me Luke."

"Peter."

"And before you ask," said Captain John, "I'm not John the Baptist."

The last two commandos did not give pseudonyms. One was silenced by a speed-slung disk of copper. As perimeter sirens blazed to life and explosive charges began rocketing out from the compound's roof, a second man was slashed and carried away.

The monsters would easily have taken the entire team—probably in less than a minute, Walter supposed—if not for the firing from the compound. The essentially random explosions were followed by distracting flashes from the creatures themselves, rendered all the more confusing by how quickly the cephalopods adapted to mimicking—on their skin, and sometimes in synchronized groups—the detonation flashes of Russian shells landing on the ground.

A mimic flashed out pallid yellow and faded to red sparks, no more than ten yards to Walter's right. He sensed something much darker and nearer and fired two shots into it. Then he hit the other, just as it went completely dark. To judge from what he knew of cephalopods, he supposed one or two bullets could not kill either of his attackers—*but at least it will give them something to think about.*

"If we ever get out of this alive," Walter said to no one in particular, "I'm quitting the deep submergence program."

"Me too," said a voice in the night. It was the captain.

The first wave of cephalopod infiltrators came onto the rooftop battlements within the shadows of detonation flashes and mimicked flashes.

Behind the makeshift battlements, two Russian commandos were carefully selecting targets among the wailing motion sensors and firing upon them. One of the commandos glanced around and halted suddenly. He listened, and died.

"What did you—?" his comrade began to say, when a Kraken embraced him from behind and, with multiple whipping snaps of its arms, began to dissect him. With a defiant whipping and snapping motion of his own, as something ropy and sharp wiggled down between the muscles and bones of one arm, he tried to end it for both of them but misfired. His wrist sent an explosive charge rocketing into the floor of the battlement.

Alan's first real indication of the human-Kraken struggle taking place overhead was a sudden push from behind, as if a giant's hand

had slapped him across the back. Along with Mc-
Queen and two others from Nesbitt's Catalina
crew, he was slapped from one side of the room to
another, with such power that the chairs to which
they had been restrained came apart, along with
the restraints. It was a strange rule of nature, but
a rule nonetheless, that human bodies tended to
fare better during explosive events than man-
made buildings and their furnishings.

When Alan sat up, he saw that, inexplicably,
he and McQueen were free and uninjured. The
room, what was left of it, was being illuminated
by the fierce orange glow of a fire that burned
not more than twenty or thirty feet away. Half of
the ceiling was gone. The wall toward which he
and the three Catalina crewmen were flung had
crumpled and come apart like rice paper. Alan noticed that McQueen and a man whose name was
unknown to him landed with their bodies halfway
into the next room.

The fourth man was not so lucky. A section of
wall had toppled onto his back, carrying with it a
slab of rebar and cement roofing that pinned his
chest to the ground. There would have been no
point in trying to free him, even though new explosions and a fire nearby were clear and present
dangers. The widest space between the roof slab
and the ceramic floor tiles was too small for Alan
to force his fingers through for leverage, much less
accommodate the width of a still-beating heart.

Directly ahead, on the other side of the crumpled wall, Cousteau and Boulle struggled in their
restraints. Alan helped McQueen to his feet

and entered the room cautiously. There were no guards. Their captors had more pressing concerns. A new explosion rattled the building and brought more pieces falling from the ceiling. Two bursts of machine gun fire followed—incoming from somewhere beyond the sentry perimeters. A handful of bullets and at least two tracer shots came in through the room's now-missing window, raking the ceiling.

"What the *hell*? Who are they fighting?" McQueen asked.

"Rescue?" Cousteau guessed.

Alan wondered why a landing party, during a mission that required stealth, would have brought a bulky machine gun, equipped with location-revealing tracers. *And why would they be firing toward us?*

He recalled a famous saying from World War II: *When the Chinese began shooting, the Japanese ducked. When the Japanese started shooting, the Chinese and the Americans ducked. When the Americans started shooting, everyone ducked.*

"I don't know, guys," Alan said at last. "I think it's a trick."

"What kind of trick?"

"We are being ambushed. Maybe we have finally managed to get the Greeks angry."

Pierre Boulle shook his head sadly and began creeping toward the space where the window had been.

"I wouldn't do that," commanded a Russian-accented voice. Dmitri arrived with Mac, Yanni, and Nesbitt in tow. Alan was relieved to see that two more of his friends were alive and uninjured.

Dmitri went to the window space. "Dawn's too many hours away," he observed. "Long night ahead. Kraken out there."

Another burst of machine gun fire, lasting no more than a split second, thudded through human flesh at the inner perimeter.

"Sounds like a Browning," the Russian said. "You thinking what I'm thinking?"

"I should hope not," Yanni replied.

Dmitri raised his head to the window again and gazed out toward the horizon. "'Yea, though I walk through the valley of the shadow of death, I shall fear no evil'—"

"Hey!" Yanni interrupted. "Hold that thought, will ya?"

July 10, 1948, Five Minutes after Moment Zero
Aircraft Carrier Intrepid

FIVE MILES OFFSHORE OF SANTORINI

Captain Christian and Lieutenant Tucker watched through binoculars, trying to make sense of what was happening near Akrotiri.

The flashes ceased, then started again, then ceased for more than a minute.

"MacCready and Nesbitt are sure to be somewhere in the middle of that," the captain said, "if they're still alive."

"Any signal from Nesbitt?"

The captain shook his head. "Nothing at all. Either it's not necessary yet or the extraction has worked. Or she's dead."

Four tracer rounds went out over the rooftops of Akrotiri.

"Are we going to send in planes?" Tucker asked.

"Bomb them in the night and let God sort them out, is not what we're here for. Hopefully, after the shooting is over, we'll get another signal from the Raccoon-jump crew—whoever they are."

"And whatever they rode in on."

"Yes—yes," Christian said. He stepped back from the rail. "Whoever they are, it's Truman who assigned them, probably before MacArthur assigned us. And there's one more thing in that regard."

"Which is?"

"MacArthur hasn't relinquished his priority here. But in their communications, the Russians are going a bit crazy about us. So, Washington's bound to know any minute." Captain Christian exhaled a sigh of relief. "Very soon, I expect we'll be under Truman's protocol."

"Support Raccoon-jump?"

More tracer fire went up near Akrotiri, silent across the intervening miles. Captain Christian had posted extra sentries, equipping some with flamethrowers. On a flight deck, this was always last-resort equipment. He hoped the creatures Tucker had burned off the deck were not part of the fight on Santorini. The Russians were challenging enough.

"Support the Raccoon team—yes," Christian said. "If there's anything left of it at dawn." He raised his binoculars and studied the fires emerging around the battle. "Meanwhile," he continued, "anything new from our two Russian pilots?"

"Same old same old. Nothing but name and rank—with many reminders about the Geneva Convention and the treatment of officers. They seem to be under the impression that there's some sort of prisoner exchange coming—like, as if they knew something before they ever took off."

"That may not be far off the mark. It seems something major has happened back home. Some sort of spy-ring roundup. Whether or not we keep any captured Russians may depend on which of our people are still alive on that island in the morning."

"And if Nesbitt sends out a call to bomb her?"

"I'm certain MacArthur would want her, and those near her, dead," Christian replied. "But I'm just as certain that she has zero knowledge about us having these two pilots—and, from the sound of it, a serious collection of other Russian prisoners back home, valuable enough for an exchange."

"But if she calls, do we send in the Hellcats?"

The captain looked toward the distant fires, watched for a few seconds, and shrugged. "I guess we'll just have to see."

July 10, 1948
10:12 P.M., *Seven Minutes after Moment Zero*
Two Miles North of Santorini

ABOARD THE *KURSK*

From this perspective, the sheer cliffs rimming the lagoon blocked Trofim Lysenko's view of the downslope toward Akrotiri, nearly ten miles away. The only information that came through was a short breach of radio silence—with a very businesslike voice announcing an attack, followed by reflections in the sky of flashes on the ground.

The single Kraken in the *Kursk*'s tank sounded suddenly like a whole nest of rattlesnakes, but the scientist knew better than to try silencing it with a spear or a pike—and besides, he needed to bring the animal home alive (along with a yet-to-be-obtained sample of the living *moctus proctus*).

Lysenko joined his captain on the bridge and paced with aggravated impatience, awaiting news from the captured MacCready compound, trying to decide if they should plot a course to a landing position near Akrotiri. But that would place them on the far side of Santorini, almost within shouting distance of the American aircraft carrier.

No, that will not serve us, Lysenko told himself. *Our mission is to capture the red miracle and anything associated with it.*

"Orders?" the captain asked.

"Take us ahead slow, one mile. Then into the lagoon."

The captain passed the order down, along with an order of his own: an open hatch on the forecastle needed to be closed, because it was leaking red light from below and he wanted the way ahead to be completely black, to avoid missing even the faintest bioluminescent flash from a Kraken.

The path was clear.

Even light from the town of Fira, high above the forward port side, provided no more distracting glimmers than a cluster of stars. Fortunately, most of the town did not even have electricity.

Two small tankers now joined the *Kursk* and its support ships. Their holds had been topped off with poisons ranging from ordinary detergent to powdered aluminum and sodium hydroxide.

Lysenko squinted into the darkness, his eyes sweeping slowly. The surface of the lagoon was dead calm, the water black as oil, except for reflected stars. The reflections winked and shimmered in summer's thick humid air, but there was not a hint of bioluminescent commotion. Even the *Kursk*'s cephalopod captive seemed to be deciding on a strategy of silent running. Abruptly it had stopped sending forth clicks and rattles through the hull.

The expedition leader sensed instinctively, but could not know for sure, that several of the beasts were already attaching themselves, noiselessly, to the ship's hull.

His intuition was correct. The Kraken were suction-grappling and climbing the steel cliff of the starboard side, seeking ingress. A porthole's glass cracked under the pressure of suckers and barbs, and at the sound of it the creatures froze, blending even more skillfully into their immediate surroundings. A sentry dog whimpered inquisitively and padded over toward one side of the deck.

Trofim Lysenko was already on the wing bridge, making another careful circuit with his eyes and his ears. Nothing. He made another circuit, and another. Still uneasy, he leaned over the starboard rail. Five Kraken were directly in his field of vision, no more than sixty feet away. He did not notice them.

"You!" he called down to one of the dog handlers. "See anything? Hear anything?"

"No. But I think the dogs *smell* something."

Stronger than German shepherds, the *Kursk*'s canine sentries were Russian black terriers, each with a sense of smell many hundreds of times more sensitive than a man's. Two more of them went to the edge of the starboard side, whining. One opened its mouth to bark a warning when tendrils and sharpened copper whirled into his face, tongue, and throat—instantly cutting the bark down to a strangled moan.

The infiltrators were not fast enough for the next dog. It lunged and howled and bit deeply before it died.

Lysenko ran onto the bridge, hit the alarm, and in almost the same motion swung a floodlamp down at the blurry commotion below. Still within that same surge of motion, he was on the mike to the nearest tanker and breaking radio silence. "Soap-bomb it—*now!*"

The tanker, only ninety feet away, responded before the Kraken had time to move. It struck them squarely, as three additional sentry dogs came galloping in for the attack. The hoses from the support ship were capable of dousing all of them at up to seven hundred pounds per square inch. The detergent cocktail was immediately debilitating and even suffocating to octopuses and their kin, but relatively harmless to humans and dogs.

The Kraken fled over the side with a series of wails unlike anything Lysenko had heard before, or imagined he would ever hear. This did not stop him, or even give him pause. He pointed a search beam into the water and saw them trying to camouflage themselves, trying to escape, but their skin was now bleached pinkish-white and peeling apart, and they moved as if blinded.

The scientist was on the mike again. "Give them the aluminum bath!"

Two more hoses came to life—one jetting sodium hydroxide, the other delivering a slurry of aluminum silt. The two substances penetrated the sea surface and the wounded cephalopods, combining to make the water and the flesh of the Kraken erupt explosively, using only a simple chemistry found in an American cleaning agent called Drano.

By this time, at least a half-dozen Kraken were swimming up from below. Uninjured, they entered the toxic brew, clearly trying to pull their burned and dying brethren away from the danger.

"Give them another shot!" Lysenko commanded. "And do not go sparingly on the poison."

He did not know that essentially anyone who had been acquainted with him for more than a few months, and who heard this call, had the very same thought but dare not speak it.

Do not go sparingly on the poison, he had said. And Trofim Lysenko would never learn how many of those around him, including the captain, wished his mother had embraced that philosophy.

July 10, 1948
10:15 P.M., *Ten Minutes after Moment Zero*
Captured MacCready Base Camp #3

SANTORINI

Mac had long ago become accustomed to the fact that real firefights, unlike the versions in John Wayne movies, often had long lulls of nothing happening, punctuated by brief outbursts of evil. Sometimes the quiet parts were the worst parts. The periods of hyperalertness during the lulls burned up a lot of adrenaline, because one never truly knew whether the fighting had finally ceased and those still alive were victorious and safe, or whether a new surge of chaos was only a breath away.

Sometimes, just when the "all clear" seemed about to be called, the real trouble revealed itself.

This was one of those times.

The nearly five-minute lull that had followed Dmitri's prayer felt longer than any hour. It ended with a series of explosions, bringing with them a growing brightness that in its own turn brought heat—and strangest of all: in moments such as this, there was actually time for Mac to take notice of objects illuminated by the afterglow of an explosion, and even to be thinking how surreal it felt to be seeing and hearing everything during the second in which he threw himself protectively over Yanni's back. After the five-minute lull was broken, Mac's mind was so busy snatching up details and analyzing them in neurological overdrive that he lived fully in a netherworld of slowed time. A hatch from an autoclave and pieces of incubation equipment landed on the floor and he recognized, only in passing and with no sense of emotion, that a Russian microbiology lab must have blown apart nearby.

It never ceased to amaze Mac how quiet the peak moments of a disaster tended to be: Dmitri throwing his body over Nesbitt, Boulle over Cousteau, with nothing louder than a grunt. No one shouted. No one screamed. They simply acted and assessed and reacted.

The exterior wall failed—just yawned open—but Mac's battle-focused senses and reflexes responded quickly enough to detect a glint of metal and begin a full-body duck-and-compress-Yanni-into-the-ground maneuver—which, in that part of a second, amounted to mere inches gained, but which also made all the difference in the world for both of them. A whizzing disk of copper cut through hair and skin near the bottom of Mac's hairline, instead of gouging a path through the base of his skull.

Utter confusion. Too much was happening

and in too many directions. The view outdoors, through the blown-apart wall, made it difficult to avoid the impression that Russian commandos were firing on their own compound. Flashes of tracer fire were coming from the direction Mac believed to be the encampment's outer perimeter. Then came a new burst of yellow-orange light, knocking away more of the wall. Half of someone's leg flew in with pulverized masonry and landed near Yanni's shoulder. The tip of a Kraken limb, split almost wide open, still gripped the leg.

The dust in the air tasted of salt.

A new lull followed, during which Yanni's hand found two spoons in the dust and gravel. She began clicking them together in a rhythm that was by now all too hauntingly familiar to Mac.

Footsteps raced toward them from outside. One of Dmitri's men stumbled in and fell onto his back. The commando's face was untouched but the rest of his body had been horribly mutilated by an explosion, or by Kraken, or by both.

Two more Russians ran in behind the dying man—uninjured. A flurry of barked orders followed them and three commandos entered the ruin with two American submariners taken prisoner.

By Mac's assessment, the Russians were still a coordinated unit despite the outbursts of full-on chaos. They were "mopping up" during a lull that seemed likely, this time, to be long-lasting.

One commando kicked the two spoons out of Yanni's hand and another pointed a gun at Mac.

Behind them, Nora Nesbitt had found a paper clip, straightened it out, and was now digging around in her mouth as if suddenly in desperate need to be using a toothpick.

What the hell is she up to now? Mac wondered.

July 10, 1948
10:35 P.M., Thirty Minutes After Moment Zero
3:35 P.M., Eastern Standard Time

WASHINGTON, D.C.

───────────────────

The brief from Albert Einstein's conference on "The Future of War" could not have been more grim. Only a few of the signatories were familiar to President Truman, including atom bomb expert Luis Alvarez, rocket scientist Wernher von Braun, and futurist Arthur C. Clarke. All forty came from different and sometimes competing fields of science and engineering, but each of them agreed on what they had signed: a Russian atom bomb might be built sooner than anyone anticipated. And then, in less than a decade, the Soviet Union might be capable of mating the bomb with a rocket. "Mutual de-nuclearization" was the recommendation; but they noted that, looking to humanity's past as an intensely territorial animal, one could expect only the worst.

Einstein noted, "If only I had truly foreseen what applications lay hidden within my shortest equation, I'd have remained a violinist and designer of refrigerators."

Finally, even without the Russian threat, the forecast was for wars to grow worse because human populations were continuing to fractionate into antagonistic groups. And worst of all, the splitting groups would inevitably be unable to migrate away from each other, and would be forced against each other, border against hardening border, by population numbers that were beginning to surge across the earth at a frightening rate.

"Even with the agricultural Green Revolution now spreading from America across much of the world," the report said, "by the time our population reaches nine billion, we may suddenly see the planet's carrying capacity drop to only seven billion. When that happens, within the lifetimes of your own children (or your grandchildren at the very latest), we will face a human rights dilemma like none our species has ever seen. And the fight will go nuclear."

So, what are they trying to tell me? Truman asked himself. *That if we don't stop curing diseases, Rome falls?*

He placed the brief into a large envelope and was marking it to be classified when Bobby arrived outside the office door and asked, "Have you heard the latest?"

The president closed the envelope. "If it's more glad tidings of the sort I've just been reading, I'd prefer you keep it to yourself."

"Well, two things: Prisoner exchange plans are getting more complicated by the hour. And the Russians have come across our lost aircraft carrier."

"*Intrepid?*"

"Yes. We've now got two of Stalin's top pilots. They came in on jets."

"We shot them down?"

"They shot at us."

"Whoa! Damn it! Somebody's got a pair of brass ones."

Bobby eased into a wide chair opposite the president. "There's more. And you're not going to like it."

July 10, 1948
11:05 P.M., *One Hour after Moment Zero*

<small>*INTREPID*, FIVE MILES OFFSHORE OF SANTORINI</small>

Barely more than a half hour after transmission of the target beacon from Nesbitt's teeth, the location had been triangulated to the fires outside of Akrotiri. Lieutenant Tucker was now on deck, watching the final preflight check of three Hellcats and their bombs. *Americans assigned to dive-bomb Americans. What could be more horrible?*

The first plane's engine was already running, ready for taxying into place, when suddenly it cut off.

Reprieve? Tucker asked himself.

Christian stepped up beside him, holding a folded sheet of paper. "Looks like the Russkies nailed our extraction team," he said. "That means more prisoners. But on our side, not counting the two we've got in the brig, the word from Washington is that we've captured some definitely high-value spy-ring people back home."

"That word's from Washington, not Tokyo—not the general?"

"Yes. Washington. MacArthur's on his own in Japan right now. Whatever's going on between those two, the general has definitely backed off from this, *one hundred percent*. It's Truman's game, now—and Admiral Rickover's show."

Tucker's shoulders relaxed as the three planes stood down from *mission-ready* to *high state of preparedness*. "So, how do we play it?"

"Prisoner exchange. Washington wants Nesbitt most of all. In her case, it's as if the Russians have captured Einstein himself. Except that, were it Einstein, I don't think they'd be saying 'dead *or* alive.' They had the same priority for a guy who worked directly with her. His name was Hata, a Japanese."

"Was?"

"The Greeks located Nesbitt's initial campsite. They found a shallow grave there. There's a Japanese in it—probably Hata."

Tucker shook his head. "Sure wish I knew what she's up to that's so important."

"Knowing *that*, died a quick death for both of us before the question could even be asked. All I've been told is that she's some sort of biologist."

"More important than if Einstein was captured?"

"Yeah. We'll never know what they're looking for out there, but at a guess, the last war began drawing to a close with nightmares the chemists unleashed over Dresden and Tokyo. It finished up with nightmares the physicists created. Next time? Guess it'll be Nesbitt's field."

"You really think there'll be a next time?"

"Look around you," the captain said. "Below these very waters are a dozen ships from World War One. They called it 'the war to end all wars.'"

"Got it," the lieutenant said. "The number came later." He looked away toward the isle of Kea, where he knew history's largest hospital ship was sunk during World War I. *The number came later*, he thought again, and kept the next obvious conclusion to himself. Lieutenant Tucker suspected that Captain Christian—who believed that projecting power was the greatest hope that America had for preventing World War III— might not want to hear his thought voiced too loudly: *That it is not our mistakes which count against our survival, but the frequency with which we repeat those same mistakes.*

July 11, 1948
Sunrise

Santorini

R. J. MacCready imagined that negotiations between the White House and the Kremlin must have been growing quite intense.

Shortly after 2:00 A.M., a helicopter from the *Intrepid* had made the first, tentative prisoner exchange. As a practice run with ground flares for guidance, the exchange ran smoothly. The two Russian pilots were landed in trade for Alan and the two Frenchmen, but Cousteau insisted on remaining behind and McQueen was traded in his place.

Two hours later, Dmitri received radio confirmation about the successful departure from LaGuardia Airport of a plane carrying three midlist Russian agents who had been swept up in what was now becoming known as "the coin-boy incident." In exchange, Walter, Captain John, and another of Nesbitt's surviving Catalina crew were "freed for reassignment" to the *Intrepid*.

Mac appreciated the strategic blunder in the trade: the Russians did not know yet that either Walter or his captain would have been worth six of Stalin's A-list spies. Identified only by well-known aliases established during the war years, they were regarded as merely two surviving members of a thoroughly botched rescue attempt.

At 4:20 A.M., they were helicoptered away from the still-smoldering encampment.

An hour after that, a dozen more Russian agents were homeward bound from New York, in exchange for Nora Nesbitt.

Again Cousteau was offered his freedom and again he insisted on remaining behind.

"Damn you, Jacques—you should have gone when you had the chance."

"You are part of my crew, as I see it. And I will not leave while even one of you is still here."

"Thanks for the thought," Yanni said. "But this isn't exactly a sinking ship, Cap'."

Mac was not so sure of that. After the 4:20 A.M. helicopter lift-off, the suddenness with which the three remaining prisoners had been marched out of the base-camp ruin and down to a secluded cove could have meant only one thing: once Nesbitt was safely landed aboard the *Intrepid*, their luck ran out. Something, Mac supposed, had snagged the very last exchange negotiation in Washington.

Either that, or we're just not important enough for Team Washington to worry their little heads about.

Under cover of morning twilight, they had been hurried aboard a launch disquietingly similar to the one Mac and Yanni saw destroyed only six days before. This time the Russians were taking no chances. The launch followed an escort boat that hosed poisons into the water.

Now they stood handcuffed under heavy guard, among the jagged, reddish-black boulders of Nea Kameni's eastern shore. One could easily imagine that the surface of the moon looked something like this. Even where the sea, over dozens of centuries, had hewn solidified lava down into gravel and mineral-rich sand, nothing grew. Unlike most volcanic islands, "the New Burnt Land" failed to be colonized by birds, trees, insects, or even weeds. Surrounded by sea life, the islet was among the deadest places on earth. Mac hoped this biological anomaly would be enough to keep the Kraken away, at least until (*oh—another oh-so-cheery thought*) they were safely transferred to one of the floating gulags in the lagoon's north.

The Russians had plenty of poison but were clearly reluctant to drive into the red volcanic springs and spray the creatures that tended to congregate there, guarding the plumes. The "red miracle" was known to be biological, so Mac was not surprised to observe a certain degree of caution against poisoning the goose that lays the golden egg. He reasoned that if Dmitri had been around these island fragments long enough to acquire at least one or two good samples, they must have been burned or lost during the previous night's battle. *Why else*, he wondered, *would their ships still be prowling the lagoon, at such risk?*

Looking up, Mac saw a glint of metal and two contrails forming behind them, in absolute silence.

"More Russians," Cousteau said.

"Yes. Two more jets—at about twenty-five thousand feet."

As if in response, three brand-new Grumman Hellcats buzzed Nea Kameni, at no more than five hundred feet. By the time they rounded Therasia, buzzed the *Kursk*, and turned toward Fira, Dmitri was scrambling down from the direction of a dormant cinder cone.

"What the hell are your people doing?" the Russian demanded.

"How should we know?" Yanni answered. "You see us with a radio here?"

Mac looked north across the lagoon and saw that the *Kursk* and a support vessel had begun steaming toward them. He looked at Dmitri quizzically.

"Time's running out," Dmitri said. "One of your carrier's escort ships is parked outside the west inlet." He nodded toward a Russian ship armed with detergent, Drano, and nozzles. "But as you see, we have more experience than your people at puzzling out how to keep the Kraken from coming aboard."

Scarcely four miles away, one side of the *Kursk*'s hull was already being sprayed.

"Strange animals," Dmitri continued. "Last night, that escort tanker sprayed five of them and before they were all dead, about five or ten more of the beasts came rushing into the poison. It's as if they crave death."

"How can you so completely misunderstand what they were doing?" said Yanni. "These are not mindless beasts. *Rescue*. Got it? The lives of their own are precious to them. They are a lot like us. Maybe—maybe they're better than us."

At the same moment Yanni was explaining to Dmitri what she believed humanity had really awakened, the clock was touching midnight in Washington. A dangerous web was being unraveled, and it was moving the president to the edge of depression. The coin-boy incident had revealed a chain of command that led to infiltrators at Los Alamos and beyond. Hendry's and Bobby's people were still following the chain, breaking it and gathering new information as they went along. The news was, as Hendry had summed it up, "definitely ungood."

If only I could have ended up anywhere but here, Truman told himself. *If only I could have remained a simple businessman, in total ignorance of what's approaching, with just a few quiet years ahead, teaching my daughter how to play the piano.*

Wishing it were somehow possible to go backward in time, and erase knowledge, President

Truman returned a telephone receiver to its cradle, then shook his head, very slowly.

"Let Hendry take a team in there," Bobby pleaded.

"That's out of the question right now. He's been waiting to hop a plane out of Bethpage but now your guy Rubenstein's revelations mean it's too late for a new op to be of any help."

"My guy. Yes. Maybe Rubenstein *is* trying to make a name for himself. And maybe he was a little overzealous, but—"

"I understand," Truman said. "Necessary evil. We had to know. We had to verify."

Bobby shook his head for the third time in as many minutes. "I hope I never have to live through a night like this again." He took a swallow of coffee. "So that's it? That quickly?"

Truman wished it were not so. "We can't give that Los Alamos duo back to Stalin," he said. "We need to find out exactly how his people did it—how Russian scientists got so close, so fast, to making their own A-bomb."

"Leaving us now with less than a year! It's still hard to believe."

"That's not even for your friend McCarthy to hear, though it's a fair bet the whole world will know soon enough. They've already built their goddamned thing. Now it's just a matter of waiting for them to test-explode it."

"We were supposed to have at least another five years. How could no one have seen this coming?"

"Some did," the president said. "Einstein and von Braun's committee saw it but I really didn't believe them. Now I'm wondering if they were right about a lot of other creepy things."

"Such as?"

"Nuclear proliferation. Nuclear showdowns. Something they call the population bomb—double the number of people we have by 1990—then another doubling, more quickly next time. And after all the seas are strip-mined of their fish, a great humanitarian crisis—and all of this beginning during the lifetimes of your children. And they think that by then it'll be more than a dozen countries armed to the teeth with A-bombs."

"They could be wrong, you know?"

"They'd better be, Bobby! It used to be drunks or prophets or people in mental institutions who warned us about the end of days. But this time it's coming from those sane and sober men with the slide rules."

"They could *still* be wrong," Bobby said.

"They'd better be," the president said again. "Did you know that I once threw the leading scientist on the Manhattan Project out of this office?"

"Oppenheimer? Really? What did he do?"

"Nothing, really. And at the same time, maybe everything. He told me that science—with all these brave new weapons coming out of the labs—was finally discovering the unforgivable sin."

Bobby said nothing. He added two more sugar cubes to his coffee, sipped quietly, and winced as if it still tasted too bitter.

The president pushed a large white envelope across the desk. "You might as well have a read of it, before you leave. A great human change, they say."

"And now the biologists are sniffing around Santorini." Bobby hefted the envelope. "And the Russians have the A-bomb."

"I'm sorry that you and your children will be in the middle of it." Truman looked out the window. The bright lights along the White House lawn cast multiple shadows from each of the cherry trees. Their growth had been impressive these past three years. "Cherry pie," he said wistfully.

"What?"

"I was thinking of Oppenheimer—and about the Atomic Bombing Survey. He interviewed a child whose entire schoolhouse flew apart, killing almost everyone inside but leaving that one girl completely uninjured. The kid remembered seeing all the cherry trees along the river blossoming the previous spring. She remembered the smell of cherry sap. And she saw the orchards of Hiroshima aflame."

Bobby looked at him sympathetically. "You need to forget about that."

The president shook his head, very stubbornly. "She said it smelled like cherry pie."

July 11, 1948
7:10 A.M.

SOUTH OF SANTORINI

How's that for your ultimate weapon?" said Elija. They were poisoned, all four of the

NR-3's engine crew; but Elija was the only one who up until now had not been feeling sick. With the seal now open between the reactor room and the cockpit compartment, the radiation aft was diluted ever so slightly by the greater volume of air, but their situation remained "Look for me tomorrow and you shall find me a very grave man."

Elija hung his head in his hands and tried to distract himself from his first sudden onset of chills. A very tired young engineer named Thomas provided a much-appreciated shift of focus from what he knew was coming: *One minute you're fine. Then you feel sick. A minute after that, you really are sick.*

Thomas held out a decoded text. "This one's in reply to our music boxes—from the captain of the *Intrepid*. Looks like a change of plan."

The signal read: "Raccoon-jump primaries being wined and dined in Presidential Suite. Come to my Eye. Don't stub your big toe."

"What the hell's he getting at?" said Thomas. He was having some difficulty staying on his feet, so the signal seemed more cryptic to him than it should have.

Elija stared at him apologetically. "'My eye,' means the *Intrepid*. They appear to have already completed the rescue—at least the major part of it. President Truman knows about us. We're being asked not to sink ourselves in deep water but go to the carrier and prepare to take towlines."

Thomas looked at his acting captain hopefully. "So, we may live through this after all."

"We're not necessarily lethal yet. If we get there

in the next couple of hours and go through a thorough hose-down, we may have a good chance."

"Might work," another engineer said hopefully. "Ever since Bikini Atoll, our carriers have been prepped to handle radiation injuries—including Dr. Nagai's ideas about regenerative cells stored in newborns' umbilical cords. The Navy's been stocking and freezing those. Best experimental medicine in the world is being done aboard carriers."

"Yes," said Elija. "It's imperative that we pull anchor and get on board the 'Eye' as soon—"

The seabed under the *NR-3*'s treads shook. Elija knew immediately that this time the sub was not being shaken by a blast or by another large cephalopod. Confidence was high that the Russians did not know where they were, or even that the sub existed. As for the cephalopods, the same vapors of heavy metal that were poisoning the crew and being pumped outside seemed to be keeping the beasts at a distance.

This time the sea itself had lurched.

Elija prepared for pump-up to positive buoyancy, looked outside, and gasped.

"Now what?"

July 11, 1948
7:12 A.M.

NEA KAMENI

P*éter un plomb?*" Cousteau muttered.
    For all that was happening around them,

Mac could not hold back a grin. The French did not ask if someone was "going crazy." To them a crazy man was said to have "broken a fuse" in his head.

This seemed an apt description for the Hellcat pilot who, while likely "going off the reservation" and with no order to do so, had dove his plane down to hilltop altitude, fired warning shots across the bow of a Russian ship, then dropped a bomb nearby. For a second, all of Nea Kameni shook— and not just from the explosion. The magma pool beneath the lagoon seemed to be acting in reply to the bomb. The earth shook again, harder this time, and for at least five full seconds—as if in warning.

Two more Hellcats buzzed directly overhead. Both circled back, made another close approach, then hurried south, waggling their wings.

Yanni looked north and pointed out a Russian jet descending. "*Péter un plomb*, for sure! How many fuses are they planning on breaking today?"

"Damned if I know," Mac replied. "*Damned* if I know."

July 11, 1948
South of Santorini

DEPTH, 230 FEET

The avalanche had mostly bypassed the *NR-3*, but the underwater landscape ahead became so unrecognizable that the old charts now seemed useless. A layer of silt hung two feet off the sea-floor. Here and there, streamers of carbon dioxide and methane were bubbling up from somewhere far below. Except for vertical wisps of silt that trailed the bubbles toward the surface, the water was surprisingly clear.

The ancient stonework where they had placed the sono-buoys was gone, and in its place the rubble of an entire port had appeared: amphorae, the contents of warehouses and guesthouses—even an ornate terra-cotta bathtub. Before them, nearly half of a Bronze Age trireme lay amid up-thrust debris. The ship's freshly exposed wood and cargo were so amazingly intact that Elija immediately forgot the aches that had begun gnawing at his bones like a thousand little rat's teeth.

Gold glinted under *NR-3*'s lamps. Even through the veil of grayish silt-mist, they saw gold every-where amid the remains of the cross-sectioned ship.

"Looks like Eighteenth Dynasty," said Thomas, clearly excited to a point of forgetting his own aches and pains. "I'm guessing somewhere be-tween the time of Hatshepsut and Tut."

"The wood looks like it's been partly burned," said Elija. He moved in closer, unlocking the sub's robot arm.

"A dock fire, you think?"

"Maybe the volcano. Who knows?" Most of the golden glimmer appeared to be concentrated around a shattered and partly melted sarcophagus that in terms of sheer beauty must once have ri-valed the jewel-encrusted coffin of the child-king popularly known as "Tut." But this coffin was built for someone very robust, very tall. And instead of being decorated with Egyptian serpents and falcons, two marine animals were represented: a leviathan and a cephalopod. As he swept away charred and waterlogged wood, Elija began to believe the object more resembled a suit of armor than a coffin. The entire head came loose at the slightest touch of the robot arm. A masterpiece of thick gold and lapis inlay, the headpiece itself was the only nonmarine animal depicted.

"That could be either Egypt or Crete," said Thomas. "The sacred bull."

As Elija tried to secure the artifact—*a king's Egyptian death mask?*—splinters of bone began to avalanche out from the rest of the armor. They looked like pieces of a human skeleton and the rotted remnants of a beef stew mixed together. "Now, Thomas, why would a man and a bull share the same coffin?"

Before he could answer, another tremor threatened more avalanches. There was little time to waste, even if not for the possibility of the sub being marooned in the next surge of silt and debris.

Elija wished he could toss away some of the Russian papers that filled the sample basket and make room for this new treasure. But the documents from the *Koresh* were a higher priority. So he pushed the golden bull's head against the top of the tray, locking down the robot arm with such force that one of the figure's ivory horns broke off. But the lockdown was secure, and Elija managed to keep the neck facing up, like the mouth of a jug. He hoped more of the strange bones lay inside the headpiece, and did not wish to spill out any of them. *The scientists will want to see this.*

They marked the position as best they could and ascended within ten feet of the surface. Radio signals were now coming in loud and clear, in three languages. Only one of them seemed really to matter:

MOUNT ELIJA, MOUNT ELIJA. ARE YOU RECEIVING? THIS IS THE EYE. PREP FOR NEW ORDERS. REPEAT. PREP FOR NEW ORDERS.

July 11, 1948
9:00 A.M.
Under American-Dominated Skies

SANTORINI PROTECTORATE,
ISLET OF NEA KAMENI

The aerial grandstanding seemed to have gone on forever. Even without the added stress of near misses overhead, thirst would *still* have been tearing at MacCready's throat. The peak of what promised to be another oppressive July afternoon was nearly four hours off, but already it was coming at them like a freight train. Today there was not even the whisper of a breeze, and the dark rocks of Nea Kameni's easternmost shore caught the rays of the sun and threw its heat back at the captives.

The dangerous farce of "playing chicken" in the sky could easily have ended in metal raining down upon the rocks—and it surely would have, if not for the skills of the pilots on both sides. Eventually the Russian jets ran low on fuel and headed north, but that provided only a brief respite.

The *Kursk* and its escorts had been approaching from Therasia scarcely faster than canoes. They were now poised only a quarter mile east of the red plumes, and were still occasionally spraying at something in the water, either real or imagined.

How long will it be till they run out of Kraken repellant? Mac wondered. As if in reply, the "spray boat" that had escorted their "prisoner transport" left the Nea Kameni shore and moved toward the plumes. *Doubtless to provide backup for one of the support tankers,* Mac thought. One of the tankers suddenly picked up speed and likewise steamed directly toward the plumes.

"I know exactly what you're thinking," Dmitri said, holstering his walkie-talkie. "But you should make a prayer for those ships, Captain Mac-Cready, because you're all going aboard. There's a scientist who wants to make an acquaintance with you . . . after he gets his samples." He paused and glanced south. Across the water, a helicopter was passing over the ruins of the Akrotiri base camp—approaching from the direction of *Intrepid*.

The earth shook again, hard enough to knock people over like bowling pins. When he hit the ground, one of the black rocks cut a gash along Mac's forehead.

"They're no use to us dead," Dmitri called out,

and ordered the prisoners' hands uncuffed, to give them at least a reasonable chance of holding their balance against the grumblings of Nea Kameni.

The submariner then motioned for two commandos to usher Yanni uphill with him. "I'm going to need her at my overlook on the plumes and their Kraken guardians. But don't worry, Mac-Cready. I can guarantee her safety."

As indeed he needs to, Mac thought. Whether or not kindness had anything to do with Dmitri's actions, he knew it was logical for the Russian to keep Yanni safe. No one besides her was better able to look down upon the lagoon and interpret every hint of where the Kraken were, and what they were doing.

Not that she's going to tell him the truth, Mac assured himself.

The *Intrepid*'s helicopter passed overhead, circled once, then made a beeline toward the *Kursk*. It buzzed the antennae and radar mast at such low altitude that had a crosswind struck, or had the pilot misjudged within a range of only two feet, pieces of rotor blades would have gone flying like guillotines into the ship's bridge and across its deck.

Mac shook his head. *Much more of this today and someone's bound to screw up badly.*

"They break a fuse!" Cousteau said.

"Exactly what I was thinking."

A pair of new and fully fueled Russian jets began circling the island—and a new swarm of Hellcats was already aloft before they arrived.

Dmitri and Yanni stopped climbing for a moment and looked around. Mac saw Yanni glance down at him, and he knew from the expression on her face that they were both having very much the same thought, as one of the Hellcats lost control in the slipstream of a Soviet jet: *Tell me this isn't the worst case of testosterone poisoning you've ever seen.*

The Hellcat dove below the cliffs of Fira Quarry halfway into a fatal spin and did not recover until it was within only two hundred feet of crashing into the lagoon. No one had ever observed a plane tipping and weaving in the vortex of a jet's wings before. It held Mac's attention for so many seconds that he did not notice the approach of a much larger plane until it was well within the boundaries of the lagoon—a B-17 Flying Fortress, coming in low and fast.

A second B-17 rounded the island fragment of Therasia in the north, flying below cliff-top altitude.

"What on earth?"

They had both been painted white, and their tails bore a hastily drawn copy of the insignia Mac had seen on Bishop Marinatos's helicopter.

"What did the bishop do?" Mac wondered aloud. "Did he go all the way up to the pope of the Greek Orthodox Church and get permission to send bombers after us?"

"I thought they were supposed to be nonviolent," Cousteau said, his voice on the very edge of being drowned out by engine noise.

"I've seen Alan kill, when he has to—and he's a Buddhist!"

"I asked him about that, with regard to Hata."

"And?"

"He said, 'I told you I'm a Buddhist. I never said I was a *good* Buddhist!'"

Mac did not hear this. The first plane was too near, and too loud—and it was dropping depth charges. The entire load followed a perfect arc over the masts of the Russian ships, directly into the red plumes.

Whatever instructions the Greeks had ferreted out of ancient prophetic texts, the bishop and his friends had evidently considered these against every clue revealed by Cousteau and anyone else who had been near the volcanic springs. The charges did not detonate until they went deep, no doubt calibrated to fall near and among the velvety red mats, on rock bottom. The second plane dropped its bombs along a more widely dispersed path—half of them missing the plumes and trailing all the way ashore and up to the volcanic cone.

The explosions felt like an insignificant series of guttural thuds, compared with what they could do. Awakened by human violence, nature responded—instantly—with violence of her own. Rocks and black dust laced with steam shot out of Nea Kameni's cinder cone in an up-rushing column that expanded hideously, drawing a curtain of smoke over the *Kursk* and its escorts.

Seconds before the veils of dust and ash hid the ships, Mac saw the sea itself exploding. Thick, oily billows rose from the place where the red plumes had been. The water in that direction boiled strangely, turning from red to black. Several Kraken floated to the surface, bleaching and dying amid the black geysers.

Overhead, the cloud from the volcano towered like a giant umbrella pine—at least five thousand feet tall and branching out. Mac realized that this was what Pliny the Elder must have seen, just before Pompeii disappeared from Roman maps.

"Yanni!"

Suddenly the whole earth seemed to be quaking and disintegrating. One of Mac and Cousteau's Russian guards disappeared beneath a dislodged boulder and another made a heroic but hopeless attempt to save the man. The rest chased after Mac as he scrabbled, stumbled, and leaped uphill toward an ever-widening chain of cracks that seemed to be spreading before him.

"Mac!" It was Yanni's voice. She was on the other side of the cracks—which were joining now to create a wider fissure. She called again through the terrestrial din and tried to make a run toward him, but Dmitri grabbed her forcefully by the wrist and cuffed her to himself.

The roar from the earth diminished to a low growl and through shifting sheets of hot mist, Mac watched a curious expression pass across Yanni's face—as if she had seen all of this before, and knew exactly what was about to happen.

One of the commandos reached him and was about to cuff him but Mac's reflexes were ever so slightly quicker and so he managed to pull away and wave. "Hey, Yanni."

"Mac . . ."

Up ahead, the fissure that separated them widened to more than thirty feet, then more than forty. Slowly, gracefully, and with surprisingly little noise—with the ease of a ship casting off from a pier—the slab of Nea Kameni on which Mac and Cousteau stood slid eastward.

"Mac, I—"

The ground dropped like an express elevator—twenty feet below sea level. All around, shock fronts forced back the sea. For what seemed like two full seconds, perhaps three or four, walls of water hovered at the edges, reminding Mac of that scene from the Bible when Moses parted the Red Sea. But today there was no such magic, and after only a few astonishing seconds of hovering, the sea closed in with a vengeance.

With uncanny rapidity, numbers were running through Cousteau's head. The walls of water were twenty feet high and were tumbling toward him as what were called "Hail Mary waves." An emergency ascent would be reasonably easy if he did not get smashed against rocks, with point-source impacts exceeding a thousand pounds per square inch. He immediately scrambled up the tallest nearby rock, realizing that he would be struck first by the wall in the north and could set himself up intentionally to be flung laterally, with the lowest probability of being dashed against any of the hundreds of shorter rocks.

"Do what I'm doing if you want to live!" he called out to the commandos.

In those seconds, he even had time to hyperventilate and begin oxygenating his blood enough for an extra edge in favor of survival, but his calculation of the pressures involved told him that he must not try to hold his breath. Far better to let the sea, as it crashed against him from at least two directions, catch him exhaling. The numbers told Cousteau that to do otherwise was to invite some hellish risks: air compressing out through the sides of the esophagus into the muscles of the neck . . . eyes blown out through their sockets.

Oh, no, no, no—butterfly says no!—as his little boy Philippe would have phrased it.

The north wave swept him off the rock before he could call this final safety tip out to the Russians. In the next second, as expected, it became impossible to tell up from down. Cousteau had time enough to hope that Mac had made the same calculations and taken the same precautions, before the north wave crashed him into the south wave.

M ac surfaced into waters white with sea-foam. Two Hellcats overflew him within pea-shooter range. Mac ignored them. He looked first toward Nea Kameni. Only two figures still moved there. Dmitri was leading Yanni away into unpredictable storms of dust. One of the Russian ships appeared to have spotted Dmitri. It weaved effortlessly in and out of the volcanic clouds. Only after Yanni and the ship vanished into the smoke did MacCready notice Cousteau treading nearby.

"Looks like we've survived the worst the island can throw at us," Cousteau said. "Until next time."

Mac gave him a quick nod and began swimming immediately toward the freshly chiseled rock face of Nea Kameni's east shore.

The French agent shouted behind him. "Not that way—stop—listen!"

He paused, and listened, and his attention was drawn immediately past Cousteau toward the cliffs of Santorini. The waves they just survived had rippled out from the avalanching mass of rock and were now crashing along the inner rim of the island crescent—here and there launching vertical jets of white sea spray from the shore. The curved, lagoon-facing coastline of Santorini was reflecting the waves whence they came, the way a parabolic mirror reflects and focuses light.

"You did not let me finish!" Cousteau warned. "The next time has already begun."

"But Yanni!"

"Yanni does not want you to commit suicide. Swim toward those rocks and the wave will fly-swat you against them."

"I've got to try."

"There won't be a piece of you big enough to feed a shrimp."

Even as a sudden current began drawing him away from Nea Kameni and toward the approaching waves—even in a moment of shocked acceptance that he now had no more power to swim against it than a cork in a tsunami—Mac's first concern was for Yanni.

He could see no trace of her, and the current was presently sweeping him away. Pumice stone floated in from the west—moving along with him in great yellow rafts.

"Swim *with* the current," Cousteau said, over a strengthening roar. "And hope it takes us to deep water fast!"

The reflection wave front was only about a mile away, barely visible as a greenish-blue line. Bearing down on Nea Kameni's east tip, it rose in frightful majesty. The wave tried to crest, then stumbled and collapsed into foaming white rapids. Up ahead, Jacques Cousteau, showing all the confidence of an Olympic athlete about to cross the finish line, moved with a sudden burst of power directly toward the wave and at the last instant dove right beneath it.

Mac copied the maneuver and once again was tumbled by multiple clashing vortexes that made it impossible to tell up from down. This time, as the roaring in his ears subsided, he was able to see light in one direction, and swam toward it.

His ears detected other sounds—carrying through the water from a distance that was difficult to determine: the clash of rocks. And hidden within the noise of the earth itself, the propellers of at least two ships, and the snap-and-click of angry Kraken.

How near are they? he wondered. According to Yanni, their communications were quite complex but right now, for Mac, breaking the code seemed childishly simple: *It's the kind of sound I'd expect if we'd just pissed into a beehive.*

When Mac broke the surface, Cousteau was twenty feet away and already swimming toward him.

"We have company," Mac warned.

"I know," said the Frenchman. He stopped to tread water and pointed east. The *NR-3*'s conning tower was rising, heading toward them at top speed. Within forty seconds she had slowed to full stop and two men on the prow were grabbing at them and pulling them aboard.

"You have to come below right now," Elija commanded. "The next surge will be weaker but we still want to be submerged when it arrives."

"Wasn't expecting to get you without shooting a whole lot of Russians," one of the rescuers said, pushing Cousteau down the hatch. He glanced up at the mile-high volcanic cloud, "but they say stuff just has a way of blowing up around you, huh?"

"Have you heard about the cephalopods?" Mac asked. "The big ones?"

"Met them," Elija said. "Unfortunately, we've got a little secret that keeps them away."

"Unfortunately?"

"Yeah. Either way, we're just about done in."

Despite the addition of another five rads, Elija's crew elected to stay behind for thirty minutes more, surfacing to periscope depth after the next wave front passed and searching Nea Kameni for Yanni and Dmitri. There were no signs of any human forms, dead or alive. The man at the flight engineer's seat detected the Russian ships racing away in multiple directions, at more than twice the *NR-3*'s maximum cruising speed.

The eruption sputtered, stalled, and began to slow down, but it continued to give the Russians everything they needed—a smoke screen of aluminum-rich volcanic dust that was playing havoc with radar. This time Hellcats were unable to spot the positions of ships, much less prisoner and captor. To fly into the dust clouds and gum up the engines was meaningless death, because there was no way of seeing more than twenty or thirty feet beyond the nose of the plane. Even under the sea, the falling ash was dense enough to complicate the interpretation of sonar.

At every opportunity, through every clearing in the ash clouds, Mac searched the shores of Nea Kameni. He prayed an agnostic's prayer (*if you're there* . . .) against the possibility of sighting dust-covered bodies. They saw none. Presumably, the Russians had Yanni.

Elija cautioned Mac and Cousteau that even with the *Intrepid* moving toward rendezvous outside the nearest inlet, they would all be taking another twenty rads before anyone was safely aboard and showering.

Twenty or twenty-five rads was close to normal for a lifetime dose from nature. Though Mac knew he and Cousteau—newly exposed to the sub's contaminated interior—could easily take that amount of radiation and probably not suffer from it, what mattered most was the rapidity with which one took those first three or four hundred rads. To keep the engineers absorbing even a few more rads, at this point in their exposure, would drive them toward depressingly diminished odds of survival.

"The Russians have her," Mac told Cousteau and the others. "She has to be alive. *Has* to be."

The waves had by now lost all of their strength and the cinder cone was also waning fast. The spectacle was still impressive, but no longer evoking images of Pompeii and Krakatoa. The lagoon was calming down and the engineers needed to be brought out of the radiation as soon as possible. All agreed that they should not provoke the fates any longer.

The shock was all the more startling, therefore, when the sea itself exploded as they sailed past the westernmost tip of Nea Kameni. Not more than a half mile astern, fountains of black steam shot sixty, eighty—a hundred stories into the sky, obliterating whatever might still have remained of the red plumes.

There were Kraken along the nearer fringe of the eruption—many of them still writhing but certainly no more alive than the severed tentacle Yanni had found aboard the Russian "fishing trawler."

Two hundred yards nearer, a type of Kraken larger than any Mac had seen before surfaced and began swimming in erratic circles. Through the periscope, Mac saw that one of its eyes appeared to be burned and unseeing. It was not alone. Smaller Kraken were moving in from cooler, more distant, and safer waters to join their brethren—more and more of them, pulling and tugging at their dead and their still-moving dead.

Mac stepped away and turned one of the sub's two periscopes over to Cousteau, who scanned the lagoon in astonishment.

"What do you see?" Mac asked him.

"A race that has been around probably as long as we have. And today, I think, we are witnessing the end of their world." The Frenchman watched until the *NR-3* was outside the lagoon and neither the Kraken nor the base of the geyser could be seen any longer. When Cousteau handed the scope over, Mac searched the land for people. He searched the horizon for ships but he did not look in the direction of the Kraken again.

"All that capability to deal out violence," Cousteau said. "And yet when it came to this, they moved toward their dying and wounded. They could have killed us. They should all, in the very least, have fled and saved themselves."

"They didn't, Jacques, because Yanni was right about them."

"I know. I expect they'll awake me the rest of my nights with this revelation: *Maybe they're better than us.*"

Report on the Brunswick Incident
Removed from Restricted Status, July 13, 1948
Royal Norwegian Navy Archives, May 6, 1930

Royal auxiliary tanker *Brunswick* was en route to Samoa among the Pacific Navigator Islands when overtaken by a large cephalopod, believed to be a squid. Animal paced *Brunswick*'s 495-foot hull in excess of ten knots, spouting jets of water. While jetting, cephalopod appeared to grow and shrink at will. Deliberately, and without provocation, it turned from what appeared to be a parallel course and attacked the *Brunswick* no fewer than three times, ramming the hull and wrapping its tentacles over portholes and gangway doors and up toward the vessel's forward well deck. Owing to hostilities between Japan and Korea and current aggression projected against Pacific Islands and shipping, *Brunswick* was provisioned with precautionary armament. Unclear how many weapons were involved in defense of ship. Animal eventually released grip and passed aft near the propellers after dispersing "huge gluts" of ink or blood. Two other large cephalopods, reportedly sighted with it, "aiding."

The Descent of Man

> *If we kill off the wild, then we are killing off a part of our souls.*
> —JANE GOODALL

> *A resolution to avoid an evil is seldom framed till the evil is so far advanced as to make avoidance impossible.*
> —THOMAS HARDY

> *All things are possible until they are proved impossible—and even the impossible may only be so, as for now.*
> —PEARL S. BUCK

PART 1

Yanni: The Quest

July 13, 1948
Soviet Research Vessel Kursk
Destination Unknown

D mitri had learned during the war that it was often depressingly necessary to leave the dead behind. After Stalingrad, he had seen how leaving loved ones behind in the ice was the least of the horrors. So he accepted that there would probably never be a chance of recovering his brother's body from damnable Santorini and bringing him home.

What he could not accept was tending to Yanni Thorne's wounds. Dmitri gently reset the splints, noting that swelling was diminishing and the joints in her hands seemed to be healing well despite the damage.

Breaking her fingers and wrists had been unnecessary, but Trofim Lysenko was very thorough with his interrogations. He was good at what he did. And he liked doing it.

The monster had intended to inflict even more painful abuse, but Dmitri had summoned every last microgram of charm, along with a willingness to—as the Americans phrased it, "eat crow"—until Lysenko brought the assault to an early stop. Additional helpings of crow permitted him to nurse Yanni back to health and render her, as promised to Lysenko, "more willingly cooperative."

"Your fingers and wrists will be perfect again," Dmitri assured her. "And I think, like your friend Nesbitt, I can guess why."

"So why are you helping me?" Yanni said. "You Mutt-and-Jeffing me? You, good cop? Lysenko, bad cop?"

"No, I don't care about your red stuff," Dmitri said slowly, softly. "Least of all does it matter if what's left of the stuff happens to heal you and Cousteau and a few Greek fishermen." Then, at a whisper, he added, "All I really care about is that the bishop got his way and blew it all to kingdom come."

"And Lysenko's Kraken, Ahab?"

"While it's alive, I can help to keep you alive."

Yanni glared back at him, looking skeptical, and perplexed. "You talk as if you're gonna die too."

"We're literally in the same boat, you and I. Do you really believe he will let either of us out of here alive? I'm as dead as you are. That is why I helped you."

Dmitri looked down at Yanni's splinted and bandaged fingers. He wanted to apologize again, but he could not get the words out. *How*, he asked himself, *did I ever come to this?*

Dmitri had followed a long, strange path from the year when one of his professors required the students to remove pineal glands from the brains of lab rats and record the effects over several weeks. After the first week, all the rats in all the students' cages were clearly suffering from the effects of the surgery—for there had been no way to remove the gland without damaging surrounding brain tissue. Dmitri could not bear witnessing (and to some degree feeling) the increasingly feeble attempts of his animals to walk, or even to feed themselves. One night he entered the lab alone and euthanized his specimens.

When Professor Cahn summoned Dmitri to her office and asked him why he had done this, he told her that he simply could not watch them suffering, could no longer listen to their uncomprehending squeals of pain. "I made the decision," he said, "and I've accepted that I will take a failing grade on my lab work."

"No, you are not failing, Dmitri. Quite the opposite, but do not tell the other students about your grade."

"How is this?"

"Because in science, humanity matters. Do not forget that."

How far I have fallen, Dmitri thought. He tried to believe he was very near to his personal worst, and could soon start again upward, but a part of him knew that he had no concept of how low the worst could really be.

He had come from sympathy for rats to wanting an intelligent beast and its entire species dead. He hoped Bishop Marinatos and the volcano had accomplished just that, but he doubted their extinction. And Lysenko, for reasons largely unknown, seemed hell-bent on keeping one of them alive, and using Yanni to learn from it.

Dmitri, like others who had come to know Lysenko, began to hate the monster, and loathe himself.

Yet, obediently, and at exactly the appointed minute, he brought Yanni to him, and to the Kraken's holding tank.

The beast Lysenko smirked indulgently and reminded Dmitri that he already knew Yanni, in accordance with a theremin transcript, as "She who talks with the animals."

Lysenko motioned Yanni toward the edge of the tank. "Now," he said. "Show me."

August 15, 1948
Admiral Rickover's Command

SUPPORT SHIP INTREPID

Officially, the NR-3 still did not exist.
Officially, immediately after the Intrepid made port, MacCready, Alan, Walter, and Cousteau disappeared into thin air.

Unofficially, the *NR-3* was scrubbed down and a crew was readied for a new shakedown cruise.

Courtesy of Cousteau's engineering, most of the outer hull was now covered in a "wet suit" of rubberized material, tailored in only three weeks to absorb and misdirect any Russian sonar aimed in its direction.

In theory, this would give the vessel a new sonar cross section, this time no larger than a barracuda.

And in practice?

NR-3 was still a "hot" boat. Despite every effort at decontamination, certain isotopes had formed permanent chemical bonds with the inner hull, and a crew could expect to receive about twice the normal human lifetime radiation dose from the sub itself if they stayed aboard for just a year.

Mac knew that it could never come down to that kind of dose for him. The admiral would not likely let his precious machine be devoted so thoroughly to a single rescue operation for a full year—or even beyond three months. And no matter what, the sub itself was not to be risked if the shore team got into trouble.

But which shore? Mac wondered. Walter and his British counterpart had ferreted out only vague clues. They knew that the *Kursk* had captured at least one of the Kraken, and it was a sure bet that Yanni was being put to work on the creature. This meant that, if taken ashore, she was somewhere with access to lots of sea water—probably similar to places where the American navy had been trying to break the code of dolphin communication.

There was no margin of error allowing for a landing near the wrong ship or the wrong sea-lab-as-public-entertainment-aquarium on the first try.

Where to land first seemed the only choice Mac had. The past three weeks were filled with worry, heartbreak, and aftereffects. During the moments in which a great chunk of island real estate collapsed under his feet in Kraken-infested waters, there had fortunately been no time to worry. Only afterward, when there was time to think about possible and actual losses, did anything next of kin to panic begin to assert itself—*and the only cure for you then*, Mac knew, *was the next mission*.

Most deep-submergence types shared the same borderline insanity level of mission focus. Even one of the reactor crew had insisted on returning from the *Intrepid*'s hospital so he could finish field-testing his replacement team. Except for a slight cold that seemed too stubborn to go completely away, Thomas insisted that he was essential for the next cruise despite his radiation dose, and his plea to join them was granted.

The weeks of training in the flight engineer's seat had kept Mac dwelling more and more on the Yanni rescue than on all that had gone (or still could go) wrong.

Captain John diverted Mac's attention back toward mission planning—"Think nothing but mission success," he had warned, "or get off my boat." Despite his declaration to Walter that if he survived Santorini, he was quitting deep submergence, the captain was once again in the pilot's seat. Alan was invited to take the navigator's post, directly across from Mac.

"I'm sorry, Alan," Mac said. "It looks like I've given you my disease. You could have continued digging up old apes with Boulle. Why not a quiet life at the museum? Why sign up again for one of the most dangerous commutes on earth?"

"Too late for me now. Interestingly, going where I could be imploded underwater or shot when I come up for air, or get eaten by strange animals, is what makes it more attractive to me."

"Besides, if we don't die in one of those ways, we might die of boredom," said Captain John.

Alan nodded, and laughed. "The greater the challenge and the trouble, the greater the urge. Also, so much greater the satisfaction, when you complete this thing that has so much risk and challenge."

Mac looked ahead. Divers were unlatching *NR-3*'s ropes. The view was mostly obscured by swarms of shrimp. "Yanni's out there somewhere," he said in a near whisper.

"Okay, friend. Let's go find her."

The Darwin Strain:

Anatomy of a Legend

August 15, 1948
Noon, Washington, D.C.

President Truman accepted the morning memo with grim resignation. The White House was in very real danger of collapse and would have to be either left to historians or else gutted and rebuilt all the way down to the basement and out to the sandstone walls.

Won't be the first gutting, he thought acidly. The most recent remodeling was courtesy of the Canadians burning down the house during that little border spat in 1814. But what most worried the president about the move was losing the wide safety perimeter around the White House. He'd already survived more botched assassination attempts than any modern president. Relocating to a two-story home along one of the city's narrow streets would aid in the efficiency of any future attempts.

During his tenure under Franklin Roosevelt and even during his first year in office, President Truman had been able to take long strolls among crowds along Pennsylvania Avenue, without any concern for his safety. And now, with the whole world entering a new and probably long-term convulsion of uncertainty, Truman expected that he was the last president to have walked freely among the people. Beginning with him, presidents might eventually become so withdrawn from their fellow Americans as to be seen and heard only on the emerging medium of television—or, as Einstein and his futurists had it, in "three-dimensional projections." Gone were the days when Calvin Coolidge took early-morning swims in the Potomac.

The president was sitting down for a late breakfast of fried eggs and coffee when Bobby entered with some doughnuts and said, "I presume you've heard about the latest rant from Senator McCarthy."

"You mean last night, or in the last hour?"

"Last twenty minutes."

"Uh-huh."

"He's caught wind of the coin-boy incident and how far along the Russians are with their bomb."

Were Truman a smoker, he'd have needed to open a new pack at this point, but he poured himself a fresh cup of coffee instead. "The kid was our best cover story—the most perfect firewall we had against anyone knowing all about the MacArthur-*Intrepid*-MacCready bullshit that's been hitting the fan."

"So far, it's working. It doesn't seem he's got a clue beyond the generic Russia problem—except for one tiny snippet that's come out through the coin-boy scuttlebutt."

"He's got a whiff of MacCready?"

"No. It's Nesbitt. Just the name. Nothing else. He wants to learn more through a subpoena."

"I'd like to see him try, Bobby."

"It probably won't come to that. Your old friend MacArthur is standing in his way."

"So, for a change my interests favor his interests." The president was about to dunk a doughnut into his coffee, but the sight of either a very small rat or a slightly overgrown mouse scuttling past the office door killed his sweet tooth.

"That poor deluded child," Truman said.

"Pardon?"

"The general never forgave me for Hiroshima and Nagasaki. As he sees it, he had spent nearly two years planning the invasion of Japan from the sea—and then in just a few days, his Operation Olympic gets ruined by a weapon I never told him existed. No amount of talking convinces the stubborn bastard that even I didn't know about it until just a few weeks earlier."

"You mean, the whole time you were vice president?"

"FDR kept the Manhattan Project secret even from me, all the way to the grave."

"And now the question is: What does the general know about Nesbitt and Santorini?"

"Something more than I know, probably." The president shook his head. "It may not matter much.

The island's crops were wiped out by more than three weeks of volcano belches and ash-falls—and so were most of the fish. People are abandoning the place by the boatload. Whatever Nesbitt and the Russians and everyone else wanted from Santorini is gone."

"And Nesbitt—MacArthur sent a war criminal in with her?"

"Yeah. A bioweapons guy: Hata. Dead now. Thank God."

"But Nesbitt," Bobby said. "I've asked around for anything I can get on her. MacArthur might have attached Hata to her team, but she wasn't in it for weapons. She was looking for something else."

"I'm sure you're right," said Truman. To judge by what little he and Captain Christian knew about Nesbitt—which was probably no more than what Patrick Hendry and Nesbitt herself believed anyone needed to know—the White House was living mostly in the ignorance of "plausible deniability."

But no secret is 100 percent leak proof, the president knew. From a Plum Island scientist who one night shared too many pitchers of beer with some biker "Grummie" friends in Bethpage had emerged rumors of a mythical lab where fruit flies lived almost forever. Not even for Truman would anyone confirm whether or not the myth was reality. He thought back to the Einstein–von Braun committee on "The Future of War." They were forecasting brave new bombs, brave new wars, and simultaneously so many brave new cures that population stress would lead to what one visionary called "the inevitability of breeder lynchings."

And then: famine and famine-induced disease—spreading worldwide and leading to the use of all those brave new bombs.

Truman pushed his eggs aside, unfinished. "Nesbitt. I think MacArthur's friends have her hidden somewhere. It's as if the earth opened up and swallowed her."

"I have a brother who once served on a mission with Nesbitt."

"Interesting," the president said. "Most interesting."

"What, specifically?"

"You want to tell me? Your brother came back from the war infected with every sort of tropical disease, and with his spine cracked practically from stem to stern. But he's doing well—right?"

"His back still gives him a really hard time now and then, but he seems to be holding up."

"Holding up? Even when I was thirty-one—no, twenty-one—I didn't have his kind of energy."

"You've lost me somewhere."

"Oh, it's nothing, really. Nothing to worry about," the president lied. "Nothing at all."

August 15, 1948
Plum Island Secondary Lab,
Ice Station Georgia Peach

PROJECT ENOCH

The first news of the morning made this the happiest day of Nora Nesbitt's career. Though they had each taken an estimated 430 rads, every member of the *NR-3* reactor crew was still alive— most of them showing signs of steadily improving health. One even felt well enough for a return to duty.

With some of the most advanced yet secretive medical research in the world being performed aboard aircraft carriers, the *Intrepid* had become the perfect extension of Nora's studies. Her newest experiment had been so secret that not even Captain Christian or General MacArthur knew the Plum Islander turned the crewmen—half of whom should have been dead or dying by now— into her own private laboratory rats. Indeed, none of the human "lab rats" knew an experiment had been performed. By rights, and in the name of a proper laboratory study, she should have administered the derivative of her own blood as a controlled experiment—meaning that half of the men would have received none of the remedy at all. Nesbitt knew enough, from the data of Hiroshima and Nagasaki, exactly what would happen to the men if she left half of them untreated. It might not be a proper scientific experiment to treat them all, but she believed that in at least this case, she must "do no harm." *Besides*, she told herself, *you owe these men.*

The next news of the morning could not have been more disturbing. Russia had already dispersed enough highly refined uranium-235 to build at least two versions of the Hiroshima bomb into four or five versions of Fort Knox.

Nora Nesbitt read the classified report and, in accordance with instructions, burned it. She found it impossible to fathom how the best day of her career, and the worst day, had become the same day. Now the nuclear arms race she most dreaded was unavoidable.

Bioweapons escalation was also bound to pick up speed.

Today she decided the only escape from civilization's march toward Armageddon was the hope of building a better future—a future too good for either side (Capitalist or Communist) to risk losing in a war.

On this day, the only escape from a future too dark to visualize was into the past.

The mysteries of Fira Quarry, *NR-3*'s "golden death mask," and the evolution of her Darwin Strain seemed as good a place as any toward which to flee.

Nora looked mournfully at Hata's half-finished machine—which they had called a "proton magnetic resonance mapper." This futuristic tool was precisely what they needed to map genetic codes, using nothing more exotic (or less brilliant) than the positions of hydrogen atoms in carbon-based molecules. Even if Nora succeeded in completing the machine (and she knew she could), a printout of genes into actual code, though rendered readable, would be no more understandable than Egyptian hieroglyphs prior to finding the code-breaking Rosetta Stone. For a long time to come there would be no such thing as a genetic Rosetta

Stone. Alan had seen to this, with the murder of Hata, the scientist most likely to have eventually made the perfect breakthrough.

Without biology's Rosetta Stone, there were too few clues from which to read how her fruit flies had become so long-lived, how ancients might have accomplished a similar feat, or what really happened with the pitiful creature behind the Santorini death mask.

We are like Neanderthals or bonobos playing with napalm, Nora reminded herself. One of her mathematician friends, whom she had tried recruiting to expand the machine's computing power, had put it another way: "We know very little and yet it is astonishing that we know so much, and still more astonishing that so little knowledge can give us so much power."

"But if we can build a genetic Rosetta Stone—if we can one day compare all the genes of all the necessary animals," Nora insisted, "we'll have all the knowledge we need."

"And good-bye," her friend replied.

Before he left, he had summed Nora up with a reprimand—"You are the kind of explorer, I fear, who would crack the world open, if you could, just to see what would happen."

She hoped that, given enough time, she could change the old genius's mind—which was why she "poisoned" his drinking glass with the same variant of the Darwin Strain that had infiltrated her own tissues, and which was presently keeping the *NR-3* engine crew alive.

Now, barring a fatal car accident or any other

unforeseen mishap, Nora expected that she and Bertrand Russell had all the time in the world. But she did not know precisely why this was so. No one did.

"The scope of our ignorance on this, and other matters of nature, is huge," she wrote in a notebook. "Knowing this is belittling. And yet it is the most precious thing we have."

Nora understood, better than most people, that from the day the first atomic bomb was exploded, scientists knew nothing at all about what protons and neutrons in the middle of an atom were really made of. And still, no one knew.

She could scarcely make a crude guess at how the strain—which she had classified as somewhere between a bacterium and a fungus—"chose" to work its strange symbiosis within human, bonobo, and Kraken bodies. She had ventured perhaps an only marginally less crude guess about how little gardens of the "scarlet *moctus proctus*" came to be maintained at both Santorini (by Kraken) and in the Himalayas (by Yeren and Cerae). She knew that the old Roman historian Pliny the Elder had written about encounters with the mysterious Cerae culture—last seen near the hot springs of a Himalayan grotto. Pliny's accounts seemed consistent with a more highly evolved version of Alan and Pierre's Fira Quarry bonobos, leading her to suspect that the ancestral Cerae had carried the organism with them from a distant shore, and very likely from the vicinity of Santorini.

And, she noted, the organism must still have

been there, near Santorini, when the pyramids were new and the first wooden ships arrived.

The gold "helmet" recovered by the *NR-3* was a work of art so beautiful that it did indeed surpass the golden death mask of "King Tut." Yet it bore enough ancient mysteries to leave even Tut's sarcophagus behind—"Forever in the little leagues," Nora told herself.

Rows of nearly microscopic, lapis-bordered hieroglyphs placed the death mask definitively within the same dynasty as Tut, but identified a queen named Kyri giving honor to another unknown historical figure, named Semut. This dedication rendered all the more perplexing the question of why Kyri or anyone else would have stuffed the interior of the headpiece with a mixture of human and animal bones.

The answer meant that the question of "the red miracle" went a little deeper than even Nora Nesbitt had at first anticipated.

Why were a man and a bull sharing the same coffin?

They weren't. The piecing together and reconstruction of only half the skull told it so. Microscope slides and comparative histology told the rest: Another civilization had indeed discovered the "red *moctus proctus*" at Santorini. It was being used there more than thirty-five centuries before the red plumes erupted onto the scene and damned near triggered a modern war. Viewed through a microscope, the semifossilized cells of bones from the headpiece were structurally identical to one another, and must therefore have belonged to a single, fully functional creature that survived into adulthood.

A chimera? Nora asked herself. *But that's impossible.*

She knew already that an organism closely related to the microbe coursing through her blood had also infected Mac, Yanni, and at least four or five other people—not counting, of course, Private McQueen, the *NR-3* crew, and Bertrand. Now she understood that someone had advanced beyond the healing of wounds and curing of diseases and discovered that the red mats could also be used to blend the genes of such distantly related creatures as a man and a bull—and somehow make it work despite the obvious obstacles.

And she told herself, *All I needed to know is that it can be done; now all I need to learn is how it was done.*

In the next moment it made no sense to her. *First the Kraken, and now?* It made no sense that the Minotaur could once have been real. It seemed impossible that, back when the pyramids were still gleaming white and clear-cut, someone had thrown open the doors to a genetic frontier far beyond anything imaginable with today's technology.

Impossible.

But there it was—like an echo from the island of Dr. Moreau. The emerging reality seemed stranger than anything H. G. Wells had tried to warn the world about.

No. None of it made any sense at all . . . without

the red hydrothermal microbe, without the Darwin Strain.

Nora Nesbitt suspected that what happened with the creature named Semut was an experiment gone wrong.

But we have the technology, she concluded. *We can get everything right this time.*

She had plenty of samples worth studying. There was, for a start (just for a start), the freeze-dried *"moctus proctus"* sample from a Himalayan grotto—the "stolen" finger that had infuriated Patricia Wynters. There was also an ample supply of the symbiotic infection in her own tissues. Life extension was beginning to look far easier than anyone had believed possible. Now, if she could unlock the secret of how to orchestrate the process of evolution, essentially instantly—even to the point of hybridizing species at will—then the agricultural advances alone might become limitless, all but guaranteeing the future security of the human species.

"Take command of our own evolutionary destiny," Nora whispered to the arctic twilight, in a moment that seemed triumphant. Standing before the lab's only window, she failed to notice the northern lights bunching together overhead and rotating on a rarely seen magnetic axis, sweeping down toward her like the spokes of a giant wheel. Instead she looked back across the past decade of her life, bit down hard on her lower lip, and dreamed of a future in which no one would ever again know the peculiar horror of watching a child die from something incurable—for it became possible to believe that she could command the destiny of nature itself, and along the way cure every disease, perhaps even create the immortal child.

She whispered to the impassive stars, "I can slow down and perhaps even reverse the human aging process. I can feel it. I am at the beginning of a fantastic adventure."

And yet, in this very same lab, within Nora's reach lay proof that the Minotaur was real, and had lived in agony.

Nora Nesbitt was a long way from being finished with the Minotaur.

And the Minotaur's bones—seething with mystery and wonder—were not through with her.

Nor was the Kraken through with her kind.

ASSN DECLASS: JANUARY 20, 2021
RE: Virginia Beach Incident

FEBRUARY 15, 1981
CAPTAIN, RUSSIAN SUBMARINE
TSIOLKOVSKY:
WE DID NOT RUN AGROUND.

REPEAT: WE DID NOT RUN AGROUND.

VESSEL DISABLED AND PULLED ONTO SHALLOW SANDBAR ZONE 32 KILOMETERS OFFSHORE BY MULTIPLE LIVING OBJECTS BINDING TO HULL.

ALL CONFIRMED BY IMAGING SONAR.

FEBRUARY 15, 1981
POTUS RESPONSE:
THIS FAIRY TALE IS UNACCEPTABLE.

THE RUSSIAN CREW IS SOLELY
RESPONSIBLE FOR A NEAR NUCLEAR
DISASTER ON AMERICAN SHORES.

MARCH 1, 1981
LT. COMMANDER ALAN J. ACKLEY, SEAL
TEAM LEADER, (SOVIET SUBMARINE
RECOVERY) RE: DAMAGE REPORT:
MISSILES (2 ARE MULTI-STAGE)
NEUTRALIZED BY RUSSIAN CREW.
WARHEADS ALSO NEUTRALIZED BY
CREW.

VISUAL EXAMINATION OF HULL
CONSISTENT WITH CREW REPORT
OF DAMAGE BY MULTIPLE OBJECTS
OF 2 TON OR GREATER MASS. SONAR
IMAGES BY CREW PRESERVED, ALSO
CONSISTENT. SEAL TEAM BETACAM OF
HULL STEALTHING MEMBRANE, ALSO
CONSISTENT. DR. G. L. VOSS EXAMINED
DAMAGED SONAR DAMPING MEMBRANE
SAMPLES FROM HULL USING LIGHT
AND SEM MICROSCOPY: CONCLUDES
DAMAGE NOT FABRICATED BY RUSSIANS
AND WAS LIKELY CAUSED BY ONE OR
MORE (UP TO "AT LEAST SEVERAL")
LARGE ANIMATE OBJECTS, SPECIES
UNKNOWN. CEPHALOPODA.

CROSS REFERENCE: MACCREADY/
THORN/COUSTEAU M016A
CROSS REFERENCE ARGO M016B
THIS IS NRBQ INDEX SHEET 1 OF 2
COUNT YOUR PAGES.
. . . .
REDACTED. COMPANY CONFIDENTIAL.
FILE M016A HAS NOT BEEN FOUND.
REDACTED. COMPANY CONFIDENTIAL.
FILE M016B HAS NOT BEEN FOUND.

THIS IS NRBQ INDEX SHEET 2 OF 2,
EYES ONLY.
SOUND JUDGMENT SHALL BE
EXERCISED AT ALL TIMES.
COUNT YOUR PAGES.
REPORT ANY MISSING PAGES TO NRBQ
AT ONCE.
COUNT YOUR PAGES.

Reality Check

> *A single gram of soil has billions of cells,*
> *thousands of species and far more genetic*
> *information than the human genome.*
> *Microbes, in a sense, rule the world: In their*
> *multitudes, they help regulate our biosphere*
> *and have profound effects on plants and*
> *animals.*
> —DAN BUCKLEY, WORLD ECONOMIC
> FORUM, 2017

> *Life on Earth is more like a verb. It*
> *repairs, maintains, and outdoes itself.*
> *And you'll see symbiosis everywhere. . . .*
> *Beneath our superficial differences we are*
> *all of us walking communities of bacteria.*
> *The world shimmers, a pointillist*
> *landscape made of tiny living beings.*
> —LYNN MARGULIS

Early on, this series of novels was conceived as a trilogy (with likely spin-offs) about an accidental cryptozoologist and his animal empath colleague. Yanni Thorne's abilities are based on some very real people known to us—including a family member, and animal psychologist Temple Grandin—who live (and manage to flourish) somewhere along what is often called the autism-Asperger's spectrum, or as some scientists, engineers, or on-the-spectrum explorers and animal behaviorists prefer to be called, *Aspies*. ("After all, the official words, [including] 'high-functioning autism disorder,' would never look good on our job applications.") Arising from such realities, some of the intense emotions described during encounters with today's *known* cephalopod species are based on the experiences of real people, not all of them Aspies (although it occasionally took an Aspie to show the way).

As with any other human group, there is much variation among people "on the spectrum." We know a string theorist who could be moved often to tears by the beauty of a mountain range or the universe hidden within the diameter of a proton. Temple Grandin shocked him by saying she could not understand, emotionally, the beauty he saw in nature. There is so much variation that even the "rule" of total social ineptitude is not universally true. The true rule: if you've met one Aspie, you can only say that you've met one Aspie.

Temple Grandin speculated that it was not the most social member of a tribe who changed history by first befriending "man's best friend" or who thought far enough outside the box to shape the first stone spear. It was probably social outcasts like Yanni, said Grandin—"Probably an

Aspie, who chipped away at rocks [or scrutinized the patterns of a wolf's behavior], while the other people socialized around the campfire. Without autism traits we might still be living in caves." Some, considered "*alien*-ish" by most people, have described "alien" the other way around. Both Grandin and the late Isaac Asimov said they often felt like anthropologists from a faraway time or place, dropped down here on earth and perplexed by alien human behavior.

If you have come away from any of these novels questioning what exactly defines an intelligent life-form, if you sometimes get the creepy feeling that humans might not always have been (and might not always be) the smartest creatures on this planet, then we've accomplished some small measure of what we have set out to do.

Each of these novels is a fable, of sorts. Although set in the 1940s, they are really about the world today, and the future. Our characters lived then, as we all live now: in someone else's yesterdays and tomorrows. Jacques Yves Cousteau understood this when he visited the isle of Santorini and viewed remnants of its lost worlds for the first time. A young Greek archaeologist who marveled at the doors to a new wilderness being thrown open by rocket scientist Werner von Braun told Cousteau that he believed humans were verging on the final conquest of nature, adding, "When God met man in Eden, he commanded, 'Subdue the Earth.'" Cousteau, one of this fable's real-life inhabitants, replied, as he often replied on such occasions: "Subdue the earth? But in order to do that, you must realize that the earth has a life of its own. And we must respect this view of life."

Cousteau's theme resonates throughout this tale.

If this novel is the first example you have come across, from the series, we planned for such possibilities. They are not meant to be read in any particular sequence. Each has been designed as a stand-alone story, with occasional crossover moments, or "Easter eggs" planted here and there.

Now, while much of what you have just read was a blend of scientific speculation and abstract fantasy, it may be fun to learn that you were simultaneously encountering much real science and history.

One result of this: no reliance here on the improbable *deus ex machina*. Though the year has been changed, a bombing run against a ship at Santorini really did trigger the central volcano to erupt, and really did allow the ship to escape. Operation High-jump was real, as was Admiral Rickover's design for the *NR-3* (a variation of which was actually built). Pliny the Elder really did record, in his *Naturalis Historia* (parts 3, 11), a "polypus" encounter, exactly as described in *The Darwin Strain*. The sinking of the *Pearl* by a large cephalopod is also recorded by history exactly as written here, as are legends and alleged sightings of, and battles with, "the Kraken," dating from World War II back to remote antiquity.

One of the great guilty pleasures in penning these tales has been to blur the line between reality and fable. In each of these novels, if a character happens to glance up at the crescent moon, you can be sure that the night sky is accurately described for that date, time, and locale on the surface of the earth.

So, now that you have traveled this far, let's look a little more closely, you and I, at the real history and the real science behind the fiction:

The *Argo* high-resolution sonar imaging system, introduced with the Prologue, is based on a very real system developed from the late 1940s onward. By 1981, when shuttle astronauts Robert Crippen and John Young met with British space scientists and oceanographers, the technology had already advanced to a level at which faint images (miles beneath the Russian submarines being observed) were identifiable as "crash sites" of sunken vessels (including the *Scorpion*, the *Thresher*, and the *Titanic*).

Significantly, as concerns our fictional heroes, this same technology revealed how extensions of the Nile and other great rivers actually carved out deep channels across the bed of the Mediterranean (during what are now known to have been a series of Mediterranean dry-outs, the latest episode ending in the great flood of 5.3 million years ago).

Large-scale geometric line patterns on seafloors have also been indicated by sonar imagery. At first glance, some of them do resemble "unnatural" or "man-made" structures. Our opinion (and the current scientific consensus view) is that all are, to near absolute certainty, natural geologic formations. However, consensus scientific opinions are sometimes proved wrong by new information and if we should be proved wrong, it will only make planet Earth's natural history a lot more mysterious and perhaps a bit more beautiful as well.

Jacques Cousteau was the first person to map the undersea typography of the Santorini Lagoon and to explore the crater in a mini-sub. His brilliance, and his actions during time-critical life-threatening situations, are as true to life as can be told, based on the firsthand eyewitness accounts of Cousteau's first American science officer, Thomas Dettweiler (of Woods Hole Oceanographic Institution and the U.S. Navy, retired).

On the discovery that became Mac's cover story for the expedition to Santorini: While no prehistoric grave of the sort has been found in Santorini's Fira Quarry (although the quarry itself is quite real, just as described), the number of branching humanlike lineages and the oldest known stone tools are becoming rather complex and being pushed progressively deeper into our past even as you read. The oldest clearly authenticated stone tools (as first published in the May 20, 2015, issue of *Nature*) date from 3.3 million years ago, with subsequent and potentially older finds now vying for the title of "oldest known." Back near the end of the twentieth century, the human family tree was believed to be rather thinly branched, sprouting (about 20 million years ago) from dryopithecine apes, through an apish fossil named "Lucy," and toward us. Late-twentieth-century sketches of the family tree appeared even thinner than Charlie Brown's classic, sad Christmas twig. However, newer fossils—more and more of them—revealed we humans to be merely a surviving limb from a once very exotic, widely branching family bush.

Even as this novel was nearing completion, new examples showed up. In one particularly fascinating coincidence, a "mystery primate," dating back to the time frame during which an extension of the Nile flowed along the deep Mediterranean desert, left its footprints on Santorini's neighbor to the south, Crete. The now-fossilized footprints (as first reported in *Nature*, September 2, 2017), were laid down 5.7 million years ago, along what might then have been a muddy alpine lakeshore. A team from Uppsala University, Sweden, discovered more than fifty of the prints concentrated in an area of scarcely more than four square yards—meaning that there were probably several such creatures, traveling as part of a troop, or lair. They walked on the soles of their feet, as might be expected of an animal that stood somewhere between chimpanzees and a more humanlike primate, or "hominin." (Note: Bonobos are more comfortable walking upright than chimpanzees.) The footprints are puzzling because, the team said, "Crete is some distance from all other sites where hominins of a similar age have been found: in Chad, Ethiopia, and Kenya. If the animal that made the prints was not a hominin, it must have been a previously unknown non-hominin primate that evolved a humanlike footprint independently."

Perhaps shedding light on the puzzle, while simultaneously rendering the deep Nile oases that aided the fictional journey of Seed's people more realistic: Branches of the Nile presently flow from Kenya's Lake Victoria, and from Ethiopia. The "Yellow Nile" formerly flowed from eastern Chad. Five and a half million years ago, winding its way north along the bottom of the great Mediterranean canyon—just as is described in this novel—the Nile really was a natural water bridge across the canyon's deserts, from Africa to Crete.

Wang (Alan) Tse-lin's odyssey is based on the experiences and writings of a real Wang Tse-lin, who disappeared (presumably murdered) during the early stages of China's civil war. We decided to give this fascinating explorer a more hopeful, "what might have been" future. "Alan's" discovery, with Pierre Boulle, of a lost branch from the hominid family bush is consistent with his life history. Educated in Chicago, he once wrote a report about his examination of a "Yeren wild man," killed by hunters in China's Gansu province. He recorded that the specimen, though apelike, also reminded him of *Homo erectus*, the tool-making "Peking Man" (a lineage believed to have been extinct since at least 230,000 B.C.). In Tse-lin's 1940 report, the

Yeren was described as "a nursing female, covered in dense grayish-red hair . . . [the] face was narrow with deep-set eyes." If the report is accurate, then Wang Tse-lin was R. J. MacCready's real-life predecessor in cryptozoology.

B eneath the surface of Santorini's lagoon, the terrain encountered by Cousteau and Dmitri is much as described in this novel. The hydrothermal springs do indeed have a history of emerging and fading, in and around the flooded volcanic crater. One spring is presently rising near the island fragment known as Therasia. During the time in which they remain active, submerged volcanic vents support exotic communities of bacteria and fungi that convert undersea deserts into biological oases. (In the deep Atlantic, we know that some of these microbes, and the eggs of certain sea creatures, can drift along the bottom for several hundred years or more, until they wash up against a friendly vent.)

The genetics of these microbes are beyond fascinating, as are their practical applications, including pharmaceutical ones. As an example, PCR technology—first used for crime lab DNA testing, and afterward to reveal everything from the ancestry of Neanderthals and Egyptian mummies to the history of your family's migration routes—came directly from chemicals produced by these extreme-environment microbes (called "extremophiles"). Similarly, the game-changing CRISPR genetic engineering tool, which brings both dreams and nightmares within human grasp, is derived from the mining of bacterial DNA.

On the genetic frontier, it becomes possible to believe that the cure of all disease is on the horizon—and perhaps even vastly extended, youthful human life-spans. But to whom shall such technology be made available? Who should play God?

Dream? Or nightmare? Which shall it be?

Early in the twenty-first century, between two Cold Wars, joint Russian-American-Canadian teams sought out new medicines among extremophiles. From hydrothermal seams near the Jordan Valley to the nooks and crannies of sunken volcanoes in the Azores, new antibiotics became available for study (including one that may act simultaneously against cancer cells). Along the way, two team members were accidentally infected by their subject matter and experienced still-unexplained (and still only anecdotal) spontaneous remissions from untreatable and life-threatening diseases. A third person (by random biological coincidence or not) appeared to have experienced remission as if by secondary (person-to-person) infection. Two cats (out of four) intentionally infected recovered from illness. One of them lasted just three months shy of age twenty-two. Other tests produced mixed results and noneffects, and have informed this fable, including the suggestion that both Yanni and Nora are infectious—which is a story for another time.

These, and related extremophiles (with regard to biomedical possibilities), are presently being

investigated at Droycon Bioconcepts in Saskatch-
ewan and the Scripps Institute of Oceanography
in the United States. (Present findings in Russia
are unknown.)

The Fatima/Lourdes syndrome: In this tale,
by the time Mac, Yanni, and Cousteau arrive
at Santorini, the hydrothermal springs have already been associated in people's minds with the
miracle waters of Fatima, Portugal, and Lourdes,
France. The connection is understandable and
even likely, given that hydrothermal pools have
been associated with faith at least as far back
as coins minted to honor the cleansing-and-
curing goddess, Hygenia, at Israel's hot springs
of Tiberias. Jerusalem's first-century B.C. healing
pools, according to the geochemist Amnon Rosenfeld, were definitely hydrothermal (volcanic)
in origin—which is not surprising, because the
entire Jordan Valley is a continental spreading
center, where a vast new ocean will exist in about
60 million years. Want to see how the Atlantic
Ocean began? Simply go to Israel and Jordan
and look around.

The first-century A.D. gospel of John seems to
echo Rosenfeld's geologic findings. In chapter 5
(verses 15–31), and in the manner of the 46th
Psalm's volcano-related "troubled" waters, the
Roman springs where Jesus was reported to have
"healed a cripple" originated with an angel who
"troubled" the waters—as in, having made the
springs hot and violent, long before Jesus arrived.

It is written that the healings began in that prior time frame. In the gospel, Jesus seems, enigmatically, to shrug off the healing of the cripple and is quoted teaching that the spring was put there, to heal, as the work of God and was not to be seen as the work of Jesus individually. In a related description, the 46th Psalm links "troubled" waters with mountains being thrown into the seas and portions of the earth itself melting (volcanism). The troubled waters, and the volcanic mountains, are also linked with end-time prophecy—which is consistent with the concerns of this fable's Greek Orthodox adversary, Bishop Marinatos.

Pierre Boulle did indeed serve as a French secret agent during World War II (for which he was awarded the Croix de Guerre). As in this novel, his mind was utterly polymathic, with interests ranging from paleontology and engineering through oceanography and spaceflight. Although we have taken the liberty of improving Boulle's mastery of English for *The Darwin Strain*, some of his fiction is well-known in America. The tune he is whistling when Yanni first meets him references Boulle's novel *The Bridge on the River Kwai* (based loosely on his experiences as a prisoner of war). He was also, with the aid of *Twilight Zone* creator Rod Serling, co-creator of the Planet of the Apes franchise. Those of you who have used smart phones to look up names and places throughout might already have discovered this and other strange connections (including an intrepid actor named Tucker), coded as a story within the story.

Descriptions of Santorini and its geology and geography are real, with very few exceptions (the Minotaur death mask and an ancient prehuman grave discovered by Boulle and Alan at the bottom of Fira Quarry). Minoan household artifacts and remains of prehistoric olive gardens have indeed been excavated from the quarry. The island has yielded up several very real, world-class archaeological sites and a submerged port dating back to the Keftiu/Minoans and 18th Dynasty Egypt (about 1630 B.C.). Discoveries include surprisingly advanced technology in ship keel design, earthquake-resistant multistory buildings, and indoor plumbing that involved upper-floor wash closets equipped with bathtubs, showers, and flush toilets. Some members of the Marinatos family, who make cameo appearances in this story, are also quite real. Their work (along with that of Cousteau and University of Rhode Island volcanologist Haraldur Sigurdsson) has added flesh to the modern world's view of seventeenth-century B.C. Santorini. That one of the authors has a family connection to the island dating back before it became a tourist attraction (including an ancestor sharing the same World War II French commendation held by Pierre Boulle) aided in providing some of the feel and even sounds and smells of mid-twentieth century Santorini.

Among the great geographic astonishments of

all time is the realization that Santorini, Crete, and the islands of Ionian Greece were once densely forested mountaintops, overlooking a vast desert. Through this desert flowed an extension of the Nile, two miles below the port of Fira and the present-day surface of the Mediterranean. Once the West African continental plate rammed into Spain and, much like the hood of a car crumpling in ultra-slow motion during a collision against a concrete wall—the "moment" this happened, a rock-solid dam was pushed up across the Strait of Gibraltar. What happened next probably developed rapidly (as seas and rivers measure time). If the strait were dammed under today's Mediterranean evaporation rates, the entire sea would dry out to a depth of two miles in "only" seven hundred years. For a while, more than 5.3 million years ago, the River Nile spilled over waterfalls so wide, and so tall, that they would have banished Niagara Falls forever to the little leagues. The Nile Falls tore through bare bedrock and ground it down to fine silt. Water slashed the earth like a sword, from Alexandria all the way south to Aswan, and created Egypt's version of the Colorado River and Grand Canyon. All those uncounted cubic miles of rock, hewn down to river silt, washed northward along the Mediterranean salt flats, laying down riverbanks of fertile, mineral-rich mud, as far away as Crete and the edge of the Devil's Hole. The former was a giant mountain, the latter a dwarf sea more than a half mile deep.

The weather patterns and oases of the deep Nile and its surroundings are based on sound scientific speculation, about a world that actually did exist in 5.33 million B.C. and which was as alien to us as another planet orbiting some far-flung star. South African mines more than two miles deep have provided a sense of how falling water droplets (raindrops) and other objects behave in an atmosphere twice the density of sea-level air, and how easily flight might be evolved under such conditions. That an unexpected animal type—in this case the phylum Mollusca (clams, slugs, squids, and their cousins)—could become the dominant life-form in an isolated, extreme environment does not lack precedent. Nearly a mile beneath the Atlantic's Atlantis Fracture Zone, white carbonate pinnacles of hydrothermal rock stand tall enough to rival the Washington Monument. Aside from creating one of the most beautiful natural vistas on earth (either above or under the sea), the pinnacles are, like our city skyscrapers, mostly empty space. The pinnacles themselves have given birth to whole ecosystems based primarily on flatworms and tiny shrimplike ostracods (the latter, famous as fossils, are mostly extinct everywhere else).

Called the "Lost City" vents, these pinnacles were the real-life inspiration for wildlife populating this tale's deep Mediterranean oases.

We are not the first to have proposed a collapsed Gibraltar Dam, and a Mediterranean Eden lost to a prehistoric deluge. The credit for *that* goes to the Roman historian and explorer Pliny the Elder. In his third volume of *Historia Naturalis*, he suggested that the Pillars of Hercules (the

Strait of Gibraltar) had broken, and the collapse of a natural dam "allowed the entrance of the ocean where it was before excluded." In this manner, a whole world disappeared, like Plato's Atlantis.

Pliny had other ideas relevant to our trilogy of fables. He knew of different elephant species once "produced" and until "recently" still being produced or evolved in Africa and India, and even on small islands in between: "As Nature is desirous, as it were, to make an exhibition for herself." Based upon bones of tiny elephants found on Crete and other Greek islands, it was easy to see how animals became isolated and were changed after surviving Pliny's flood. In Syria, fourth century B.C. coins dedicated to King Seleucus depict Athena surveying a herd of elephants standing only half the height of people. Some are represented either with horns on their heads or with multiple trunks. Pliny understood this and other changes in the shapes of living creatures—understood this, and more. Even before he was born, the emperor Octavian/Augustus had explored the concept of species rising and then falling into extinction. Offshore of modern day Sorrento, Italy, he had built a famous Hall of Giants that actually reads (as described in *The Twelve Caesars*, Augustus—paragraph 74) like history's first-known dinosaur museum: "At Capri," wrote the Roman historian Suetonius, "Augustus had collected the huge skeletons of extinct sea and land monsters popularly known as 'giants' bones." At least one Augustan coin depicts a creature with ridges running the length of its spine, along with a curious mixture of sauropod and birdlike features—as if fleshed out from a skeleton by an ancient Roman predecessor of Charles R. Knight.

You may find it a bit odd to be reading about concepts of extinction and evolution dating back to ancient Rome and the Greek islands. But these ideas far antedated Darwin. What Darwin added was the first mathematical model describing rates and modes of change (biology's equivalent to Einstein's core equations defining rates and modes for mass-energy, relativity, and the ultimate fate of the universe). What Darwin gave us was the basic skeleton to which knowledge of genetics later applied flesh and form—in essence, some core equations defining the ultimate biological fate of earth.

The bio-computational leaps made by some of the wildlife in this story, at least in the case of the cephalopods, have in real life been turning out to be a little stranger than we humans have imagined. It becomes possible now to wonder if cephalopod evolution toward greater intelligence even needs a "Darwin Strain." After we introduced an intensely symbiotic, bio-computational microbe in *The Himalayan Codex* (involving feedback regulation by constantly shifting RNA software), the April 6, 2017, issue of the journal *Cell* published a paper in which scientific understanding was (once again) catching up with and perhaps exceeding fiction: the discovery of rapid RNA editing in *cephalopods*. This involved extensive recoding specific to three of the most intelligent, behaviorally complex octopus and cuttlefish species presently known. More than 60 percent of the proteins governing the neurochemistry and structure of their brains is subject to essentially continual RNA recoding—with the potential, as in this fable, to leapfrog over some of the usual mathematics in Darwinian variation and selection. By contrast, other animals, running the spectrum from fruit flies to dolphins and us, have recoding taking place in one small fraction of 1 percent of our RNA. Viewed in this light, an octopus not only begins to look more alien than ever before, but it finally turns the textbook dogma of DNA and RNA being the genetic hardware completely on its head. We've had it backward all along. DNA and RNA are the software, not the hardware. (Protein is the hardware.)

The real-life behavior of cephalopods, and especially as observed among certain cuttlefish and octopus species, is fantastic almost beyond words. In this fable, we have (for the "Kraken") increased known cephalopod abilities to match some old legends dating back past Viking Kraken stories and Pliny's "polypus," all the way back through myths about Homer's description of a shape-shifting, self-camouflaging sea monster with features quite reminiscent of cephalopods.

When describing cephalopod behavior in the field and in the lab, there was no need to exaggerate. Two very good nonfiction introductions to these wonders of the world are Sy Montgomery's *The Soul of an Octopus* (Atria, 2015) and Peter Godfrey-Smith's *Other Minds: The Octopus, the Sea, and the Deep Origins of Consciousness* (Farrar, Straus & Giroux, 2016). Though they are traditionally believed to be solitary animals, Godfrey-Smith has recorded two first occurrences of an octopus species forming communities—apparently as an opportunistic consequence of human activity in the sea (garbage dumping), leading to a rudimentary but expanding form of architecture.

In a region of the Indian Ocean where the *Pearl* was reported to have been sunk by a "squid," Jacques Cousteau and his fellow ocean explorer Arthur C. Clarke really did encounter a little cephalopod that darted at their face-masks with the startling mimicry of a poisonous lionfish. After the divers flinched, it dropped to the bottom, instantly changing shape and color to match the surrounding coral. The camouflaging capabilities of *known* cephalopods are nothing short of amazing. We know of a cuttlefish that, when placed in a laboratory test tank with checkerboard flooring, shifted with astonishing rapidity to a checkerboard pattern that rendered it somewhere between completely invisible and the translucence of glass with mild flaws (depending on viewing angle and whether the animal decided to move). Most scuba divers have probably been watched by a cephalopod at very close range and never known it.

In the Atlantic, at the hydrothermal vents of Menez Gwen, a large Humboldt squid, about the size of a man, attacked the bright lights of a Russian Mir-1 submersible in 2003, causing some damage.

NASA's Kevin Hand was aboard to film the incident. A characteristic of Humboldt squids is that they flash stripes and geometric shapes across their bodies, sometimes flashing as alternating groups of animals, to create visual confusion. The Mir incident occurred at a depth of little more than a half mile. The animal was first sighted lurking on the other side of swirling, partly obscuring, and blurring veils of hydrothermal water. Flashing suddenly to pure white (interpreted more as an indicator of curiosity than angry red), "it came at the Mir like a torpedo and started smacking and pulling at the lights." When the Humboldt was finished, it retreated toward the warm veils, spread out all ten arms to make itself look quite large—"Felt like it was giving us the finger, times ten"—then darted away and vanished.

During an earlier dive, at 2.5 miles, explorer and undersea cinematographer Ralph White saw what he believed to be a very large cephalopod, but it "disappeared suddenly in billows of sediment, wanting to get out of Dodge." Evidently it disliked the submersible's lights as much as the Humboldt. At this same depth, another apparent cephalopod responded to Mir-2 with a display to rival the sub's own floodlights. A later examination of the video revealed what appeared to be a gently curving lateral line of dull green bioluminescent "lanterns," the line being vaguely reminiscent of a cuttlefish in side view (with the added mystery that this visitor, if a cuttlefish, was at least twenty feet long). Topside, one of the engineers said that the lights reminded him of a machine crossed with an animal, then joked at the invertebrate zoologists: "It's like one of those ink blot tests the psychologists use. You people see cephalopods everywhere—which means you'd be just the people to film an underwater foo-fighter for real and think you discovered some new kind of squid."

One thing that can be said for certain, about the ever-black—and especially about the volcanic springs of the deep—is that new species of cephalopods are being encountered almost as a matter of routine. As White once said, "It's *Planet of the Cephalopods* down there."

During a "White expedition," one of the biologists (one of many explorers who, like Yanni, is "on the spectrum") came away from a twenty-minute encounter with a new species of octopus, in tears—describing "the most profound loneliness" after the animal departed. The scientist taught others how to interact with the strange visitors, and some came away with the same unmistakable impression one has after looking into the eyes of an elephant or an orangutan. You are never quite the same again, because you can never escape the feeling that while it looks into you, it is having thoughts of its own. (See human responses to a deep ocean robot probe encounter in the 2003 Disney–James Cameron documentary, *Aliens of the Deep*.)

As for the scientist who realized, "They know when you are looking," this too is real. At Woods Hole Oceanographic Institution (as reported in the *Washington Post*, 3/2/2019) biologist Bret Grasse noticed that he was being continually squirted in the back of his head, when he turned away from his habitat for cuttlefish and began working on something else. Each time this happened, when he looked back at the source of the squirting, the cephalopods were sitting innocently on the bottom of the tank, in the positions he had last observed them. Finally, Grasse made use of his smart phone's selfie function, looking back over his shoulder as if through a mirror, as the cuttlefish snuck up to the water's surface, fired off a volley of well-aimed squirts, and returned to their original positions on the bottom during the split second it would have taken him to turn around.

In 2019, Mindy Weisberger reported (on *Live Science*, 3/19/2019) that one octopus, evidently feeling content enough to sleep out in the open, in its laboratory tide pool habitat, appeared to be dreaming flashing patterns of star-shaped geometric figures.

Woods Hole scientists, meanwhile, confirmed that secondary brains and neural nets are spread throughout the octopoid body and are high-functioning. Unlike a human limb, a severed octopus arm has long been known to scurry away from hydrochloric acid and other toxins. At Woods Hole, several scientists working closely with these organisms have turned against surgical experimentation, and long ago stopped eating them.

Supporters of commercial octopus farming have begun campaigning against cephalopod intelligence, calling the idea "nonsense" and "fake science cultism," asserting that they, like oysters, belong only on the dinner plate. Increasingly, this argument is based on claims that an octopus will fail (so far) to meet certain human standards of intelligence. Until some octopuses were observed using coconut shell halves for shelter, and carrying them away in apparent anticipation of future use, they appeared to have failed at the intelligence markers of tool use and anticipating the future in reasonable detail. Marine biologist James Wood answered would-be octopus ranchers (in *Smithsonian*, Ocean, on-line): "So you think you're smarter than a cephalopod?" He asked his readers to imagine setting intelligence markers for humans, by the standards of an octopus. So, the octopus thinks, "All right. I'm going to make an intelligence test for humans, because they show a little bit of promise, in a very few ways." And the first question the octopus comes up with is this: "How many color patterns can your severed arm produce in one second?"

Much as biochemist Cyril Ponnamperuma suggested that we might have to develop a gradational approach to the definition of life (as between a protocell, a virus, and a cell), we may also need a pH scale for intelligence. The division of life on earth into thinking and nonthinking is artificial, convenient for distinguishing such extreme cases as a human and a clam, but quite inappropriate when dismissing a mountain gorilla that learns sign language, or a "lowly" octopus that unscrews jars and expresses complex patterns on its skin (some decipherable, possibly, as emotions), or a pod of orca whales that develops its own distinct dialect (in a language still undecipherable). The spectrum of animal minds, ours among them, may require something analogous to the words "acid" and "base" as used in chemistry. While sodium hydroxide is distinctly alkaline, the hydrochloric acid in your stomach is a powerful acid. But in between these two extremes exists a whole spectrum of variable strength. The chemists have pushed aside rigid (and untenable) categories by inventing the pH scale—the measure of "hydrogen ion concentration." In this way, all the observed phenomena can be described as a quantity, or a placeholder on the spectrum. We may have to invent a similar quantity to avoid any vagueness (or worse, assumptions) that might arise from applying the terms "human" and "dumb animal."

As a civilization hoping to survive its nuclear adolescence, striving to become truly adult, and to explore far beyond earth, the sidestepping of a terrible mistake may ultimately depend on understanding a new spectrum.

We know of a biologist who studied a species of intensely mimetic cuttlefish that could instantly sprout thorny red shapes along the surface of its body—"Seeming to enjoy scaring us by looking like something that just stepped out of hell." One day, she was certain it had tried to mimic her own face—"Or, rather, half-a-face." Amid a convergence of fleshy red thorns, and for a fleeting moment, the scientist was certain that she saw a human brow, eye, cheek, and half of her own smile.

Looking around, it would be a great mistake to deny that other animals—including mammals, certain highly evolved birds, and even a "lowly" octopus—can know emotions and consciousness, albeit sometimes via a consciousness quite alien to our way of thinking.

The theremin device was an actual ancestor of synthesizers, electric guitars, and every other electronic musical instrument. Its Russian inventor, Leon Theremin, became very popular in the United States. His instruments contributed to the soundtracks of films ranging from *Spellbound* and *Rocketship XM* to the animal calls in *The Birds*. Behind the music, Theremin and his machines were historical oddities, because the inventor was simultaneously a Russian spy. This novel's Theremin-based listening devices were quite real during the first Cold War. One was actually presented (disguised as a gift) to the U.S. ambassador to the Soviet Union and functioned for seven years until accidentally broken (and revealed as a "bug"). Contrary to the stereotype of humorless Russian spies, the little espionage machine had been named "the Thing." The sounds Leon Theremin created became the eerie music that amplified the moods of isolation and paranoia in both film versions of *The Thing*—which, as some of you might have noticed, is a story for another time (including the fate of young Robert Jerry MacCready, who, in 1948, had not been born yet).

Trofim Lysenko is introduced very much as he actually was, and we have led him to behave in a manner consistent with the real historical figure, if thrown into this extraordinary event. First you meet the man. Then, very quickly, the monster within the man.

Dmitri Chernov, though a fictional character, is based on a combination of several real Russian naval officers and one former KGB agent. The Nesbitt character (like Mac) is a composite of several civilian scientists who have sailed with American marines, often on high-risk "cruises." Like marines, Chernov and Nesbitt have one feature in common: they are entirely mission focused. And in many cases, such people have seen too much.

Chernov's "best bar in town" mathematics: reality. By the end of the twentieth century, real spies learned how to sidestep this phenomenon.

The four ancient apocalyptic books cited by Bishop Marinatos (including *The Apocalypse of the Egyptians*) actually do exist. Several were in fact excavated during the 1940s, including Egypt's "Nag Hammadi Library." The buried Egyptian library includes several texts that were preserved (and over many centuries duplicated by hand-copying) within the Greek Orthodox Church.

Some of the original texts date back to the earliest Judeo-Christians, and to the Christian-like "Gnostic" churches. Several such texts, as cited in *The Darwin Strain* (including references to fiery red "dragons" rising out of the sea) are echoed in Revelation (4, 12–15, and 18). Since its formation, the Vatican's Jesuit order has preserved many apocryphal texts (declared heretical under Emperor Constantine's committees, after A.D. 325). By tradition, these have been consulted for comparison with miracles involving the sudden appearance of springs with curative powers, as in the cases of Lourdes and Fatima. Thus it is a safe bet that if the Kraken and the Santorini springs really did arise in a manner anything like this fable, in 1948 (or even today), they would have been scrutinized and suspected by the religious authorities in the very same way.

The "coin boy" incident: Yes, this is based on something that really happened.

The newsboy was thirteen-year-old Jimmy Bozart. Although the actual event occurred in 1953 instead of 1948, the real Jimmy did indeed receive a hollowed-out nickel containing a Russian microfilm after selling copies of the *Brooklyn Daily Eagle*. (The McCarthy-era red scare excerpts cited from the paper are actual for that July day in 1948.) At home, Jimmy magnified the microfilm through a lamp and lens, really did discover lines of coded numbers, and notified detectives. The mistakenly spent nickel led back to some "enlightening answers" to "many questions" about how Russian spy rings operated.

Jimmy received a reward from the government and went to college at Rensselaer Polytechnic Institute (not coincidentally, a favored location for CIA talent scouts, through the 1980s). During an intensive study of the commodities markets, and as his between-classes hobby, Jimmy made his first fortune while still a teen by investing some of his reward money in the Texas Gulf mining company. He redesigned vending machines (made another fortune), designed a rocket or two (made no money there), then naively crossed paths with some of Jack "Sparks" Ruby's money-laundering colleagues after building some nightclubs (almost got "a big time-out" there). Jimmy made his next fortune in New York and Florida real estate, having followed advice of a future U.S. president on "the art of the deal."

About 2015, Jimmy asked the FBI if he could buy his nickel back, at "*any*" price. He was told, "Nyet."

Kitano Hata is a composite of two actual war criminals, one of whom (Shiro Ishii) was known as "Black Sun" (as in the Chinese film by that title released in 1987). The horrors of the Unit 731 bioweapons facility have not been exaggerated beyond what they were in real life (not in *The Darwin Strain*, nor in its prequel, *Hell's Gate*). The real "Black Sun" did, in life as well as in this fable, survive under General MacArthur's protection. He eventually built many children's hospitals and dedicated himself to other charitable acts—having accepted a Bible from MacArthur and embraced Christianity as the only religion that offered forgiveness for his sins. In China today, with regard to "Black Sun" and Field Marshall Shunroku Hata (who survived with flash burns from the first atomic bomb), the people really do say, "No one should waste his spit on either of their graves." Field Marshal Hata, responsible for more than a quarter million murders, died of natural causes at advanced old age, unrepentant.

The Truman White House really was falling apart from within, and really did have to be completely gutted to the outer walls, in a process that included a bulldozer in the basement, hidden from public view. Much of the post-1814 White House wood (installed after a previous gutting resulting from the War of 1812) ended up buried under what is now a baseball park. Reconstruction and renovation were finally completed when First lady Jaqueline Kennedy presented her famous color television tour of the White House.

Although the MacCready events to which Truman must respond are fictional, his reactions to several other 1945–48 events (including the Russian problem and the predictions of Einstein) are realistically described. The portrayal of President Truman's way of interacting with people (including RFK and the futurists) was informed by Arthur M. Schlesinger (regarding the Kennedys) and by Harry Truman's grandson Clifton Truman Daniel.

Clifton has said his grandfather never spoke about the atomic bomb at home—"*But*," he added, "that's partly because I never asked." Although President Truman had once threatened "a nuclear rain of ruin," his real feelings might have been a little different from what most people suppose, according to correspondence discovered by Clifton and his friend Masahiro Sasaki (which was read and broadcast on C-SPAN 3 on November 19, 2015, from the Truman Presidential Library's Paper Crane Dedication ceremony). About the letter and its context: Near the war's end, a senator had sent a telegram cheering the "rain of ruin," and he called upon the president for the more expansive use of atom bombs. Truman's letter was written the day after Nagasaki, with still not a whisper of surrender coming from Japan. History now knows that Truman knew (and certainly did not want anyone else to know) that America was fresh out of atom bombs. The president also knew that at least two new bombs were in the manufacturing pipeline, scarcely more than two weeks away. Additionally, he was receiving reports from scientists (based on sand melted into glass and flash-burned wildlife miles from the July 16, 1945, bomb test in New Mexico) that thousands of people, "those not incinerated," must have been flash-burn irradiated—"Hideously so, and instantly"—out to several miles from the centers of Hiroshima and Nagasaki.

Knowing this, and embedded in one of history's

loneliest moments, Truman replied: "I know that Japan is a terribly cruel and uncivilized nation in warfare. But I cannot bring myself to believe that because they are beasts we should, ourselves, act in the same way. For myself, I certainly regret the necessity of wiping out whole populations because of the pig-headedness of the leaders of the nation. And for your information, I'm not going to do it, unless it is absolutely necessary. It is my opinion that after the Russians enter into the [Pacific] war, the Japanese will very shortly fall down. My objective is to save as many American lives as possible. But I also have humane feelings for the women and children in Japan. Sincerely yours, Harry Truman."

The background history of Jack ("Sparks") Ruby and Meyer Lansky: reality.

Bernard the rat: a true story.

Professor Cahn and the lesson of the lab rats: a true story.

Operation High-jump: Although the timing of maneuvers has been extended from 1947 into 1948, to more ideally match the MacCready adventure, High-jump really did involve aircraft, ships (albeit not our secret mission of *Intrepid*), and five thousand men in Antarctic war games and long-term settlement experiments. Although one offshoot of High-jump was permanent Antarctic research stations and many Explorer's Club mission flags, the primary objective was to practice for defense against a Russian invasion across the Arctic Circle—just as in this fable. Cover stories included an actual research station being built, with plans for power to be provided by a portable nuclear reactor. (The *"NR-3"*–style reactor was in fact built and shipped, but it needed a continually reliable supply of liquid water to cool its core. To freeze-dry the scientific story of what went wrong, suffice to say that somewhat like Napoleon and Hitler when they decided to invade Russia in the wintertime, somebody forgot to check the winter weather forecasts.) Much of the actual misinformation circulated around Operation High-jump—everything from the search for Nazi foo-fighters to Hitler's "hollow earth" mind rot—has accidentally infiltrated and persists to this day in UFO legend and myth. Archival records that emerged from Moscow between the two Cold Wars revealed that Russia was not fooled by any of it. Meanwhile, the actual demise of the so-called Fourth Reich, prior to 1948, is in fact exactly as described in *The Darwin Strain*.

Pliny the Elder's "polypus" is not exaggerated at all beyond what Pliny actually wrote. The Viking saga version of the "Kraken" is also quoted as originally written. The July 4, 1874, story in the London *Times*, about the sinking of a schooner near Sri Lanka by a large cephalopod, is reproduced exactly as reported. The *Brunswick* incident is also based on a real report (the actual date of the incident was May 6, 1930).

A review of the 2003 video of "an unprovoked attack on a *Mir* submersible, by a Humboldt squid" surprised some observers because the creature approached with its head and arms facing forward—"Just like the squid attack in the movie, *20,000 Leagues Under the Sea*," observed one scientist. "How did Walt Disney know?"

Disney did manage to get a lot right, except perhaps for the translation. In Jules Verne's novel, the creature is more akin to Pliny's "polypus"— called a *poulpe* in the original French. *Poulpe* is an octopus, not a squid. The "squid" monster appeared in a different novel: Ian Fleming's *Dr. No*.

The legend of Odysseus's encounter with Scylla is quoted accurately from Homer. The same monster appears in several forms on coins of the Roman Republic, from at least 270 B.C. through a posthumous memorialization (35 B.C.) of Pompey's fears about conquest from the sea. The creature's upper body was typically a nude woman, occasionally represented as youthful "Athena" holding a Gorgon's shield and wearing a gown suggestive of writhing tentacles. Other times, the lower extremities were tentacles outright, often terminating in fish tails—literally a chimera made from three different creatures. In Greco-Roman mythology, Scylla was a beautiful nymph transformed into a monster. On a Pompey coin, the lower part of her body is a multiheaded dragon, rising from the sea with serpent's tails and the faces of humans and dogs (for a dreadfully beautiful animation of what Romans imagined, see John Carpenter's film *The Thing*). A variation on this multiheaded sea-dragon imagery—already quite familiar to Romans by the time Judeo-Christians set out to convert the Gentiles—appears to have made its way into the Roman-Christian book of Revelation and into much apocryphal religious literature and art. An example of this can be found on the island at the center of our fable.

Clinging to the cliff sides of Santorini's "Mesa Vouno" is a church dedicated to Saint George, the dragon-slaying patron saint of England. Newcomers to early paintings and carvings of the dragon, having often heard stories of a towering fire-breathing monster, are often surprised to see that the dragon seems to be writhing and in retreat and is pitifully small—so small that George would have had to climb down from his horse to kill the beast by stabbing it or crushing it under the heel of one boot. Saint George's dragon seems to have undergone many transformations during centuries of retellings and repaintings, each of them fascinating in its own right. The story of Saint George riding in on a horse and rescuing a princess from sacrifice to a sea monster closely (and possibly not coincidentally) echoes the ancient narrative of Perseus riding in on the winged horse, Pegasus, to rescue the princess Andromeda from a sea dragon.

The historical Saint George was scourged and beheaded about A.D. 303, near the end of an anti-

Christian purge initiated by Emperor Diocletian. The *Roman Catholic Encyclopedia* cites narratives of pilgrims dedicating their first church to George within only a few years of his execution. Along the eastern shore of the Black Sea, where Saint George was originally said to have defeated the dragon, he was deified by the country that became Georgia. Saint George was officially canonized under Pope Gelasins I in A.D. 494 (a time in which Rome was fading and stories about the knights of King Arthur were just on the very cusp of originating). The earliest clearly defined textual stories of Saint George encountering a sea dragon record prior song-stories and pilgrimage tales in a Roman province of northern Turkey (bordering Georgia). The stories reached the British Isles by A.D. 650 (and later expanded to include Saint George resurrecting from the grave and joining British knights in victorious battle).

Northern Greece's Vinica icons, dating from about A.D. 730, are the first known to visually portray Saint George (and other saints, including Mary Magdalene's brother, Philip) slaying evil "dragons." In this case, the dragons are little knots of snakes and tentacles with human heads. Saint George is shown riding in on a horse, with a lance held high above a cowering evil serpent's nest. Here's where it gets complicated: Because Pliny's nephew was kind to the earliest Christians during times of oppression, his works were preserved by the churches, copied, and widely distributed. This may explain why several of the sea dragons depicted in religious paintings of Saint

George have long, ropy forearms, multiple coiled tails, and even wings that sometimes more resemble the arms of Pliny's "polypus" than anything capable of flapping. These creatures are also surprisingly small, compared to Saint George's horse.

If (and this is a big if) the sea dragon originated in the imagery of a real octopus mixed in with Pliny's version, then a legend originating along the Black Sea about a water serpent to whom a town sacrificed virgins until a saint came along and speared it makes a certain amount of sense. The octopus is uncommon in the Black Sea (especially along its eastern shore), and it becomes easy to imagine how, though smaller than a horse, one of the lamb-sized species—or even a smaller, more ordinary individual—dwelling among submerged rocks near a port and glimpsed by people not likely to have seen one before would frighten the villagers. Easily associated or confused with Tethys and other Triton sea gods of Emperor Diocletian's time, or with the serpent features of Christianity's dragons, this would not be the first time that villagers began drowning their virgin daughters and sacrificing them to the sea.

In all early paintings, and in many dating from the eighteenth century, the terrifying sea beast is much smaller than Saint George's horse (only centuries later did it swell to *Godzilla* or *Game of Thrones* proportions). The dragon in the Santorini church, like the one that came to be engraved under the sword and hooves of Saint George's charge, as depicted on the British sovereign, is consistent with most eighteenth-century dragon imagery.

The story committed to writing in Great Britain's *Golden Legend* (A.D. 1275) is more consistent with the "polypus" and our Santorini Kraken: "Where St. George slew the dragon, there sprang up a fountain of living water, which healeth sick people that drank thereof."

To better serve MacCready's mission to Santorini, we did take the liberty of pulling the World War II aircraft carrier *Intrepid* out of mothballs a little earlier than history records. Actual history reports that having survived five kamikaze attacks and one torpedo strike, the "Fighting I" was officially retired as part of the reserve fleet in 1947, and recommissioned for refitting in 1952. At the birth of the jet age, she became the first carrier to launch planes using steam-catapults, before deploying to the Mediterranean Fleet. During the space race between the United States and Russia, the carrier assisted in the pickups of astronauts Scott Carpenter, John Young, and Gus Grissom. The ship did conduct exercises deep within the margin of polar climate (in operations similar to High-jump) during the 1970s. Her final port of call was New York City, where she became a world-class air and space museum. In 2002 and 2003, the carrier's well-shielded offices were temporarily reactivated, for a final military operation that included Navy medical and New York Fire Department planning for dirty-bomb protocols. Her final spaceflight-related duty was receipt of the space shuttle *Enterprise*—which had passed its airstrip approach and landing proof-of-concept test (1977) with Apollo 13 astronaut Fred Haise at the helm.

The nuclear mini-sub *NR-3* is based on Admiral Rickover's original designs for what became the fantastic vessel *NR-1*. The environment inside deep-diving mini-subs (also called submersibles) is based in this story on multiple firsthand experiences by colleagues who have actually lived in the *NR-1*, have descended more than two miles in the vessel's "cousins," and even survived a volcanic event/landslide and temporary stranding on the bottom of the sea—much as described in this tale.

Agent Number T070 was a real-life OSS agent who served during World War II with his British counterpart, Ian Fleming. "T070" went on to write *A Night to Remember* and *Day of Infamy* (the book that became the film classic *Tora! Tora! Tora!*). His real name was Walter Lord. At war's end, he participated in the interrogations of Hitler's architect Albert Speer ("Speer only *pretended* at being the repentant Nazi"); a surviving pilot who flew the raid on Pearl Harbor ("the start of a friendship"); and German physicist Werner Heisenberg ("an unsung hero, perhaps, who sabotaged the German atomic bomb project from within . . . Heisenberg could not believe we actually built and dropped the thing"). During the war, Lord knew the retired baseball star and polymathic genius Moe Berg, valued for his intensely photographic memory and fluency in multiple languages. In late 1944, Berg had been assigned by the OSS to kill Heisenberg at a Zurich conference and at the last moment declined to do so (leaving Lord and others somewhat perplexed, for many months). Berg continued working for a while with the postwar descendant of OSS, the CIA, and was instrumental in analysis of Tito in Yugoslavia. Ian Fleming went on to write *Chitty Chitty Bang Bang* and also created James Bond, based on his friend Walter, himself, and several other World War II agents (among them Berg, who had gathered much information in Italy about Eberhart Sanger's plans to bomb America from orbit with a piloted predecessor to the space shuttle, in a manner consistent with certain Bond villains). The namesake of Fleming's semifictional character was a real-life vertebrate zoologist who had written one of his favorite books: *Birds of the West Indies*. Little was ever told of the World War II period in Fleming's life, or Lord's, aside from a few humorous anecdotes and bits of declassified history that went into their books. In 1992, when a *New York Times* writer approached Walter Lord about a biography and the birth stages of the CIA, Lord said, "Never want to relive that. It's too depressing a story to tell." Moe Berg, when asked to write an autobiography, had said the same thing.

Nora Nesbitt's James Bond–like tooth gadget, designed to call in a self-silencing strike on a captured scientist and anyone who might be interrogating her, really existed. We know a colleague who actually (and voluntarily) had one temporarily installed.

The volcano and the bombs: an event much like the eruption that led to Yanni's capture, and the escape of the ship that captured her, actually did occur at Nea Kameni, at the center of Santorini Lagoon.

On September 18, 1940, one of Mussolini's bombers attacked a freighter after it departed from the port of Fira for Athens. As in our fable, the ship was passing just north of Nea Kameni, in the region of on-again, off-again hot-water plumes that had been erupting since 1865. As in our fable, all of the bombs missed the ship, and hit the volcanic equivalent of a neurological trigger point instead. For the first and only time in history, a bombing raid instantly triggered a volcanic explosion, with columns of ash and steam towering more than a mile above the island and drawing a smoke screen over the freighter. The crew of the bomber radioed that they had apparently struck a ship full of munitions. Rome radio broadcasts proudly announced the victory, but the citizens of Santorini and Therasia offered a toast in the direction of the volcano. They had seen the ship emerge from beneath the smoke screen and exit the lagoon unharmed. Throughout the war, Nea Kameni continued to cough boulders and dust into the air almost daily. The waters around it steamed and swirled, one afternoon milky white or yellow, the next morning green, or violet, or scarlet.

The Virginia Beach incident: The stranding of a Russian submarine and damage to its rubberized hull by an unknown giant cephalopod is a composite event, informed by three actual incidents. The first event's biological results were reported by J. C. Scott in *U.S. Naval Institute Proceedings* (August 1978, p. 106). This involved a collision of the U.S.S. *Stein* (a *Knox*-class destroyer escort). During a mission in 1978, the rubberized skin over a submerged dome of monitoring equipment was damaged by contact with a large mass that gouged and slashed away nearly 10 percent of the dome surface. The remaining skin contained several hundred broken barbs and "hooked claws," morphologically consistent in every way with "teeth" rimming the suction cups of certain cephalopods. They differed only by a matter of degree. These "teeth" were much larger than those from any known cephalopod.

In a separate, non-"Kraken" related event of the period, known as the Vela Incident of September 22, 1979, a satellite detected the distinctive flash signature of a low-yield tactical nuclear weapon at 40 degrees south latitude in the Indian Ocean, off the coast of South Africa. During a wreckage search, a standoff developed between submersible-equipped ships of the United States and Russia. Meanwhile, there were concerns in

Australia and New Zealand that radioactive fallout was approaching. Washington assured Canberra and Wellington that the flash had nothing at all to do with nuclear testing by either of the two suspected nations, Israel or South Africa. This was the truth, but only part of the truth. The rest of the story involved what at that time was classified under the category "Russian unscheduled energetic disassembly" of a nuclear device—or, "Oops, that atomic bomb was not supposed to go off then and there" (U.S. Naval Research Laboratory, Albright, 1994).

The fallout path shot straight through Australia's south island of Tasmania and reached New Zealand's capital, where some of the radioactive debris came down with the rain. In the spring of 1980—helping to kick-start the Australia–New Zealand *nuclear-free zone* movement—plant species known to respond quickly to low-level radiation came up displaying spectacular mutations (strange clovers, and crown chrysanthemums with multiple flower centers on the outside, ringing central clusters of petals). This led to the discovery of isotopes in the thyroids of sheep and a lot of political outlet hitting the fan. While children collected seven- and eight-leaved clovers, the Virginia Beach incident of February 1981 occurred.

This third mishap contributed mightily to America and Russia deciding to reduce the probability of blundering into a nuclear war by vastly pushing down the number of nuclear weapons in the arsenals (initially by 80 percent). The program was called START (Strategic Arms Reduction

Treaty). As Harry Truman would undoubtedly have observed: "A good start. We should START, and START again."

The Vela Incident and the real Virginia Beach incident (which, except for the "here's looking at you, squid" moment, happened much as described) were two of three Russian mishaps at sea that led novelist and honorary CIA publicist Tom Clancy to write his classic, *The Hunt for Red October*.

O n the very real genetic frontier, it seems almost inevitable that we will be able to cure almost every disease, to vastly extend human life spans, reengineer life, and even turn the *Jurassic Park* recipe into something quite real.

Some of our colleagues, concerned with the possibilities of wars generated by overpopulation, are looking toward Mars as a possible relief valve for earth.

Hopefully, these novels convey a point: we do not live on a disposable planet.

Fortunately, contrasted against a time when major, problem-solving technological breakthroughs came every three years (at the turn of the century), they now come every three months. And the rate is accelerating.

There is plenty to hope for, if our species is wise, and pays attention.

But as anyone who studies Rome in the time of Pliny will see, the loss of liberty and the threat of the fall were always lurking no more than a generation away.

Rome fell with its engineers in possession of multiple water-powered grain mills with their paddles arranged in rows. It fell in possession of steam pumps, ball bearings, and multiple gear-shift devices (among them the famed Antikythera mechanism). As near as we can tell from history and archaeology, if anyone ever connected them together to run a steam engine on wheels, or on a boat, no one paid attention.

It's easy to mock the Romans for where they went wrong, but future generations, if we become the next archaeological mystery, may mock us for the same reasons.

Dmitri Chernov observed, sooner or later, every civilization is archaeology. Every civilization becomes a ghost story.

It does not have to be that way.

We simply have to live up to our species name: *sapiens*—"Wise."

We can do better than merely "be fit" and "survive."

We have the potential to excel.

And if we are unwise, if we become the next Atlantis legend, then there will be no words more poignant as an epitaph than "What might have been."

Acknowledgments

JRF: I wish to thank, equally (1) my teachers and (2) friends in the USN and USMC and related expeditions. Among the latter, I carry with me, forever alive in my memories, those who did not make it back to shore. Ohana. Ohana.

I acknowledge warmly, over the course of many years, the people of Santorini, including the Marinatos family, members of the Greek Orthodox Church, Yaron Niski, and Petros Mantouvalos. Much gratitude also to James Cameron, Walter Lord, Robert Ballard, former Cousteau science officer Tom Dettweiler, Clifton Truman Daniel, and the real-life "coin boy."

Thanks also to Gillian MacKenzie, our incomparable editor Lyssa Keusch, her assistant Mireya Chiriboga, and Patricia J. Wynne.

A personal shout-out to our veterans—and to all first responders, past, present, and future.

B.S. thanks Janet and Billy Schutt, John Hermanson, Darrin Lunde, Kathy Kennedy, Gillian MacKenzie, Leslie Nesbitt Sittlow, Don Peterson, Nancy Simmons, Carol Steinberg, Patricia J. Wynne, and Lyssa Keusch.

Selected Bibliography

Amir, Sumayah. "Octopuses, Squids, and Cuttlefish Can Edit Their RNA," *Science News*, April 7, 2017. Also on this subject, at increasing depth of technical exposition: Steph Yin, "A Genetic Oddity May Give Octopuses and Squids Their Smarts," *New York Times*, Science, April 6, 2017, citing the journal *Cell*: Liscovitch-Bauer, et al. "Trade-off between Transcriptome Plasticity and Genome Evolution in Cephalopods." https://www.cell.com/cell/fulltext/S0092 –8674(17)30344–6.

Ball, Philip. "When the Mediterranean was a Desert." *Nature*, August 12, 1999.

Cullimore, Roy. (on Droycon Bioconcepts and bacterial/fungal/archaea "super-organisms," an introduction) "Gigantic New Super Organism with 'Social Intelligence' Is Devouring the Titanic." Oceanexplorer.noaa.gov, April 14, 2011.

Gierliński, Gerard D., et al. "Possible Hominin Footprints from the Late Miocene (c 5.7 Million Years Ago) of Crete?" *Proceedings of the Geologists' Association*. DOI: 10.1016/j.pgeola .2017.07.006.

Godfrey-Smith, Peter. *Other Minds: The Octopus, the Sea, and the Deep Origins of Consciousness*. New York: Farrar, Straus & Giroux, 2016.

Guarino, Ben. "Inside the Grand and Sometimes Slimy Plan to Turn Octopuses Into Lab Animals," *Washington Post*, March 2, 2019.

Hanlon, Roger, et al. *Octopus, Squid, and Cuttlefish: A Visual, Scientific Guide to the Oceans' Most Advanced Invertebrates*. Chicago: University of Chicago Press, 2018.

Marinatos, Nanno. *Santorini: The Island of the Volcano*. Athens and New York: Mathioulakis, 2003. For Santorini in film, see *Atlantis Rising*. National Geographic Channel, 90 minutes, 2017.

Marschall, Ken. "The Exploration of the HMS Britannic: A Tour Aboard the NR-1," *The Titanic Commutator* (vol. 20, no. 1, available on Amazon), 1996, and submersibles in film, including the Lost City hydrothermal vent "microbial wonder world" in James Cameron, *Aliens of the Deep* (Disney, 2005).

Meyer, M. W. et al. *The Nag Hammadi Scriptures: The Revised and Updated Translation of Sacred Gnostic Texts Complete in One Volume*. New York: HarperOne, 2009. On the relevance of the orthodox bishop and what he thought MacCready needed to know about the books of the Apocalypse, readers may be interested in translations of this buried Gnostic library, including the *Apocalypse of the Egyptians*.

Montgomery, Sy. *The Soul of an Octopus*. New York: Atria, 2015.

Weinberger, Mindy. "This Octopus's Dreams (Maybe) Were Written All Over Its Body," *Live Science*, March 12, 2019.